2cool2btrue

2cool2btrue

simon brooke

ORION

First published in Great Britain in 2003 by Orion Books
an imprint of The Orion Publishing Group
Orion House, 5 Upper St Martin's Lane, London WC2H 9EA

A CIP catalogue record for this book is
available from the British Library

ISBN (hardback) 0 75284 762 7
ISBN (trade paperback) 0 75284 763 5

Typeset by Deltatype Ltd, Birkenhead

Printed and bound in Great Britain by
Clays Ltd, St Ives plc

For my mum and dad

Humankind cannot bear very much reality

T.S. ELIOT

I would like to thank my editor Kate Mills at Orion as well as Nicky Jeanes and Emily Furniss for their hard work on my behalf. Thanks also go to my agent Elizabeth Wright at Darley Anderson for all her advice and support.

The Fraud Squad were extremely helpful and provided me with some useful information about how they operate. I would particularly like to thank Detective Constable Terry Davis for all the help he gave and I'm very grateful to him for allowing me to accompany him and the team on a raid. It must be said that he and his officers are nothing like my character DCI Slapton and their courtesy and politeness – even to the people they were arresting – was unstinting.

I would also like to thank the National Missing Persons Helpline and the National Drugs Helpline for their help in my research.

One

My problem, says the girl [illegible]
[illegible] my [illegible]

[illegible]

[illegible] and finds that she [illegible]
[illegible] all the [illegible]

[illegible] in the girl's [illegible]
[illegible]

[illegible] to people [illegible]

I know this room so well [illegible]
[illegible] and [illegible]
[illegible]
the empty water [illegible]
[illegible]

chapter one

'My problem,' says the girl sitting opposite me, 'is that my celebrity status is overtaking my acting credentials.'

She is talking to a red-haired girl sitting next to her who is nodding gently and absent-mindedly running her hand up and down her leg.

'Mmmm,' says the red-haired girl, obviously partly concerned about this dilemma and partly preoccupied with the fact that it will be her turn in a moment.

The girl with the problem has recently appeared in a commercial mini-series for shampoo. You know the one – she's just moved into a new flat and finds that she hasn't brought her shampoo, or it's got lost amongst all the boxes or something and so, with just a towel wrapped round her, she knocks on the door of the flat opposite and the bloke who opens the door, a really smug bastard, looks her up and down and lets her borrow his.

I reflect on the girl's CV-versus-fame problem for a moment then realise I'm staring. Still, perhaps when you're the Thick 'n' Glossy girl you're used to people staring.

I know this room so well: the groovy pink leather settees, slightly worn now and marked in a couple of places with biro, MTV playing silently on a monitor in the corner, the bored, hip girls on reception, the empty water machine which invites everyone who doesn't have the obligatory bottle of Evian to go up to it, realise that in fact it's empty and then walk away, trying to look cool. Looking cool at all times is the most important thing about being in this room.

Another model walks in and gives his name to the girl at the desk. 'Jake Cooper, Models UK, here for the Sunseeker ad.'

She consults a list, ticks off his name and says, 'Okay Jake, darling, just take a seat and fill out the release form, will you?'

'Ta,' he says, practising his 1,000-watt smile ready for the casting director. He turns to find a place to sit, the smile dimming to about 250 watts as he sees the number of other models waiting ahead of him. Then the power is turned up a bit more as he sees someone he knows.

'Hey, sweetie,' he says to a girl who is combing her hair in a boredom-induced trance.

'Hi, honey,' she says, looking up at him as he kisses her on both cheeks. 'How's it going?'

'Great,' he says, as if it would be anything else. 'Yeah. You?'

'Great.'

'Busy?'

'Yeah, pretty,' she says. Diplomatic answer: no one is going to say, 'No, dead, actually,' are they? But you can't say 'I'm working every day – it's just mad' because no one would believe you. 'You?' she asks.

'Yeah, not bad,' he says, nodding thoughtfully. Then he launches his Exocet: 'Yeah, got the Ford Cirrus campaign, so I'm off to Sicily next month to shoot it.' He knows very well the effect this will have. Two or three other guys look up casually to see who picked up that job after all. It was a biggie – three days of casting, hundreds of guys and thousands of pounds. Why didn't I get it? Perhaps they were looking for someone dark, I reason. That's probably why they called in so many blond models. Other guys around me, dark and blond, are checking him out discreetly. He basks in their, well, all right, *our* envious loathing for a moment and then carries on. 'Did you ever see the pictures from that job we did together?'

'Oh, *don't*,' says the girl. 'The agency sent me the brochure. Why do they always choose the worst shots? That one where you're picking me up? And carrying me across the grass? I look like I've got this huge nose.'

'Yeah,' he says. They both laugh. But now he is staring at her nose.

Her laughter dries up after a few seconds and she says, 'And I haven't, have I?' As if it were absurd, obviously.

But he is still staring at her nose. Actually it *is* quite large. Yeah, that's a big conk for a model. Another girl looks up from the blockbuster novel she is reading and surreptitiously checks out the first girl's nose. As she looks down at her book again, she gratuitously wipes around her own nostrils with a long, slim finger. Just checking.

'It just looks like it, doesn't it?' says the girl, her voice betraying a degree of panic now. 'In the picture. It's daft.'

Jake Cooper is still mesmerised. 'Yeah, it does,' he says at last. 'Yeah, I mean, it's just the picture. I mean not really in the picture, either. It's a lovely nose. That's a great picture. No, honestly. I'd put it in your book if I were you,' he says, patting his own portfolio which he has already removed from his rucksack ready for when he goes in. 'He goes in'? Makes it sound like a military assault on enemy-held territory. Ridiculous. What a daft comparison.

This is far more terrifying than that.

I turn back to my paper and sense once again the edgy atmosphere as other models read novels or magazines or consult A-to-Zs, locating their next casting. Some stare into space or smile at people they half-know, while we all secretly wish everyone else would just sod off and die so that we could get this job.

Another guy comes in, gives his name and flashes a grin that he's obviously used a hundred times before to charm various casting directors and girls on reception.

'Here, you go, Ben, my darling,' says the receptionist.

He takes his form and then makes a joke about the dying flowers on the desk.

'What?' she says, looking up from the list of names.

'You need someone to buy you some more flowers,' he says again, nodding at the drooping white tulips in the vase.

'Eh? Oh, yeah. I think the office manager does it,' she says vaguely, looking back to her list.

He gives a little embarrassed sniff of a laugh and then goes to sit down. The *Schadenfreude* is palpable as the rest of the models, oh, all right, *us*, again, enjoy his discomfort. Yeah, practise your charm somewhere else, mate.

Rather conveniently, by the time I've got to the crossword and discovered that I haven't got a pen, the casting room door opens and the girl on the desk says, 'Charlie, babe, your turn.' I practise my own 1,000-watt smile on her but she has turned back to answer the phone.

The guy coming out, a huge South African I've met before, holds the door open for me and I try it out on him instead. He looks vaguely alarmed.

I walk in and am immediately blinded by the lights. Just behind them I can see the shadows of people, including presumably the director and the client. The only person I know is the casting director, Angie.

'Hi Charlie, darling,' she says, taking her huge glasses off her head and shaking her greying, bobbed hair free. We double-kiss. This familiarity – after all, I'm an old hand at this game, aren't I? – makes me feel much better. My smile feels slightly more genuine, slightly less fixed, when I use it again. She introduces me to various other disembodied voices from the darkness behind the lights. I say 'hi', hoping I'm looking in the right direction.

'Okay, ident just for the record, sweets. Name and agency,' says Angie, who I can just see, looking down at a monitor. I make sure I'm standing on the little masking-tape cross on the carpet and look up.

'Charlie Barrett. Jet Models,' I tell the glassy eye of the camera as if I'd just asked it to marry me.

'Beautiful,' says Angie. 'Can we see your profile, Charlie, love?'

'Sure,' I say confidently, and turn to the left and then the right, taking my time, a slight, jocular wobble to the head, making it clear that I'm not only perfectly self-assured but I'm actually quite enjoying this whole daft, familiar business.

'Luv-leee,' says Angie. My smile almost seems real now. 'Okay, love, take your clothes off down to your undies.' However genuine, that smile must have evaporated pretty quickly. With a very tight timetable to keep too, Angie obviously notices my slight hesitation. 'This is for a beach scene. Didn't they tell you?'

Sunseeker Holidays. Makes sense, I suppose. You might take your clothes off. The only problem is that I'm wearing an age-old pair of white (oh, go on then, slightly grey) M&S undies because they were the only ones that were clean. It's not even as if I'm going to get a trip out of this – no need to go to a beach with today's new technology. All the glamour and expense of a studio in Acton for a half-day. My image (if I get the job and somehow I don't think I'm going to now) will be superimposed onto powdery yellow sand thanks to a special computer image-enhancement program.

Modern technology, eh? Damn it to hell.

Suddenly I can make out four girls squashed onto the settee to whom I haven't been introduced but who are now staring sullenly at me, and I remember the South African hunk whose turn it was just before mine.

God, I'm too old for this.

I really am, though.

I take the stairs three at a time. I don't care if I break my neck, I've just got to get out of here. I step out into the street and make for the tube.

It's been on my mind for a while. At thirty, I reckon I'm ready for a job that not only has better long-term prospects but also provides a greater mental challenge than the ability to remember a name and address and to respond to a request to move your head to the right a bit. But I'm also spurred on by the morbid fear of spending my twilight years doing chunky pullover ads for *Reader's Digest*. It'll be easy-to-get-out-of baths and Stannah stairlifts before you know it.

It's been fun, I must admit. I've earned quite a lot of money for doing very little. I've travelled, often business class. Stayed in nice hotels. I've met some fun people and often thought to myself, What a ridiculous way to make a living, which is probably the best attitude you can have towards any job. I've stopped crowds in the City modelling suits – secretaries shouting risqué comments, men looking on, contemptuous but intrigued, wondering what I've got that they haven't – and I've entertained picnickers in Battersea Park while doing a fashion shoot.

I've travelled across Kenyan game reserves (aftershave) and I've curled up on settees with girls in soft sweaters holding mugs of coffee (empty, of course) in loft apartments to sell life insurance. I've cruised the Caribbean and got paid for it – the only drawback being that we were weren't allowed in the pool or the top deck or some of the lounges because technically we were suppliers to the cruise company or something.

I've been married countless times and sometimes at some really beautiful churches. Should it ever happen for real, I'll be well prepared and able to discuss with my intended all the best venues in which to get hitched in central London. I think my favourite would be Farm Street, Mayfair. That was a lovely wedding. A sunny afternoon in May. The groom wore a Jasper Conran suit and the bride, a tall Irish lesbian called Fennoula or something, looked stunning in an ivory satin dress with a train. Two of the bridesmaids were lovely but the third, whose mother was having a row with her agency about travel expenses, was not such a sweetie.

I get home to my flat in Chiswick and let myself in to find my gorgeous girlfriend on the phone. Sitting on the kitchen unit she is saying, 'Uh, huh,' and stretching out a smooth, tanned, never-ending leg, letting her shoe hang off her toes. I throw my keys down on the counter, get down on one knee and look up at her. She smiles down at me, half anxious, half thrilled.

Lauren's legs have been photographed protruding elegantly from the door of a quarter-million-pound sports car, slightly soaped in a shower cubicle and with a scarf sliding down them to prove that a certain hair removal cream lasts longer than shaving or waxing. If any commercial or any press advertisement requires a classy blonde girl with long, beautiful legs, Lauren's the one they go for. She was in that advert for aftershave with the swarthy bloke sniffing the underside of her knee, and the hair mousse commercial where the girl walks into the restaurant in a shimmering red dress and causes havoc with waiters dropping their trays and male customers being rebuked by their girlfriends as they ogle her.

I touch her skin with my lips, enjoying the unperfumed, unself-conscious, natural smell of her for a moment. Then I slip off her shoe and kiss around her foot. I hear her gasp and tell the person at the other end, 'Nothing.' I run my hand round the gentle curve of her calf and then move my lips up her shin, hovering over the skin, stopping occasionally to kiss her. She gasps again. 'Yep. Look, I'll have to go.' I bite her knee gently and then move my mouth round behind it. 'No, of course. Don't worry. Ah, listen, gotta go.' I kiss around to the front of her thigh and squeeze it a little more aggressively as I push her skirt up. 'Oh, erm. Yes, I'm fine. I think Charlie's coming, that's all.' I look up again and give her a wide-eyed goofy look of 'You bet.' I begin to bite her inner thigh gently. 'He's down here, I mean, he's here. Okay, okay, bye, Mum.' She clicks off and puts down the portable.

I look up again quickly. 'That was your mum! Oh, shit, why didn't you say?'

'What could I say?' she laughs. 'Gotta go Mum, Charlie's slowly bringing me to orgasm?'

I smile, then stand up and pull her against me roughly. 'She'd know what a good prospective son-in-law she's got.'

'Easy tiger,' says Lauren. 'You're still just the boyfriend. Don't go getting ideas above your station.' Then she smiles and begins to kiss me. Our lips still touching, I lift her up and carry her to the bedroom.

'Do think you got it then?' she says, curled up, nestling her back into me in bed after we've made love.

'What?' I say sleepily to the back of her head.

'The Sunseeker thing.'

'No, I mean, I don't know. They didn't say anything, obviously. Actually I think I probably buggered it up. The agency didn't tell me they wanted to do body shots so I was wearing some horrible old undies.'

'Oh, Charlie, you must check these things, I told you,' says Lauren, turning round. 'Always ask if there are any special clothing requirements and always wear good underwear in any case. You've got tons of pants.'

'But you haven't washed them,' I explain sweetly.

She gives me an admonishing tap on the nose. 'It was pretty obvious that they wanted to see bodies if it was for a holiday brochure.'

'I suppose so, I just wasn't thinking. Anyway, why do you ask whether I've got it or not? Can't a man come home and make love to his woman, just because he feels like it, whether he's had a successful day or a crap one?'

'I'm not your *woman*. I just wondered if that's why you're in such a good mood, that's all.'

'I just am, I suppose. I shouldn't be – the casting was pretty bloody embarrassing.'

She looks at me and then says, 'Why do you always go into these things with a such a negative frame of mind?'

'I don't.'

'You do. It's always "Why have they put me up for this one? It's not me," or "God, I made such a fool of myself." You should walk into every casting thinking to yourself, "I'm the one they're looking for," "I'm the perfect person for this job." Then you'll get it. It's all about positive thinking.'

'Is that what you do?'

'Yeah, of course I do.'

'Why don't you always get it then?'

'Because . . . oh, shut up.' She squeezes my cheek hard and kisses me, then gets up to have a shower.

I look at my watch. Nearly five o'clock. Time for a drink? Or a cup of tea? Big decisions. Drink? Tea? Drink? Tea? I find a cool place for my feet across Lauren's side of the bed and lie back with my hands behind my head. I can still smell her on me. Drink? Tea? Tea? Drink?

'Lauren?'

'What?' she calls from the shower.

'Shall I have a drink or a cuppa tea?'

'Whaaaat?' The water stops for a moment.

'I said shall I have a drink or a cup of tea?'

'Have a cup of tea – it's too early to start drinking. And make me one too, will you?' The water starts again.

Well, that's that decided. Now all I have to do is get up and do it. I turn over and see myself in the mirrors on the wardrobe. Do I look too old to call myself a model? 'Course not. One of the few advantages of being a bloke in this business is that you can go on for years. More character. The downside is that people think you're either gay or stupid, or both, but at least you can go on working and getting decent-paying jobs for longer than women can.

Except that they're probably adverts for incontinence pants.

The mirrors along our built-in wardrobe doors were there when we first moved in, and we immediately decided to remove them because they're so naff, but somehow we never got round to it. My mates had a good laugh when they first saw them.

'Bit more subtle than putting them on the ceiling, I suppose,' said Mike, giving me a leering smile.

'You can tell he's a bloody model,' said Becky. 'Vain or what, Charles?'

Laughing, I explained that we really *were* going to get rid of them.

What would Mike and Becky and others say if they saw we still had them? They haven't been round here for ages.

When we first moved in, sometimes as we were making love, I

would catch Lauren looking across at these mirrors, at the images of the two of us entwined. Her long legs around me, or her perfect breasts cupped in my hands as she straddled me. At first I wasn't sure whether to be embarrassed or annoyed. Was she looking at me or at herself? Was it because the sex was so good? Or was it because it was so boring that she needed some sort of extra stimulation? Was she enjoying it or being subtly critical – making a note to work her thighs a bit more at the gym or advise me to keep off the beer and chips for a while.

Now, sometimes I glance across too. There I am with my girlfriend, almost like a stranger, kissing her stomach, moving down her long, honey-tanned body, holding myself above her on my elbows as I push my way into her, slowly, conscientiously kissing her breasts. My own, private version of those articles you find in men's health and fitness magazines called things like 'How to achieve the ultimate climax' or 'How to give your woman the best time ever in bed'. Or just a home-made porn movie with me starring and directing. Sometimes I look over at the same time Lauren does and our eyes meet. We exchange a glance of love, lust, intimacy through the glass.

Our whole home is beautiful, I must say. It's Lauren's work, of course. A ground-floor flat in a large Victorian house off Chiswick High Road, it has scrubbed pine floors, whitewashed walls, big Roy Lichtenstein-style prints, plus little things she has picked up from antique shops and from a visit a few years ago to Morocco. She did all the research about freighting the things home. Spoke to couriers, checked up on the paperwork, got a good deal. Bullied, begged, bribed her way through it. People love our flat as soon as they walk in. I tell them 'It's all down to Lauren,' and they say 'Yeah, I can believe that.'

The sound of my mobile ringing shakes me out of my reverie.

'Ye-e-e-llow,' I say.

'Charlie?'

'Speaking. Karyn. How are you?'

'Good, darling. How did the Sunseekers casting go?'

'Oh, pretty crap, actually.'

'Really? Why?'

'I was wearing these really disgusting old undies . . .'

'How lovely – I'm just visualising them. Anyway, you knew it was for a body shot, didn't you?'

'No.'

'Oh, Charlie, you did.'

'Penny gave me the details.'

'Oh, I see.'

Penny might be Karyn's boss at the agency and a frighteningly tough businesswoman who can screw every penny out of a client for a model – and every penny out of a model for her agency – but her ability to pass on the simplest bits of information for any casting or job is negligible.

'I think she was probably too pissed again,' I explain.

Karyn giggles. 'Very possibly. Anyway, this is *me* giving you a casting so you know it will be totally correct in every detail.'

'If you say so.'

'I do say so. Now, got a pen?'

'Hang on, let me get out of bed.'

'Tough job being a model, isn't it?' snaps Karyn. 'Come on, I've got other people to talk to before six.'

'Ooh, 'scuse me. Right. Here we go. Shoot.'

'It's to go to 11a Kenworth Mews, W11, to see a guy called Dave Howland. It's advertising for a new dotcom company—'

'I thought they'd all gone under.'

'Fortunately for you matey, they haven't. This one is just launching and they need some advertising and some images for their homepage, which is where we come in.'

'Jolly good.'

'So it's any time between ten and twelve tomorrow. Go smart casual, you know, like a young entrepreneur.'

'I'm going to get this job,' I tell her, remembering Lauren's sensible words.

''Course you are dear,' says Karyn with exaggerated condescension. 'Just make sure you're wearing clean pants.'

chapter two

I am the face of Lord James cigarettes.

In Uruguay, that is. Laughing, talking to my friends, getting the girl, sipping a cocktail, elegantly smoking a cigarette – my picture appears in magazines and billboards from Montevideo to Punta del Este. I'm on the side of the buses as they snort and push their way through the swirling exhaust fumes and jostling traffic on stiflingly hot days in the palm-filled squares, past crumbling former colonial mansions and along newly built express ways. Peasant women from the outlying regions and girls from Spanish Catholic schools in stripy uniforms get on these buses, and they must sometimes look up at my face smiling down at them.

Do those women really believe that I am some British aristo who likes nothing more than to enjoy a relaxing ciggie with his smart friends? Do those schoolgirls giggle and wonder who I am, what I'm like in real life and where I live? Or do they think I'm just another tosser in a stupid ad? (Obviously I hope not – although in strictly moral terms, it is probably more acceptable than their being so overwhelmed with my handsome face and the mood of effortless elegance that I embody that they actually start smoking the disgusting things I'm advertising.)

And when those buses go back to their corrugated-iron sheds at night in the outskirts of the city I'm still smiling, smoking, talking to my friends, my face inches away from my face on another bus or pressed up against the image of a dark-haired woman advertising a Brazilian soap opera.

So, although I've never been to Uruguay and I don't particularly want to go, I suppose that if I walked down the street in Montevideo, somebody would stop, stare, nudge someone else and say, 'Hey, that's the guy from the Lord James ads.' That's fame, you see: someone knows you even if you don't know them.

People have done it to me in Britain. I was once standing on a tube station platform when two women with shopping bags looked across at me and began to giggle. I smiled back, slightly bemused. Then I checked my fly and rubbed my mouth just to make sure that it didn't still have toothpaste on it or something. What's their problem? I thought, irritably. It was only when I turned round that I noticed a huge poster behind me on the tube station wall: my face looking up at a stewardess in an advertisement for a business class airline seat.

With my swept-back blond hair, linen suit and smooth, tanned skin I'm also the face of Lord James cigarettes in Paraguay, Ecuador, New Guinea and various specified southern states of Brazil and associated territories for poster, print and point-of-sale advertising, with no specific conditions attached until June 2005 when the licence will have to be renewed. And, if it is (oh, please, oh, please), I'll get another big, fat cheque – for doing absolutely nothing.

I remember being in the agency when the call came to say that I had got the job. Since it was the end of the day one of the girls dashed out to the corner shop and bought a bottle of Australian Chardonnay. We toasted my success with our plastic cups.

'Well done, darling,' said Karyn, kissing me on the lips.

'Thanks, babe,' I said, putting my arm round her waist, knowing it looked pretty cool but hoping all the same that it was okay by her.

Penny also kissed me on the lips so that I could taste her bright red lipstick as well as the stale alcohol on her breath from her lunchtime session. 'Congrats, darling,' she growled at me. 'You're an absolute bloody star. Isn't he, everyone?'

There were murmurs of agreement from all around me.

I'd never been in the agency before when one of these big jobs came through. Previously I'd just be told about it on the phone so I wasn't sure of the etiquette; whether to say 'thanks' to them for helping me or just look pleased with myself. I suddenly felt rather embarrassed at being the centre of attention. It's not like I could explain how I got the role, what special skill or strategy I'd employed. I just turned up at the casting, showed some guy my book, let them take a polaroid of me as they always do for some unfathomable reason, even though they've got my card with half a dozen pictures on it anyway, said 'Thanks very much' and went home. But somehow I did it. So there I was. The man of the hour.

'Hey, bud!' Brad, one of the girls' bookers, gave me the high five model handshake, a giant pec moving under his skin-tight 'army' T-shirt. 'Mr Uruguay!' It wasn't very funny really, but we all laughed, glad to have something to laugh about. Then we stood in silence and everyone sipped, eyes looking for someone to speak next.

I took a deep breath. 'I could do with a cigarette,' I said. 'Shame I don't smoke.'

Everyone laughed again.

'Sophisticated, confident, European' the brief from the ad people had said. That's me. Well, if they say so, who am I to argue?

I arrive at the casting early because I know it'll get busier later, old pro that I am. Unfortunately lots of other old pros are there too, having had the same idea. But perhaps the other reason I'm usually early for these things is simply that I hate hanging around with other models. I nod hallo to a few familiar faces and have a brief chat with a red-headed Glaswegian guy called Brian. I did a job with him a few months ago when we both spent an afternoon in a brand new office in Docklands poring over a laptop computer and then shaking hands – doing what is known in the trade as the 'grip and grin'.

On the way here I've been doing Lauren's thing and telling myself I'm the man they're looking for and that this is the perfect job for me, but I always feel a bit of a berk doing it – thank goodness no one can hear me. Unless, of course, I'm actually talking out loud. The clients are late, natch. At nearly half past ten, when the room is beginning to fill up and I've read most of my paper and am sliding a creased old copy of *Men's Health* out from under a precarious pile of magazines on the coffee table, two thirtysomething guys burst in. One gushes apologies at everyone and tells us that his breakfast meeting ran over, the other stands back and offers a quiet 'So sorry' to the girl running the casting.

She offers them both coffee and the talkative guy reacts as if she's just left him her house in her will. They are shown into another room, Mr Verbosity still apologising and thanking everyone in sight. Somehow the collective malevolence radiating from us models – especially those of us who have now been here for nearly three-quarters of an hour – escapes him, and he just grins wildly at us.

'Sorry guys,' he says lightly. We smile back absolution with varying degrees of sincerity, each thinking, just shut up and get on with it, you incompetent tosser. The other guy seems to pick up this vibe and looks genuinely embarrassed, shuffling nervously.

I'm fourth in. There is a strict order in these matters, even if no one is keeping a list. First come, first served. Anyone who tries to get ahead risks being ripped limb from limb by their fellow models. Got to get off to another casting? Haven't we all, mate? Got a job in half an hour? Go and do it then. Car on a meter? Should have taken the bus. Need urgent dialysis? Bite on a towel, bud. You can steal my money, take my girlfriend, shoot my dog, but don't *ever* try and get ahead of me in a casting.

I walk in and say, 'Hello, Charlie Barrett. Good to meet you.'

'Charlie. Excellent. Piers,' says the talkative one, extending a hand. 'My associate, Guy.'

I shake hands with him too and then pass them my book. It's the standard format: good, strong head shot at the front, then a mixture of fashion, lifestyle, business – me with suit, looking at watch, staring down into laptop, walking fast with another guy – then a bit of young dad stuff with a girl and a four-year-old plus a couple of my weddings. They flick through and I give them my well-rehearsed anecdotes: 'That was actually taken at seven in the morning, even though I'm wearing a DJ', 'That kid was such a brat', 'The girl I'm with there presents something on Sky TV now', and 'That one? Thanks. Actually the photographer got really drunk at lunchtime, I'm just amazed it's in focus. Ha, ha.'

Piers laughs uproariously and Guy asks more questions. They ask me how long I've been modelling and I tell them: since I left university.

'What did you read?' says Piers, obviously surprised that someone in such a brainless profession could have gone to university. Don't worry about it, Piers, I'm used to it.

'Marketing. At Leeds,' I tell him.

'Really? Why are you . . .?'

'In this daft game?' I laugh. Does that sound too cynical? Oops, never mind – plenty more jobs out there. 'I thought I'd do it for a while after university and, well, here am I eight years later.'

'It's a form of marketing, I suppose,' says Guy.

'Yeah, I suppose it is,' I say, hoping to recover the situation.

'All right, Charlie, that's splendid,' says Piers. 'Absolutely fantastic. Great pictures. Thanks very much for coming in to see us.'

'Thanks, Charlie,' says Guy.

I smile, take my book back and then it's the next bloke's turn.

First come first served is how I first met Lauren. I'd seen her a couple of times before at castings. Even in a room dotted with stunning women you couldn't fail to spot Lauren. There was something about her manner and her self-assurance. She certainly knew how to make an entrance, too; she breezed in as if she was doing a catwalk show, ignoring looks of interest from the boys and depressed resentment from the girls.

It was a casting for a new type of mobile phone. Europe-wide. Lots of money. Even more models up for it. She gave her name, turned round without looking at anybody else and found a seat. Then she dipped into her bag and took out a book called *Know the Market: Choosing the best ISA for you*. What? I thought. Around her other female models were reading *Marie Claire* or novels about girls with fat thighs, a Chardonnay habit and no boyfriends. This girl even seemed to be enjoying her improving tome. She took a pen out of her bag and made a note in the margin. She ran a hand through her long blonde hair. I remember thinking that this was a face that could sell almost anything. Lauren's beauty is sort of immediate and easily accessible. There is nothing quirky or unconventional about it, she has the kind of large bluey-grey eyes, long straight nose, clear skin, even white teeth and sensual mouth that any girl would want.

I knew I was staring and I knew she would sense it and look up in a moment, but I didn't care. In fact her eyes didn't move away from her book so I went back to my own reading matter – a mindless thriller. A few moments later I realised that there was some discussion going on about whose turn it was next because one girl had arrived late but had been allowed to go in early. I could sense the tension rising. The girl at the desk was checking her list and muttering, 'Just hang on a sec . . . what was your name again?' Another model said something about being before someone else and having to be away by four because she had to pick up her daughter from her boyfriend. Lauren was also looking up from her book now. I wasn't that bothered. I had all day with nothing else to do and the sight of a model cat-fight always amuses me. But suddenly Lauren was speaking and the others were quiet.

'It's you next, then you, because you agreed to let her go ahead,' she said, talking to another girl. 'And then you, followed by me. Okay?'

Whether that was the right order or not, there was something about Lauren's confident tone that prohibited any further discussion. A challenge to 'Argue with that, if you dare' seemed to hang in the air as the other models decided slowly that it probably made sense. Lauren went back to her book and everyone else fell silent, either satisfied or terrified.

Fucking hell, I thought. Luckily my turn came before hers and I hung around afterwards, clutching my rucksack and an A-to-Z, pretending that I was just in the process of leaving and, hey, gosh, you got another casting, too? I'd also thought of mentioning something about ISAs but I couldn't think of anything intelligent or funny to say about them. Know any ISA jokes, anyone?

In fact she nearly breezed past me so I had rush after her and catch her up.

'Hi,' I said.

'Oh, hello,' she said, looking slightly surprised.

'You were just in that casting, weren't you?' I had hoped to do this a bit more subtly but I was in for it now and there was no turning back.

'Yes,' she said, not having to add, 'Were you? I didn't notice you.'

'Erm, how did it go?'

She stopped walking and turned to look at me properly.

'Not bad. I don't think I got it, though, I think I'm too English-looking for the kind of girl they were after. I asked the casting director which countries it's being sold to and I got the impression they wanted someone more American, more West Coast, sort of a Laura Dern or a Cameron Diaz.'

'Yes,' I said dumbly.

'How about you?'

Well in my case, the agency told me to go and I'd gone. That was it. 'Erm, seemed okay, but I don't think I got it either.'

She looked at me for a moment. Then she said, 'Never mind, you always learn something about your look and the potential market for it at every casting, I think, don't you?'

'Yes, I suppose so.' She smiled (patronisingly?) and then carried on walking. I heard myself calling after her, 'I wondered, actually, whether you'd like to go for a drink sometime?'

She stopped again and then slowly walked back towards me. 'What's your name?' she asked.

'Erm.' Oh shit, what is my name? I thought, panic gripping me like an anaconda. 'Charlie, Charlie Barrett,' I said at last. It sounded like I'd just made it up. That *was* right, wasn't it? Yeah, Charlie Barrett, that's me.

'Thing is, Charlie Barrett, I'm booked up all this week—'

'Ohrightnoproblemsureofcoursejustwonderednevermind,' I spewed elegantly.

'But I could do lunch on Wednesday.'

'Lunch?'

'Yeah, why not? You do *have* lunch, don't you?'

'Yes, I have lunch every Wednesday,' I said. It was supposed to be a joke but I'm still not sure how it sounded.

'Give me your number and I'll ring you in the morning to confirm where and when,' she said.

I thought, Oh I see, that's a nice way to do it. You won't ring, you'll accidentally lose it and I'll be too embarrassed to mention it if we ever meet again at a casting. Slightly despondently, I gave her my number and expected nothing.

But she did ring me. We went out to a little restaurant in Soho where she had fish and salad because she was on a high protein/low carb diet. I ordered chicken kiev. I didn't particularly want it but I'd been too busy talking to look at the menu, and when the waiter came it was the first thing I saw.

'You're not doing any swimwear stuff at the moment,' she said as I gave my order.

'How do you mean?'

'Chicken kiev, all that butter.'

'Oh right, no, no not really.'

'That's the thing about boys, you never have to watch your diet, do you?' she said.

'No, I suppose not. I just tend to eat any old thing,' I said, laughing oafishly.

'You're lucky, you've got a naturally slim build,' she said. Was there just a flicker of a smile across her face as she realised the effect that this innocent observation was having on me? I mean, it was a compliment, wasn't it? 'I bet you never put on weight, do you?'

'Yeah,' I said. 'I mean no, not really.'

She definitely smiled this time. 'Do you do much sport or go to the gym?'

'Swimming. And I play football on Saturdays.' I watched her snap off a piece of bread-stick. 'Why are you laughing?'

She laughed more. 'Because you sound like a little boy talking about your hobbies to a friend of your mum's or something.' She laughed again. 'I didn't mean to make it sound like that.'

'I collect stamps, too.'

She stopped smiling and looked unsure for a moment as though she felt she ought to say something polite about philately.

I let the confusion continue for a moment. Then I said, 'I'm joking.' She laughed – amused by my joke or her own gullibility? Who cares? Lauren 1. Charlie 1.

I loved the way she loved being annoyed by my teasing. It was like playing along with my silly jokes made her cross but she couldn't help it. Even if nothing had ever come of this romantically, I'd have learnt something about how to market myself as a model, how to buy an ISA, how to negotiate with hotels to get the best room-rate and how to fillet a fish.

That makes the rest of our conversation sound so tedious, but it wasn't. Lauren was just so on the ball. About everything. Opinionated, perceptive, and funny too. Everything interested her and she had strong views on every subject.

Later, having asked about my background and career, she told me about hers: she had done A-levels, two As and a B, but had decided to put off going to college because she wanted to see something of the world. She had known she had the potential to be a model, so she decided this would be a good way of earning money while she figured out what she really wanted to do with her life.

'I just couldn't work for anyone, could you? I've always needed to be my own boss,' she said.

'I don't know, never done it really,' I told her. 'Work generally doesn't, you know, do it for me.'

She stopped the expert filleting of her seabass and looked at me again. Was I being serious? I wasn't sure. I was just giving her a provocative, enigmatic look which always works well in shots for women's magazines, when my chicken kiev, into which I'd just stuck my knife, spurted melted butter across the table at her. It exploded. All over this beautiful, elegant woman. In the middle of the restaurant. On our first date. Hot, liquid butter, flecked with chopped parsley, dripping down her cream linen dress. A huge, yellow smear. The restaurant seemed to go silent. Or was that just the strange hissing noise in my ears, the kind you get before you faint?

Eventually I managed to drag my eyes away from the stain and look up at her face. She was expressionless. Then she rolled her eyes (oh, God, not a good sign, surely. Why? Why me? Why now?) and suddenly smiled.

'Charlie Barrett,' she said. 'You are a fuckwit.'

Waiters fluttered around. The owner's wife was consulted. Napkins were produced. Advice was given. We finally ate, although on my part every mouthful was torture. As we ordered coffee and I emptied her sachet of sugar as well as my own into my cappuccino, it occurred to me that not only could she carry off almost any situation – anything that life, figuratively speaking, or me, literally speaking, could ever throw at her – but I'd never be lost or bored with this woman. I was right. Lauren has an inbuilt compass so she always knows exactly where she is going, and at that moment I decided I wanted to tag along.

As we walked through the restaurant she had an even greater effect on our fellow customers than she had had in the casting. The butter stain looked, at a cursory glance, like a pattern on the dress and she gave the impression that she really didn't care at all about it. Garlic butter appliqué? Oh, it's very in this season, didn't you know?

I held the door open for her and she swept out, putting on her sunglasses as she did so.

'Are you around next week?' I asked her, assuming she'd give me a polite, polished brush off, the kind of thing a girl as stunning as her would have to say to men about two or three times a day. Especially to one who has just covered her with the contents of a chicken kiev.

But she didn't.

'Actually, we could do something tomorrow,' she said.

'Oh, right, I thought you were busy all . . .' What the fuck was I doing? Trying to put her off?

'Yes, I was,' she said. 'But I've decided to cancel.'

chapter three

I arrive at the job early, with a selection of trendy young businessman's clothes as instructed. I've brought a navy blue suit, a long-sleeved polo shirt, a black T-shirt, a cream button-down collar shirt and a French cuffed navy blue number with matching cufflinks. One thing about this job is that you need a large wardrobe – although mirrors on it aren't compulsory. Oh, God, those mirrors. It happened again last night. Perhaps we can't do it without the use of mirrors any more. We don't smoke, natch, but we do use mirrors to create an illusion.

Lauren, needless to say, has put her wardrobe together with military precision over the years she's been modelling. Her side of the hanging space contains suits, skirts, blouses and casual clothes to fit every occasion: busy executive, young mother, seductive girl in bed, sensible woman in the kitchen. All perfectly appropriate for her colouring and build, all tax deductible. Lauren does her own accountancy. She also does mine, now.

I, needless to say, have chosen my work clothing with absolutely no thought or skill whatsoever. Most of it is stuff I wear anyway, stuff I've rushed out and bought the day before a job, stuff I've borrowed from friends and sort of forgotten to return, stuff I got cheap at Primark because I know I need it, plus a couple of things I've nicked from fashion shoots: 'Where *is* that grey T-shirt?' one harassed stylist asked me after a job. I shrugged my shoulders. 'Dunno, search me,' I said, knowing that if she did she'd find the missing item in my bag. Oh, shut up! They've got thousands of them. On the other hand, I've also been chased down the road by a stylist to return a pair of socks that I'd forgotten to take off. It's tit for tat.

But this is a suit job. Smart, confident and on the ball. Huh, I wonder what that feels like. It's the job from the casting the other day, the dotcom job.

'Clever boy,' said Karyn when she rang to tell me I'd got it. 'I knew you looked like a dotcommer.'

'What? You mean broke, washed up and and desperate.'

'What's the matter with you? What happened to your get-up-and-go?'

'It got up and went.'

'Oh, Charlie. Don't be so cynical.'

Perhaps it's beginning to show.

'Sorry, Karyn. I'm delighted. How much is it again?' I know that will encourage me, even minus agency commission.

'Fifteen hundred, and you're worth every penny of it.'

'You say the sweetest things.'

We're shooting it at a massive loft apartment overlooking the river in Battersea. Sun is flooding in, the clothes they have brought for me, having spurned my own motley collection, are actually really cool – lots of Prada, Ermenegildo Zegna and Dries Van Noten. They've even managed to get the right sizes in some cases. It often amazes me that although all my sizes are clearly printed on my card in UK and European versions and we confirm them before the job, the stylists always manage to get the wrong ones. It must be on their list of things to do: 1) Bring iron. 2) Polish up shoes. 3) Make sure model's clothes don't fit.

Moan, moan. Sorry.

Piers bursts in, late again, just as we're going through the wardrobe and the photographer's assistant, a fat guy called Benny with Joe 90 specs, is putting up the lights.

'Morning, gang,' he sings at us, his fruity voice filling the whole cathedral-like void of the apartment. There is no way any of us can match his enthusiasm so our responses sound decidedly downbeat. 'What have we got for our cool young businessman to wear?'

He dives into the neatly laid-out wardrobe and starts throwing the things around, much to the annoyance of the stylist, Hilary, a tall, willowy girl who is frightfully posh and has just been telling me about working on the latest Joseph Fiennes movie. 'He's like such a total sweetie, yeah?' I feel I should apologise for being just a nondescript model doing some crappy advertising shoot.

'This is great,' says Piers, pulling out a black Prada shirt and holding it up. 'This is very "2cool". Guy! Very "2cool", don't you think?'

Guy, who is talking intently to the photographer, looks over and nods.

'I haven't ironed that yet,' says Hilary, snatching it back.

'You need a dark suit too, like this,' Piers informs me, ignoring Hilary and grabbing a jacket off the rack. 'Yep, perfect.'

'He can't wear all that black, he'll just disappear in the picture,' says Hilary, failing to catch the trousers as they slide off the hanger.

'Excellent,' says Piers, dumping the whole lot on her and marching over to Guy and the photographer, presumably to cock things up there too.

Hilary runs her hands through her hair and says quietly, 'Just keep that twat away from me, will you?'

'Yes, ma'am,' I tell her, picking up the trousers.

I always get on well with stylists and make-up artists, even though make-up takes thirty seconds for boys – just a bit of powder to stop us shining, and something to cover up any spots and shaving cuts that have chosen to appear that morning. Remember those unwelcome but very noticeable visitors on the day of a teenage party? Well, the bigger the modelling job the more likely they are to pop up – literally.

Perhaps because this isn't exactly a massive job, there are none of the little buggers in evidence, which means I spend even less time with the make-up artist, an Eastern European girl with a round, pale face whose name I don't catch.

The only time I've ever lost my temper with a wardrobe person was when I was doing a show for Paul Costello. My dresser rabbited on endlessly about the new flat she was buying with her boyfriend, and I only just had time to let her rip off one set of clothes and help me put a suit on ready to go out again. I did my stuff, sauntering down the catwalk (or runway as we call it in the biz, just to make it clear that we are *in* the biz) and came back ready to change into the next outfit on the rail. It was only when I reached down to take off my trousers that I realised she had sent me off there and back without my fly done up.

'Oh, fuck,' I hissed. 'How embarrassing. How could you do that?'

'Look, mate,' she said, thrusting a jacket at me, 'there are some places where only *your* hands go.'

The thing about these shoots is that as a model you have almost nothing to do all day until the very last minute when the photographer, art director, client and God knows who else who feels like a day out of the office decides that they are ready for you. So you sit around and chat with strangers. By the end of the day you sometimes find that you know almost all there is to know about someone you had never met before that morning and might never meet again.

This shoot is relatively painless. They only need three different pictures, apparently. It still manages to take all day, of course. I talk to Piers and Guy quite a bit in between shots. They're actually nice guys. They're interested in what it's like to be a model and I ask a bit about their new venture.

'I thought dotcoms were all finished,' I say, smiling to show I'm being deliberately provocative.

'The first generation certainly are,' says Piers. 'It's all about timing. Those guys thundered in without thinking and everybody – banks, investment houses, venture capitalists – just poured money at them in a sort of blind panic, but if you looked at the business plans very often there were no obvious revenue streams.'

Guy says, 'We're about building stable business models—'

'With carefully targeted audiences and correct market positioning,' jumps in Piers.

'We're looking to create market synergies with appropriate trading partners,' says Guy, looking at me intensely as if he's willing me to challenge him or ask him to elaborate.

Instead I say, 'That seems very sensible.'

Lunch is a vast selection of sandwiches, cold chicken and salads. It's one of the best lunches I've ever had on a job. There are fruit juices and a kind of mineral water I haven't seen before. According to the label it comes from newly melted snows and glaciers at the tip of the Andes. The rain from which this snow was made fell before the industrial revolution and so it is exceptionally pure, it says. Glacial Purity. What does that mean? I hold it up to the light. Glacial Purity. I like the sound of that. Mind you, when I see the menu and the receipts for the food and notice that it's six pounds a bottle, I'd have to really like it.

We finish just before five.

'We're wrapped, guys, well done,' says the photographer, a small, dapper man in black with a cap of salt-and-pepper grey hair.

'We're wrapped everyone,' echoes Piers.

'Thank you, Piers,' says Hilary, venomously folding clothes.

I take off my suit, put it back on the rack and then start to put on my own clothes.

'Can I have a word, Charlie?' says Guy.

'Sure,' I say, assuming that he and Piers are going to ask me to do some more work for them without the agency – freelance, you might say. I'm not particularly averse to it; Penny has done very well out of me. Besides, it happens. Everyone does it.

Sure enough, he guides me to one corner of the huge, open plan living room and says quietly, 'We wondered if you'd be interested in working for us.'

'Mmm, could be.' Play it cool, see what they want and what kind of rates they'll pay. What would Lauren ask?

'We think you're the kind of guy we're looking for for our venture, you know, just from talking to you today,' says Piers. 'You've got the right look, the right manner.'

'So, you want to do something without the agency?' I ask, as if suddenly I'm not so sure about this and will need to be convinced – and remunerated adequately.

They exchange glances.

'Yeah,' says Guy, laughing gently. 'We'd like you to help with our marketing.'

I let it sink in for a moment. 'Really? You mean *not* modelling.' I'm not handing out flyers, that's for sure.

They laugh a bit more this time.

'No, full-time marketing,' says Piers, his dark brown eyes fixing me. 'I get the feeling you're pretty bored with this game, aren't you?'

'New challenge?' suggests Guy, raising his eyebrows.

'You've got a degree you haven't used yet,' says Piers.

I think about it for a moment. This is a proper job they're talking about. I'm about to ask whether I'll have to wear a suit, then realise that I should probably find out about something a little more serious such as private health insurance or non-contributory pension schemes or something. Instead I just say, 'Ummm.'

'Well, think it over,' says Guy, handing me a card.

'It does sound very interesting,' I say, trying not to sound like a complete dingbat. 'It's just that I haven't done any marketing for, well, since I was at university.'

'Oh, you've got the basics,' says Piers. 'This thing can really market itself.'

'Anyway, the important thing,' says Guy, 'is that you've got the personality and the look. We've done the hard work, what we need is someone to charm the investors and customers, schmooze the media a bit. We'll brief you on the company and what we're doing. We'd like you to be the face of 2cool2btrue dot com.'

'2cool2btrue?'

'Dot com,' adds Guy, helpfully.

'It's a second-generation internet venture, learning from the mistakes of the first,' says Piers.

'Yeah, you said. But what does it do, exactly?'

'Have you got a moment now to talk about it? Shall we go for a drink somewhere?' says Guy.

We find a quiet pub across the road and Piers buys three Cokes while Guy begins their presentation. By this time, I'm over the initial shock, a bit more switched on. I decide to play devil's advocate a bit.

'So what's different about 2cool2btrue? I mean, what's your unique selling point?' I ask.

'I thought you'd forgotten all your marketing stuff,' says Piers, setting down the drinks. 'USPs already, I'm impressed.'

Guy ignores him and pauses for thought for a moment. 'Image is everything these days, isn't it?' he begins, putting his hands together as if in prayer. 'Labels, market positioning, brands are what counts. No one, well hardly anyone, buys things today because they *need* them or because they're the cheapest, or whatever. They buy a product because of what it says about them. Look at advertising in the fifties and sixties and even the seventies – it was all about things working better than their competitors—'

'Or being cheaper,' interjects Piers.

'Exactly, or being cheaper, but no one really cares about that nowadays.'

'Mmm,' I say. It all makes sense to me, but I decide to keep looking sceptical.

'Now it's the label. You buy Armani, Mercedes, Nike or Apple Mac or Smeg cookers or whatever not because they're better put-together or they fit you, and certainly not because they're cheaper, but because you want to be seen with them.'

'Take your trainers,' says Piers.

I look down quickly at them.

'What make are they?'

'Nike,' I say, pretending to have to look.

'But lots of other people make them – why not George at Asda, for instance?'

'What make of jeans are those?' asks Guy.

'Levis. Engineered.'

'Why not M&S? Their jeans are just the same, only slightly cheaper.'

'Because you'd feel like a middle-aged man,' suggests Piers.

'What kind of car do you drive?'

'I don't. Don't need one.'

'Okay, your dad. Volvo? Audi?'

'Not a good example,' I say.

'Oh, sorry, is he . . .?' Guy asks, awkwardly.

'Dead?' says Piers.

'No, he's not, he's alive, very alive. Too alive, if anything. Anyway, he drives a Porsche.'

'Ah ha,' says Guy. 'Middlescent?'

'Mm?'

'Middle-aged man trying to be an adolescent,' he explains.

'Sort of,' I groan at the thought of him.

'Underwear?' says Piers.

I don't really want to think about my dad in his underwear, actually, but Piers is off.

'Armani pants are really just like anyone else's – M&S or John Lewis, except that they say "Armani" on them. Or 2(x)ist if you're really cool. And, of course, only you know that when you're wearing them, don't you?'

'Yes,' I say. Because I do. Like now. Like Lauren says, always wear good underwear to a job.

'So it's all about the label, the image. Brand image is so important. Armani will not let just *anyone* sell their underwear, for example. If you want them to supply you, they'll come and inspect your shop to make sure that you're not some pile-it-high, sell-it-cheap merchant in Leyton High Road.'

'Okay,' says Guy. 'So you get the idea. At the beginning of the third millennium, the label is what counts. Look,' he points out of the window at two black kids walking past. 'See that? "Dolce & Gabbana" all over their T-shirts. People don't even want designs these days: the label is the design. The label has to be visible – the bigger the better.'

'That's why these companies are diversifying; you can now buy Armani for the home, Ralph Lauren paint. You'll soon be able to buy their food.' I think of the Harvey Nichols coffee and chocolates I bought the other day for Lauren's mum when we went over for lunch.

'Everything must have a label, otherwise we're just not interested,' says Piers.

'So 2cool2btrue is a label.'

'Exactly,' says Piers. 'Think of an ultra-chic, upmarket website.'

'Like Armani dot com?'

'Armani dot com is just the web presence of the company.'

'Well, Mercedes must have a pretty cool site.'

'But again, it's just the website of a smart car company, not a smart website in its own right,' says Piers.

'2cool2btrue dot com will be the web equivalent of Armani, Prada, Rolls-Royce, *Wallpaper**,' explains Guy.

'You'll be proud to have it on your Favourites list.'

'Your boss will be *impressed* when he sees you visiting it at work.'

'What will you sell, then? Clothes?' I ask, playing with a beer mat.

'A whole lifestyle experience,' says Guy.

'People will be able to *live* 2cool2btrue.'

'They'll *want* to live it.'

'People like you.'

'People who want to *be* like you.'

'Very flattering,' I offer, mainly just to halt the tide for a second.

'Nothing of the sort,' says Guy, 'It's just effective marketing. 2cool will be the smartest, coolest, hippest thing in cyberspace and *you* will be the human face of it.'

I gaze up at a sign saying 'Bar Snacks: Cod Almighty – tasty bite-size battered cod pieces served with our own tartar sauce. £3.95. Vegetable lasagne served with chips and salad. Dressing of your choice. £4.95.'

A large-screen TV is playing American football at the back, slightly out of focus. An old man with a pint of mild is trying to watch it, brow creased with confusion and irritation at the mystifying, blurred images. He reaches over almost painfully to tap ash into a huge, grubby, plastic ashtray emblazoned with Castlemaine xxx. Pubs, when he was a lad, had pianos, ham rolls under a glass dome, and busty, blowsy landladies, not big-screen all-sports cable television and Australian backpackers wearing T-shirts with the pub's corporate owners' logo and a name badge.

Glacial Purity. Six pounds a bottle.

chapter four

'I think it sounds like an excellent opportunity. Pass me the balsamic vinegar,' says Lauren.

'It does sound quite exciting, doesn't it?' I do as she says. 'But I'm just a bit wary; it all seems a bit too clever, somehow.'

'That's probably what somebody said about television, or the internet,' she says.

'And half a dozen other crackpot schemes we've never heard anything more about.'

'Oh, Charlie, this isn't balsamic vinegar, it's washing up liquid.'

'Is it? Sorry. Here you go. I *am* interested – just a little bit sceptical.'

'Well, nothing ventured, nothing gained. I think this is an opportunity staring you in the face,' says Lauren, picking some basil leaves off the plant on the window sill which is now bathed in the low, evening sunlight. 'Check it out. If the worst comes to the worst you just go back to modelling.'

'True.'

'Anyway, I had some interesting news today,' she says, in a bashful, little girl kind of way.

'Do tell,' I say, aware that we've been talking about me for the last half an hour.

'We-e-e-ell, you remember that audition tape I did for the shopping channel?'

'Yeah, did you get it?'

'Not that particular one, but I'm actually quite glad. That is a bit naff, I think. Anyway, they showed it to this other producer and he thought it was great. He thought I had real screen presence.'

'That's brilliant,' I say, coming round from the other side of the work top where we are both cooking – well Lauren is cooking up dinner and I'm cocking it up.

'He said I was, oh, what was it? "Warm but authoritative".'

'That's you,' I say, turning her away from the chopping board and putting my arms around her.

'Don't take the piss, Charlie, this is serious,' she says crossly, slapping my shoulder.

'I *am* being serious. That *is* you. You *are* friendly but authoritative.'

'Warm but authoritative.'

'Yeah, whatever. Exactly,' I say, kissing her neck.

'Well, don't you think that's good?'

'Yeah, I do. So what's next?'

'He wants me to go in and discuss some programme ideas with him and some of his colleagues later this week.'

'That's great. What kind of programme ideas? Who for?'

'We don't know yet, but they'll probably be lifestyle or property related. Perhaps something like *Changing Rooms* or *Ready Steady Cook* but with a new twist.'

'Brilliant. You mean for the BBC or Channel Four or something?'

'It would probably start off on cable but then it could transfer to terrestrial at a later date,' she says, letting the jargon roll off her tongue.

'Hey, you could do something for 2cool.'

'A tie-in? It might work, mightn't it? I'll suggest it.' We both chop and stir in silence for a moment, then she says, 'So you're going to do this thing then?'

'Yeah,' I say, realising that I've already made up my mind. 'Yeah, I am. What have I got to lose? They're going to pay 35,000 pounds a year and if the whole thing crashes I'll just go back to modelling, like you say. Or I might even set up my own website.'

'Mmm,' she says. Dinner is actually ready now: grilled organic chicken, penne with home-made tomato sauce and salad of rocket, cherry tomatoes, shaved parmesan and balsamic vinegar dressing. But somehow we're not ready to eat yet, too lost in thought and excited by the prospects of our future career plans stretching out before us.

'I think we should do it, both of us,' says Lauren looking across at me. 'I think it's time we made a change.'

'Here's to new careers,' I say, holding up my glass.

*

I only got into modelling because a friend of mine from university wanted to do it. Paul was very good-looking with his wavy, dark hair and Tom Cruise eyes, and he knew it. He was planning to take a year off after we graduated and had decided to try and earn some money as a model. He suggested I have a go, too. I wasn't that bothered, in fact I didn't really fancy the idea very much but I told him I'd come with him. So we both got some pictures taken by a photographer he'd had recommended to him and we took them to a few agencies. Obviously we didn't tell anyone.

We started at the top and not surprisingly were told that we both had a great look but it wasn't quite right for them at the moment.

'Never mind,' I said, assuming we'd knock it on the head and go and work in a bar or photocopying in an office like most of our friends. But Paul wanted to try some other agencies, so one hot afternoon in July, A-to-Z and travelcard in hand, feeling like a complete berk, I followed him from one address to another. On one occasion, just as we were leaving a girl called to us.

'Sorry, excuse me a minute.'

Paul froze. This was it, at last, a break – someone had seen what the others had missed, someone ready to take a punt, trust an instinct. The girl looked closely at him and said, 'Can you leave this at reception on your way out,' as she handed him a large envelope. Whether it was simply economy of effort on a hot day or just casual sadism, I don't know, but, either way, I was already pretty sick of this.

Then, after I had been so keen to leave yet another large, sun-flooded room full of beautiful people talking on the phone and surrounded by photographs of even more beautiful people, that I had walked into the stationery cupboard instead of out onto the landing, still saying, 'Okay, thanks anyway, g'bye. No problem, thanks,' I secretly decided I'd do just one more of these and then leave Paul to it.

So, finally, we visited a woman called Penny who was based in an attic in a street just off the King's Road in Chelsea. She was on her own apart from a very pretty-looking Oriental bloke in a black polo neck, and a rather jolly-hockey-sticks girl in a faded denim jacket. Cig in mouth, she flicked through Paul's cards at ninety miles an hour as the others had done and said they were really great but they weren't quite right for her at the moment. Then she looked at mine.

But this time she did it at thirty miles per hour and then showed them to the Oriental bloke. He looked through as well, looked up at me, raised his eyebrows at her and nodded and then handed them back. Then she called over to the girl to get a portfolio. She began to slide them into it, taking a moment to choose the best order for them.

'Okay, lovey, you'll have to get some more done and we'll need to talk about a card,' she said as she pushed my stupid, naff, amateur pictures into plastic wallets inside the black, shiny book with *JET* written in big red letters over the front. Still with the cig in her mouth, its ash wilting precariously now, she showed me a contract and told me to sign at the bottom, which I did in a slight daze, with the pen the girl gave me as I opened my mouth to ask for one. Paul looked on as we both realised that weirdly enough, at the end of this long, hot, exhausting day, our faces glazed with perspiration and pollution, I had done it. I had entered the world of modelling, even though I wasn't really sure I wanted to.

Afterwards Paul was dismissive. 'Never mind, mate, thanks for coming along with me,' he said over a very welcome cold beer in the Chelsea Potter in the King's Road.

'No problem,' I said, just wishing we could swap places. He obviously wanted it so much and I just wasn't that bothered.

Penny's agency grew, moved to bigger offices, took on more people, and my career has sort of taken off with it over the past eight years. My current booker, Karyn, joined three years ago and we speak almost every day. We sometimes go out for a drink, and I was the first person she rang after she split up with her boyfriend. She came over for dinner, which should have been fun, but she and Lauren didn't seem to get on, so I don't mention one to the other now.

Am I good-looking? Well, I must have something, although I'm never quite sure what it is. When I first started working, one girl said to me thoughtfully, 'You've got the kind of face I'd like to see if I was lost in a foreign railway station and I didn't speak the language.'

I think that's a compliment.

Having waved modelling goodbye – perhaps only temporarily, of course – my first day in my new job, on the second floor of a building in Soho, drags a bit because there is so little for me to do.

The office itself has maroon walls and all the desks are heavy constructions in dark wood which contrast beautifully with our white and clear perspex, state of the art Apple Macs, I notice. That, somehow, can't be a coincidence. There is a sort of fresco painted on the ceiling. Piers has already explained that the room is intended to look cool but understated and cost effective, to make it clear to our investors and trading partners that all their money is going into the product. Whatever that is.

He shows me my desk.

My desk.

What my parents always wanted. Okay, I'm not wearing a suit but I've still got a desk with a phone on it. Their reaction when I told them that I was going to start modelling was every bit as joyous as if I'd said I was going to join a monastery or become a Bangkok ladyboy. I kept trying to explain that I was just going to do it for a while until I worked out what I wanted in the way of a career. Their sad, anxious looks every time the subject was raised drove me bonkers with irritation.

'What shall we tell our friends when they ask what you're doing now?' said my mum as if this was the final, clinching argument against this whole daft idea.

'Just tell them I'm dead,' I shouted as I headed upstairs to my room, now more determined than ever to do it, and to succeed at it just to spite them. What better driving force for a career could you hope for than revenge on your parents?

They relented slightly when they saw that I was making a living and enjoying it – that being the order of importance to them. I just worry sometimes that my career decision is what made my dad turn out the way he did.

I haven't actually told the agency about my new job. You know, just in case. Well, I told Karyn. She said she couldn't believe it and she was very sad but she wished me all the luck in the world. In the end we agreed that I wouldn't go to castings unless they were 'requests', in other words the client has specifically asked to see me but if jobs came up she would definitely pass them on and I'd take a day off to do them.

I sign another form about being a director and then get introduced to a guy called Zac who is the technical whiz, as Piers puts it. Zac sits in a corner surrounded by two giant computer screens, a number of keyboards, a computer graphics drawing board, some CPUs and an explosive spaghetti of wires and cables.

He avoids my gaze shyly as we shake hands and says in an American accent, 'Welcome aboard, bud.'

'Thanks. This all looks pretty impressive,' I say, less out of interest and more by way of conversation.

'It is,' Zac tells me. He strokes the giant Apple Mac between us. 'These are some of the most sophisticated software packages ever devised running on state-of-the-art equipment and we're using it all to create the most beautiful images and the most exciting experience, ever, on the internet.'

Stunned by this visionary speech, I let his words sink in for a moment.

'We're all on a journey here at 2cool,' says Piers quietly from over my shoulder.

I consider this thought too.

Our secretary is Scarlett. She has bright pink dreadlocks and is wearing a yellow angora cardigan, a tartan mini-skirt and jelly sandles. I find myself looking her up and down but she doesn't seem offended. I suppose if you dress like that you must be used to people giving you a stunned once-over whenever they meet you.

'Hi Charlie,' she says over a firm handshake. 'Welcome to 2cool.'

'Thank you,' I smile, trying to make up for my discourteous gawping. 'So what's your background, then, Scarlett?' It turns out that she used to work in film post-production but has decided that the internet will take over from conventional movie production and marketing very soon as the principal creative medium of the future.

I'm about to ask, 'Won't people still want to go to the cinema together?' but it seems churlish, and besides, Piers has thrown a pile of glossy magazines on my new desk and is asking me to find products and services that 2cool would have 'a natural market affinity with'.

I start to look through them but almost immediately he gives me a list of things we 'need' for the office, such as a stereo system, a visiting masseuse, laptops for him and Guy, and a couple of company cars because apparently we won't look good arriving at potential affinity partners' offices in a battered old cab. He also asks me to find out about trips to Mauritius and some spas in East Asia. 'We're going to have to get away from here, all of us, at some point, and brainstorm. You know, get some distance from this office so that we can see the wood for the trees.'

I like the idea of brainstorming and seeing wood rather than trees while two babes give me a simultaneous massage in a bamboo hut set on stilts above the rippling, azure waters of a secluded lagoon, but I'm not quite sure how to arrange it – or the stereo or the laptops.

Piers looks slightly surprised and annoyed. 'Just ring them up, get them to send the stuff over and tell them to bill us.'

'Oh, okay.'

'It's standard purchasing procedure, Charlie.'

Nervously, I call a few of the luxury goods suppliers on the list Piers has given me. Amazingly they agree, promising the goods within the next four working days. Soon clothes, more office furniture, sophisticated computers, even a couple of watches to replace my Swatch jobbie are on their way over to us.

And to think I'm getting paid for this.

At lunchtime I go with Scarlett to get a sandwich.

'I'm a vegan,' she says, heading for an organic, vegetarian café and takeaway called Wild World which apparently offers 'Sustenance for the body, mind and soul'.

'I'm an omnivore,' I tell her.

'Is that like being Jewish? Does that mean you can't eat certain things?' she asks.

'Er, no,' I say, feeling slightly embarrassed at toying with her obviously heartfelt views. 'You know, omnivore – like some animals.'

'Oh, right, so you can only, like, eat some animals. Which ones, for instance?'

'No, I mean, I'm not a herbivore. *I* eat anything.'

'I see,' she says, with a toss of her dreadlocked head. I remember at this point that I'm supposed to a spokesman for the company. Perhaps communication isn't my thing, after all.

In the end we both get sandwiches: cheese and tomato for me and houmous and alfalfa sprouts for her, and she buys me a tiny shot of wheatgrass which, she explains, contains the equivalent nutrients of six tons of green vegetables or something.

It's the most disgusting thing I've ever tasted.

'We're still at the early stages,' I tell Lauren that evening as we sit on our white settee, sipping Frascati. I'm saying this as much to reassure myself as to explain it to her. I still don't know exactly what 2cool2btrue.com actually does but Piers and Guy keep telling me that 'it will become clear very soon' or 'all will be revealed'.

'I think it's all very exciting. I'm so proud of you,' says Lauren. Then she adds, 'Like you say, even if it doesn't work out, you've given your best shot and anyway, nothing ventured, nothing gained.'

Did I say that?

'So how did your meeting with thingy go?'

'With Peter?'

'What's his name again?'

'Peter Beaumont-Crowther.'

'Bit of a mouthful.' She ignores my less than complimentary remark and carries on. I squeeze her arm by way of apology for belittling her fledgling TV career.

'They want me to do some more screen tests and go on a TV presentation course.'

'Really? That's great. They're really going to invest some money in you then.'

'Yeah, because I'm worth it.'

'Isn't that a line from an ad campaign?'

'Yeah. I was in it, remember?'

chapter five

'Hello? Keith?' says my mum.

'Hi, Mum,' I say, holding the receiver under my chin as I turn down the stereo which I'm playing at full blast because Lauren is out at a meeting with Peter, the people upstairs are on holiday, and the people downstairs don't count because they have a 'Nuclear Power? No Thanks!' poster on their living room windows and leave their rubbish lying around the bins.

'Keith?' says my mum again. She isn't actually bonkers. I was christened Keith by my parents but Penny changed it to Charlie because she thought it sounded smarter, classier, and that it completed the whole package. (Lauren is actually Lorraine but she made the decision to change her name as part of her 'personal marketing proposition', as she put it at our first lunch.)

'Hi, that's better. How are you, Mum?'

The important thing to know about my mum is that she is one of those women who keeps a tissue up her sleeve.

'Oh, okay, I just thought I'd ring and check you're all right.' This is mother-speak for (a) it's been three geological eras since you've rung me and (b) I worry about you, you know that, don't you?

'I'm fine. I've got a new job,' I add triumphantly, hoping that this will lift the conversation a bit.

'Oh? What a modelling job? The lady across the road saw you in that advert for . . . what was it? Chocolates?'

'No, it's nothing to do with modelling. I'm the marketing director for a new internet company,' I tell her, as suddenly it hits me. God, I am, and all! I'd better ask about getting some cards printed.

'Oh.' There is a pause. Please, please don't drag it down, Mum. Please sound happy about it. Please don't irritate me and make me say something unkind and then feel guilty. Finally she mutters with a glimmer of enthusiasm, 'How exciting.' I'm grateful for the effort, at least.

'Yeah, I just started this week. I'll see how it goes. If it folds I can still go back to modelling or find something else,' I explain as a concession to her disapproval of my usual work.

'They haven't asked you to put up any money, then?'

'No. You're joking, I wouldn't do that,' I tell her confidently.

'Good. Very sensible. What does it do, then? Haven't all the internet companies gone bankrupt?' she asks.

'It's a second-generation dotcom,' I inform her, getting up and looking out of the window as I talk. 'These guys have learned from the mistakes of the first lot. We're building stable business models with identifiable revenue streams.' I know it's going over her head, but that doesn't really matter. Besides, isn't it every child's innate need to impress their parents? And to confuse them – to make it clear that the world has moved on from them and their experiences of it.

'Oh, I don't know about these things. Just make sure they don't ask you for any money.'

I laugh. ''Course I won't. Even I'm not *that* daft.'

'Mmm.' Thanks, Mum. 'Lauren okay?'

'She's fine, I'll send her your love. She's out tonight. She's at a meeting. She's going to become a TV presenter.'

'Gosh, really? Will we see her on the telly?'

'Hope so.'

'Tell me when and I'll set the video.'

I laugh again. 'You'll be invited to the party.'

There is a pause. I know what's coming next but we've got to go through it.

'Have you heard from . . .?'

'Not recently,' I say briskly. 'But I'll give him a call and tell him about my new job.'

'Oh, right. I'm sure he'd like to hear.'

'I'm sure . . . bye then.'

'Bye.' We both hang on the line for a moment.

'I love you Mum . . . oh, don't cry . . . I'll come and see you very soon, I promise. Bye.'

*

I do feel guilty about my mum, stuck on her own in that little house now that they've sold the family home. My sister tells me not to worry about her, that she is getting better and after all it's been nearly seven years since her life was turned upside down. I remember the doctor, though, when Mum and I went to see him.

'It's not *clinical* depression,' he said as if to cheer us up.

'Just *ordinary* depression?' I said, my angry sarcasm hitting him with the impact of a paper plane against a brick wall. He was already writing out a prescription for her.

'Er, yes,' he muttered, scribbling away. Just ordinary, crushing, grinding, paralysing depression that made her burst into tears in Sainsbury's or lie awake every night for two months till her head ached and her eyes stung all day.

I arrive at the office at ten the next day. Piers and Guy are already in and on the phone. They nod 'Good morning'. I sit down at my desk and realise that I haven't really got anything much to do. I've flicked through all the magazines Piers gave me and put yellow Post-it notes against all the advertisements and articles relating to posh or smart things that I think might be right for 2cool. In fact, of course, that is just about everything, so all the magazines now have tatty, yellow fringes.

Most of the stuff I've ordered won't be here for a couple of days. I could ring that travel agent Piers told me about, Madonna's favourite, apparently (they're so smart that they're ex-directory) and chase up our Mauritian spa trips.

'Morning, champ,' says Piers when he gets off the phone. 'Sorry about that – been on to Hong Kong since five this morning. They're very excited. You know how they love their luxury and labels in Honkers.'

'Was that the money men or the retailers?' I ask, trying to sound a bit more switched on today, a little less easily impressed.

'Both really,' says Piers, taking aim at the bin with his Starbucks cup. He runs his hand through his thick, dark hair and shuts his eyes for a moment, screwing up his face with its strong features and permanently flushed cheeks. 'Investors and marketing people seem to love the whole concept.' The cup hits the bin, dances around the rim a bit and finally falls in, splattering coffee dregs up the wall. Piers punches the air in a movement that turns into a stretch and a yawn.

'Yep, see, that's the thing about 2cool. It has no national borders, like all labels these days, but even more so because it's internet-based. Anyone, anywhere in the world can be 2cool2btrue at any time of the day or night.' He performs a sort of pirouette and stretches again. 'At any one time around the world, a broker in Manhattan, a designer in Cannes, a . . . a . . . an entrepreneur in Hong Kong, even someone in sub-Saharan Africa can be 2cool.'

'Sub-Saharan Africa?'

'Yeah, why not?'

'Well,' I say. 'That's not really our market, is it? I mean, wouldn't they be more interested in food or something?'

'Perhaps. However, people need more than food to live.'

'Yeah, but it's usually a good starting point—'

'The point about the Third World, Charlie, is that the people in it are becoming the planet's workshop. We don't actually make things in the First World any more. Your Nike trainers, your Levis, your Apple Mac – they're manufactured in the Philippines or India or somewhere.'

'By children,' I suggest, but Piers is off again.

'Do you know what we *do* manufacture in the First World? Brands! We make the brands and they take care of those little details like the products they go on.'

'Hi, Charlie, how are you?' says Guy as he puts the phone down. 'Piers, we need to get something over to Li Ka Shing's people by midday.'

'Right you are,' says Piers, diving to his computer.

'Got some coffee, Charlie?' asks Piers.

'No, fine, thanks,' I tell him.

'Listen,' says Guy, coming round to the front of his desk and sitting on it. 'We've scored a bit of a PR coup. Piers knows a journalist on the *Post* and she's agreed to do a piece about the site. She's coming in today to meet us and I want you to take her out to lunch and tell her about the whole concept.'

'Yeah, sure,' I say, hoping I sound more confident than I feel. I can probably manage the overall concept, the big picture. It's the details I'm not so hot on. At this rate we'll have run out of things to talk about before we've even ordered. I hope she's been somewhere nice on holiday recently, otherwise we'll have absolutely nothing to say to each other.

'You know what we're all about here.'

'I think so, Guy. I just wondered, you're, er, you're not coming along as well then?'

'No, matey, this is your territory. She's arriving here at quarter to one. Just take her out and talk to her. Scarlett's already booked a table for you both at one o'clock at Dekonstruktion. Oh, nearly forgot, here's your 2cool credit card.' He grabs an envelope off his desk and slides out some pieces of paper along with a Mastercard. It has 'Charlie Barrett, 2cool2btrue.com' embossed on it.

I run my finger over the lettering appreciatively, but then a thought strikes me. 'Charlie's not my real name, it's actually Keith, Keith Barrett.'

'Is it?' Guy seems unconcerned.

'Charlie is, was, just my modelling name.'

'Don't worry about that, it's the 2cool bit that counts. We'll have our own cards soon – none of this tacky Mastercard shit. What kind of a logo is that? About as smart as Doritos.'

The journalist arrives ten minutes late. I'm on the phone organising some plants for the office from a company that rents them out. Piers has given me certain varieties that are very '2cool' and the woman is making a note of them and pointing out that they are very expensive as well as being difficult to maintain. She asks for a large deposit which I decide to allow Scarlett to sort out.

When I put the phone down, Guy introduces us.

'Nora, this is Charlie, our marketing director,' says Guy. We shake hands.

'Nora Benthall,' says the girl, smiling.

'Hi Nora,' I say. 'Good to meet you.' I smile too, about 750 watts, which is friendly but not too obviously designed to impress. She is a bit younger than me, late twenties, perhaps. She has dark red hair, pale skin, a small mouth and big brown eyes behind a pair of black-framed glasses. But what *is* she wearing? It looks like she has raided an Oxfam shop: baggy purple satin trousers, big army boots, a sort of New Romantic shirt that looks like it came from a jumble sale, and a loud, checked brown and yellow coat.

Has no one else noticed? Perhaps they're just a bit more subtle than me and have not checked her out so blatantly. Hearing

Scarlett's voice on the phone reminds me that this is getting to be a habit.

'Do you want to have a quick look at the site, Nora, before you and Charlie go off?' says Piers.

'Love to,' says Nora, looking at him expectantly. I thought so – there is a definitely a subtle American accent there. She spins round to check out the software bit of the office and her coat catches something on Scarlett's desk. Scarlett grabs it and looks daggers at her but Nora is oblivious to it.

Zac, who has arrived by now, sighs to make it clear that showing his baby to an audience of the uninitiated like this is a total pain in the arse and taps at his keyboard. The big screen of the huge Mac that we are all peering at bursts into life. 2cool2btrue seems to grow from nothing in the distance and then comes forward until we are overtaken by one of the 'o's of 'cool'. There are images of groovy young people in bars, shots of signs saying 'Fifth Avenue', 'Bond Street' and 'Via Veneto' interspersed with pictures of Madonna, Hugh Grant, Lady Helen Windsor and Martin Luther King. Then there are shots of beautiful people in what looks like the Art Deco area of Miami before we're transported to a modern airport lounge in some part of Scandinavia where a pale-skinned girl with long blonde hair gives us a curious, lingering stare. Suddenly there is newsreel footage of Woodstock and the riots at Penn State and then a rave in Ibiza. There are catwalk shows and finally stills of some tosser relaxing in a huge loft apartment overlooking a river and working on his laptop as he reclines on a Charles Eames chair.

'Hey, that's you,' says Nora, prodding me. Quite hard, actually.

'Oh, yeah,' I mutter. I hate seeing myself in pictures, even in such august company.

'That's really cool,' says Nora when it has finished.

'It needs some tweaking and we want to make it all completely interactive, of course,' says Piers.

'Everyone who logs on will be able to customise the site to fit in with their own interests and requirements,' says Guy.

'And aspirations,' adds Piers.

'After you've logged on a few times the site will be able to identify your own personal, individual interests together with your activity and retail patterns and actually offer you things that it thinks you'll be interested in or that you probably need to know about,' Guy tells her, eyes wide with excitement.

I feel I should be making notes.

'Okay, thanks, Zac,' says Piers.

Zac makes a tiny movement with his head to acknowledge their belated gratitude as he races the mouse around its pad and hits a couple of keys.

'That's some site,' says Nora as we make our way down the street to the restaurant.

'Well, I think it's the whole concept that's so exciting,' I hear myself saying.

'Kids'll love it,' she says, as if she isn't one of them, of course.

'It's very much of its time, I think, you know, after all the dotcom hysteria that surrounded the first generation of internet entrepreneurs.'

'Wasn't all that business just crazy?'

'Absurd.'

Scarlett has got us a nice quiet corner table at Dekonstruktion, this week's scorchingly hip restaurant. After we have ordered tuna carpaccio followed by steak and kidney pudding for her, and smoked wild boar on a bed of pak choi and then Alaskan cod tagine for me, she says the one thing that I really I don't want to hear above all else.

'So, you used to be a male model.'

'Model,' I correct her. 'I used to be a model. Unless, that is, you're a lady journalist.'

She is unembarrassed. 'Oh, I'm no lady.'

I decide not to wait for the standard 'Do you shave your chest?' line (to which the answer is no, never) and change tack.

'Is that an American accent you've got there?'

'Does it still show? When I go back to the States all my friends say I talk like the Queen.'

'I thought I heard it,' I smile, trying to smooth over the male model faux pas and also, I have to admit, to avoid discussing 2cool in case she guesses that I haven't really got a clue what I'm talking about.

'My father's American and I grew up mostly in New York but then

I came to London to work after I left journalism school about ten years ago.'

'Do you like it at the *Post*?'

'Uh huh, it's pretty cool. I mostly get to do things like "Which of these women is most likely to suffer from cellulite in five years' time?" and "Men who spend more on beauty products than their wives do". You know, the big issues.' She gesticulates with the fork she has picked up and inadvertently stabs a passing waiter in the arm. He tuts prissily but Nora continues regardless, clearly unaware of what she has done. 'Plus a few celebrity interviews.'

'Really? Like who?'

'Oh, Debbie Harry the other week.'

'What was she like?'

'Big head.'

'I bet a lot of these people are really conceited.'

Nora looks at me. 'No, she has a big head.' She spreads her hands around her face to make the point.

'Oh, right.' That communication thing again.

'They mainly employ me to take the piss,' Nora is saying. 'But this is quite a fun story by comparison. I think it'll be pretty big.'

'If it all works out,' I say, consciously lowering expectations a bit.

'Sure, but even if you all fall on your asses, it'll still be interesting.'

I smile. 'You'll still get a story.'

'Sure. A better one, in a way.'

I try to work out whether she is being deliberately provocative or whether she simply doesn't appreciate how annoying that sounds, but her innocent smile gives nothing away.

'You know Piers already?'

'Piers? Er, yeah, we've known each other for a long time. He's quite a guy – never stops.'

'A real ideas man.'

'Always.'

Our food arrives and I'm quite relieved to have something to concentrate on.

'So why'd you give up the male, I mean, the modelling?'

'This seemed like an interesting project. They asked me. I'd been modelling for eight years or so; it seemed like the right time to change career.'

'What experience do you have in internet entrepreneurship?'

'None,' I tell her confidently, deciding that I'd better make a virtue of it. 'That's the point in a way, I've come to it fresh, no preconceptions, no baggage. Like I said, we're a second-generation dotcom, we've drawn a line in the sand after the first wave and learned from their mistakes.' Way to go, Charlie! *I* almost believe me.

'What experience have you got in marketing?' she asks, shovelling food into her mouth as if she hasn't eaten for a week.

'I've got a degree in it.'

'That all?'

Her bluntness takes me by surprise but I get back into my stride. 'Well, to be a successful model, you have to market yourself effectively. After all, you're selling yourself as a distinct product at every casting and when you do a job you have to be in tune mentally with whatever you're selling, be it fashion or . . . I don't know, office furniture or holidays,' I waffle fluently, cobbling together some of the things Piers, Guy and Lauren have said to me recently. Sounds good, anyway – we're on a roll here.

'Suppose so. What kind of things did you model?'

I really want to get away from the modelling thing so I say quickly, 'Clothes, holidays, laptop computers; but this is a more exciting challenge.'

'I think I've seen your face. Did you do that one for a bank or something where you're walking across a station concourse while everyone else is in slow motion.'

'Yes. So what else are you writing at the moment?' I ask pointedly as the waiter, thankfully not the one she's just stabbed, takes our plates.

'I've got to interview a woman this afternoon who's just discovered that her husband is married to three other women.' She looks up at me over the top of her heavy glasses, then pushes aside a stray hair that has fallen out of place as she has been shovelling her food.

'*Three* other women?'

'I know, I suppose if you're going to do these things you might as well do it big, go for it.'

'Why not? Do it in style.'

'Even if you fall on your ass,' she says, taking a sip of wine.

We leave the restaurant at gone three o'clock. I can't believe where the time has gone but I'm just relieved it has. As we make for the door, Nora manages to take out another waiter, this time by walking into him as he is carrying a stack of dirty plates. She is telling me about a piece she did some time ago about people who have married their old school teachers, walking fast through the crowded restaurant, turning her head round completely to talk to me. I try and warn her about where she is headed but perhaps she doesn't notice or she cottons on just too late and so either way, seconds later there are plates everywhere, one of which slides elegantly down the back of a woman I recognise as a TV weather presenter.

'Oh, no,' says Nora, only mildly concerned. 'Did I do that? I'm *so* sorry.'

The weather presenter's face has what could be described as a black cloud on it. She looks slightly absurd, glowering at Nora, her familiar smiley features now contorted with fury while she tries to see what kind of damage the dirty plate has done to the back of her bright pink jacket.

'Shit. What a mess,' says Nora. Is she enjoying this? 'Don't worry,' she says, 'that kind of fabric dry cleans really well. I had a jacket like that – last year.'

The recipient of her helpful observation opens her mouth to say something but is speechless.

'Just send the bill to the restaurant, I would,' says Nora, touching her shoulder kindly.

I say goodbye to Nora at the top of the street and suggest she gives me a ring if she has any questions. She says she will, and that the piece should be in the paper on Monday.

As soon as I get back to the office I brief Guy and Piers on the lunch. They seem pleased with how it went although I miss out the final disastrous episode.

'She should be a useful ally in the PR campaign,' says Piers. 'I met her recently at a dinner party and I thought she could be helpful to us.'

I think about this for a moment. 'I thought you'd known each other for quite a while.'

Piers looks surprised. 'Yeah, yeah. I meant met her *again*.'

'Right, next thing on the agenda for you, mate, is the launch party,' says Guy. 'We've booked Frederica's – do you know it?'

'That big place in Berkeley Square?'

'Yep, we've got the whole place. It's all booked for next Friday.'

'A week tomorrow?'

'Yep, hope you can make it,' says Guy, only half-joking.

'Oh, yes, of course. That's brilliant,' I say, genuinely impressed.

'Our PR company have developed a guest list for us. Can you look over it and let us know about any thoughts you have, anyone else you think we should ask? Ta.'

Scarlett hands me a file with lists of names and their organisations. There are newspapers and magazines – *Vogue, Harpers and Queen, Tatler, GQ, Esquire, Wallpaper**, some TV presenters and a batch of celebs, most of whom I've heard of, with a note of their agencies, and some models with agencies and figures next to them. 'Sophia Kendall – £5,000,' says one.

'Is she doing a shoot for us?' I ask Scarlett, pointing to her name.

'No, that's her attendance fee.'

'What? She's being paid for coming to our party?'

'Yep. For . . .' she runs her finger further along the line, pushing mine out of the way, until she finds what she's looking for. 'For a minimum of fifty-five minutes. Any less and she's in breach of contract.'

'Any larger?' I ask, not really interested but thinking vaguely of overtime – every model's first thought (after travel expenses and buyouts).

'Sophia won't be here for thirty seconds more than her contract states; our doormen will time her entry and departure,' says Scarlett, rolling her eyes towards her eyebrow ring.

There are other names on the list: aristo model Henrietta Banbury (£4,000, one hour ten minutes), *Blue Peter* presenter Sarah Jones (two hours subject to other commitments on the evening, exact timing to be decided with agent by 5 p.m., £2,000). And, oh fuck, the weather presenter in the pink jacket. Well, the pink, brown, yellow and red jacket. She'll be pleased to see me. I can't help smiling at her fee: £500.

'Simon Smith, the PR, is coming in at four to talk us through it and to confirm the other arrangements,' says Scarlett.

'Simon Smith,' I murmur, really just trying to cope with all the names and information being fired at me.

'Yes,' says Scarlett, picking up her phone. 'He's a tosser.'

*

Simon Smith from The Communications Game seems like a nice bloke, although he does engage in what appears to be an amateur arm-wrestling match with Piers. They call each other 'wanker', 'arse face' and 'donkey bollocks' before he sits down with me.

'We've invited A-list celebs and movers and shakers. People like Richard Branson, Jonathan Ross, Rik Mayall,' he explains, staring me hard in the face.

He fiddles with his silk cufflinks as I whizz down the list and nod approvingly.

'Anyone we should add?'

'Um, there are a couple. One is the TV producer Peter Beaumont-Crowther – you've heard of him?'

'Oh, yes, of course,' says Simon, scribbling on the list.

'And the other is my girlfriend, Lauren.'

Simon and Scarlett exchange glances and I wonder if I've overstepped the mark. For God's sake, it's one person in 2,000.

'She usually comes to parties free of charge,' I say deadpan, realising what a terrible lost money-making opportunity this is for her.

'Splendid,' says Simon, shuffling the papers together. 'I think you've approved the menus, haven't you?'

'I haven't,' I say. It comes out slightly petulantly so I add, 'I wouldn't mind having a look.'

Silently Scarlett takes out another file and I read through the menu of Japanese-style black cod, poached sea urchins, miniature smoked reindeer soufflés. Champagnes: Pol Roger, Laurent Perrier, Krug. Price per head: £250.

'Bloody hell! £250? Times 2,000 people. That's . . .'

'Half a million quid,' says Scarlett calmly.

chapter six

'When did you hear?' I ask Lauren.

'I got back from a casting this afternoon. I was just putting my key in the door when my mobile went and it was Peter.'

'So what's it for again?' We're lying on the settee. We've just made love. Lauren told me about her audition within seconds of my getting through the door and then pounced on me. We did it in the living room – something we haven't done for ages. Well, not since we, I mean Lauren, had the settee dry cleaned. The mirror here is an antique, faded Venetian job resting on the white limestone mantelpiece. I sometimes wonder if the people who come for dinner or to our parties (Lauren loves entertaining) that we actually live the scrubbed pine, neutral coloured, elegantly understated, sunlit lifestyle we spend so much of our time advertising. Sometimes even I'm not quite sure where our work ends and our real lives begin.

I push my face into her breasts, kissing and biting them gently.

'Charlieeeee,' she says, pushing me away. 'Stop it. Aren't you interested?'

'Of course I am. I told you, I'm so pleased for you babe, honestly. What's the show again? Sort of a dating thing?'

'Well, each week we take an ordinary person and the idea is that a group of experts – psychologists, agony aunts and other people – assess who would be the right boy or girl to go out with that person, and then I have to find one with the help of their friends, on the street, at a club, at work.'

'That's great. How many are up for it?'

'There are just three of us. I got through the first two rounds just on the strength of my audition tape alone.'

'You're a star. I told you.'

'How was your day?' she asks, rearranging her hair and sniffing it for some reason. Must be a girlie thing. I sniff my armpit in reply and tell her, 'Pretty busy. I had lunch with this journo who's going to write something about the site.'

'That's good. Did you fix that up?'

'No, Piers did. She was bloody weird. Dressed like a tramp; bizarre clothes that didn't match, *wouldn't* match anything really.' I can see her now, sitting opposite me at the table. Intense and provocative. Totally unselfconscious. I've never felt quite so closely observed. Even casting directors don't look at you that deeply, they just check out your face, but she seemed to be going further. Probing, penetrating. Was she taking the piss throughout the whole meal? Or is that how she is with everyone? She must be clever. When I asked her about her career she told me she went to Vasser and Columbia journalism school. Perhaps if you're as bright as her it's tempting to take the piss out of everyone else, the less bright of this world. Especially a former *male* model who's trying to persuade you that he works for the planet's coolest website.

'And?'

'Erm,' I'm shaken out of my unexpected reverie. 'Erm, oh God, and then, when we were leaving she crashed into this waiter,' I laugh. 'Just smashed into him. Plates flying. Food everywhere.' I tell her about the weather presenter. 'It was so funny, Nora, this journalist, was like "Hey, ho! These things happen."'

Lauren says, 'God, how embarrassing. I'd have died. That woman, what's her name?, should have sued for the dry-cleaning costs, or even the whole jacket. You'd have loads of witnesses.'

'It was *funny*,' I say. I suppose you had to be there. With Nora, still intent on carrying on her conversation, oblivious to the chaos she had just caused.

'Sounds more dangerous than funny.'

'You know me, I've just got a strange sense of humour.' I begin to kiss her breasts, tasting the slight salty sweat on them, feeling myself get hard again.

'Oh, well,' says Lauren, looking down at me and squeezing my ear, which she knows I like. 'Makes a change from you throwing food all over the woman you're having lunch with.'

I smile sarcastically. 'You still think that was an accident.'

She makes a face and pushes me away.

'I think we should celebrate our successful weeks – do something fun on Saturday,' I say. 'Let's hire one of those thirty-pound-a-day cars and drive into the country. It's going to be lovely this weekend. We could go to—'

'I can't, hon, I've got to practise for this next audition,' she says, getting up and putting her bra back on.

'Oh, okay.' I look at her, looking at herself in the one reflective spot of the antique mirror. Is this how it's going to be with the new career? Weekends spent practising for auditions? What shall *I* do? I used to spend Saturday afternoons playing football with some old mates from university, a couple of other models, a guy called James who everyone thought was a friend of everyone else but who, it turned out, was pretty good in goal. Then we'd go to a pub in Barnes, the game contracting and the drinking expanding depending on the weather, how many of us turned up and how energetic those that did felt. I wonder if they still play?

When Lauren and I bought this place my Saturdays were suddenly spent at Ikea, Habitat and The Pier, or painting and sanding under her direction, or just holding the end of things while Lauren made comments like 'Oh, watch what you're doing, will you?'

'It'll take *all* Saturday, will it?' I ask in rather a small voice.

'Sorry?' Lauren is running her fingers over the mantelpiece and looking irritably at the resultant thin film of dust. Was it my week for dusting? Well, if there's still dust around, it probably was.

'It's not going to take all day, is it? Why don't we go out on Saturday evening and celebrate. I'll book La Trompette, shall I?'

'Charlie,' she says, turning round.

Oh, fuck, now what? It's just a bit of dust, for God's sake.

'What's happening on Saturday night?' Phew, acquitted on dust charges, anyway.

'This is something I should know about, isn't it?' I surmise. Accurately, as it happens.

'Yes, Saturday night, I told you.'

'You didn't.'

'Oh, Charlie,' she says, shaking her head, trying not to smile. 'I told you weeks ago: dinner. Tim and Sally, Mark and Sarah, and I've invited Peter too.'

'You didn't tell me.' Okay, perhaps she did, but I'm a bloke and I'm no good with these things.

'I bloody well did, sieve brain. I assume you can make it.'

'Yes, of course I can. Sorry babe.'

'It's not your fault, you're just a boy.'

'Guilty, m'lud. I mean, m'lady.'

She takes my face in her hands and kisses me deeply. 'I love you.'

'Love you, too.'

'Even if your memory is crap – and your dusting's abysmal.'

While Lauren is doing her audition practice, I decide to make a duty call and go and see my dad. Dad lives in Docklands now and he is very happy for me to come round to his flat, I mean 'place'. As long as it's not too early that is.

He works in advertising. Ten years ago he set up an agency with two colleagues half his age. Dad is actually an accountant and was working with them in a big agency balancing the books and looking for tax breaks, but when these two guys – Cambridge educated, off-the-wall twenty-somethings who exist in a world of street-fashion labels, pop culture and wall-to-wall irony – decided to go solo, they realised that his dull, safe financial know-how could form an essential bedrock to the company and so they invited him to join them.

Needless to say, my mum wasn't keen. She pointed out the risks of starting a new business with reference to her auntie, who had opened a wool shop in Lewes in the seventies and failed, reminded him that he was comfortably on his way to retirement, and just sighed a lot when these two arguments failed to convince him. I think it was her retirement point that actually clinched it for him and made him go out and do it.

He pointed out that he had just about paid off the mortgage, the children had left home and, after all, nothing ventured, nothing gained. He didn't mention the real reason: mid-life crisis. But then perhaps he wasn't aware of it.

The new company, Matthewman Kendall Barrett (the order of names should tell you something) won a clutch of big accounts with their cheeky, irreverent approach, grabbed some headlines in *Campaign* magazine, provoked a couple of outcries from the *Daily Mail* over risqué copy lines and then quickly floated. Suddenly my dad was fifty and a millionaire. He decided to get a new wardrobe and a new car. He got rid of his old suits, his Volvo estate and his wife, and set up home in a Docklands penthouse flat that has its own lift, speakers in the ceiling and panoramic views of the Thames – just beyond some corrugated-iron sheds and a double-glazing storage depot, that is.

Getting there is near impossible: you have to go to a perpetually windswept DLR station and then ring for a taxi which takes you along the dual carriageways through the post-industrial wasteland to a shimmering white residential Fort Knox which has a surly security guard and a 'marketing suite' which is permanently open.

Dad has had a number of girlfriends since he left my mum, but to be honest I tend to get them confused: they're all thirty years younger than him, all blonde, all leggy and have names that end in 'i' like Linzi, Leoni, Nikki and Toni. I'm sure most of them put a smiley face in the dot of the 'i' when they sign their names, although none of them has ever written to me.

Amongst other things, my dad bought a coffee table supported by the kneeling fibreglass figure of a naked woman in a leather basque which he proudly showed to me when I went over there once. Holding our shots of frozen flavoured vodka, we circled it, studying it intensely.

'Sexy, eh?' said my old man, eyeing up the cellulite free, rock hard curves of her behind in a way that still makes me shudder slightly.

'I think it's supposed to be ironic, Dad,' I said uneasily, trying to make out the woman's expression. He walked round to get a better view of her face too.

'Yeah, whatever,' he said.

When I finally penetrate the security and arrive at my dad's flat, he has obviously just got up and is still in a sort of kimono thing. My initial reaction is to say 'I think you're a bit old for that, aren't you?' but then, of course, that observation applies to his entire life, so really what's the point? Dad thinks he is Hugh Heffner made over by Stussy. My sister says that he is more Austin Powers meets Burton's.

'Hey, Charlie,' he says, hugging me and slapping me on the back. Unlike my mother, Dad does call me Charlie and he seems to really like the name. Whose idea was Keith, anyway? But I still call him Dad, not Jared, as he sometimes asks me to. I suppose Jared is similar to John, but then it was John who was married to my mother and fathered me so I'm a bit sensitive about that.

'Hi, Dad,' I say, wandering in and looking around with a mixture of intrigue and trepidation for his latest purchase. 'Pool table's gone.'

'Mmm? Oh, yeah, took up too much space,' he tells me, his voice echoing around the barn-like emptiness. 'Want some coffee?'

'That'd be great,' I say, drifting around and looking out at the view. In the distance a tractor is pushing something into a hole and a crane moves almost imperceptibly against the shimmering skeins of cloud.

'How do you have it?' he asks, looking slightly apprehensively at a black and chrome espresso machine the size of a nuclear power station.

'White with a couple of sugars, please.' I wouldn't expect him to remember that.

'Espresso? Cappuccino? Latte? Ristretto?'

'Rigoletto? Ravioli? Ravenelli? Oh, I don't know, just white coffee would be great, thank you.'

'O . . . kay' says the non-streak-bronzed barista. 'Erm . . .' He yanks the handle off and looks for somewhere to bang out the dregs. He looks along the line of identical, minimalist, brushed stainless steel cupboard doors and chooses one. His smile indicates that this is the one with the bin.

'I can have instant, Dad, honestly, whatever's easiest.'

'Nope, nope, this is no problem . . . honestly,' he says, mesmerised by the line of dials and buttons. He presses one and suddenly boiling water begins to trickle down into the grate below. He leaps back and curses again.

Just then an angel appears and saves us: a beautiful girl, straw-blonde hair cascading over her shoulders, wearing only a baggy white T-shirt and a pair of tiny panties wanders into the vast living area, the shadows of the window frames slipping over her shoulders and clearly visible breasts as she glides along, hips swaying. She comes up behind Dad, puts her arms around him, reaches up to kiss his neck and then gently, silently and confidently takes charge of the coffee machine.

Two minutes later we're all drinking wonderful lattes.

'Very good,' I tell the girl to break the ice.

'This is Kari,' says Dad over his chunky American Retro mug. No, I don't think I've met this one before, which is very possible since I haven't seen my dad for nearly three weeks.

'Charlie,' I say. I'm never sure whether to admit I'm the son or just let them assume that I'm a cool young dude my dad happens to know – his dealer, perhaps.

The girl smiles back from the black leather settee, her legs luxuriously folded up under her. Like father like son: me and my dad both have the same taste in women. Except that his are usually ten years younger than mine.

'Good coffee,' I say again to the sphinx-like Kari.

'Should be,' says Dad proudly. 'Kari works in Caffè Nero, don't you, carina?' Presumably after school. 'So what's this new job?' he asks, turning to me.

'I've jacked the modelling in. I did a shoot for an internet company last week and they offered me a job as marketing manager, I mean, marketing director.'

'Director? You've got equity in this thing?'

'Er, no. How do you mean? Have I invested something? No. I'm just on a salary.'

'That's good.'

'I thought I'd wait,' I say, enjoying this paternal approval.

'What's it called?'

'2cool2btrue dot com.'

'Right, heard of them.'

'Really? Have you?'

'Oh, yeah, there's quite a bit of talk in the creative and media industry about them at the moment,' says Dad levelly. 'Sort of a lifestyle site or something isn't it?'

'That's right. It's a second-generation website. It's going to be the first of the truly aspirational internet *brands*. You know, the web equivalent of Gucci or Louis Vuitton.'

'Interesting,' says Dad.

'I think it will be.'

'All life consists of a label of one kind or another,' says Dad, running his fingers through Kari's hair as she stares at silent MTV on the massive TV screen.

As I leave a couple of hours later, it occurs to me that it would sometimes be nice to have a dad who mowed the lawn on Saturday before falling asleep in front of the cricket, and spent Sunday mornings in the loo with the papers, but then you can't choose your parents.

I do some shopping in town on the way home and then, because it's quite near to Chiswick anyway, drop in at the pub in Barnes we used to meet at post-Saturday-afternoon footy. I walk in, avoiding the gaze of the girl at the bar, and look around for the old gang. But they're not there. I do another quick tour just in case I've missed them or don't recognise them and then I stroll back over the bridge to Hammersmith and get the bus to Chiswick.

It's nearly seven when I let myself in. I smell cooking and hear Lauren laughing. I leave my bags in the hall and wander into the kitchen. She is sitting on the work top, swinging her legs and laughing at some middle-aged bloke who is stirring something on our hob and telling her a story.

'So this girl's reading the bloody autocue as fast as she can and the director's shouting, "For God's sake. . . ."' He trails off as he sees me. 'Hello. You must be Charlie. I'm Peter, Peter Beaumont-Crowther,' he says extending a hand.

'Hi, Peter,' I say. I've just realised that I really can't be bothered with this. I just want to lie in front of the telly with Lauren and a good bottle of wine and a crap video. I look down at what he's cooking.

Lauren fills the silence.

'Peter came to Sainsbury's with me after we'd finished and it turns out he makes this chicken casserole thing. I thought it sounded delicious so I bullied him into doing it.' They both laugh. I know Lauren on charm mode so well. It's just a bit unnerving to see it happening in our kitchen. I'm not sure who is the target of it, me or Peter.

'It's a kind of chicken cacciatora but with a few *secret* ingredients,' Peter tells me, raising his eyebrows.

The first thing that strikes me about him is 'Why don't you get a haircut?' His hair flops forward and he is constantly sweeping it back with his hands. He has a pudgy, fleshy face, big lips and a sharp nose, and he's just a bit too smooth for my liking.

'Smells great,' I say and leave the room. I'm kicking my trainers off in the bedroom when Lauren comes in. She watches me for a moment as I take my T-shirt off.

'What's the matter?' she asks from the door.

It's decision time: I can either go for a fully fledged sulk which is what I feel like but which would make tonight a hell of an effort for both of us and probably result in at least forty-eight hours of awkward silences and bickering, or I can just give in and be a good boy. I choose the latter.

'Sorry, babe, I'm just knackered.'

Lauren sensibly meets me halfway. 'That's all right.' She puts her arms round me, whispering in my ear. 'Sorry about this. Peter insisted we try his chicken thing and you know I've got to be nice to him.'

'I know. I'm just going to have a shower and then I'll be fine.'

''kay,' she says. She kisses me. 'Hurry up, though, the others will be here in a minute.'

I'm about to walk out of the bedroom naked as any man would naturally do in his own flat, but then I remember about Peter. Oh, sod it, I do it anyway.

chapter seven

I'm such a devoted boyfriend/crawler/good actor/spineless wonder or mixture of all four that I even ask to taste Peter's stupid bloody chicken creation.

'Mmm,' I say, licking my lips as he holds the spoon inches away from my mouth, his hand poised underneath it to catch the drips. 'That's delicious.' In fact it's just about okay. It tastes like chicken casserole with tinned tomatoes in it to me. 'Babe, have you tasted this?' I say, deciding to put my back into this crawling.

'Yep, good, isn't it?' says Lauren who is slicing courgettes at the other end of the kitchen. I know I'll get my reward for this tonight.

Peter is smiling knowingly. Oh, leave it alone, you smarmy pillock. It's just bloody chicken.

'Can't wait,' I say moving away, having done my duty. Getting drinks and laying the table is the limit of my culinary ability. Besides, it's not a good idea to get in the way of Lauren while she is cooking unless she tells you to.

Sarah is relating her favourite dinner-party anecdote.

'So I came back early one day because I had to pick up a file I'd accidentally left on the dining table,' she tells Peter in her heavy, throaty, thirty-Marlborough-Lights-a-day voice. She is the only smoker that Lauren allows in the house and she revels in this privilege. 'And I know the cleaner is there obviously because it's a Tuesday. So I put my head round the door to say hallo and let her know I'm not a burglar or a mad rapist, and there she is doing the washing up at the kitchen sink.' She pauses. 'Topless.' She punctuates her punchline with a slurp of wine.

'No!' Peter is leering across the table in disbelief.

'Seriously. And she's not exactly Kate Moss either, yeah?'

Peter roars with laughter. 'What was she doing?' he asks.

'It's just for cleaning the glasses,' I explain, twisting two imaginary glasses over my own chest.

Peter roars again. 'What did you do?'

'What *could* I do? I just said "Oh, hi, Janet, could you do the oven please if you get a moment?"'

'But preferably not with your tits,' adds Sarah's husband, Mark.

More guffawing from Peter.

'Oh, not that awful cleaner story,' says Lauren, entering the room with two more bottles of wine and a basket of warm, rosemary-infused foccacia which we immediately fall on.

'Cleaners are such a problem, aren't they?' says Sally. Everyone nods and mumbles agreement. Then Sally says, 'The woman next to us has a Brazilian.'

I can't help it: 'Have you looked?'

Sarah is howling with laughter. 'I think Sally's talking about her cleaner, Charlie,' she says. 'Not her bikini line.'

'Oh, right, sorry,' I groan, overdoing it. There is a pause while Sarah and Peter try to control themselves.

'Ooh, can I help you, Lauren?' says Sally suddenly, always glad to lend a hand. Whenever she and her husband Tim come over, Sally seems to spend more time in our kitchen than most of the appliances.

'No Sally, honestly, sit down, thank you. Charlie can do it.'

'Charlie's doing the wine,' says Sally. 'Here you are.' She gets up. I let her. After all, I've done my bit with the brown-nosing casserole appreciation.

'So Peter, you're in television,' says Mark who does something with futures in the City that we've all given up trying to understand a long time ago.

'Yes,' says Peter. 'I run a company called Freak Productions.'

'What kind of thing do you make?' asks Sarah, obviously feeling she should repay him after his tremendous reception for her cleaner story. At least I'll find out a little bit more about Lauren's New Best Friend without actually having to talk to him.

'Mainly lifestyle programmes, like *Ready Steady Cook*.'

'You make *Ready Steady Cook*?' says Sarah. 'I *love* that programme.'

'Er, no, but programmes like it,' says Peter. 'I do one for a cable channel where a celebrity chef comes round to your house and makes over all your boring, ordinary food, takes it up a peg or two. So if you're giving your kids beans on toast, for example, he'll make it really special by adding some extra ingredients or showing you how to make your own beans on toast with real Cannelloni beans, fresh tomato sauce and newly baked sourdough bread.'

'Oh, right. You must really learn something,' says Sarah. She mulls it over while Peter looks on, delighted at the brilliance of his baby. 'But on the other hand I think I'd be tempted to say, "Okay, you try keeping a three-year-old and a five-year-old from killing each other while you piss about with Cannelloni beans and skinning tomatoes." You know what I mean?'

But apparently Peter doesn't. Tim, who has also been listening to the exchange and who deals in commercial property, doesn't really do jokes, unless they come from a client. So there is only one person now roaring with laughter in the room. Oh, dear, it's me.

'It'd be wasted on our kids,' says Mark, inadvertently twisting the knife, I mean the reinforced steel, Sebatier cook's paring knife, in the wound.

Fortunately at that moment Lauren and Sally come back in, each with a tray full of starters arranged on small plates.

'. . . it's called centre height,' Lauren is saying to Sally. 'The idea is that you arrange the dish so that it's raised at the centre – looks more dramatic, more interesting, then it's so easy, you just chop up a packet of herbs and sprinkle them over. Gives it a more professional appearance in no time.'

'That's another thing we do,' says Peter. 'We give little tips on how to get that professional look.'

'Oh, that would be useful,' says Sarah, clearly feeling guilty about her last joke. I know she couldn't give a toss, though, and so I'm trying not to laugh again.

Over the main course, the others ask Lauren about her new career and she smiles knowingly at Peter. Then they ask about my new venture. Mark doesn't say anything, even though I address most of my comments to him. He nods in an interested but non-committal way.

I make my usual contribution to the meal by taking the dinner plates into the kitchen and putting them in the dishwasher. Then I carefully take the Patisserie Valerie *tart aux fraises* out of its box. Two things are racing certainties at this point: one is that I'll nearly drop it – which I do, breaking the crust slightly – shit! Lauren will notice, even if no one else does. The other is that Mummy's Little Helper will make an appearance.

'Can I do anything?' asks Sally from behind me.

'No, it's fine, honestly. No problem. Thanks.'

'Are you sure?' she asks, her voice rising another octave.

'Yes, honestly. It's very kind, Sally, but there's no need.'

'Really? I feel so guilty leaving you out here doing all this while we're in there having a good time.' I'm probably having a better time loading the dirty dishwasher and struggling with an uncooperative *tarte aux fraises* than I would be in there, but I don't say it.

'No, I know my place, Sally. The old kitchen porter.'

'Oh, you are good.' Oh, you are annoying. 'Are you sure?'

'Oh, go on then, clean the oven, will you?'

There is a silence from Sally as I crush up the tart box and bash it down into the overflowing bin. Obviously not my funniest line ever. But when I turn round, Sally, in her pearls and immaculate Thomas Pink shirt and pressed blue jeans is peering anxiously into the oven.

chapter eight

On the way to the tube station on Monday morning I grab a copy of the *Post* to see Nora's piece. I have to read through quite a bit of other stuff before I find it and by this stage I'm sitting on the train, so when I say, 'Oh, shit,' loudly, quite a few people around me notice.

The first thing I see is a picture of me. It's from a job I did last year, or the year before, for some Swedish fashion house. I'm in a white linen shirt with most of the buttons undone and an old pair of jeans and cowboy boots, lying back against a huge, moss-covered log in a wood, hair ruffled, giving it the old three-quarters-to-camera, frowny 'come to bed' look. I hated the picture when I first saw it and never even put it in my book. Now coupled with the headline 'At last . . . the net nerd gets sexy', I hate it even more.

It's huge – across nearly two whole pages. There are other pictures, including one of me in a tux which is taken from a catalogue, and another featuring me on a beach, wearing some stupid bright yellow trunks, I was originally advertising a holiday brochure, but now my 'family' have been carefully cut out so I look like an extra from *Baywatch*.

If the pictures are toe curling, the text is worse:

> *The blond, six-foot hunk is self-effacing when I ask about his involvement with the new site. 'I think they've just employed me because I've got the right look, you know, classy, cool,' he says.*

Did I? Possibly, during lunch at some point, but I was being sarcastic. Tongue in cheek. Didn't she understand that? Well-aired observations about Americans and irony flit through my mind.

You won't know his name but you'll know his handsome face – and his well-toned body – from hundreds of advertisements and commercials around the world for a variety of luxury products, ranging from designer-label clothing to fast cars. Charlie Barrett is one of Britain's most successful male models . . .

No, I'm not – and I told her not to use the phrase '*male* model'.

Over lunch at his favourite restaurant, the mind-bogglingly hip Dekonstruktion in Soho, haunt of celebrities and the media world's most beautiful people, he explains a bit more about how the site, dubbed 'the coolest thing in cyberspace', will work. 'It's a second-generation site so we've learnt from the mistakes of the net pioneers.'

I've never used that phrase in my life.

'It'll be the first web designer label,' explains Barrett. 'But what about the Gucci and Prada websites?' I ask.

No, you didn't.

'Ah,' he says, his deep blue eyes flashing with excitement, 'they are just luxury products with a website, this will be a website that is itself a luxury product. It's a global village of cool. Your boss will actually be impressed to see you surfing it at work.' With his chiselled jaw and elegantly swept back mane of blond hair, Barrett, who lives in trendy Chiswick with his model turned TV presenter girlfriend . . .

When did *that* happen?

. . . is something of a designer label himself. But he has now decided to turn his back on the modelling world . . .

I can't wait for Penny to read that.

. . . and to trade on his good looks and his cool, self-assured manner in order to bring his lifestyle of elegance and hip sophistication to a wider audience.

'It's very aspirational,' he says, using one of the marketing men's favourite buzzwords. Now we can all aspire to be like Charlie Barrett.

Feeling light-headed with the initial shock, and anger welling up inside me, I fold up the paper as the woman next to me quickly goes back to her book after allowing herself one final glance at my face.

I get off at Piccadilly Circus and feel, or at least imagine I feel, thousands of pairs of eyes on me. I've been stopped in bars, at the gym and even on the street before with the question, 'Aren't you the bloke from—?' Or, 'Sorry, but aren't you in that ad for—?' It goes with the territory and it can even be quite funny sometimes, depending on who makes the comment and what kind of mood you're in, but 'Hang on, aren't you that vain, arrogant tosser in today's *Post*?' isn't quite as much fun somehow.

As I open the door of the office, Scarlett and Piers, who are the only ones in, cheer in unison.

'Our media star,' says Piers, beaming.

'You mean your media twat.'

'What's the matter?'

'I don't think he likes the piece, Piers,' says Scarlett dryly.

'Don't you? Why not?'

'Why not? It's just so fucking embarrassing.'

'Is it? Why? Where?'

'The pictures, for a start, and all this shit about me being Mr Super Cool, drop-dead elegant . . .'

'I liked the picture,' says Scarlett. 'Nice bod, honey. Is is true that male models—?'

'No, it's not. Well *I* don't, anyway.'

'Look, Charlie,' says Piers, putting an arm round my shoulder and walking me over to my desk. 'I'd be lying if I said we didn't employ you for the way you look, but it's much more than that. It's your style, your presence, the way you wear your clothes, the way you carry yourself . . . you're our . . . what's the word, Lettie?'

'Muse,' says Scarlett, scraping the bottom of a yogurt pot with a plastic spoon.

'That's it, you're our muse. We want to create a website, oh, more than that, a lifestyle, a *façon de vivre* for people who want to be like you.' He pauses for effect. 'That's why that piece is so good, so important.'

'But, Piers, I look like a total bullshitter and a total tit,' I say, shaking his arm off me and sitting down heavily.

He puts his hands on my desk, leans over and looks at me. 'Charlie, you think you do because you're a nice guy, a modest sort of bloke who is embarrassed by this kind of adulation, okay? But believe me, to the ordinary punters out there, to those *Post* readers, you're the smartest, hippest thing ever. You simply *are* 2cool2btrue. You represent what they want to be, what they want a piece of. This is exactly what our target audience is looking for. Aspirational! You said it yourself.'

I get some water out of the fridge. It's that six quid a bottle stuff. Glacial Purity. Actually, I never mentioned the word 'aspirational' to Nora. Did I?

I ring Nora at the *Post*'s office just to see if I can at least ask why she wrote what she did, but funnily enough she is not around.

'Who? Nora?' There is a laugh. 'No, she's sort of out at the moment.'

'Sort of out?' What does that mean? Just generally out of it?

'She will be back later. Can I take a message?'

'Yes, please. Could you ask her to ring Charlie Barrett?'

'Will do.'

'Ta.' I put the phone down. Can't that girl even be *out* in a normal way?

Lauren rings towards lunchtime. She has just done a casting and someone we both know pointed out the article to her.

'Oh, don't! Who was it?'

'Jo Preston.'

'Shit. What do you think of it?'

'Well . . .'

'Oh, fuck, don't say "Well".'

'Are they pleased at the office?'

'At 2cool? Yeah, Piers is delighted.'

'Well, that's what I was going to say – that's the important thing. If they're pleased then you're doing your job.'

'I suppose so.'

'Cheer up. I'll save a copy for my mum. Love you. See you tonight.'

Karyn also rings to tell me she has seen it, as indeed has Penny.

'What are you going to tell her?' asks Karyn.

'Well, I'd better be honest I suppose.'

'Why?' says Karyn.

I laugh. 'You're right, Penny's never been much into honesty, has she?'

'Why don't you just say that it doesn't change your relationship with us greatly and that you can still do the occasional job. Penny will hate to see you go.'

'You're right, I've been dreading telling her.'

'I'll put you through to her now. Let me just see if she's in her office . . . er . . . yep. Okay, just tell her what we agreed and don't say anything more. Ring me back and let me know how it goes, if you want.'

'Ta, babe.'

There are a few minutes of a dance track and then Penny picks up.

'Hello, Charlie.' She is curt.

'Hi, Penny, how are you?'

'Fine.' Oh, shit.

'I suppose you saw that piece in the *Post* today,' I begin, flattering her that she is on the ball and reads more than *OK* and her stars.

'Yes, I did, Charlie. I was rather surprised, I must say.'

'Yes, it all happened rather quickly.'

'It must have done.'

'I wasn't sure initially how much of a commitment this job was going to be or even if it was going to be full-time,' I explain, glad that the others are out at lunch and can't hear this statement.

'Well, is it?'

'Yes, yes, it is, but they're giving me quite a bit of freedom, so obviously if any good jobs come up . . .' I decide not to be too specific here.

'Okay, we'll see how it goes,' she growls. 'A lot of clients will be very disappointed about this but I suppose we could say something like you're available by special arrangement only and hope that works. I can't promise anything, though, and don't come running back here when it all goes tits up.'

'No, sure. Well, as you say, we'll see how it goes. That's great.' Then I play my only trump. 'Obviously we'll be using Jet models whenever possible.'

She hardly skips a beat. 'We'd be very happy to work with you.'

'Great. Thanks Penny.'

'Bye.'

She hangs up and so do I after I've made a face and stuck two fingers up at the receiver.

'Oh, she could have been a lot worse,' Karyn points out when I ring her back later on the mobile and she pops out onto the fire escape to talk. 'You know how it is. Remember Paul Sommers.'

Paul Sommers, an affable Australian, was caught doing some 'freelance' work for a shifty photographer. The pictures ended up being used everywhere and eventually Penny saw them. She screamed at Paul across the office, 'You'll never model in London again!' and threw his cards at him. In fact he went back home, got into some soap and now he's coining it, but no one wants to feel the full, Concorde-engine force of Penny's wrath.

I try to get on with some work such as finalising the details for the party and chasing the PR company for a draft of the press release. Perhaps Lauren is right. And even Piers. I might not like the coverage, but it might be right for the target audience, whatever I think. All the same: 'chiselled jaw', 'well-toned body' . . . Oh, God!

On Tuesday after lunch, when Scarlett is out having a cranial massage and Zac is . . . well, just not in the office, I ring my dad on his mobile.

'I thought it was great – very positive coverage.'

'I thought I looked like a tit.'

'Yeah, but it's not aimed at you, is it? Think of your target audience.'

'So what? I still look pretty daft. Everyone I know will be laughing at me.'

'Not when you make a mill or two out of this thing. Look, I've got to run. I've got a busy morning ahead of me.'

'What do you mean "morning"? It's afternoon. Where are you?'

'I'm in New York. Someone faxed that piece over to me yesterday, as soon as it appeared. We're just keeping an eye on 2cool.'

'Okay, give me a ring when you get home again. Come and find me. I'll be in hiding up in the hills.'

'Will do. Don't worry, like I said, it's brilliant brand positioning.'

It's this comment and the realisation that he saw the piece not because of any paternal pride or interest but because of the commercial opportunity associated with it that makes me snap at him.

'I'm not a brand, I'm your son,' I point out. But he has gone and I'm left shouting to no one across thousands of miles of empty air.

Our fantastically cool and expensive stereo arrives later that day and a bloke spends a couple of hours installing it, asking if I have any idea how state-of-the-art this thing is. I say I don't, but can I get Radio Two on it? He doesn't see the joke and talks about watts per channel and digital quality sound reproduction or something just as wanky.

Bags of clothes are delivered from the 2cool stylist, and Scarlett and I have some fun trying trying them on while Piers is out lunching someone at Le Caprice and Guy is doing the same at the Savoy Grill. Later, a couple of crates of champagne are dropped off which have apparently been ordered for entertaining in the office. Before I can stop her, Scarlett has decided that we need some entertainment and she opens one.

Other than that there is very little to do for the most of the week. I begin to learn something, though, that all my friends who went to work in offices after school and university learnt many years ago: the art of paper shuffling and time killing. Scarlett and I go for organic juices and Shiatsu massages and even spend a couple of hours shopping on Wednesday with our 2cool credit cards: a Hugo Boss shirt for me and an outfit for her from a shop called Sceeech! for a lesbian wedding she is going to on Saturday.

On Thursday Piers takes me for what he describes as a fact-finding trip to Bond Street and Harrods.

'This ghastly tat is just the kind of thing we're *not* about,' he says very loudly in Harrods' Room of Luxury.

A few shoppers look round in surprise. I pretend to be one of them.

'Harrods is what Gucci and Pierre Cardin were in the seventies when they licensed themselves to anything and everything,' explains Piers. 'You've got to guard a brand with your life. After all, it *is* your life, well, your livelihood anyway.'

We move into another area of the shop, part of the menswear department, and Piers picks up some ties and drops them.

'Crap display!' he bellows.

Partly to hide my embarrassment I say, 'I'm just going to the loo, Piers, shall I see you back here in five minutes?'

'A piss?' he roars. 'Yeah, I could do with one, too.'

'I think the Gents is down there,' I whisper. At the urinals Piers continues to lecture me on luxury-goods marketing.

'They're called "ostentatious goods". Part of the attraction is the high price – people feel they're treating themselves whenever they buy something like that, or they just feel good because they know other people can't afford them. It's that old tag-line "reassuringly expensive".'

Piers even pees fast – his jet could cut slate. Mine is a pathetic, old man's trickle by comparison. Piers finishes, looks down to see if I'm going (yes, I'm going as fast as I can!) and then spins round to wash his hands.

We sprint out of the shop, Piers managing to make a couple of telephone calls between the inner and outer set of doors at the entrance. As we dash further down Knightsbridge we pass a beggar on the street outside, patterned shawl and skirt blowing in the breeze generated by the cars, hand extended, face set in the usual contorted mask of desperation and pleading. A drugged baby lies slumped in her arms. I look away, embarrassed, uncertain whether to give her money or not.

'See, *that* is bad market positioning,' says Piers, dialling another number on his mobile. It takes a moment for me to realise that he is talking about the woman we've both seen.

'What?'

'No one is going to give her money there. They're either hard-hearted bastards who don't care, or they've only got plastic on them. She should try the King's Road or somewhere like that, where there are lots of kids around who are into that sort of thing, you know, begging and busking.'

Later we pass a young guy begging with a painfully thin mongrel on the end of a piece of rope, who shakes a tatty McDonald's cup at us. Again I look away but Piers tells him, 'Oh, eat your dog.'

*

''Iya,' says Lauren. 'Good day?'

'Pretty quiet. I've just been finalising things for the launch party on Friday night. It should be spectacular. Scarlett and I did a final tour of the place this morning. The money they're spending – three bands, giant video walls to show the site as it goes live, thousands of staff, cars to pick up the VIP guests, and the food budget – I told you, didn't I? 250 pounds a head. Even the guy at Frederica's said it was one of the most amazing menus he'd ever seen.'

'Grea',' says Lauren, opening a bottle of Merlot.

'What did you say?'

'I's like that's really cool, yeah?'

'Why are you talking like that?' I laugh, slightly spooked.

'Well, the thing is, Pe'er says my accent is a bi' too cu' crystal, yeah? A bit too Received Pronunciation, and I should troy fla'ening it ou' a bi'.'

'You're joking! You sound like you're an American doing a terrible lovable cockney routine.'

'Well, thanks for the encouragement,' she says, slamming the corkscrew down on the work surface and turning to get the glasses.

'Sorry, it's just . . . why?'

'I'm going for this presen'ers job on Friday, yeah? And it's a bit more stree'y? A bit more cu'ing edge, and so Pe'er's worried my accent might coun' against me.'

'But I thought you were warm and, what was it? authoritative or something?' I ask, taking a welcome mouthful of wine.

'Oh, I am, but for this part I just need something different, a new string to my bow,' she says normally.

'I liked your old strings,' I say sulkily.

'Oh, honestly, Charlie, I'm no going to do i' f'rever, just for a few days while I ge' into it, yeah?'

'All right, Eliza Doolittle,' I say, lifting Lauren's simple cotton dress over her head. 'Now, lawks-a-mercy, let's have a bath and get that soot off you.'

chapter nine

On Friday I arrive back at the club just before seven and try to smile confidently in a you-know-who-I-am kind of way at a bloke in a DJ with an earpiece and a headset. He lets me in impassively. The party is planned to start at eight but I've been here all afternoon, watching the giant video walls go up while armies of glasses spread across white tablecloths and plates pile up ready for the buffet. Cables and control boxes appear then disappear as they are neatly tucked away. In fact, I haven't had to do much because Simon Smith, our PR man, and his assistant Charlotte, have been organising most of the activities.

The morning was spent with Scarlett and a couple of Simon's colleagues arranging for a fleet of nearly a hundred Mercedes and BMWs from every chauffeur-drive company in London to pick up our VIP guests and take them back home again afterwards. On their return journey they'll find a 2cool goodie bag, featuring amongst other things an Italian designed crocodile-skin mobile phone holder, a bottle of Krug especially labelled *poil de chien* (hair of the dog – geddit?) and a pair of Luttoxica sunglasses to protect the really hung-over.

A little envelope contains complementary treatments at spas such as the Dorchester, Aveda, Molton Brown and Bliss. There is a little coke container with each VIP's own monogram on it, created by one of Mayfair's finest royal warranted silversmiths. Poor old buffers were told the little solid sterling silver tube with its miniature scoop was for snuff. Ah, bless, as Scarlett put it when they agreed.

Now I'm back on duty wearing a black Armani suit and dark grey Costume National shirt with Tim Little shoes I bought on my 2cool credit card.

Simon is still shouting at people and consulting a clipboard when I get back. It seems Heaven, the decorator, is giving him a hard time about some delivery. Over the last two weeks of working in an office I've discovered that the thing to do in these situations is to concentrate on doing some small job. It makes you look busy, it keeps you out of the way and at least you can point to something you've done if anyone asks. Not that they have so far. In this case my small achievement is telling two guys where to put some potted plants.

'Two, two. Testing. Two, two,' says a voice from behind me, but when I look around I can see no one. A techie guy laughs at my confusion and explains: 'It's a new sound system. There are 300 miniature speakers around the place, tucked away in flower arrangements and places like here . . .' He reaches up and pulls out what looks like a black matchbox from behind a picture. 'So wherever you are it sounds like someone next to you is talking, rather than all that shitty sound quality you get with tannoys booming and distorting across the room.'

Suddenly sequences of the new, updated website flash on to the screens. One telly in the wall of monitors isn't working and remains obstinately blacked out, like a missing tooth in a smile. The techie tuts and yells something to his mate.

'I told you they were your responsibility,' Simon is saying.

'Hal*lo*? Are you not hearing me? My responsibility was to *buy* them. *Your* responsibility to *get* them here,' spits Heaven, lovingly enunciating every venomous syllable.

Simon consults his clipboard but, finding no solace in it says, 'Well, I would have thought *buying* them would have included actually, you know, *getting* them here.'

'Not when I had no budget for transport and the shop doesn't deliver. I would have thought that was obvious,' says Heaven, hands on hips, edging slowly closer to Simon, who is pretending that he is not remotely interested in this conversation. Finally Heaven is so far into his adversary's personal space that Simon has to say something.

'Well, at the end of the day it's your problem. You're responsible for candles and you haven't got them.' Nyah, nyah, nyah, nyah, nyah, goes unsaid. The two face each other for a few moments.

'Oh, working with you is just hell,' says Heaven.

At that moment Piers arrives. 'Fingertip control?' he says, rubbing his hands together. Heaven and Simon give him a poisonous look but he is impervious to it and rearranges some of the exotic flowers, admiring his irrelevant handiwork. 'How's it going Charlie?'

'Fine, no problem. Should be ready in plenty of time, shouldn't we, Simon?'

It's supposed to be supportive but Simon obviously doesn't see it that way. His jaw locks and he shudders slightly before spitting out, 'No problem.'

'Great,' says Piers.

'Huh! Give him a clipboard and suddenly he thinks he's bloody Stalin,' yells Heaven from across the room. Simon begins to talk to Piers. 'Poncey public school twat!' adds Heaven for good measure.

'You will *never* work for The Communications Game again,' says Simon with dignity.

'Good!' yells back Heaven. 'I wouldn't want to!' He turns round to concentrate on something else. 'Oh, for God's sake, sprinkle love, sprinkle,' he shouts at one of his terrified staff. 'If I'd wanted that much glitter on it I'd have given you a bloody shovel.'

'Splendid,' says Piers.

At two minutes to eight it looks like we're finally there. Waiters and waitresses are milling around with full drinks trays, moving into position around the main reception room. One is showing another the underside of his shoe for some reason. An older waitress with rather exaggerated eye make-up sidles up to me and says, 'What time does overtime start?'

'Midnight,' I tell her.

'Oh, good, thanks,' she says. I've actually no idea but I suppose I ought to know. The candlesticks, I discover, have arrived because the owner of the shop was persuaded (and bribed) to come back and open it especially so that they could be biked over to us. Now the huge, gilt gothic pieces with their towering black candles are placed on each table along with white lilies and black tulips.

Hundreds, well not hundreds but it seems like it, of girls with flicky blonde hair and names like Arabella and Louisa who work for The Communications Game arrive suddenly and introduce themselves to me, saying how exciting it all is and how much they're enjoying working on the account.

Lauren arrives with Peter just after half past eight as we agreed. She looks stunning: a cream coloured dress and simple gold chain. Peter is wearing a maroon velvet smoking jacket and spotted bow tie, and looks like he's just walked off the stage of an amateur dramatic society production of *The Mouse Trap*.

'Hi, babe,' says Lauren.

'You look great,' I say, putting an arm round her and kissing her on the lips.

'Thought I be'er make an effor',' she says.

'You're not going to do that all night?' I half-beg, half-command her.

'Oh, don't worry,' she laughs. 'It's been driving Charlie bonkers,' she tells Peter. 'No, I didn't get it, babe. Peter thinks they wanted someone a bit more in your face, a bit more off the wall.'

'A bit more Sara Cox or Davina McCall,' says Peter knowingly.

'Right,' I say, thanking God I'm not going out with someone 'in your face'. 'What was the programme exactly?'

'It's a proposal I put to E4,' says Peter, glad to be able to take the lead here. 'The idea is that it's a bit like *This Is Your Life*, only it's *This Is Your Sex Life*, at least that's the working title. We find a celeb and reintroduce them to everyone they've ever had sex with, from the person they first lost their virginity to, to long-term lovers and one-night stands. The guests rate them and tell some funny stories.'

'But E4 didn't like it,' I say, unsurprised.

'Oh, no,' says Peter. 'They love the *concept*, it's just—' Just Lauren they don't like? 'They just haven't found the right presenter yet.'

'That's not you is it, really?' I tell Lauren rather than ask her.

'No, probably not. But Peter's got some other projects in the pipeline for me,' says Lauren, who I notice is standing next to him, not me. Anyone who didn't know us might think that *they* were the couple rather than her and me. I'm about to try and angle myself nearer to her and get my arm round her again when Guy approaches us.

'Hi, Charlie, looking pretty sharp tonight,' he says, beaming.

'Thanks. From someone who knows so much about labels and style that's quite a compliment. Looking pretty good yourself. Er, Guy, this is my girlfriend, Lauren Tate, and this is . . .' I know I should say a friend of *ours*, not friend of *hers* but it just sticks in my gullet so I say, 'Peter Beaumont-Crowther.'

'Pleased to meet you,' says Guy, shaking hands with them both warmly and taking in Lauren, I note proudly. 'Charlie, mate, I need to introduce you to some people. Can I, er, steal you away for a sec?'

'Of course,' I say.

'Sorry, duty calls,' grins Guy at Lauren and Peter. 'Very nice to meet you, look forward to seeing you later; perhaps we can have a proper chat then. Have a great evening.'

Lauren and Peter smile generously as Guy leads me away. I turn briefly to tell Lauren I'll catch up with her later but Peter has already moved round to talk to her, standing between us so that she can't see me any more.

I meet a couple of very dry money men from New York to whom Guy talks for most of the time as if I might put my foot in it. By this time the place is really filling up. The girls from The Communications Game grab me every few seconds and say, 'Charlie, I'd really like you to meet . . .' or 'Charlie, do you know . . .?' or 'Charlie, you *must* meet . . .' Marketing people from the smart brands, editors of glossy magazines, style journalists, design celebs appear, tell me how much they're enjoying themselves and how excited they are about the site, how they loved the piece in the *Post*, then they give me a card and suggest we have lunch, dinner, breakfast or drinks before disappearing back into the crowd to be replaced by another well-moisturised, expertly made-up, non-streak bronzed face.

'How's it going?' says Guy to me anxiously at one point.

'Very well,' I say.

'Good, good,' he says, looking around us. 'Everyone happy, everyone enjoying themselves?'

'Yep. I've met so many new people, all really excited about it all.'

'Mmm? Good,' says Guy, looking around in the other direction, rather distractedly.

'These people, er, where are they?' I say, fiddling around with the mass of cards I've assembled. 'They want to do a promotion with us. Develop some synergies,' I explain, repeating the woman's phrase.

Guy looks down at the card for a moment and then sniffs. 'Huh! It's a possibility. I'm not quite sure that they're 2cool material, though.'

'Oh, okay.'

'Good stuff, champ,' he says, diving back into the crowd.

I go to get another drink and notice Lauren and Peter talking to two gay guys. It dawns on me who Peter reminds me of – Barry Humphries. Not as Dame Edna or Sir Les but just in civvies, just himself. It also dawns on me that they look like a couple. My girlfriend with Barry Humphries. I begin to move over to them but Arabella or Sophie, or whatever the hell her name is, grabs me and introduces me to someone from an in-flight magazine. When I finally escape Lauren and Peter have disappeared. I am looking around to see if there is anyone else I should speak to, when I notice Nora talking to a tall guy with floppy hair.

She immediately sees me and I decide to go over and say hello. I still haven't managed to speak to her since the article so it might be useful to share a few candid thoughts.

'Hi, Charlie,' she says, extending a hand.

'Hello,' I say coolly.

'This is Rupert. Rupert works for Cartier.'

'No, I don't,' says Rupert. 'I work for Sotheby's.'

'Do you? How interesting,' says Nora as if she has just met him.

'Don't worry,' I tell him. 'Accuracy's not her thing.'

'Isn't it?' she says sweetly. 'Here, Charlie, you haven't got a drink.' She sticks her hand out to a passing waitress but moves rather too quickly and immediately glasses begin to fall like dominoes on the tray. The waitress squeals in horror and tries to steady herself but she is soon covered with red and white wine, champagne and orange juice. As is Rupert who has tried to help her.

'Oh, you're soaked,' says Nora who like me seems to have escaped the deluge of booze.

'I think I'd better go and dry off in the Gents,' Rupert says as calmly as he can.

'Don't worry, just go to reception. We've had some spare jackets put aside just in case,' I tell him – one useful thing I did discover from Simon Smith. I check that the waitress is all right. She says 'Fine, thanks,' looking malevolently at Nora, and then disappears into the kitchen where they are presumably used to this sort of casualty.

'Well done,' I tell Nora.

'I can't believe that woman's a waitress,' says Nora, watching her go.

'Why not?'

'She's so clumsy.'

'*She's* so clumsy.'

'Yes, didn't you see her? You would have thought a waitress could at least keep a bunch of glasses on a tray. Poor woman, it must be her first night or something.'

I open my mouth but nothing comes out.

'So, nice party,' she says.

'Thanks.' She is wearing a maroon velvet dress, long-sleeved but backless, and her hair is up. There is a chunky, hippy chain around her neck. She does look pretty good, actually. I remember Lauren once telling me that in many ways it doesn't matter what you wear, as long as you wear it with confidence and feel comfortable in it. Nora seems to feel pretty pleased about her outfit.

Despite this I decide to plunge straight in. 'I saw the article.'

'Oh, yeah, Monday's piece. Did you like it?'

'No, frankly, I didn't.'

She looks surprised. 'Really, why not? Did I get something wrong?'

'Yeah, most of it.'

'Oh, my God, no. I hate getting things wrong. Which bits?'

'The whole thing. It was so naff. It made me look like a complete smarmy, arrogant tit. How did you find those pictures?'

'Oh, the picture desk do all that kind of thing. I liked the one of you in the white shirt, though. What was that for?'

'Oh, just a fashion shoot I did ages ago.'

'"Oh, just a fashion shoot", he says. So cool,' she laughs.

'It was just a job. But it was the article as well: "the blond, six-foot hunk is self-effacing".'

'Well, you are.'

'And what about "They employed me because I've got the right look – classy, cool."' It's not difficult to show her how painful those words are for me.

'Well, you did say that, in a manner of speaking. Over lunch.'

'What?'

'Anyway, I'm really sorry if you didn't like the piece. My editor loved it and I thought it was very positive really. Just what Piers wanted.'

'Piers told you to write that?'

'He didn't tell me exactly what to write, obviously, but he did give me the spin beforehand, told me all about the site, and then I pitched the story to my editor and she said to write it like that. I couldn't *not* do it.'

'It was all Piers's idea, all that stuff?'

'Yup. Well, most of it.'

'And you just wrote what you were told.'

'Charlie,' she says, suddenly serious. 'I've got to keep my boss happy. That's the way it goes. You want to please Guy and Piers, I want to please my editor. If I don't she'll fire me – it's as simple as that.'

I think about it for a moment. I've really only had to please Penny and Karyn in the past, by going to castings and turning up at jobs on time properly shaven and with my hair washed, but, talking to my friends who have worked for companies I think I know what she means about pleasing the tosser in the glass-surrounded office.

I look at her for a moment, trying to decide what it must be like to be Nora Benthall. To be very bright, but still have to please your boss by writing clichéd guff that is only marginally connected to reality, to be so amazingly clumsy (is that why I'm standing some distance away from her?) and to have a dress sense which somehow doesn't correspond with what you see in the shops, with what your friends wear or what appears in any magazine but that you are perfectly confident about and comfortable with.

'So where were you when I rang?' I ask. 'Why were you "sort of" out?'

She grimaces. 'I was keeping a low profile.'

'From me?'

'Oh, no, like I said, I tried to ring you but 2cool isn't in the phone book yet and I only had Piers's mobile. He said he'd get you to call me but obviously he didn't pass on the message.'

'Obviously not.' Thanks Piers. I make a mental note to ask him about that when I see him. 'So you were just avoiding someone else you'd libelled?'

'No, no,' she says, holding her glass in both hands and looking away while she begins her story. 'It's really embarrassing, actually. I'd just done something really stupid.'

'Something else?'

'Something else?'

'I mean in addition to that article.'

'Oh, not that again.'

'So what was it you did that was really stupid?'

'I was sending this email to my friend Gemma saying, "I'm going to the Ladies, meet you there". You know, it was for a girlie chat. Thing is we both quite fancy this guy in the office. I'm sure he's gay but never mind. Anyway, unfortunately, her last name is Allworthy. That's not the unfortunate bit, after all it's quite a nice name, isn't it? Don't you think? Allworthy.'

'Lovely,' I say, wondering where the hell this story is going.

'No, the unfortunate bit is that instead of clicking on "Allworthy, Gemma" in the "Send To" box, I clicked on "All Staff".'

She pauses.

'So all the staff at the newspaper got an email from you inviting them to meet you in the loo?'

'Basically, yes.'

I consider it for a moment. Then I realise that actually it's probably the funniest thing I've heard all night, all week, and I find myself almost crying with laughter. When I look back at her, wiping my eyes, she has a 'What can you do?' expression on her face.

'So did anyone turn up?' I ask her, not too seriously.

'Well, I'm told that quite a few people did. Even the boys from the mail room were sticking their noses round the door out of interest. I think they thought drugs were involved. Apparently the fashion editor went, but she doesn't have a lot to do at the moment because there aren't any shows on, as you know. Who else? A couple of people from the newsdesk popped in. Actually it was quite sweet – the editor's secretary emailed me back to say that he couldn't come because he had a lunch booked with the home secretary.'

'Has he no sense of priorities?' I demand.

'He'll never get anywhere in journalism with that attitude,' says Nora.

Just then the music pauses and there is a kind of fanfare from the rather spookily placed mini-speakers around us. 'Ladies and gentlemen,' says a voice. '*This* is 2cool2btrue dot com.'

Suddenly the video wall is alive. To the sound of some chilled-out instrumental beat which rises and turns into a dance anthem, we see some of the images I saw in the office but which are now enhanced. They seem to appear out of nowhere and disappear by blending into each other, drawing us in and spinning us round. I almost feel like I'm losing my balance at one point.

You can tell how impressed people are with the graphics and the breathtaking special effects by the fact that after the show there is a stunned silence before the applause begins.

Guy then appears and says, as if he means it, 'Wow'.

There is a ripple of laughter from the audience and then he begins to speak without notes about the importance of labels and branding in the third millennium, singling out, sometimes admiringly and sometimes teasingly but always charmingly, representatives amongst the audience from Vogue, Dunhill, Tanner Krolle, Rolls-Royce, Salvatore Ferragamo and Cartier amongst others. Then he moves on to his theory that what they have done for clothes, accessories, cars, electronics, and watches, 2cool will now do for the internet. He is self-deprecating about his knowledge of internet technology, and even more so when he talks about dotcom startups – and closedowns – to the further amusement of the audience, but then he talks about why 2cool will be different.

I look around me as he speaks. There are certainly some very clever people here and many of them look intrigued, heads to one side, brows furrowed, eyes narrowed, shrewdly. Not necessarily wowed – they're obviously too cool, too blasé for that – but they certainly seem interested by this rather serious, intense young man with pale skin and piercing eyes, his dark hair receding into a widow's peak, and his slight stoop. He looks more like a political speech-writer or a City economist than an entrepreneur, let alone a style guru. Perhaps that is why his audience is so gripped – he is not one of them, but he certainly has a certain nervy, edgy charisma.

Beside me is Nora. Eyes fixed in an intense, shrewd gaze that I have not seen before. She seems to be weighing up every word and analysing it, somehow thinking beyond it. I ought to ask her if she's going to write this up as an article. Is that what she's thinking? She looks away from Guy for a moment and sees me watching her. We smile at each other uncertainly.

Embarrassing. Never mind, I could just be checking her reaction along with everyone else's like any good marketing man.

But I'm wondering why she is called Nora. Funny name, Nora. Kind of name your great aunt is called. She sure is a strange girl. Inviting the entire office to meet her in the loo! Is she really that daft? I can't tell. Anyway, why should I care that she fancies some bloke in the office?

Apparently slightly taken aback and overwhelmed by the enthusiastic reception he generates, Guy mutters some thanks and hands over to Piers before walking off the stage. He's the least smart, cool thing about the whole evening and yet somehow by far the most intriguing. Piers, by contrast, is confident and relaxed. He introduces himself, makes a few obvious but funny jokes about dotcoms and designer labels and then explains that food is about to be served, but first he would like to express the company's gratitude to a few people for making tonight such a success.

'I'd especially like to thank Simon and Charlotte from The Communications Game, who have put in so much hard work this evening,' says Piers. 'Simon, take a bow, matey, well done.' There is a round of polite applause as people begin to look over to where the food is coming from.

'Fuckin' arse wipe,' hisses a voice next to me. It's Heaven.

'And also to Charlotte. Charlotte . . . where is she?' A spotlight swivels round and falls on a small, timid-looking girl wearing a pink ball dress obviously designed for someone bigger and more outgoing. 'Here she is. Well done, Charlotte. You've done a splendid job here tonight.' Charlotte beams, some people begin to applaud. 'And I know you haven't been well the last couple of days.' Her smile weakens. 'Poor Charlotte.' The smile evaporates altogether. 'Chronic diarrhoea,' booms Piers sympathetically. 'Sounds like it must have been awful.' Charlotte's face is frozen in a mixture of horror and a desperate supplication to Piers to just fucking shut up. 'Can't have been much fun but glad you've made it tonight.' A couple of people move discreetly but noticeably away from her. 'And . . . er . . . let's just hope there's plenty of Imodium or something in that beautiful handbag she's carrying,' adds Piers for good measure.

I can't bring myself to look back at Charlotte but I am sure she is now on her way to the Ladies either to cry her eyes out or to . . . well, I find myself hoping, like Piers, that the Imodium is working.

I turn to ask Nora what she thinks, as much as anything to explain my staring at her in that very obvious way during the presentation, but she has turned to talk to someone else.

'Hey, you look great this evening,' she says to someone just out of view behind a pillar. I look round to see who it is and recognise her instantly. Instead of appearing flattered, the weather woman looks alarmed by Nora's compliment and moves away quickly.

After the speeches, I congratulate Zac, who has made no effort in his dress at all tonight – baggy combats and tie-dyed, sleeveless green T-shirt with the words 'Eat the Poor' on it. He mutters something and crams some food into his mouth as if he hasn't eaten for a week. Then I try and find Lauren. She and Peter are also getting some food so I grab a plate and join them.

'What do you think?' I ask casually.

'Pretty bloody amazing,' says Lauren. 'That film is incredible – I didn't know it was possible to do that.'

I smile modestly. I wait for her to kiss me but she just shakes her head in wonderment.

'Very impressive,' says Peter. 'Is that PictureMark they're using?'

'Is it what?'

'For those dissolves in between the stills and the principal sequences – is it PictureMark they've used there? I'd heard it can do things like that, even in an off-line edit.'

'It's PictureMark Super,' I lie blithely, chasing a giant tiger prawn around my plate and catching it elegantly before I stab it, feeling the fork push its way in and the flesh satisfyingly giving way to the sharp metal. 'Do you want to dance, babe?' I suggest. 'They've imported this guy specially from New York. He's only here for a few hours, then he's off to Ibiza. We're paying him fifty grand for it. Can you believe it?'

'Not yet,' she says. 'Peter wants me to meet this woman from . . . where is she from?'

'Channel Five. They're looking for new programme talent.'

'I'll introduce you if you want,' I say. 'I've just been talking to her. She wants to do a promotion with us.'

'Don't worry,' says Peter. 'We were at Cambridge together. She's an old, old mate.'

'Sure,' I say and walk off. There must be a way to separate Lauren from him, perhaps with a crow bar, I think as I wander around the room. I suddenly realise that the girls on the soundtrack arranged by the ultra-cool DJ are groaning:

'Hey, babe.
Do you wanna ride me?
Do you wanna come inside me?'

Perhaps I'm just getting old, but that is bloody rude isn't it? Suddenly someone slaps me on the back.

'How's it going?'

It's Piers.

'Great,' I say miserably.

'Splendid,' he bawls.

I find myself talking to a woman from an expensive shoe company.

'Think Jimmy Choo on acid,' she says.

'Okay.' I don't think I could imagine that even if *I* was on acid.

'Think classic with a surrealist twist.'

'Right.'

'We're talking deconstructionism taken to its logical, terrifying conclusion – in terms of slingbacks, anyway.'

'I see.' I wish I did have some acid now.

Suddenly she takes a step further towards me and says, 'After all, you know what they say: "Shoes are the windows of the soul".'

'It *is* all pretty impressive isn't it?' I say to Lauren as she nestles under my shoulder in the car on our way home. It's gone four and we were almost the last to leave. Guy and Piers are still chatting up the remaining potential investors and partners. Peter is talking to some 'old mates' from the beeb and Nora must have gone without saying goodbye to me.

'Oh, yes, it's amazing. Your friend Guy certainly knows his stuff.'

'He's brilliant. So . . . what's the word? Cerebral. I think that's why they like him. They sense that here is someone with something new, something different to offer. Did you have a good time?'

'We did, yeah.'

We? What's with this *we*?

'Peter enjoyed himself too, did he?'

'Yes, it turned out he knew quite a few people there. Mind you he knows so many people.' Now that his name has been introduced again it feels as if he is in the car with us, crammed on the back seat. The atmosphere is suddenly soured. My arm's going to sleep a bit anyway so I pull it out from under Lauren's head, perhaps a bit more roughly than I had intended. We sit in silence as the car speeds along Knightsbridge.

Finally Lauren says, 'Who was that strange-looking girl you were talking to?'

'Which strange-looking girl?' I ask unnecessarily.

'The one in the maroon dress. You seemed to be having a great laugh at one point.'

'Oh, her. That's that journalist who wrote the piece in the *Post*.'

'Oh.' There is a pause as shop windows fly past, their reflections dancing over us. A few late-night stragglers walk backwards looking for cabs and night buses or joke with their mates, while others stagger around drunk. 'Well, you seemed to be giving her a good talking-to like you said you would.'

Lauren's sarcasm hangs in the air like a challenge. I try to neutralise it.

'We discussed the piece and she explained why she'd written it.'

Silence.

'And that's that?'

Silence.

'What do you want me to say? We discussed it. I told her what I thought of it, she told me why she'd written it the way she had and that was that. Piers asked her to do it like that apparently.'

Silence. With Peter *and* Nora in the car with us now, things are getting very cramped and uncomfortable.

'I see.'

Silence.

'Look, I've got to keep her onside. She'll be very useful.'

'Huh. What for?'

'For promoting the site. Now let's leave it shall we?'

'What's her name again?'

'Nora. Nora Benthall.'

'Never heard of her,' says Lauren. 'She's obviously slept her way to the bottom.'

Lauren and I get ready for bed in silence. When I get in she has her back to me. I wriggle over to her and put an arm round her. She mutters something about being tired.

chapter ten

It takes me ages to get to sleep. My mind is still buzzing from the party. I've got lunches arranged from now until the end of my life and there is a stack of business cards on the dressing table. I can still hear the voices: 'So exciting', 'Excellent product', 'So looking forward to doing business with you', 'You certainly have a wonderful proposition here', 'Tremendous opportunities for developing synergies'. Or something like that. Smart people, rich people, powerful people, famous people asking for a piece of the action, a piece of me.

The light wakes me up. I reach round instinctively for Lauren, looking for some lazy Saturday morning sex. The kind where you don't mind if you come or not. But she's not there. The curtains are open already. I squint my eyes up against the harsh, unforgiving light. I can smell coffee. I fumble for my watch and check the time: just before eleven. I get up and stumble into the kitchen. Lauren is chewing on a piece of toast and flicking through the newspaper. I come up and put my arms round her, nestling into her hair and kissing her neck.

'Morning, hon,' she says quietly, still reading the paper.

'You're up early,' I say, wandering over to the fridge.

'Mmm? Yeah, I know, we've got access to a studio today, so I'm going to do some autocue practice.'

'What? Today? But you were at it last Saturday.'

'Yes. That's when the studio's free. Do you know how much these things cost to rent? Thousands. Thank goodness Peter knows someone who said we could borrow it for nothing.'

'So you're going to a studio this Saturday as well?' A pretty pointless summary of the situation, but I want her to understand how ridiculous it is that she's working all day, given that we've seen so little of each other over the last week or so. Instead she takes the opposite view.

'Yes, like I say, it makes obvious sense.'

'When will you be finished?'

'I don't know. When I've had enough. When Peter thinks I've done all I can.'

'Will you be back by five?' I ask, drinking orange juice out of the carton because I know it will annoy her.

'I don't know, Charlie, please don't pressurise me.' I turn up the sulk meter a bit more. She comes over to me and studies me for a moment, then she laughs. 'You look like a little boy with your hair all messed up.'

I narrow my eyes at her with mock crossness.

She laughs again, takes the carton out of my hand, puts it back and then says, 'What am I going to do with you?'

I look into her eyes, pull her towards me and say, 'I can think of one thing.'

She pinches my cheek and giggles. 'That'll have to wait.' She pulls away. 'I'm going to be late.'

I catch her arm but, instead of asking her what she wants to do tonight I find myself saying, 'Do you love me?'

She pushes my hair out of my eyes.

''Course I do.'

I pick up the paper after Lauren has gone and begin to flick through it, making my way towards the sport to see whether Chelsea are at home. Halfway through there is an article by Nora along with a picture of her, looking cheekily over her black-framed glasses. It's called 'Why I'll never marry a man who waxes his behind'. I have to read the title twice to make sure I've got it right. The piece is about how women hate male vanity and how she and her friends (who are her friends? Other clever, barmy women with strange names? Or does she just invent them too?) would rather have a man with shaggy nose hair than one who spends hours in the bathroom cutting it with his nail scissors. It seems that her friend Amanda, who works in marketing, once went out with a bloke who waxed his bum – hence the headline. My buttocks clench at the thought of it. They clench even tighter as I read on.

Male models shave their chests. Can you imagine a greater turn off? Most women I know like curling their fingers around a light dusting of chest hair. The idea of a waxed, fake-tanned chest is about as attractive as low-calorie, frozen risotto compared to the real thing, oozing wickedly butter and parmesan and eaten overlooking the Canale Grande.

I finish the paper and go into the living room. Now where did Nora get the inspiration for that? I'm not being vain, it's just an obvious connection. Actually I did know a guy who shaved his chest. Gary had the kind of body that looked like it had been carved out of granite at the dawn of time. Underpants were his speciality. I still see him – well, his six-pack and lovingly sculpted (and shaved) pecs – on packets in department stores. He told me that he was once doing a shoot and just as the client arrived he felt himself getting a hard-on. Desperately he tried to think about his tax return or Alan Titchmarsh but it had no effect. As six women from the client company entered the room he found himself saluting them through their soon-to-be-launched cotton and lycra microfibre-mix knitted trunks.

I flick on children's Saturday morning television and watch, feeling rather confused and out of it. After a phone-in in which Leanne from Burnley correctly identifies Ronan Keating's star sign and wins a baseball cap and a CD, a girl band comes on:

'Oh babe, the cat's out of the bag.
Your love's become a drag.'

I rub my chin, trying to decide whether to have a shave. Sod it. It's Saturday.

At about seven I ring Lauren on her mobile. I've been avoiding doing it all day, not wanting to pester her like the good boy that I am, but now I've had enough. I want to know what we're going to do this evening. I want to spend it with her.

I get her voicemail and, with superhuman effort, manage to sound casual and friendly. 'Hi babe, just wondered what time you thought you'd be finished.' I wait nearly an hour and then decide to go for a run because I can feel anger rising from deep within me and I can't think how else to release it, other than yelling at her when she rings, or just throwing things around the flat. But that would just make things worse and I simply can't bear to do that, although part of me feels I should. Perhaps I would if I were a real man, not just an ex-male-model now working in the virtual glamour business.

I only run for twenty minutes or so, just round the block, but laziness – and the sight of other couples walking along hand in hand – draws me back home. It's just long enough, though, for Lauren to have called.

'Hi babe, are you there . . . Charlie . . . Charlie? Okay, well just to say sorry I couldn't talk to you just now, had to turn my phone off. But listen, babe, we've bumped into some friends of Peter's and they've offered to take us to dinner, so I'm just going to have a quick bite to eat with them, but I won't be late. Sorry about this, but I'll make it up to you tomorrow night I promise. Love you.'

I have a shower, during which I find myself singing that stupid girl band song from children's television. I knew it would get stuck in my mind when I heard it.

I put my bathrobe on and go into the kitchen. There is no wine in the fridge and the only stuff in the cupboard is a Châteauneuf du Pape which we bought last year in France and promised to drink on a special occasion. I shut the cupboard and begin to wonder whether I can be arsed to get dressed and go up the road to the off-licence and buy another.

I can't, so I open the cupboard again and take the expensive, slightly dusty bottle out.

I don't bother to get a coaster and, glass in hand, I flop down on the settee and switch on the telly. I flick between channels and watch Davina McCall explaining to a group of lads with viciously gelled hair and River Island shirts, and girls with diamond nose studs, exactly how they can earn points and what they can do with them. 'But,' she explains from behind a huge perspex lectern bathed in a ghostly blue light, 'if someone from the opposing team gets the answer before you then you have to give them half as many points as your total so far, although you can of course challenge them to gamble their bonus points provided they haven't earned any bonus points this round. Okay?'

I must be getting old because I can't understand a word of it, so I switch off and throw the remote down next to me. The flat is suddenly silent. I get up, shuffle morosely over to the music centre and flick through the CDs. Opera highlights, Ministry of Sound Chill Out sessions, Dido, the best of Frank Sinatra, jazz compilations. They're all Lauren's. Where did mine go? I go back into the bedroom and reach up to the top shelf of the wardrobe where there are some boxes of my stuff from before I moved in with Lauren. She didn't seem to like any of my music and so it all got tidied up into these cardboard boxes along with photographs from college and various other personal effects from My Life Before Lauren.

I flick through the cassettes and find Suzanne Vega. I don't know why but I've always had a bit of a thing for a chick with an acoustic guitar. I stick the tape in the machine, turn up the volume and let her plaintive, melancholy voice fill the room. Then I take a big gulp of expensive wine and lie back, committing aural adultery.

chapter eleven

I'm the first in the office on Monday morning, just before nine. There is a pile of letters waiting on the mat. I scoop them up and put them onto Scarlett's desk. Then I realise that I might as well open them, partly because I am, after all, one of the team, so I have every right to. And I've got nothing else to do. There is nothing very exciting amongst them – just routine correspondence from the phone company, the computer people and the landlord.

There are also letters of welcome from the bank. Quite a few banks actually, including some in the Cayman Islands and Monte Carlo, thanking 2cool for using their services and promising that they are always on hand to help us. And there are some bills, lots of bills in fact, most of which come from the do on Friday night but also from taxi companies, stationers and a florist. Even our in-house masseur, whom I don't seem to have had the benefit of yet – Scarlett and I had to go down the road for our treatments, although admittedly we charged them to 2cool. There is something from a Paris *chocolatier* which seems a bit bizarre, as well as invoices from The Communications Game and various Bond Street stores.

'Morning,' says Guy, striding in with a coffee in his hand. 'How are you, Charlie? Good weekend?'

'Yeah, great thanks,' I lie. 'You?'

'Erm, yes, yes good,' he says, eyeing the pile of post.

'Recovered from Friday?' I say by way of conversation, suddenly feeling a bit shy of him now that there are just the two of us in the office.

'Eh? Friday, oh yes, of course. We had breakfast afterwards with some of those money men. Most of them were still working on West Coast time, so they weren't that bothered about going to bed at all really – look, why don't you just shove all that crap on Scarlett's desk, let her deal with it?' he says, snatching the sheaf of letters from in front of me and thrusting them into Scarlett's in-tray.

'I don't mind going through them,' I say. 'At least until Scarlett gets in.'

'No, don't you worry about that. Your time would be better spent chasing up some of the valuable contacts we made on Friday night. Look, let's work up a list of people to see, get some lunches planned, set up some meetings with the potential 2cool partner organisations, shall we?'

'Sure,' I say.

Later that morning, a range of specially imported Italian crockery and cutlery is delivered, as is a huge cappuccino machine. We all look at it appreciatively as it's being plumbed in, but then realise that we can't actually be arsed to use it so we'll just stick to Caffè Nero round the corner.

'I got you a wheatgrass shot,' says Scarlett, putting the tiny plastic container carefully down on my desk as she arrives just after half past ten. 'I've already had a double.'

'You're such a health freak,' I tell her.

'Yeah, I know, but I dropped two Es on Saturday night and I just *cannot* get my shit together today,' she explains.

Piers bursts in at lunchtime. He's just driven up from Gloucestershire, he enthuses, where's he been staying with friends who are all very excited about the new site. A girl called Suzie, who does PR for a newly launched line of luxury French silks, thinks they might be able to work together, he tells me, so will I ring her? He throws a business card at me, but before I can ask exactly what he envisages us doing together Zac calls him over to show off some new visuals on the computer, and he goes into paroxysms of delight. 'Have you seen this, Guy?' he asks. 'Here Charlie, look at this new gizmo our brilliant techno-whiz here has cooked up. It's just . . . just . . .'

'2cool2btrue?' asks Scarlett.

'Yes, yes,' says Piers. 'It is, that's exactly it.'

We crowd around the monitor in Zac's corner of the room to watch a new computer graphic which allows us to sit inside the new Bentley sports car and imagine we are being driven in it. We then 'drive' into a virtual mall and a chauffeur in the form of Oddjob from Goldfinger ('I wanted someone who was instantly recognisable, an iconic chauffeur,' explains Zac morosely) reaches out, picks up items and hands them over to us in the back seat.

'You can sit in the front if you prefer,' he says. He taps away at the keyboard and suddenly we are alongside Oddjob. 'Or you can swap places with him if you'd prefer to drive.'

'Absolutely fan-fucking-tastic,' says Piers.

But Guy just says, 'Great. Look, I need to talk to you, Piers. Erm, let's step outside for a moment.'

The three of us 2coolers remaining exchange glances.

'That's incredible, Zac,' says Scarlett, standing up straight and going over to her own desk. 'Even better with an E hangover.'

'Most hi-res graphics look better if you're slightly drug-fucked,' says Zac, racing his mouse around its pad.

'That's true. I think I need something to jump-start me a bit. I'm just going to get a shot of wheatgrass,' says Scarlett.

'You've already had a double this morning,' I tell her.

'Have I? Christ I have, haven't I?' She sits down and taps away at her keyboard a bit. Then she says, 'Spiruleena, that's what I need.'

'What?'

'Spiruleena,' she says. 'It's a nutrient derived from algae.'

'Yum,' I say.

'It's the dog's bollocks. Want some?'

'I'd rather have a ginger, carrot and apple.' I can't believe I've just asked for this, as if I'm offering it as a sane alternative.

'Sure. Zac?'

'Doctor Pepper, please.'

'Have you any idea how much sugar there is in those things? Like a ton in every mouthful.'

'That's what keeps me sweet.'

Scarlett looks completely mystified. As she opens the door to leave, Guy and Piers come back in.

'Where are you going?' asks Guy.

'Bikini wax,' she tells him. Guy opens his mouth to say something but then just looks away, embarrassed. Piers throws himself down in his chair and stares at his desk for a moment.

'Everything all right?' I ask, partly out of genuine concern and partly to point out that hurried meetings outside in the corridor with no subsequent explanation aren't exactly good for staff morale.

Piers opens his mouth but Guy speaks. 'Fine. We just needed to talk about the second tranche of financing.'

'Sure,' I say, relieved.

Then Piers opens a drawer of his desk. 'Taste this,' he says. He holds up a jagged piece of dark chocolate. I take it from him, put it in my mouth and let the familiar sweet, cloying sensation flood over my tongue.

Piers is watching me. 'Just imagine – something that tastes like chocolate, feels like chocolate and yet has no calories whatsoever.'

'That's incredible,' I say, running my tongue over my teeth. I swallow hard in near disbelief. 'Every woman in the country – and lots of men too – would go mad for this stuff. What is it?'

He looks at me for a moment, slightly confused, slightly disappointed.

'Well, it *is* chocolate actually,' he says, throwing the bar back in the drawer. 'But just imagine if you had something that wasn't chocolate but tasted like that.'

Now it's my turn to look confused and disappointed. 'Right, yeah, it would be . . . great.' I try and redeem the situation. 'Very marketable.'

'It would, absolutely, *very* marketable,' says Piers, getting back into his stride. He gets up from his desk and moves over to the window. 'You see, Charlie . . .' and he is off again.

I spend the day making appointments to meet some of the people whose cards I collected at the party, and take the opportunity to leave that evening when Scarlett does, just after six.

'Do you think everything's okay?' I ask as we step out of the front door and into the street.

'How do you mean?' she says.

'You know, with the company, with 2cool?'

'Yeah. Why shouldn't it be?'

'I didn't like that hurried meeting Guy and Piers had this morning. They sounded distinctly worried.'

'Oh, that. Well, they both cheered up later in the day, didn't they?'

'I suppose so.'

'Don't worry. Media projects, especially major ones like this, require a huge initial cash outlay. It all comes out in the wash.'

'Does it? I suppose the important thing is that the investors still have confidence.'

'Oh, yes. They're not going to pull the rug from under our feet. They know that this is a second-generation e-commerce operation and has the potential to be, like, a *major* money spinner. Most of them are just bursting to get back into the whole net business as soon as possible, anyway.'

'I just couldn't help noticing how much money we're spending, like the party on Friday and things.' I hadn't originally planned to say all this to her, but what the hell. 'And all those bills this morning. And those bank accounts in the Cayman Islands. What's that all about?'

'Look, don't worry. It's the same in the film business. Most creative industries are like this. It's what they call the J curve, or the V trajectory or the U bend or something.'

'If you say so,' I mutter, even less reassured. We march out of Old Compton Street into Charing Cross Road, our speed and Scarlett's bright red dreadlocks terrifying some ageing Japanese tourists.

'People who are really closely involved in the development of a project often get cold feet at this stage,' says Scarlett. She's probably right. 'I mean, my sister, yeah?' she says. 'She's a stylist, works with *Dazed and Confused* and does a lot of pop videos, yeah? Anyway, she's bought a cat, yeah? And it just won't go into the kitchen. Any other part of the flat, no problem, but the kitchen? It's like it's spooked or something. It's the same thing, yeah?'

We walk along in silence for a moment. It's no good. I've got to ask her.

'How is that the same thing as 2cool's financial situation?'

'How's what the same thing?'

'Your sister and her cat.'

Scarlett stops for a moment, thinks, and then carries on walking. 'Oh shit, sorry, did I say that? That's the E talking again. Don't worry, I should be okay by Thursday.'

I can't wait.

We get to Leicester Square tube station and as she walks towards the Northern Line barrier I say to her, 'Bye, then, see you tomorrow.'

She looks around and then, apparently slightly surprised that I'm not coming all the way home with her, calls to me, ''Kay babe. Stay beautiful, yeah?'

God, I hope no one heard that.

That evening I go to see my mum. It says something about my relationship with Lauren at the moment that I think an evening with my mum would be more fun than one spent with her. I take the tube to Barnet but give up on the bus and take a minicab into the tightly knit pattern of streets in which she now lives. After they split my dad more or less gave her the family home since, thanks to the power of advertising, or its financial clout anyway, he didn't need it any more. My sister regarded this piece of thoughtless generosity as the final insult.

'How could I live in that place without him?' pointed out my mum as the tears dripped into her tea.

So now she lives in a small thirties-style semi in a quiet, nondescript street. It's actually so nondescript that it always takes me a moment to confirm that it really is the right house and the right street.

She opens the door on the chain and then lets me in. She's getting liver spots on her hands, I notice.

'Hi, Mum,' I say, bending down to kiss her on the cheek.

'Hello, dear,' she whispers.

'Brought you some flowers.'

'Oh.' She takes them from me. 'I'm not sure if I've got a vase big enough for these.'

'Oh, well.' I mentally roll my eyeballs.

'Well, it's very kind. I'll put them in something. Now do you want a cup of tea?'

'I've brought some wine as well,' I tell her, holding up a bottle of Australian Chardonnay. We always go through the 'Tea? I've brought some wine,' script.

'Wine? Really? Oh, well, how nice,' she says as usual.

We have shepherd's pie, peas and diced carrots sitting opposite each other in her spotless kitchen, and I listen to her prattle on about the neighbours I don't know and about my brother-in-law and how well he's doing at work but how she wishes he would spend more time at home with my sister and the baby. She asks how Lauren is, and I look down at my plate as I say, 'Fine, fine.'

'And how's the new job going?' she finally asks, as she stirs a saucepan full of rice pudding, and I wonder why she never uses the microwave I bought her for Christmas two years ago. I'm sure we ate better than this when we were growing up – ratatouille and spaghetti carbonara even made an appearance when I came home from university – but it's as if she has withdrawn into a sort of culinary nostalgia, resorting to the familiar comfort food of her childhood.

'It's going very well,' I tell her, as much to convince myself as anything. 'We had an incredible launch party on Friday at Frederica's, this ritzy nightclub in Berkeley Square,' I say, adding my own footnotes. 'And now it's officially up and running. You can actually visit the site if you want to. Go and use one of the machines down at the library. Here, I'll write the address down.'

'I know where the library is,' she says indignantly.

I laugh gently. 'No, I meant the address of the website, so you know what to type in.'

'Oh, don't worry. I'm not much good with computers. The woman in the post office was saying she still can't use hers properly and I said "Don't look at me".' She laughs sadly.

'Oh, go on, Mum, have a look.' I'm slightly offended that she won't even check it out. 'It's incredible – amazing graphics.'

'Graphics? You mean the pictures?'

'Yeah, it looks fantastic.'

'Oh, okay. I'll have a go. I've got to take a couple of books back anyway. Actually, there's a new – what are they called? – cypher café on the high street. I could go there and have a coffee, a latte or whatever it is they drink now.'

'Yeah, that's a good idea. You'll love it, Mum. It's incredible, what they've done.'

'Do you want jam in it?' she asks, carefully spooning rice pudding into two bowls that she has heated in the oven.

'Please. You can go virtual shopping on Bond Street or Fifth Avenue and find out what's hip in Hong Kong or Melbourne at the moment.'

'Oh, and that's right up my street, isn't it?' We both laugh at the idea and I'm glad to see that she doesn't dissolve into tears this time.

*

I get in and watch Lauren sleeping silently. I take my clothes off, brush my teeth, look at myself in the mirror and decide that with those ads for comfy cardigans and geriatric baths looming I was right to make the career change.

chapter twelve

'Sweetie, can you change the channel? I can't stand any more of this crap,' I mutter at Lauren from my position on the settee.

'Where's the controller?' she asks, curled up in a chair next to me.

'Down on the floor, I think.'

She tuts. 'If you get any lazier, you wouldn't bother to breathe.' She finds the elusive remote on the floor and throws it onto my stomach.

'Ouf! I think you've broken some ribs.'

'Good.'

But before I can switch channels the phone rings and she reaches over and picks it up. It's my mum.

'Hello Sheila. How are you?' says Lauren, looking across at me with a face which says 'get ready to take this off me very soon'. They chat briefly and then Lauren says, 'Anyway, nice to talk to you, Sheila. Take care now. He's just here.'

'Hi, Mum,' I say, taking the receiver from Lauren's outstretched hand and still looking at the television.

'Hello, dear. Everything all right?'

'Yep, fine thanks.'

'Good, good.' There is a pause.

'What is it, Mum?' I ask, sitting up.

'Well, I had a look at your website—'

'Great, what did you think?'

'It was er . . . the pictures, you know the graphics, were very exciting, like you said. Everyone in the library was very impressed.'

'Good,' I smile, enjoying the idea that we had fans in her local library – definitely the 2cool target audience. Not.

'And those clothes: very smart. I liked one of the skirts by that

Italian designer, expect for the price, of course. Do people really spend that much money on a skirt?'

'Oh, yeah, you'd be amazed.'

'Incredible. Anyway, we looked at what was, you know, trendy, like you said and then . . .'

'Yeah?'

'Well, the thing is Charlie, we went on the bit that said "Extra Curricula" and . . .'

'Sorry, which bit?'

'The little thing called "Extra Curricula", you know the . . . what's it? The icon. The cursor turned into a little hand like it does and we clicked on it and then we found these pictures . . .'

'What pictures?'

'Charlie, I don't know about these things and I'm sure you know what you're doing . . .'

'Mum, what pictures?'

'Charlie, you must know.'

I sit up and reach for the telly controller. Even Lauren is watching me now.

'No, what pictures?'

She takes a deep breath. 'Pornographic pictures.'

'What? Porn? On the site?'

'Yes, dear, didn't you know?'

I look to Lauren for some reason but she just gives me a questioning frown.

'No, I didn't. Listen Mum, are you sure you went to the right site?'

'Oh, yes, everything else was there like you said.'

'2cool2btrue dot com' I spell it out for her just in case.

'Yes, you wrote down it here. I'm looking at it.'

'Somebody's hacked into the site.'

'You mean, like . . . like burglars.'

'Yes, exactly. Oh, God, Mum. I'm so sorry about this. How embarrassing. I hope the people you were with didn't see it all.'

'Oh, they did, we were all looking.'

'Oh, God.'

'Don't worry, I think the head librarian was very interested in it. He spent ages, you know, checking things. He was still at it when I left.' She laughs shyly.

I laugh a bit too, mainly to encourage her, like I always do, but also to show that it's all right, I'm a professional, I can handle this little hiccup.

'Oh, hell's teeth. Listen, I'll tell the others. Thanks for letting me know. I'd better ring them now, actually. Love you. Speak to you soon.'

I click off and get up to find Guy's mobile number.

'Someone's put porn pictures on the 2cool website?' asks Lauren.

'Yep, looks like it,' I mutter, leaving the room.

'Oh, my God,' she laughs. 'Let's have a look.'

'It's not funny,' I tell her.

In the bedroom, before ringing Guy, I switch on my computer and log in just to check that my mum is right. Sure enough, along the options along the left-hand side is a new one, 'Extra Curricula'. I click on the icon and am immediately presented with pictures of girls lying back exposing their crotches, grasping their tits in wide-eyed amazement as if they'd never seen them before, and others with men and women, women and women and men and men having sex together. Most look like they were taken recently but some have a grainy, seventies quality, and some a harsh, lip-glossed, heavily blushered look of the eighties about them.

I'm stunned for a moment. I haven't been so unaroused by naked flesh since a biology lesson. Then I ring both Guy's and Piers's mobiles to warn them. I get voicemails on each of them so I leave messages telling them what I've discovered and asking them to ring me at home if they want, otherwise we can discuss it in the office tomorrow.

'Oh, yeah,' says Guy when I mention it to him the next morning.

'So, you did get my message?' I ask, dropping a newspaper on my desk. 'About the porn thing?'

Instead of being shocked and angry as I had expected, he simply refers me to Piers, who says what I'm sort of dreading by now.

'Good, eh? Zac put them on yesterday.'

'What?'

'Zac's been sourcing them over the last few days. We've even had some done specially. He uploaded them yesterday.'

'You knew?'

'Yeah, of course,' says Piers, draining his coffee and crushing the cardboard cup with obvious satisfaction.

'Look, I don't like this. How the hell can you say that porn pics are too cool to be true?'

'Oh, Charlie—' says Piers with a sad smile.

'Oh, Charlie nothing! Why the fuck didn't I know?'

'Piers should have told you,' says Guy. 'Listen mate, I'm really sorry about this but sometimes things move so quickly in this game.'

Piers is looking slightly miffed about being dumped on but finally even he realises that this is his role in Operation Keep Charlie Sweet.

'We need to keep each other informed of what's going on all the time, after all, we're supposed to be in the communications business, aren't we?' adds Guy.

There is a deafening slurping sound as Scarlett finishes her juice and looks meaningfully at him.

'We certainly bloody should, but what the hell has porn got to do with our site?' I ask.

'Thing is, Charlie, porn is what drives the internet. Eighty per cent of internet searches are for pornography,' explains Piers.

'But why do *we* have to get involved in it?'

'Because it's part of modern consumerism,' says Guy, looking up from his computer.

'Oh, that's so eighties,' howls Scarlett, looking at her own screen. 'Look at the blusher and that lip-gloss. And that one's pure seventies. I love the long beads and the afro hair, and is that a Biba print in the background? Zac, these are brilliant.'

'Thing is, Charlie,' says Piers, and I find myself spinning back to him, 'we're treating these pictures humorously. They're not for spotty teenage boys to drool over, they're part of modern-day life. We're exposed to porn of one kind or another every day – just look at a Gucci or a Häagen-Dazs ad, for goodness' sake. We're just having a laugh at it here.'

Once again everyone seems to be in the know and have reached a consensus except me.

'Ironic porn,' explains Scarlett. 'Everyone's doing it. My friend Maria, yeah? She's a performance artist. She's made a couple of porno movies. You know, ironically.'

'What? Sort of fucking in inverted commas?'

My sarcasm is wasted on Scarlett.

'They're really funny – crappy sets, sound quality so bad that you can hardly hear what they're saying, awful dialogue. At one point she says something like "But I'm a good girl from a convent school; can you teach me to be bad?"' Scarlett and Zac yell with laughter. 'The guy she was doing it with – he was a fine art student or something – had these, like, huge sideburns. And a gold medallion. And she was wearing false eyelashes like, you know, spiders? And a huge blonde hairpiece. It was *so* funny.'

'And she actually had sex with this guy?' laughs Zac enthusiastically. 'Full penetration?'

'Yeah, shaved her minge down to a Brazilian. Did all that "Oh, my God, my God. You're so big!" bollocks.' Scarlett runs her hands through her hair, closes her eyes, opens her mouth, licks her lips and throws her head backwards, arching her back ecstatically. Zac looks on, thrilled. I've got a horrible feeling that he is turned on in a decidedly non-ironic way.

'She's, like, really creative,' explains Scarlett, now mercifully out of character again. 'They had to go all the way. It was a condition of their grant.'

'Look, porn is porn,' I tell them.

'And what's the moral *minority* going to do about it?' sneers Zac. I give him an evil stare.

'But we've had some of these girls shot specially,' says Piers. 'They appreciate the irony.'

'Oh, she looks very ironic,' I say, pointing to a girl on my screen in patent leather high heels and a long pearl necklace, spreading her legs wide and grasping her huge man-made breasts as if they might just go off at any minute.

'But that's a classic porn mag pose. *Mayfair*, *Penthouse*, circa 1973. 2cool readers are immediately going to appreciate the historical reference,' grins Piers enthusiastically. 'Anyway, those shoes are specially acquired Manolo Blahniks. How many porn mags use Manolo Blahniks?'

I'm lost for words.

'You never done any nudey stuff then, Charlie?' asks Zac, from a near horizontal position behind his desk.

'Oh, don't be disgusting.'

'Bit of skin?'

'I said no.'

'What about that pic in the *Post*?'

I sigh deeply. 'That was to advertise a holiday. There was a woman and a couple of kids in the original photograph. They just cut them out.'

'You looked kinda cute in those groovy little swimmies.'

'Fancy me then, do you?'

''Fraid not bud, just wondering why they used you.'

'In that picture? Why not? I was a model.'

'Exactly.'

'What's that supposed to mean?'

Zac flicks a pen up in the air and catches it. 'Well, why not some old guy with a beer belly and a hairy back?'

'Because . . . well, because you obviously use good-looking people in advertising.' My phone begins to ring but I ignore it and let Scarlett get it.

'Oh, right. Good-looking people . . . showing off their nice bodies . . . in sexy poses?' asks Zac, innocently.

Oh, very clever.

'It's not the same, it's not obscene . . . I'm wearing swimming trunks,' I tell him sulkily. He carries on flicking the pen in the air and smiling victoriously at me. I'm just wondering how things could get worse when fate obliges.

'It's Nora Benthall for you,' says Scarlett, holding up her receiver. I look around at Piers and Guy, who nod for me to take it.

'Hey, Charlie,' says Nora.

'Hello,' I say stiffly.

'How's it going?'

'Fine, how are you?' I say with an effort, aware that four pairs of ears are trained on me, however busy their owners seem to be with other tasks. This will be a test of my communications skills, and my overall professionalism, I realise.

'Good thanks. Listen Charlie, I was just looking at the site and I noticed that there's a new section on it.'

I can imagine that cheeky – dare I say it? – ironic smile at the other end of the phone.

'Yes?'

'Extra Curricula or something? Well, it seems kind of rude to me. I'm just doing a little piece about it, you know, the threat of cyber porn and . . .'

'Yes?'

'I was wondering why you'd done it? Not very "too cool" is it?

How do you answer the allegation that you're already going downmarket and you've gone for the lowest common denominator: pornography.'

Oh, God, I'm really tempted to agree with her. I pause for a moment just to build up a little tension amongst my colleagues. Guy so obviously isn't reading that piece of paper. 'That's right, Nora, we just thought "Fuck it! Sex sells" and decided to put lots of porn on the site, but I hope you like the boots – they're real Manolo Blahniks.'

I take a deep breath.

'It's obviously ironic,' I say.

Around me there is a silent but noticeable feeling of relief as the others realise that I'm going to play ball.

'Pornography is now in the mainstream. It's all around us, part of the consumer experience. You've got to remember that the 2cool audience is one of the most sophisticated on the net, they appreciate this kind of stuff for its, er . . .' Before I can turn to him for help, Guy immediately mouths 'cultural significance' at me. 'Cultural significance. They can put it into context.'

'Uh, uh? Really,' says Nora, obviously scribbling away.

'Yeah, of course. It's not there for a bunch of adolescent boys to wa— I mean, drool over.' I look meaningfully at Zac but he is tapping at his keyboard and checking something on the screen.

'So you don't think this is offensive?'

'No, because our audience gets the joke,' I explain. 'It's taking the piss, I mean, it's poking fun at porn itself.'

'Okay, ironic porn. Interesting concept.'

'Interesting concepts are what 2cool is all about,' I tell her. Guy gives me a thumbs-up and I begin to feel that I have finally managed to beat Nora and him in one go. I decide to quit while I'm ahead. 'Hope that all makes sense.'

'Sure. If that's what you want to say.'

'Yep, that's about it,' I tell her.

'Okay, thanks very much, Charlie. Speak soon. Bye.'

'Bye.' I put the phone down.

Piers immediately gives me a round of applause.

'Well done,' says Scarlett. 'Wheatgrass?'

I'd prefer a drink.

*

When I see the piece in the paper the next day while sitting on the tube, I feel relieved but quite removed from the whole thing. Detached, neutral.

> *Designer website 2cool2btrue.com was branded 'sleazy and degrading' yesterday following revelations that it contains blatantly pornographic images. Women's groups and morality campaigners condemned the recently launched website, which describes itself as 'the coolest thing in cyberspace', for featuring full-frontal images of nude women and men.*
>
> *Mary Fairfax of NetWatch said, 'It's basically just a porn site. Children who are looking for things to buy could easily stumble across these pictures. They're also highly offensive to women.'*
>
> *But Charlie Barrett, the former top male model heading up the site, defended the use of nudity. 'Pornography is now in the mainstream. It's all around us, part of the consumer experience. These pictures are poking fun at porn itself. Our audience gets the joke.'*

I can't help smiling at the idea that I am 'heading up the site'. Guy and Piers will love that. But why am I *still* a former male model? On the other hand, they can't complain about the quote. It sounds pretty good. I quite like being a spokesman. At least there are no pictures of me this time.

In the office I'm greeted as something of a hero. Everyone has a copy of the *Post*.

'Excellent publicity,' says Piers, tapping the article.

'Perfect positioning,' Guy tells me. 'You got the message across beautifully.'

'Mate of mine in the City says all the traders are already looking at the site,' says Piers. 'It's all part of the marketing mix along with the Ferrari Testarossa and the Armani suits.'

'I see,' I say, sitting down at my desk. 'I suppose you guys know what you're doing.'

'Oh, Zac, tell him,' says Piers.

The perpetually horizontal Zac, who has just got to, please God, *got* to fall off his chair on to his authentically distressed antique 501-clad arse, takes the floor.

'Some company IT systems have filters these days that can, like you know, sense excessive areas of skin tone in an incoming email or website and block them so that people at their desks can't check out porno pics at work,' he explains. 'But I've included this little gizmo in the 2cool site protocol to override them.'

'Incredible, eh?' says Piers. 'Ours is the only T & A that most of my pals on the trading floors can actually look at while they're at work.'

'I'm so proud,' I tell him.

'Zac, you're a genius' says Scarlett. 'A gentleman, a scholar – and a pornographer.'

'I revel in your laudatory portraiture,' says Zac, finishing off a Dr Pepper and stamping on the tin rather unnecessarily.

Did he detect her sarcasm? Was he being sarcastic in return? Perhaps she wasn't being sarcastic after all? Perhaps it was just ironic? Perhaps *he* was being ironic too? Perhaps she was being sarcastic and he was being ironic in return? Perhaps I've OD'd on irony so much recently that I just can't recognise it any more.

Later that morning Guy tells me that he wants me to develop my relationship with Nora.

'What relationship?'

He looks slightly startled.

'You've established a good working relationship with her, haven't you?'

'Erm, I suppose so. Yes, she's a useful contact, isn't she?'

'Exactly. Anyway, apparently she also freelances for *Esquire* and various other magazines, you know, like *High Life* and *Elle* and things, so we need to cultivate her a bit.'

'Oh, okay.'

'We've done a deal with this new bar in Clerkenwell,' says Guy in his silky smooth sales voice. 'Take her there one evening this week. It'll be a nice contrast to the 'Extra Curricula' section, make the point that the pictures are just one part of the package and that whatever those moral crusaders say, we're the coolest, smartest thing in cyberspace.'

'Evening?'

'Yes, you don't mind working the occasional evening do you? Come in later the next day, if you want,' he says as if I'm being a 'job's worth' about it.

'No, evenings are fine,' I tell him.

What *is* wrong with an evening, anyway? Just a quiet bottle of wine, bit of a chat . . . cosy bar, settee in the corner. Oh, for God's sake. It's just a drink for work. Like Lauren and Peter do every now and then. Somehow that doesn't make it any better.

'Yes, okay,' I say. 'It's useful for coverage isn't it? I mean, if we can get her to write articles for some other magazines it might be helpful, especially *High Life*, that's the British Airways in-flight mag, isn't it?' But I'm gabbling, chattering away, protesting too much.

'Just take her there for a drink at this place and, you know . . .'

'Show her a good time,' says Scarlett lecherously from the other side of the room.

chapter thirteen

As it happens, Nora's packed diary means that she can only make that evening so we arrange to meet at 7 p.m. at the bar Guy has suggested. She manages to make it sound like a bit of a drag. I'm tempted to say that I'm only doing it because I've been asked to, but I don't. I ring Lauren and let her know that I won't be home till late. Well, not that late, quite early in fact.

'It's a work thing,' I say. 'Very boring. I've got to charm this journalist because Piers wants her to write something else about us in another magazine.'

'Oh, okay. I see.'

'Sorry about this.'

'Don't worry. If they want you to meet her you'd better do it.'

'You out with Peter?' I ask, trying to change the subject but sounding like I'm making a point.

'Peter? No, he's in New York at the moment. Make sure you keep the receipt – and charge them for a taxi home.'

'Will do. What're you doing tonight, then?' I'm pleased that just for once she's not seeing that twat, but I'm disappointed that we won't be able to enjoy a quiet evening alone together.

'Nothing.'

'Okay. Why don't you give Sarah a ring or something, have a girls' night out.'

'Why would I want a girls' night out?' She laughs.

'I don't know – might be fun.' Why is this developing into a row?

'No, I'll just potter around the flat. I've got to sort out some paperwork, actually.'

'Oh, right, good idea.'

There is a pause and I'm about to check again that she doesn't mind about tonight, but then I hear her talking to someone else.

'Babe, listen gotta go, they're ready to shoot again.'

'Love you.'

'You too.' She ends the call.

Nora is late. I'm waiting at the bar, talking to the owner who is struggling to explain the concept behind it.

'It's very now,' he says.

'Yeah,' I say, encouragingly.

'Its look is very much of its time, very *fin de siècle.*'

'Yeah, looks like it.'

'But it doesn't take itself too seriously. See this bar: pure antique aluminium. Came from an old brasserie in Paris – so it's *fin de siècle,* well the last *siècle.*'

'Really? I love it,' I say, rubbing my fingers over it. He does the same. We both caress the cold, smeary metal as he tries to think of something else to say about the place and I wish to God Nora would hurry up and get here.

I listen to the music on the sound system for a while. It's a boy band:

'Babe, there's one thing you must do,
If you want to get to heaven above,
Don't ask what your love can do for you,
Ask what you can do for your love,

they sing.

The guy who owns the joint is just telling me about the colour scheme when she walks in.

No apology. 'Couldn't you have chosen somewhere more inconvenient?' She smiles. 'I know a bar in Aberdeen that's slightly nearer.'

I ignore her remark, mainly because the bar owner looks rather upset about the idea that his place is so off the beaten track.

'This is Jim, the owner,' I say pointedly. 'He was just telling me about the decor.'

'I was just saying it's very now,' begins Jim again. I'm actually slightly relieved when Nora slams her bag down on the floor and says, 'I'm sure it is. Can I have a G and T – a large one.'

'Okay,' says Jim, slightly miffed that he won't get a chance to do his spiel. 'What can I get you, Charlie?'

'I'll have a beer,' I say.

He offers me some new Thai beer that is exclusive to the place.

'Very 2cool,' says Nora, cleaning her glasses on her silk scarf and looking around her.

'Yeah, we've done a deal with them. A sort of synergy thing,' I explain, hoping she won't press me on this as I've no idea what I'm talking about. What did Guy say again? Oh, yes. 'Even though we're a virtual concept we know that we also need to have a real dimension, a physical presence.' Or something like that.

Nora is looking at me, nodding her head slightly and giving me that knowing, piss-taking look.

'You see?' I say, as Jim hands us our drinks.

'Not really,' she says, taking a large mouthful.

'Well . . .'

'Oh, don't bother. I'm used to hearing things I don't understand and just nodding and looking interested. Anyway, I'm bored with 2cool, aren't you?'

'Er, no, not really.'

'Oh, perhaps I've just got a short attention span.'

'Wouldn't surprise me. Anyway, why did you come if you don't want to talk about the site?' I ask, fool that I am.

Nora swallows a mouthful of G and T and raises her eyebrows at me.

'Okay, how was your day at work? Any more embarrassing emails?' I say quickly.

'No, thank goodness. I managed to go a whole day without embarrassing myself – apart from a little incident with a cup of coffee which wasn't my fault. If people will leave them lying around on their desks . . .'

'What are you writing about at the moment?'

'Erm, I've been interviewing Lara Trewin, you know, that actress. She's set up a homeopathic hospital for animals at her farm in Sussex. Went down there. That's why I'm a bit late.'

'Oh, interesting.'

'No. Ludicrous. I *so* ripped the piss out of her,' says Nora, taking a large gulp of G and T. 'Mmm. I needed that.'

We talk a bit more about her writing and 2cool and I pepper the conversation with references to Lauren and our flat, how long we've been going out together and the surprise trip to Venice I'm organising for her birthday.

'Venice,' says Nora, shaking her empty glass at Jim. 'Ah, La Serenissima.'

'Yes,' I say, irritated that she can make even my wonderful, inspired, romantic gesture sound vaguely ridiculous. Perhaps she's just jealous. Yeah, that's it.

'It's stunning actually. God, I'm picking up that English habit of saying "actually" every five seconds. No, it *is* beautiful. Don't go in the summer, though, go in the winter when it's deserted and grey and foggy. It's sort of sinister.'

'I'm not sure we want a sinister holiday.'

'No, no, you're missing the point – that's the real Venice. Mysterious, decaying, inscrutable, corrupt. Hey, you should meet my friend Peta; she studied art history there. Says the place is impossible to know unless you've been there for at least a year. All the best restaurants are hidden behind closed doors; tourists never notice them.'

'I'm sure we'll find them,' I tell her through thin lips.

'Sorry, didn't want to put a downer on it. You'll have a great time, I bet,' she says, touching my knee. 'Hey, I'll get Peta to email you some places to go, some of those hidden restaurants. Harry's bar. You must go there. Just have a drink—'

'A bellini.'

'That's the one. Don't eat there, though; it's a rip off. But for a drink it's great, with the waiters in their white jackets and the dark panelled walls. It was one of Hemingway's favourites, wasn't it? Oh, it'll be great, I wish I was going.'

Why not? I can imagine what effect that would have on Lauren.

'So why did you leave the States and come here?' I ask her.

'I thought it might be fun. Change of scene. Get away from a country where the sixteen-inch chilli dog is considered haute cuisine, and where only five per cent of the population hold a passport, which is, coincidentally, the same number that believe they've been abducted by aliens at some point in their lives.'

It sounds like a frequently repeated rant. I wonder how often she makes this kind of comment. I smile.

'But mainly because my then boyfriend came over here. And promptly dumped me.'

'Oh, I'm sorry.'

'Don't be!' she says, a little too emphatically. 'I'm so much better off without him. He was a tosser, as you'd say, started working for a glossy men's magazine here and decided he needed a glossy men's girlfriend to go with it.'

'You're pretty glossy, though,' I laugh. I'm not sure what I mean by that.

'Thanks,' she beams.

By the time we leave it is much later than I had realised and it is pouring with rain.

'How are you getting home?' I ask her.

'Taxi I suppose,' she says, looking in vain around the deserted, rainy streets for one.

'Sure, let's find you a cab then. Where do you live?'

'Notting Hill.'

'Very nice.'

'I only moved there because of the film. Looked like a nice place – all those gorgeous movie stars and bumbling, charming, floppy-haired Englishmen wandering around spilling things every five minutes. Where do you live?'

'Chiswick.'

'Oh, I know, friend of mine who works at the BBC lives there. It's just a bit further out west than me isn't it? We may as well share a cab.'

Yes, we may as well. How convenient.

We eventually find a cab. In fact Nora hails him by throwing herself in the road in front of him. She lives in a flat in Oxford Gardens, off Ladbroke Grove.

'I'll just see the lady in,' I shout to the cab driver.

'Oh, how charming, how Hugh Grant. It must be the effect of Notting Hill,' says Nora, opening the door. 'You don't have to.'

'Better to be on the safe side,' I tell her manfully.

We walk up the garden path past the overflowing bins, lager cans and Sainsbury's bags. Nora opens her bag while telling me about a diet she's doing a piece on which consists of eating only fruit in the morning and corn on the cob in the evening. She is still ferreting around in her shiny pink retro-kitsch vinyl handbag after some time, and I look round just to reassure the cab driver and check that he doesn't give up the ghost and leave without me.

'We've got three women who have been on it for a month and we're checking their progress. One fell off the wagon last week and had a Mars bar but that makes it more interesting in a way. She felt terrible about it though—'

'Um, Nora, have you got your key?'

'Somewhere. Men are so lucky not being afflicted with these things – handbags I mean – I can never find anything in here.'

I'd been quite enjoying watching Nora feel shy, self-conscious about me being on her doorstep. For once this bright, aggressive girl is out of her depth, not in control. Now, though, her nervous gabbling is making me nervous. What's she worried about? I'm not coming in for coffee. This isn't a date, after all.

'Here it is,' she says, holding up a couple of keys on a ring. 'Phew! That's a relief. Well, night then.'

'Night Nora. See you soon,' I tell the back of her head as she opens the front door and disappears inside.

In the taxi back I try to decide which is worse – smart, sneering Nora or shy, nervous Nora. Both are pretty hard to deal with.

The next day we have a meeting with our new PR company.

'What happened to Simon and The Communications Game?' I ask Guy.

'They were appropriate for the launch, for the financing and corporate positioning, but now we need a luxury goods specialist,' he says. 'Someone who really knows how luxury goods work.'

Two blonde girls called Lucinda and Annabella from a company called Glambusters arrive dead on eleven carrying Louis Vuitton briefcases and we gather around Guy's desk.

'Before we start, can I just say how thrilled we are to be working on this project,' says one of them while the other agrees. 'It's a dream account for us.'

'Well, we're very glad you've agreed to help us,' says Guy.

'And we're very glad to be helping you,' says the other blonde girl, nodding vigorously.

'And I'm very glad that you're very glad about us being glad that you've agreed to work with us,' I add. It's supposed to be a joke (obviously) but the others just smile and nod in agreement at me. I realise that Guy just doesn't do jokes. Life is too serious for him.

We plan some more parties and a develop a press release distribution list. I have an idea for a competition which the others really like.

'We thought you might do some surveys too,' says Annabella (or is it Lucinda?).

'Yes,' says her colleague. 'They're always good for easy publicity. We thought of one showing that thirty per cent of men these days spend more on clothes than their wives or girlfriends.'

'That's a great idea,' says Guy.

'It could also show that fifty per cent of those wives and girlfriends actually resent it. You know, get a bit of a battle of the sexes going.'

'Great,' says Guy.

'Sorry, did you say you've *done* this survey?' I ask.

'No,' says Annabella. 'We'd do it and then publish the results.'

'But how do you know the results before you've done the survey?' I ask.

Annabella looks at Guy for a moment. 'Well obviously you don't do these kinds of surveys unless you know roughly what the results are going to be.'

'Don't you?'

'Yes, you want to find something fun and controversial and newsworthy. There's no point in doing an investigation that finds that most women like shopping and most men don't, for instance – everyone knows that.'

'We'll still ask our site visitors to take part in the survey. We'll put it in the What'scool page, I think, but we'll make sure that when we've finished it, in, say a week's time, that we've got the right result.'

'Oh, sure, of course,' I agree.

'We'll do a Sunday for Monday release on it,' says Annabella. She turns to the slowest ship in the convoy. 'I mean we'll send it out on Sunday for the Monday papers because Monday is a very quiet news day and they're always desperate for something,' she explains to me.

'Great,' I tell her.

chapter fourteen

I'm cooking dinner because apparently it's my turn. Lauren is talking to guess who? on the phone. She is laughing and saying something about 'No, I don't believe you. Get away! No!' As a result I'm chopping the peppers a little more aggressively than is strictly necessary and after a few minutes the inevitable happens. It's not a serious cut but it does start to bleed profusely and it makes me feel a little bit sick – especially when I hear Lauren again.

'*Peter!* You're outrageous! What did she say? Mmm? She's got a point.' Lauren giggles seductively. 'Well, she *has*.'

I go out into the hallway and present my bleeding finger to Lauren. 'Plasters?' I mouth.

She winces at the sight of my injury. 'Listen, can you hang on a minute Peter, Charlie's cut himself. No, not seriously. It's nothing. I'll be right back. What did you do?' she says, putting down the phone.

'I was just cutting these peppers. It'll be ready in a minute,' I add by way of hint that she had better finish her cosy little chat.

'You know where the plasters are, Charlie.' She opens a cupboard and takes out a First Aid box which I probably have seen before at some point 'What are we having?'

'My ratatouille thing with pasta.' It's my special, well just about the only thing I can knock up that's edible. Peter might have his chicken thing but I've got my sautéed peppers, tomatoes, onions and garlic thing.

'Great,' she says, putting a plaster on my finger. 'I'll come and give you a hand when I've finished with PBC.'

'Who?'

'Peter – Peter Beaumont-Crowther. PBC. That's what people call him.'

Yeah, amongst other things.

'Okay,' I mutter and go back to my chopping.

True to her word, Lauren comes in a few minutes later and takes over the cooking as I know she will. At the same time she prepares the dinner she manages to make a plate of little bruschetta, some with chopped tomatoes and basil and some with creamed artichoke. I pour us both a glass of Orvieto. Has anyone, anywhere in the world, been cooked for by someone as wonderful as Lauren? I ask myself as I sip my wine. And had a plaster put on by them?

'How did your drink go with that journalist?' she asks, stirring and chopping.

'Fine. We didn't talk much about the site in the end . . . but . . . erm . . .' Oh, oh, wrong answer. I can't decide whether I'm relieved or disappointed that Lauren makes no reaction to my confession. 'We might be able to give her some more stories. We're going to do a survey about shopping and they've already decided on the result, can you believe it? They're going to find that thirty per cent of men spend more money on clothes than their wives or girlfriends.'

'That can't be right,' says Lauren without looking up. 'Never mind, I suppose if you're going to do these surveys you've got to find something interesting to say, something newsworthy, haven't you?'

'I'm sure Nora will be able get a piece out of it.'

'Nora? Was she that slightly weird woman at the launch party? The one in that bizarre Mortitia Addams dress that you were having such a laugh with?'

'Nora, yes,' I say defensively.

'Was it her you were having a drink with last night then?'

'Yes. I told you.'

'No, you said a journalist.'

'I didn't mention her name but so what?'

'This is almost ready.'

The adrenalin is flowing now. I've finally made Lauren jealous.

'What's the matter? You can hardly complain after your conversation just now with Peter.'

Oh, what the fuck! Let's go the whole hog.

'Charlie, what *are* you on about?' Lauren looks up from her cooking.

'You know – giggle, giggle!'

'Don't be ridiculous. Peter is a friend and we're just having a chat.'

'Sounded like a very cosy chat to me.'

'Don't be absurd. I think this whole website thing is getting on top of you,' says Lauren.

'Perhaps it is, but I think this whole PBC/TV presenter thing is getting on top of you,' I snap back, but it's the last word that pushes it too far: 'Literally.'

She looks at me for a moment. 'I'm going out,' she says quietly.

I watch her go. Then I put my glass down and go after her. She is in the bedroom putting on her coat.

'I'm sorry,' I say quietly. She ignores me and opens the cupboard to find her shoes. 'I said I'm sorry.'

'I heard what you said.' I gently close the wardrobe door. 'Excuse me. I'm trying to get my shoes.'

'Please don't get your shoes. Please don't go out.' She avoids my eyes. 'I'm sorry I said that about you and Peter.' I know I'm making some progress now so I press on.

She looks up. 'I don't know why you've got such a thing about him. I've got to do this for my career. I told you.'

'Yeah, you said.'

'Why are you so jealous of him all the time?'

'Because . . . because he sees more of you than I do these days.'

She runs her hand through my hair. 'Oh, Charlie.'

'I don't want to lose you.'

'You're not going to lose me.' She plays with my hair some more and begins to massage my ear gently. 'But don't expect me to give up this part of my life. It's very important. Don't make me choose between you and my career, it's not fair.'

'I know.'

She takes off her coat again, along with the rest of her clothes and, deciding that dinner can wait, we end up having great 'make-up' sex. I watch us momentarily in the mirror and think again how lucky I am.

Scarlett offers me a shot of some dark brown liquid when she gets into the office the next day.

'What's this?' I say, eyeing it with disdain.

'It's called maruca. It's made of peat extract or something.'

'What does it do?'

'Gives you energy, detoxes and, erm, what else did they say? Oh, yes, boosts your melatonin levels. Makes you feel good.'

I shrug my shoulders and knock it back. It's sort of earthy initially but then the aftertaste kicks in – like farts mixed with rotting rubbish.

'Aaargh!' I gasp, looking around for something to rescue my taste buds with.

'Hey, that's my Dr Pepper!' says Zac.

I let the sweet, fizzy liquid rinse away the taste of shit and rotting vegetables and then hand the can back to him. Once I've got over the experience I look at Scarlett.

'Oh, my God. How can you drink that stuff?' I mutter, still swallowing hard.

'I don't. I've never tasted it before. I thought I'd try it out on you first.'

'Oh, ta, Scarlett.'

She smiles sweetly and answers the phone.

'2cool2btrue, can I help you? Guy? No, he's not in yet, I'm afraid. No, he's not either. Can I take a message? Okay, all right, babe, I'll get one of them to call you. Bye.'

'Where are they? It's gone ten,' I ask when she's put the phone down.

'I dunno, but I'll get them to report to your study when they get in, shall I?' she says.

'All right, I'm just saying.'

'What's this thing down here at the bottom of the screen?' I ask Zac a bit later.

With lightning speed in response to my question he mumbles, 'What you talking about?'

'This thing, this little icon at the bottom right hand on the home page? "Digitally Enhanced Hyper Resolution Graphics System". What the hell does that mean?'

'It means shag-all, as you Brits would put it.'

'Nothing? You mean it doesn't do anything? Why have you put it in there then?'

'Cos it looks cool, man. People think it's a new bit of kit, something that no one else has.'

'You just made it up?'

'Yup.'

'I still think it should be Enhanced Hyper Resolution Digital Graphics System,' says Scarlett. 'Rolls off the tongue better.'

'Well, you're wrong, little lady,' says Zac, not bothering to look up at her. 'I'll do the hi-tech stuff and you stick to rolling things off your tongue.'

Scarlett gives him a sarcastic smile. 'Oh, Zac, I'm sure you'll be a much nicer, more relaxed person when you finally lose your virginity.'

Fortunately the phone rings and I get it. It's someone asking for Guy or Piers again. They're quite insistent but all I can do is take a message.

'Where *are* they? I'm going to ring their mobiles,' I tell the others.

'Give them a piece of your mind,' says Zac.

Just at that moment the door swings open and Piers sweeps in.

'Sorry I'm late everybody – bit of a night of it last night.'

'No problem,' I say. 'Quite a few people have been calling for you, that's all.'

'I bet they have. Well, we've done it!' he announces, looking around at us excitedly.

'What? You and Guy last night?' asks Scarlett, raising an eyebrow.

'No. What?' says Piers. 'No, *we've* done it – all of you! 2cool! We've reached our two months' target of half a million hits in just three weeks.'

'Excellent,' I tell him. 'That's brilliant.'

'Cool,' says Scarlett. 'Too cool, in fact.'

Zac says nothing, but since he wouldn't have had anything pleasant or encouraging to say this is probably a good thing.

'That's brilliant,' I say again.

'Isn't it? Well done team.' The team looks slightly embarrassed at his hearty praise. 'Excellent. Yes, well done. Now I could do with something to bring me back to life after last night.'

'Yeah, you look terrible,' says Scarlett, obviously not just being rude on this occasion. 'Have you slept at all?'

'No, to be honest I haven't much,' says Piers with a slightly false, hearty laugh. 'I'll go to that place you're always off to along the road, what's it called?'

'Wild World,' I tell him.

'That's right, I'll get a juice or something.'

'No,' says Scarlett, 'get a yourself a maruca – it'll do you a world of good.'

'Hey, guess what? We've beaten our target at work,' I tell Lauren that evening as we snuggle up on the settee after supper. 'We were supposed to take two months to get half a million hits but we've done it in just three weeks.'

'Nice going, babe,' she says, turning her face round in my lap to kiss me.

'It is pretty good, isn't it. All down to the marketing of course.'

'Of course. You should make sure you keep all the press cuttings and file them.'

'That's a good idea. I think Scarlett or the PRs do it.'

'No, I mean for your own file so you've got something to show future employers.'

'That's a *very* good idea. You're so sensible. Hey, let's go out and celebrate tomorrow night. I'll book a table somewhere.' Lauren doesn't say anything. 'What about that new place down by the river?'

'I'm actually seeing Peter tomorrow night.'

'Oh, okay,' I say in a small voice.

'Charlie, I'm sorry. He's been in New York for the last few days and we've got a lot to catch up on.'

'Sure.'

'You know this thing means a lot to me, don't you?' She sits up and looks at me. 'I'm bored with modelling. You've made a successful career move. It's not really fair, is it, to try and stop me?'

'No, 'course not babe.'

'Friday night, I promise. We'll do something really cool.'

chapter fifteen

By midday the next day neither Piers nor Guy are in, and I seem to be the only one vaguely bothered about it. Neither mobiles are answering this time either so I decide we'd better find them.

'Scarlett. Scarlett.' I try waving at her.

'Hang on bud, I'll send her an email,' says Zac, being helpful for once.

'Don't worry,' I tell him, getting up.

I tap her on the shoulder and she jumps. 'What, for goodness' sake?' she says, taking off her headphones and switching off her Discman.

'I was just thinking it's odd that we haven't seen Piers yet this morning and we haven't seen Guy for nearly two days.'

'No, that's true,' says Scarlett. 'Perhaps they're at a meeting. Let me check their diaries.'

'I think we ought to have heard something though, don't you?'

'Erm, let me just have a look at what they've got booked in at the moment,' murmurs Scarlett, tapping away and glancing at her screen.

'No, you're right, there's nothing here in their diaries, so they've obviously been murdered.'

'Thanks Scarlett, very helpful.'

'Oh, I'm just kidding, don't worry, Charlie. They'll ring in soon I'm sure.'

'I suppose so, but it just bugs me that they piss off like this. Someone must know where they are – haven't they got friends or something?'

'You've met them,' says Zac.

'They must do,' says Scarlett. 'Let me ring their home numbers.'

A few moments later she reports that both answer machines are on.

'Like I said, they'll be in later, I'm sure,' she says, putting back her headphones.

I look round at Zac who is, as usual, nearly horizontal with one leg crossed loosely over the other. He's wearing a T-shirt that says 'Lesbian in a man's body'. He shrugs his shoulders and looks back to his screen.

I decide to go out and get a cappuccino.

By mid-afternoon, I'm quietly satisfied that I *was* right to worry, unlike the others, but at the same time I'm decidedly unnerved. We've all left more messages for them everywhere we can think of.

'Mind you, creative people *are* like that,' says Scarlett. 'When I worked in the music business people would disappear for days and then just turn up again. They're highly sensitive, highly strung.'

'Really? What they hell had they been doing?'

Scarlett thinks about it. 'Drugs usually.'

I'm the last to leave the office. I ring my old mate Ben, and we decide to go for a pint. We were at college together but then he got a sensible job in the City. He's read about the site.

'Saw that picture of you in the paper. You looked a right tosser, if you don't mind me saying,' he tells me over a beer.

'No, you're right, I did look like a tosser.'

'How's it going then with this thing?'

'Really well,' I say, wondering whether to be honest. 'We've hit our target for visitors.'

'What are your margins like?'

'Margins?'

'*Profit* margins.'

'Oh, yeah of course. Profit margins.'

He smiles. 'Well, how are they?'

'Too early to tell . . . oh, all right, fuck off, smarty pants. I don't know. I don't really have a lot to do with that.'

The smile turns more patronising. 'Let me get this straight: you're the marketing director and you don't know much about the profit margins.'

'It's early days, we'll have to wait and see.'

'What about the projections? I mean the profit projections—'

'I know what you mean. Look, Ben, all right, I don't know but I'm sure they're healthy.'

'What about the business plan?'

'Bugger the business plan, I don't know.'

'Okay, just wondered. You should ask your fellow directors, though. What are their names? Piers and Guy?'

'Yeah, you're right, perhaps I will.'

Except there's one slight problem. I turn the conversation round to him and his new job at the bank.

By the time I get back to the flat it's gone ten and Lauren still isn't home from seeing Peter, so I make myself some baked beans on toast with extra butter and tomato ketchup.

I wake up feeling cold and uncomfortable on the settee. There is something I don't recognise on the telly. The reason I've woken up is that Lauren has just come in.

'Oh, hi hon, you still up?' she says, kicking off her shoes.

'Yeah,' I groan, 'must have fallen asleep.'

'Come on, let's get you to bed.'

'Sure.' I yawn and stretch. 'What time is it?'

'Erm, just after three.'

'What?'

'Just after three. You fell asleep in front of the telly.'

'Never mind about me, where have *you* been all this time?'

In the cold, blue, flickering light of the telly Lauren looks surprised and irritated.

'What do you mean, "Where have I been?"'

'It's bloody three o'clock in the morning, I thought you were just going for a drink or something.'

'Then we had something to eat and then we went to a club Peter's a member of.'

'Till this time?'

'Yes, *Dad*.'

'Sorry, it's just a bit late, that's all.' I pull myself up feeling groggy and dizzy.

'I'm getting a bit fed up with this, Charlie. I told you I was seeing

Peter tonight and I don't expect you to be holding a stopwatch against me.'

She walks out and I sit back down again with my head in my hands.

Next day there is still no sign of Piers and Guy.

'I'm going to their homes,' I tell Scarlett.

'Good idea. I can't think of anything else to do,' she says seriously. Scarlett serious. Now I'm really worried.

'What about your friend Nora?' says Zac.

'What about her?'

'She knows Piers, doesn't she?'

'Actually she does, doesn't she? She might have some idea where he is or at least who might know.'

I ring her.

'Hey Charlie, thanks for the other night. It was nice.'

'Yeah, it was, wasn't it? Nora, I was just wondering if you'd heard anything from Piers.'

'Piers? No, why?'

'He seems to have disappeared. And Guy. We haven't heard from either of them for days.'

'Really? What, nothing?'

'No, they haven't been into the office. We've tried to track them down on their mobiles but there's no answer.'

'How bizarre.'

'It is a bit, isn't it? Never mind, just wondered if you'd heard anything. You do know Piers anyway, don't you?'

'Yes, I do. Look, I'll try to get hold of some of his other friends.'

'Thanks Nora, let me know if you hear anything.'

She sounds distracted for a moment. 'Yes, of course. Sorry, when did you last see them?'

'Piers came in on Thursday but we haven't seen Guy at all since Wednesday.'

'Mmm. Almost all week. And no one's heard anything from them?'

'No. Nothing.'

'Bit worrying isn't it?'

'It is a bit. Anyway, as I say, if you hear anything just give me a ring.'

'Yep, will do. Do you think the site will suffer without them? They are the leading lights aren't they?'

'They developed the concept, that's true.'

'And raised the finance.'

'Yes. Anyway, as I say, it was just in case you hear something.'

'Sure, sure. So it's just the three of you left.'

'Yeah, well no. Not *left* as such; I'm sure Guy and Piers will be back soon. I just wish they'd told us where they were going, that's all.'

'Are you going to their homes?'

'Might as well, have a quick look around, see if there's any sign of life.'

'Where do they live?'

'Guy lives in Chelsea and—'

'Piers lives in Fulham, doesn't he?'

'Er, yeah, that's right. Anyway—'

'What about the police?'

'I'm not sure. It's difficult. I don't want to alarm people unnecessarily. I think we'll give it a few more days. Presumably if they're missing their family or friends would do that.'

'That's true.'

'Anyway, I'll keep you informed.'

'What's Zac's surname again?'

'Zac's surname? What's that got to do with anything? Nora, you're not going to write about this in the bloody paper are you?'

'Well, I don't know. I mean, it might help, mightn't it?'

'Help bugger up the whole thing completely, you mean. Look, you'd better not.'

'Okay,' she says half-heartedly.

'Nora, please don't.'

'Oh, honestly Charlie.'

'I said "don't"!'

'And I heard you. I'd better make some calls. I'll let you know what I find out.'

I set off to Chelsea first of all, having made the others promise to call me the minute they hear something. I'm sure everything's fine but it's beginning to dawn on me that of three of us 'left' as Nora puts it, I'm the only one with any sort of responsibility or common sense. I realise that the suit I'm wearing today is Armando Basi, bought by

2cool, and that most of what I wear these days comes from the company, via our stylists or via my smart, new, totally transparent, 2cool-branded credit card. Like I say, I'm sure it's all kosher and above board, but if there were something, well, dodgy, I'd have to admit that I've had my fair share of goodies from this little operation. Even my skin is glowing from a free facial, courtesy of a new men's grooming studio we've hooked up with.

Guy lives in a basement flat not far from South Kensington tube station. I walk down a tiny staircase and peer into the window. The living room itself is traditionally furnished with an old chesterfield couch, patterned rug and some repro landscape paintings. There is a fireplace with some china ornaments on it and some invitations. Next to it is a large telly.

On the floor, on the Chesterfield settee, on the shelves either side of the chimney breast and on almost every available space, are piles of paper and magazines. Hundreds of them. Thousands probably. Some neatly stacked up, some toppling over. A sock hangs limply out of one pile. There are precariously balanced towers of thick glossy magazines all around the floor and on the coffee table, which must make watching telly almost impossible.

There is not much else I can do, other than knock on the window hard and shout through the letterbox. As I do, a gentle gust of cold, stale air greets me. If anything, this visit has made me feel more anxious.

There is no answer from Piers's small terraced house in Fulham, either. He has the same kind of country-house-in-a-London-box furniture but the place is sort of casually messy, not maniacally so. Again I bang on the window and do some pointless shouting before setting off along the street. I ring Scarlett and tell her that I've drawn a blank and I'm coming back to the office. After I finish the call, something makes me turn just before I've got to the main road, and I see a bloke taking photographs. He looks pretty professional – angler's jacket full of gear, automatic rewind on his camera, another camera around his neck.

He is definitely shooting Piers's house.

The next day, Saturday, for once I'm up before Lauren is awake and I dash out to buy the *Post*. Walking back to the flat I begin to flick through. There is nothing on the first few pages. I smile at a picture of someone I know from my old agency, advertising a laptop by looking harassed as he walks across an airport concourse. What a crap shot. That guy just cannot act. But when I turn the next page there is a massive picture of me, plus one of Piers, next to a smaller one of his house.

I feel like I've been kicked in the stomach. I have to stop and take a deep breath before I can read it.

EXCLUSIVE

2Cool Two Go Missing

Hyper-cool website 2cool2btrue.com was in chaos last night following revelations that its two leading lights, Guy Watkins and Piers Gough-Pugh, have disappeared. Watkins and Gough-Pugh have been missing nearly a week.

Questions were being asked about the location of the two marketing whiz-kids whose website has grabbed the attention of the nation's smartest young things and boasts a host of celebrity fans. Some commentators have been arguing that 2cool has even signalled a return of business confidence in the internet.

With only three members of staff left to run the website – which has signed deals with a host of designer labels and luxury goods manufacturers – experts were yesterday predicting that it would be difficult for the company to build on its remarkably successful launch, which followed a party at Frederica's nightclub in Berkeley Square, attended by rock star Sir Josh Langdon and aristo model Henrietta Banbury amongst others. The site recently revealed that it has already received half a million 'hits' after just three weeks' trading.

Speaking exclusively to the Post, *the face of the new site, former male model Charlie Barrett said, 'We're all very worried indeed. We haven't seen Guy since Monday and Piers since Tuesday. It's difficult because they're the ones who developed the concept and raised the finance.'*

Gough-Pugh, a former City trader and financier, was not at his £500,000 Fulham house yesterday. One neighbour said, 'He's a nice young man, always very polite and charming. He's been working long hours so he doesn't seem to have much time for friends.'

Barrett has not yet reported the disappearance of the two to police because of concerns that the news might affect the image and financial position of the site. However, a spokeswoman for the Metropolitan Police Missing Persons Unit confirmed, 'If we are contacted we will take the case as seriously as we always do with any report of a missing person.'

By the time I get back to the flat, Lauren is pottering around the kitchen.

'You're up early,' she says in a sleep-croaky voice.

'Yeah, there was something in the paper today about Piers and Guy.'

'You're kidding.'

I open it again and present it to her. Seeing my stupid face grinning at us makes me feel sick again. I turn away to carry on making the coffee. By the time it is dripping through the filter Lauren has finished reading the piece.

'Well?' I ask.

'Doesn't look good, does it? Why haven't you contacted the police?'

'Well, why should I? Haven't they got friends or family or something?'

'How would I know?' She opens the fridge and takes out the orange juice.

'Yeah, okay. I'll ring the police on Monday. Can't do any harm. Sod's law they'll come back if I do.'

'Why did you say all this to the paper?'

'I didn't. I, oh, for God's sake, I rang Nora because she knows Piers anyway and I just wondered—'

'Did *she* write it?' asks Lauren, snatching back the paper. 'Oh, well, what did you expect? You ring a journalist, tell her all this and expect her not to write about it?'

'All right, I know, I'm completely stupid. I thought she might be able to separate her professional life from her private life.'

'You thought you could trust a journalist?'

'I was ringing her as a friend.'

Oh shit, that doesn't sound right.

Lauren laughs irritably and rolls her eyes. 'I'm going to have a shower.'

I decide to ring my dad and get some advice from him. A girl answers the phone with a sleepy voice.

'Hallo, is John there?'

'Qui? Who?'

I've definitely got the right number – it's on speed dial – so I persist.

'Sorry, is Jared there?'

'No, er, no, he run.'

'What? He's gone for a run? Okay, ask him to call his son when he gets back, will you?'

'Er, call?'

'Oh, fuck.' I'm actually quite used to this now so I run through the usual list of possibilities. 'Parlez-vous français?'

'Er, sorry?'

'Habla usted español?'

'Er?'

'Parla italiano?'

'Er, sorry?'

My Serbo-Croat – usually a good bet these days – has deserted me, but fortunately at that moment my dad takes the phone from her.

'Hello?'

'Hi, it's me, Charlie. Are you around this morning?'

'Yeah, sure, we were going shopping but we can do that later. Everything all right?'

'Not really.' My throat suddenly feels a bit tight.

'You and Lauren?'

'Erm, partly. There's a piece in the paper today about the site; Guy and Piers, the guys who started it, the guys I work for – they've disappeared.'

'Disappeared?'

'Look, can we meet for coffee or something?'

We arrange to meet for breakfast at a new restaurant in Knightsbridge which specialises in a mixture of French and Thai food. I manage to extract a normal cappuccino out of them and wait for my pop who is fashionably late.

'Hiya,' he says, slapping my arm. 'This is Marika, Mari for short.'

'Hello,' I smile. She is tall with long blonde hair – you know the deal. 'Where are you from?'

She looks confused for a moment and then my dad rescues her.

'Hungary,' he says proudly. 'Or somewhere like that.'

I make a mental note to get a Hungarian phrase book.

Dad has fresh fruit and yogurt, I have a couple of muffin things which apparently have some Far Eastern connection although you could hardly tell, and Mari eats for a week: omelette with Thai spiced prawns, muffins, croissants, toast and some sort of porridge-like thing with passionfruit in it. I show Dad the cutting from the *Post*.

'Why did you say all this?' he asks.

'Oh, fuck. I know, I'm so naive. She knows Piers, so I thought she might be able to help as a friend. How can she stab me in the back like that? I asked her not to.'

'Charlie, she's a journalist.'

I look down at my plate.

He squeezes my shoulder. 'Hey. It's okay; so you learnt a lesson in business.'

'Yeah, I s'pose so.'

'First thing you've got to do is try and find these guys. I'll put out some feelers too. I'll find out more about them.'

'Thanks, Dad.'

'What are the books looking like?'

'What?'

My dad smiles sadly. 'What kind of financial shape is the company in?'

'We've achieved our two-monthly target of hits in just three weeks.'

'Yeah, yeah, great, but are those visitors spending money?'

'It's not just about people spending money—'

'Charlie, listen, son, it's *always* about people spending money.'

'Erm, I don't know. I've never looked at the financial side of it.'

There is a flicker of concern across my dad's immaculate, tanned, moisturised face. Is he wearing eyeliner again today? Never mind, I've got slightly more important things to worry about.

'You'd better have a look first thing on Monday.'

'Okay.'

'You're not a director are you?'

'Er, yeah.'

'You are.' Suddenly he looks more serious. And I wanted him to be proud of me. 'So you're a signatory on the chequebooks?'

'I don't think so.'

'Have you ever signed a cheque?'

'A few, of course, for some of the suppliers.'

My dad looks thoughtfully at me. 'I'm sure you're fine if you've still got the invoices and things then, but you've got to be careful you don't implicate yourself in anything.'

'No, of course.'

'You realise that as a director, you're legally responsible. If it can be proved that you've acted negligently or fraudulently you can be prosecuted or sued.'

I suddenly feel slightly sick. Like when I was a kid and I got stopped by the police for throwing stones and breaking the windows of an empty factory down the road. It was the naughtiest thing I had ever done – until now.

'Really?'

'Don't worry. I'm sure it won't come to that, but watch out, hey, son,' he says kindly, reaching across and patting me on the shoulder. 'And if you've got any questions, just give me a call.'

'Will do, sure.'

'Can they carry on paying you?'

'Yes, for the time being. Scarlett, who also works there, checked with the bank, and the account that our salaries come out of looks pretty healthy at the moment.' I don't like to think about what state the other accounts 2cool has around the world might be in.

'Well, that's one good thing.' Dad smiles broadly and then reaches across and squeezes my shoulder again. 'Mari and I are going shopping. Wanna come?'

chapter sixteen

The conversation with my dad gives me a sleepless night. Lauren tuts and moans as I turn over yet again. I can see myself being portrayed suddenly on some TV documentary as a crook. I've defrauded people. Interviews with angry creditors and innocent investors who were taken in by me. I think of the money we've been spending.

I suppose the most I can hope for is that I look naive, not criminal.

On Sunday, Lauren and I go to a lunchtime barbecue in Clapham with some other models from the agency and some friends of hers. Sarah and Mark are there, and as we stand by the French windows, glasses of Merlot in hand we have a quiet, conspiratorial laugh together about how much – Sh!! – we actually *hate* barbecues.

'Botulism in a bun,' says Sarah, taking a drag of a ciggie and watching our host manfully trying to flip a crumbling home-made hamburger with an unwieldy kitchen utensil while being advised by his spouse.

Then she asks, 'So, how's the new job going?'

'Bit difficult at the moment,' I say, looking out at the garden.

'Oh, sorry to hear that.' There is a pause. 'Don't want to talk about it?'

'Not really.'

'Sure. Look, Mark and I were thinking, why don't you and Lauren come and spend a weekend with us at my parents' place in France. Go on! It would be a laugh. Lots of lovely food and wine. Sunshine and swimming. Watching my parents bickering. Great spectator sport.'

I laugh. 'I'd love to. I mean, we'd love to. I'll go and ask her in a minute. Thanks.'

*

To avoid talking to anyone else about the site and answering the inevitable questions, I end up playing with the kids. Jack, who is two, and Lily, who is five, invent a game with some pebbles, toy cars and dollies and it keeps them occupied for hours. Me too.

'You're so good with the children. Everyone's very grateful to you for keeping them quiet,' says a woman I don't know as she carries some dirty plates over my head into the kitchen.

When we get back there are two messages on the answer machine. My heart leaps. Perhaps, finally a call from Guy and Piers. The first is from Lauren's mum, just ringing for a chat and sending me her love, and the second is from my old mate Becky whom I haven't seen for years.

'Hi, Charlie. It's Becky. Long time no speak. Hope you're well. Just ringing to say that I've had a baby. Louise Emily. Just over seven pounds. The father is a guy called Daniel, don't think you've met him. We've been going out for two years. Not yet got around to the marriage thing – on my list of things to do, though. Sure we will. Always wanted to see Vegas!' She laughs. 'Anyway, come and meet her! It would be really nice to see you.' She sends her love and leaves a number.

Becky and I had a mini-fling just before I met Lauren. It could have been my child, in another life. I could have been a father. I remember the woman at the party: 'You're so good with children.' So is Lauren actually, but then she is good at most things so perhaps it doesn't really count.

On Monday I wait until lunchtime to make absolutely sure that Guy and Piers really aren't coming into the office again, and then I tell Scarlett I'm going to ring the police.

'Good idea,' she says. Serious Scarlett is really frightening me now.

I decide not to ring 999. After all, it's not really an emergency is it? Well, not yet. I didn't sleep much on Saturday night after my conversation with Dad. Somehow reporting Guy and Piers missing will make it official: we really are in trouble, but, on the other hand, it also feels like I'm doing the right thing.

I speak to someone at the Met's Missing Persons Unit. A woman with a kind voice takes all the details. She seems slightly surprised when I explain that I'm calling about *two* people.

'Two? Oh, right. Are they in a relationship?'

'With each other? No. Well, just a business relationship.'

'I see. What relation are you to either of them?'

'I work with them. *For* them.' Suddenly, following the conversation with my father, the distinction seems very important.

'Let me just check the database to make sure we haven't had anyone else reporting them missing already.' She taps away for a moment and then says, 'No. Funny. Usually it's family and friends that report it first. Have you spoken to these men's relations or people they know outside work?'

'We don't know of anyone,' I say, deciding not to mention Nora.

'Oh, okay.'

'Does this sound a bit odd?' I ask.

'Odd? Erm, not really. Men in their late twenties, early thirties, are one of the most likely groups of people to disappear, actually. Them and teenage girls.'

'Right.'

'On the other hand, we don't know that they have really disappeared. Sometimes people just go off without telling anyone – they forget or suddenly decide they need to get away from it all.'

'I know how they feel.'

'Don't we all? We'll carry out our own investigations and as soon as we hear something we'll let you know.'

'Thanks.' She gives me the number of the Missing Persons Helpline and I hang up.

'Well?' says Scarlett.

'You heard what I told her, what more can we do?'

'Why don't you ring Nora Benthall about that piece?'

'I don't trust myself not to yell abuse at her.'

'So? Yell abuse at her.'

I look at Scarlett for a moment while I think it over and then I ring Nora's number.

'Hey, Charlie,' she says, bright as ever.

'Thanks for the piece on Saturday.'

'No worries.'

'Nora, I'm being sarcastic.'

'Why? What's wrong? It'll help find them.'

'I asked you *not* to write it.'

'Charlie, you can't tell me what I can and can't write. It's a good story. We've already had a couple of calls about it.'

'Really?'

'Yeah, hang on, let me find them. Jenny, where's that note about those calls? Thanks. Right . . . oh, perhaps we need to wait a little bit longer.'

'Why? What do they say?'

'A Mr Hampson from Birmingham called in to say that it serves you right for worshipping mammon and you'll all go to hell—'

'Great, very helpful.'

'And someone called Jeremy from Southampton rang. He wants to know where you got the shirt you're wearing in that picture because he'd like to get one too.'

'Oh, case solved then.'

'Okay, I admit those probably aren't going to produce very good leads but someone else might crop up.'

'Well, call me when they do. You owe me, all right?' I tell her and put the phone down.

'So?' asks Scarlett. I can hardly bear to repeat the conversation but I do for hers and Zac's benefit. She thinks about it for a moment and then says, 'Well, if you don't mind me saying . . . that shirt was horrible. Why would anyone want one like it?'

'What are you on about?'

Zac is smirking.

'Glad you think it's funny you, you sniggering nerd.'

He bursts out laughing.

'Am I the only one who gets what's happening?' I ask. 'A lot of money has disappeared here. Am I the only one who actually realises that this whole thing is collapsing around our ears?'

Zac stops laughing, sits up and leans across his desk. 'No, bud,' he says. 'You're the only one who ever thought it wouldn't.'

I go out and walk up and down the street for a while to regain my composure. What does Zac know? Cynical, sneering net nerd. Nobby no mates. But I *am* the most visible aspect of this site, aren't I? Spokesman, frontman. The embodiment of 2cool. Muse? Fall guy? Director more to the fucking point. I did sign some cheques, six, in fact. I counted them as soon as I got back to the office on Monday after talking to my dad. Over £40,000-worth. Oh, for fuck's sake. If

2cool's crashed in flames then so have I. And very, very publicly. I could go to prison for it.

Images of a celebrity trial begin to flood into my mind. Stories of our spending. Me arriving in a van at the Old Bailey. Is that right? Would that happen? Or would it be a smaller court? Who cares? My old mates at the agency reading about me and gossiping at castings as my case goes on. Penny smiling grimly in that little office of hers. My poor mum. It would kill her.

I ring Lauren's number but get her voicemail. I leave a short message asking her to call me when she can. We've hardly spoken over the last few days. After the party on Sunday she went into town to do some shopping and I came back to the flat and watched telly. I really need to talk although I know what she'll say.

I go into a newsagent. On the front of a women's magazine are a guy and a girl from my old agency. Smiling, hugging, gazing adoringly at each other, so in love. Well, in love for £100 an hour on a Thursday morning in a studio in Clerkenwell, hair and make-up provided, but no wardrobe at that price so bring your own selection of smart-casual tops. Not a lot of money but a nice cover shot for your book.

I ring Karyn at the agency.

'Hey, how are you?' Not saying my name out loud, I notice.

'All right. How's it going? Busy?'

'Yeah, it is quite.' I didn't want to hear that. 'You?'

'Did you see the piece in the *Post* on Saturday?'

'Yes, Penny pointed it out.'

'Oh, shit.'

'Difficult times?'

'You could say.'

'So where *are* these guys? Derr! Sorry, obviously you don't know but it does seem very odd, doesn't it? They've really just disappeared into thin air, then?'

'Yep. It's too weird.'

'You sound down.'

'Just a bit. It's all a bit worrying, you know. I'm sure it'll be fine.' I feel I have to add the last comment so that she doesn't think I'm a complete crook. Or a naive pillock. 'Anyway, you're busy, then.'

'Yeah, pretty. Little jobs.' The kind I used to moan about and turn my nose up at. Suddenly they sound safe and familiar. Boring but manageable.

'Better than nothing,' I say, hoping it doesn't sound like I'm angling for something.

'You never used to say that,' says Karyn, teasingly.

'Yeah, I know.' There is a pause. I nearly ask about going back. It does sound tempting – so much easier after the stress of 2cool.

'A couple of people have been asking about you.'

'Really? That's nice.'

'Penny's a bit funny about it, though. Keeps suggesting other models.'

'No, of course. Well, she'll be even funnier about it now.'

'Probably. She's out to lunch with a client today so she'll be totally smashed when she gets back.'

'Good old Penny.'

'Give me a ring if you want to have a drink sometime, Charlie.'

'Will do. Take care babe.'

I go back to the office after half an hour or so. Fortunately Zac has gone to lunch. Scarlett is on the phone.

'No, you'll get your cheque, I promise. It's just that we're up to our eyes at the moment and our, er, accounts department has got a bit behind. No, they're not here at the moment but I'll pass your message on. Well, I can't comment on press stories. You believe whatever you like, but as soon as they come back I'll get them to sign the cheque and we'll bike it straight over. Okay, will do. Bye.' She puts the phone down. 'Honestly, some people. Money, money, money. Don't they know there's more to life?'

'Have we had a lot of calls like that?'

'Quite a few. Well, quite a lot actually. But what can we do? I don't know where the chequebooks are.'

'Even if we find them I certainly don't want to go signing any more until I've spoken to Guy and Piers and seen the bank statements. Let's look in their desks, see if we can find these statements and the chequebooks.'

'I feel a bit funny about rummaging around while they're not here.'

I laugh bitterly. 'Yeah, but where the hell are they? Anyway, I'm also a director. I just want to see the figures.' Saying that, I realise that I don't. 'Come on, Scarlett, someone's got to do it. This is getting silly.' Not to mention frightening.

'Okay.' She goes over to the end of the room where Guy's and Piers's desks are. I've checked the surface of the desks a hundred times over the last few days for clues as to their whereabouts but I've never looked inside the neo-industrial filing cabinets that surround them.

'I'll need to get into their computers too,' I tell her as she gets the keys.

'They're password protected and I don't know—'

'Where's Zac?'

'At lunch. Playing pinball across the road.'

'Ring him and get him over here, can you? Ta.'

I open the first drawer of one of the filing cabinets and almost gasp in shock. Hundreds of bits of paper are stuffed into it. Most of the suspension files are hanging off their rails, documents squashed down between them. I pick out a piece of paper at random. It's a bill for red roses. £350-worth from a smart florist in Notting Hill. I flatten it out and put it carefully onto Piers's desk. Slowly I pull out another piece of paper, dislodging a few others and sending them cascading onto the floor. This one is a receipt for a couple of suits and trousers from the press office of an Italian design house. 'Sample loan. Please return in good condition to London Press Office by 20 June'. Three weeks ago. I look around hopelessly as if the suits might be hanging up somewhere.

There are bills, invoices and statements of account from clothing companies, taxi firms, stationers, restaurants, PR companies, event organisers, video production people and hotels, as well as plenty of well-known designer names. Many of them are red bills and final demands. There is even one for a model agency I know. £3,500 a day shoot fee and usage agreement.

Some bills are for hundreds, some for thousands and some for tens of thousands. Others are for forty or fifty quid. Many are related to the launch party. Others I recognise from things that have just appeared in the office or been mentioned by the others.

I begin to try and sort them in date order but I'm soon running out of desk space. There are big ones, small ones. Some are on coloured paper and some are handwritten. There are ones with familiar logos and addresses and ones where even the type of goods isn't apparent. Who the hell is Watson Blencowe? And what are 'professional services'?

'Hey, dudes,' says Zac as he strolls in.

'Have you seen these?' I ask. He looks across at the papers in my hand.

'Oh, hello, twenty-first century calling. Why do people still do it on these bits of paper? Haven't these people even heard of ecommerce . . .?' But his voice trails off as he nears the desks and sees the other drawers full of papers. 'Holy sssshit.' Zac serious. Now I'm really scared.

'Why didn't we notice this?' I ask the others, sheaves of papers in both hands.

They stare in silence for a moment and then Scarlett says, 'Because they were always in the office before us and still working after we'd all left?'

At that moment the phone rings again. She answers it and as soon as she starts, 'Yes, your invoice has been logged and you'll get a cheque very soon,' the three of us exchange glances. Eventually she puts the phone down.

'Zac, we need to get into their computers.'

'No problemo,' says Zac, but without his usual chilled bravado. He sits down at Guy's desk and switches on the machine. Then he kicks his foot against something, looks under the desk and says, 'Oh, shit.' He pulls out another box, overflowing with invoices.

'Oh, my God, how could anyone spend money so fast?' I ask the world in general.

'They *have* been working eighteen hours a day for the last few months,' points out Scarlett. 'Shop till you pop, you know.' I pull out some more bits of paper. 'And . . . we've all been doing our fair share,' she adds.

I think of my new suits, cars everywhere, the champagne we've got into the habit of opening at five o'clock.

'Okay,' says Zac from the other desk. 'We're in.'

In what, I don't know. There are files of letters, games, lists, press releases and finally some spreadsheets. But even these don't say much. Lists of amounts with dates and names, most of which mean nothing to me. I look down them just in case. The money has certainly been pouring in – until recently, anyway.

'Don't they have bank statements?' I ask Scarlett.

'I don't know, I suppose so. Actually I have opened letters with bank statements in.'

'So have I, come to think of it,' I tell her. I remember Guy grabbing them off me a couple of weeks ago. No wonder he didn't want me to see them. Was it all going wrong even back then?

We ignore the phones and spend another few hours rooting around the desks for some evidence of any sort of correspondence from the bank, but we find only more invoices. Some envelopes, I realise to my horror, are full of things that have been ordered by me. I stuff them back in a drawer.

My mobile rings and it's Lauren.

'Hi, babe,' I sigh.

'Hi. Got your message. What's the matter? You sound really down.'

'Just this money thing. I'm trying to sort out the invoices and bank statements here. Look, I'll be late tonight – I'm going to try and get this stuff in some kind of order if I can.'

'Okay, I'm seeing, erm, seeing Peter tonight, anyway.'

'Yeah,' I say, without having to add, 'thought you might be.'

'He wants me to watch some of the tapes I've made recently to see where I can improve my performance.'

I'm tempted to make a cutting remark about Peter and her performance but I decide against it. I'm just so pissed off.

A few minutes later my phone rings again.

'Hi Charlie, can you talk?' says Nora.

'Sure,' I tell her, trying to sound cheerful, learning from my last mistake.

'Good, listen. I've gotta be quick because I'm on deadline but a couple of people, *sane* people, that is, have called in about Piers and Guy.'

'Really?' Some good news at last.

'Yeah. Okay. Piers's parents live in South Africa and he doesn't see them much which is I suppose why they haven't reported anything yet. I've broken the news to them and I told them I'd pass on anything I could. You haven't heard anything?'

'No, nothing.'

'Okay. Guy's parents are both dead unfortunately and his only blood relative is an older brother who's an entomologist in the Galapagos Islands. We're trying to contact him at the moment.'

Somehow the kind of thing you'd expect of Guy. 'But, and this is a bit of good news, there's a party tomorrow night—'

'Nora, I'm not really in the mood, thanks anyway—'

'No, banana brain! It's being thrown by . . . by, here it is, Sir James Huntsman, whose son and daughter are friends of Piers. I've got us invited – my friend Anna knows them. I say we go along and do some snooping, okay?'

'And I say this isn't *Scooby Doo*, you know.'

'I know, Fred, but we might as well go along and talk to some people, see what we can find out.'

'What the hell are we going to find out?'

'Haven't you got any sense of curiosity?'

'Haven't you got any sense?'

'It can't do any harm, can it?'

'I suppose not. If we turn up anything though, we go straight to the police.'

'Oh, sure,' she says unconvincingly.

'We don't publish it.'

'Well, that depends.'

'All right, I'm not going then.'

'Don't be silly, Charlie, you can't stop me writing about any conversations I might happen to have with anyone.'

'Okay, but don't include me.'

The party is at an address off Kensington High Street. We agree to meet in a pub nearby at 8 p.m. I'm past feeling nervous about it.

By about seven, Scarlett, Zac and I have got most of the receipts in some sort of order. They are now spread across Guy's and Piers's desks as well as mine and Scarlett's with the most up-to-date being lined up against one wall of the office. The monotonous process of sorting them by date order and category – the biggest of which is miscellaneous – has almost put us into a kind of trance, but now that we can see the full extent of 2cool's financial predicament spread around the office we're numbed by it.

I tell the others to go home.

'Don't stay too late, hey?' says Scarlett, stroking my cheek.

'No, don't worry, I just want to have another look at those spreadsheets and check a few names and things. See you tomorrow.'

I make myself a cup of coffee to keep me awake and begin to read through the spreadsheets that Zac has printed out for me from the other computers. I realise that part of the reason I want to sort this out is because I want to show my dad that my first proper job hasn't been a total fiasco. I want to show him that I've saved it, or least done all I can to stop it going under and walked away with a clean conscience and the knowledge that I did my best, that I learnt something from it. No criminal record would also be nice.

He got used to my doing the modelling thing after a while, but I know he was never particularly proud of the career path his only son had chosen.

I'm still there at ten when the buzzer for the outside door goes. I walk across the office which is now in darkness apart from the light over my desk. I pick up the entry phone.

'Hello?'

'Pizza.'

'Pizza? I didn't order a pizza.'

'Er, you sure?'

'Yeah, honestly. Sorry, bye.'

I put the phone back. It buzzes again before I've got to my desk.

'You definitely didn't order a pizza?' says a voice above the street noise.

'Yeah, really, I'd remember.'

'Oh, well, it must be a mistake. Look, someone ordered a pizza and I'm only going to have to take it back. You might as well have it.'

I realise that I won't eat anything any other way tonight. 'If you're sure. Thanks. Come up. Second floor.'

I buzz him in and stand by the door of the office, waiting for him to come up the stairs. After a few moments a guy in leathers with a black crash helmet appears. He doesn't look like a pizza delivery man, not least because he doesn't seem to have a pizza with him. I'm just pondering this when his hand comes up and pushes me hard in the chest, sending me staggering back into the office.

'Oi,' he says.

My heart is pounding with shock as well as the impact. 'Oh, fuck! Who are you? What do you want?' I gasp, trying to get my breath back.

'Oi,' he says again.

'What do you mean?' I'm suddenly offended as well as frightened. Who the hell does he think he is?

'I mean some of your creditors want their money and they're not going to wait for it.'

'All right, all right. We'll pay everyone as soon as we can. Just bear with us.'

'Yeah, well, listen, some of them aren't going to just hang around, see?' He moves towards me menacingly. 'Ow!' He's managed to walk into the desk in the semi-darkness of the office, made more obscure by his helmet. 'Aw, fuck that hurt,' he says, holding his thigh.

'Are you all right?' I ask.

'Shut up!' he bellows, still nursing his upper leg and limping around on it. 'Anyway, yeah, er, right. Like I said, some of your creditors aren't going to wait for their money, okay?' he snaps, pointing a gloved finger at me.

'Well, tell me who they are and we'll make sure they're on the list.'

'What? I'm not telling you who they are, am I? Just make sure you pay up – and fast. Got it?'

He goes to thump me again but I step back quickly and he half-misses so his intended assault ends up as a sort of tap on the shoulder as if we were playing tag. Looks like I'm it now.

'Remember what I said.'

On his way out he glances around for something to smash up to make his point but, with nothing to hand, he ends up just tossing some invoices on to the floor. Then he turns back to leave but walks into the half-open door. 'Ow, fuck!' He stumbles back, stunned. Then he leaves and slams it behind him.

I close my eyes and take a deep breath, telling myself I'm okay. I'm not hurt, just a bit shocked.

But then suddenly there is a terrible thumping, followed by a crashing sound and a voice roaring in anger. For a moment I think he must have smashed up something in the stairwell as a final act of intimidation. Then I realise that there really isn't anything much you could damage out there. I open the office door a crack and peep out. Nothing. I look further out and realise that he's fallen downstairs.

chapter seventeen

I leave the office shortly afterwards and take a taxi home, where I have a large drink. Whisky for a change. As far as gangland muscle goes, my assailant was pretty incompetent. Poor bugger, he's going to have a horrible bruise on his leg tomorrow. Perhaps I should tell the police now? I laugh sadly at the idea that they'd easily be able to identify the man. Just round up the usual suspects and check their legs for nasty contusions.

I don't hear Lauren come in.

'Hi,' she says. 'Why are you sitting in the dark?'

Am I? I must have forgotten to put the lights on. Perhaps I don't want anyone to know I'm at home.

'Sorry, I didn't notice.'

She switches them on and closes the curtains. 'Are you all right?' She sits down on the settee next to me and gives me peck on the cheek.

'I was working late tonight, like I said, and this bloke came in and tried to beat me up.'

'What?' She sits up and looks at me. 'Are you hurt?'

'No, no. I'm fine.' Casually my hand wanders up to my chest where he shoved me. I can hardly feel anything there at all. 'He's in a worse state than I am, I think.'

'What? You're kidding. You attacked him back?'

I laugh. 'I didn't have to. He walked into a desk and then into the door – and then he fell downstairs.' Relief and delayed shock makes me laugh even more.

Lauren is deadly serious. 'Charlie, this is awful. You've got to get out of this. Let's call the police and tell them. I don't want you going to that office tomorrow. It's not safe.' She stops for a moment. 'This puts a whole new perspective on the Guy and Piers thing, doesn't it? Perhaps they've been . . .'

'Murdered?' I say. And then I burst out laughing.

'What's the matter with you? It's not funny.'

'No, sorry, it's not. Perhaps I'm still in shock or something.'

She stands up and looks thoughtful. 'I think you should keep away from this whole thing. It's doing you no good.'

'I just want to try and sort it out.'

'Charlie, it's beyond that. Can't you see? Look what it's doing to your image. Who's going to employ you as a model, or anything else, after this publicity?'

She's right in a way. As always. But there is one very strong argument against her.

'Babe, I'm a director. I've signed cheques. My dad says . . . my dad says that if someone could prove that I was negligent or dishonest I could be prosecuted. I could be in deep shit.'

She looks horrified. 'But you haven't done anything wrong, have you? *Have* you?'

'No, of course not. Well, I've been spending money, but we all have. Piers and Guy told us to.' I wonder how that would stand up in court. I'm sick of thinking about it, so I ask, 'How did it go with Peter tonight?'

Lauren is still staring intently at me. 'Peter?' she says. 'Okay. Yeah, fine. There's a new proposal he's got in with the At Home channel for a DIY makeover thing.'

'Sounds interesting,' I say, staring at the fireplace.

'Should be.'

'Tell me about it.'

'The idea is that a decorator does over someone's house while a celebrity chef cooks them dinner.'

I smile. 'Great. And what did you do tonight?'

'We went to the studio again. Peter wanted me to work on my technique.'

I smirk. 'And is he pleased with your *technique*?'

'Yes.' She pauses. 'What's so funny?'

'Oh, nothing.' I feel her watching me. 'Why don't you show *me* your technique?'

There is another pause and she says, 'I just don't understand you any more, Charlie.'

A few moments later the spare duvet and a couple of pillows are delivered in silence.

I sleep fitfully on the settee. The Couch of Correction, as Sarah calls it when she makes Mark sleep on theirs. I don't feel particularly redeemed the next morning, though. I finally get up about seven, have a quick wash and shave and get the tube back to the office, taking in a cappuccino and an almond croissant from the café next door.

I let myself in and stare at the spreadsheets again. Lauren's right. It's hopeless. Names, amounts and dates are all neatly laid out. I recognise quite a few of them. Sir Josh Langdon, of course, and some other pop stars, plus some big names from the City, some designers and theatre people, but so what? It doesn't explain where the money actually is, does it? When the post arrives, as well as the usual final demands and invitations to luxury-goods launches there are two bank statements: one from a bank in Monaco (overdrawn to the tune of a few hundred thou), the other from a bank in the Cayman Islands (in credit, whoopee, £13.47).

I'm just putting these on a pile when the phone rings.

'Could I speak to Mr Barrett, please?' says a gruff male voice. I curse myself for picking it up.

'Speaking.'

'Oh, good morning, Mr Barrett, this is Detective Inspector Slapton from the Metropolitan Police. I wondered if I could talk to you about the disappearance of your colleagues.'

'Yes, of course. I'm around at the office all of today.'

'Okay, shall we make it, let me see, eleven?'

'That's fine with me.' I give them the address. 'Have you got any news about them, then?'

'About their whereabouts? No.'

'Oh, I've also already spoken to someone in your office.'

'Have you? Which office?'

'Missing Persons.'

'Eh? Oh, sorry, no, I'm not Missing Persons,' he says. 'I'm from the Fraud Squad.'

I've warned Scarlett and Zac that the police will be coming over and might want to talk to them. Zac shrugs and nods. Scarlett says, 'Oh, okay,' and then takes something out of her desk, leaves the room with it and a few moments later we hear the lavatory flushing.

Somehow that would have been the least of our worries.

I also tell them about being attacked. 'I think none of us should be in the office on our own, well, neither of you,' I say, hoping I sound braver than I feel.

Scarlett is looking at my face. 'What did he do then?'

'He didn't hit me in the face but he punched me in the chest.'

'Break any ribs?'

'No, well, I don't think so.'

'Oh, not serious then.'

'Scarlett, I wasn't actually beaten to a pulp,' I say. My masculine pride seems to be getting roughed over worse now than last night.

'But they might come back for more. That was obviously just a warning.'

'Okay,' she says, clearly unimpressed. 'Gonna tell the filth?'

Detective Inspector Slapton and a younger colleague, PC Newton, arrive dead on 11 a.m. We shake hands and I suggest that we sit at the settee and armchairs in one corner of the office. Scarlett offers to make us some coffee. The older policeman can't hide his disdain for her red dreadlocks, purple shades and leopardskin mini-skirt, while his colleague looks at her in awe.

'Thanks very much for taking the time to see us,' says Slapton.

'No problem. Glad to help if we can.' I suddenly wonder if I should have a solicitor present or something.

As if he has read my thoughts Slapton says, 'Just some general questions to help us with our investigation. Nothing to worry about.'

'Sure,' I say.

He asks about how I met Piers and Guy, how I came to work for them, what the site does, about the launch party, about what I do at 2cool, and Scarlett's and Zac's roles. When we come onto the financial element, which is obviously what he is really interested in, my total ignorance saves me. To almost every question I can truthfully answer, 'I don't know,' or 'I was never involved in that.'

'But you *are* a director,' says Slapton at one point.

'Er, yes but obviously I concentrated on the marketing and presentation.'

'What about board meetings?' asks Slapton. A look in his eye suggests that he knows the answer to this one.

A look of panic, which must have flitted across my face in response, confirms it. 'We didn't really have any, not formal ones, anyway. Things have been moving too fast.'

I just hope they believe me.

Slapton lets the information sink in and then asks, 'And the site's still up and running isn't it?'

'Yes, yes it is.' Remembering my job description, as if it still mattered, I say to him, 'Would you like to have a look?'

'Why not. We haven't really had a chance to see what all the fuss is about.'

I lead them over to Zac's desk. We catch him slightly unawares and it takes him a moment to get out of a war game he is playing but he gives the two policemen a guided tour of 2cool2btrue.com – avoiding the porn pages. They seem slightly bemused for most of the time but suitably impressed with the graphics and the funky tricks that Zac shows them. For some reason they end up reading an article about champagne glasses.

'Here's one for you, sir,' says Newton to Slapton. 'Apparently flutes are out for drinking champagne; we'll all be sipping from saucers this season. Just your sort of thing.'

'I think we've still got the saucer kind from the first time around, a wedding present or something,' says Slapton.

'You're all right then,' laughs Newton.

It's supposed to be tongue in cheek, you berks, I think. We're not really suggesting it's a serious issue. Well, I'm not anyway.

They also laugh at our survey about men spending more on clothes than their female partners.

'Not in our house they don't,' says DI Slapton.

As Zac takes them around the site, there are some gratuitous shots of the police shooting protesters at Penn State University, the significance of which is clearly not lost on our visitors.

'Very impressive,' says Slapton. 'I leave all this computer stuff to my son. He's a real whiz at it. Personally, I can't do much more than look at my files. Isn't that right?' he asks his sidekick.

'Yes,' says Newton.

'I'd be quite happy to stick with a typewriter.'

'He can't even get his emails half the time,' says Newton. 'Usually the whole office gets involved. In fact, he doesn't even know—'

'Er, thank you,' says his superior pointedly. The younger policeman falls silent and looks at the ground.

'I hope I've been helpful,' I say, pretty convinced that I haven't.

'Oh, yes. Either myself or my colleague,' he says, shooting Newton another withering look, 'will be in touch if we have any more questions.'

'Sure. I'm around.'

I lead them to the door, suddenly aware of how desperate I am for them to leave so that I can relax.

'So, from male model to computer whiz,' says Slapton as we stand in the open doorway.

'Hardly,' I laugh. He nods thoughtfully, looking at me hard, eyes boring into me so that I have to look away.

'Perhaps myself and PC Newton here should set ourselves up as models – call ourselves Ugly Bastards Incorporated or something.'

I laugh again. What the hell am I supposed to say to that? I've already clocked Slapton's face with its broken veins, the cuts and stray hairs where he hasn't shaved properly, his bloodshot eyes, the chest hair poking up over the top of his collar, and his stomach bulging through his cheap shirt. Call me vain but how can anyone let themselves go like that?

'Oh, no, modelling isn't all it's cracked up to be, believe me,' I mutter, opening the door. 'That's why I got out of it.'

'Spending a whole day doing nothing except hanging around with beautiful women?' he says. 'Eh? Can't be bad.'

'Well, it does have its good points,' I laugh. 'Anyway, great, thanks very much. Bye.'

I close the door and rest my head on it for a moment, at which point a voice from across the room snorts sarcastically, 'Well, it does have its good points, fnurr, fnurr.'

'Oh, fucking hell, Scarlett, what else was I supposed to say? At least we haven't been arrested.'

'I know,' she says. 'What a fucking waste of gear. They didn't even search me this time.'

chapter eighteen

It's black tie, this do at Sir James Huntsman's, as if it wasn't a pain in the arse enough already. Usually Lauren ties my bow tie for me after I've cursed and sworn for a while but this time I don't want to even ask her. She's cooking herself an omelette in the kitchen and I leave her to it.

The final attempt looks like I've at least made an effort although the breeze from a butterfly wing in South America will probably cause it to unfurl again.

'Bye, then,' I tell her. 'I won't be back too late.'

'Okay,' she says without looking round, her fork suspended in mid-air and her legs crossed as she sits at a stool by the breakfast bar, reading a magazine while she eats. That I'm going to this thing with Nora hasn't helped relations between us. Added to which is the fact that instead of getting out of the whole 2cool mess, I seem to be wading in even deeper.

Even though it's warm outside I'm wearing a mac so that I don't look too conspicuous. I'm five minutes early at the pub and I order a whisky for my nerves. Then another. The juke-box comes on and a bloke begins to sing in a thin, tremulous voice:

'It's truth, yeah, yeah, that has to be repeated:
Our love united, yeah, babe, can never be defeated.'

Nora, funnily enough, is late.

'Sorry,' she says, spotting me at the bar. 'We had a bit of a crisis at work. Hey, you look great.'

'Thanks, so do you.'

She's wearing a black lacy dress, sort of Edwardian, with some heavy costume jewellery and dark red lipstick.

'We're running a little news piece on your survey about men spending more on clothes than women, you'll be glad to hear. Editor loves it.'

'Great,' I say. I suppose 2cool might as well carry on generating news – perhaps even positive stuff – until it is finally closed down for good. I've decided to say nothing to Nora about the Fraud Squad visit.

'I think it's a crap story, so obviously my editor but *loves* 2cool which is good for you, and for me, I suppose.'

'I suppose so.'

'Now, tactics for tonight. Let's start with a large G and T.'

I call the barman over and give her order plus another whisky for myself.

'So what are the tactics, beyond a large gin and tonic?' I ask.

'Well, I say we mingle, okay? We've been invited by a friend of mine called Anna. She'll be there so we'll say hello to her and she'll introduce us to Huntsman's children and, hopefully, some other friends of Piers, and we'll chat 'em up and see what we can find out.'

'Sounds simple enough. So who's this Huntsman geezer, then? His name's familiar.'

'He's a financier. Mainly property but also a bit in oil and airlines. Came to Britain as a kid from Poland or somewhere. You know the story – no money, name like a bad hand at Scrabble. Got a job in the post room of a bank or something, changed his original name to Huntsman and built it up from there.'

'I see.'

She clinks her glass against mine and then starts off again. 'Incidentally I've found out a little bit more about Piers's past business activities.'

'Dodgy?'

'A bit.'

'Oh, God, like what?'

'Well. There was one where, let me remember this right, oh yes, he'd employ out-of-work actors to come round and cook dinner for you and then stay and eat it with you and make witty conversation.

An instant dining companion. You could even order two or three of them and have your own dinner party if you had the money.'

'And no friends. That sounds quite above board.'

'Well, apparently the most popular part of the service was where a girl came round, cooked you a delicious dinner with wine, made charming conversation – and then had sex with you.'

'Very nice.'

'The vice squad put a stop to that one.'

'Spoilsports.'

Sir James Huntsman welcomes us with bored, superficial charm as we move along a sort of receiving line.

'Hello, good evening. How nice of you to come,' he drawls. White-haired and florid but tall and slim, he has no trace of a Polish accent. I'm about to thank him for inviting me and explain that I'm a friend of his children's friend Anna, when he turns to the person behind me and says, 'Hello, good evening. How nice of you to come.'

'Hello, Pamela Huntsman. Lovely to meet you,' says Lady Huntsman. She is a tall, thin woman with great cheekbones. She reminds me of someone called Diana at my agency who has cornered the mature women's market and does a brisk trade in smart, older travellers and elegant grandmothers. The only difference is that Lady Huntsman's hair seems to be back-combed to within an inch of its life, so she looks like she's just been electrocuted. 'We're relying on you young ones to get the party going,' she says.

'Oh, Charlie'll get it swinging, he's known for it,' says Nora, giving her a huge wink. I'm so fazed by this comment that I just stare at Lady Huntsman.

'Super,' she says, and turns to the next person.

'What the hell did you say that for?' I ask her when we've moved away from Lady H sufficiently.

'So she'll remember you.'

'She certainly will. Right, where's your friend, then?'

'Can't see her.'

'What does she look like?'

'Sort of short with dark hair.'

'Okay, keep an eye out for her. Do you want a drink?'

'Gasping. Oh, look here's a tray and some nibbles. Grab 'em.'

Knowing Nora's relationship with waiters and trays I hold her back for a moment.

'Now, what do you want?' I ask her.

'Champagne, please,' she says, looking surprised.

Carefully I pick up a glass of champagne and hand it to her. Before I can stop her she reaches for a smoked salmon thing. My heart stands still for a moment but she seems to manage to pick it up without sending the rest flying.

I take a glass of bubbly too and ask her, 'How do we introduce the subject of Piers, and what if someone recognises me or knows your name? And why would they tell us, anyway?'

She tuts. 'Well, they're not going to say, "Actually, since you ask, he's gone to Acapulco" or "Oh, of course, he's hiding in my attic" are they?'

'No, so what are they going to say?'

She rolls her eyes. Why do I always feel like a dumbo with Nora even though I'm usually the one making sense?

'I need another one of these to think.'

She drains her glass and reaches over to another tray. I close my eyes ready for the inevitable but when I look back she is holding a full glass and looking thoughtful.

'The point is, Charlie, that people like to gossip, like to show off their knowledge. You find it all the time as a journalist. You think "Why would anyone want to tell me that?" But they do. We'll just chat and pick up some clues, get to know something more. As I say, you'd be amazed how much people are willing to gossip even when they know they shouldn't.'

'Yeah, we'll see.'

'Knowledge is power and people like to feel powerful,' she says, looking up at me with wide eyes. 'They love reading something in the papers the next day and knowing that they contributed to it, that they're part of the story.'

'Mmm, I suppose so.'

She looks around us and then says, 'Did you know that the cocktail party was invented in 1924 by Alec Waugh, brother of Evelyn?'

'No. Was it?'

'One of the great inventions.'

'Up there with the steam engine and television.'

'Far more useful, though. Thought you could work it into the conversation somewhere. Break the ice a bit.'

She takes another large mouthful of champagne. I've hardly touched my glass.

'Do you always drink this much?'

'Only when I'm nervous,' she explains.

'Now you're making *me* nervous.'

'Don't be! Big boy like you, look at the talent around here. You're bound to score.'

'Ha, ha! I'm not single, you know that,' I say pointedly.

'I know, that's what makes you extra attractive – to these Sloaney girls I mean. Anyway, let's split up and get snooping.'

'Yes, Velma. *Scooby Doo,* you know—'

'Yeah, I get it. Now, let's mingle, mingle.'

I push my way gently through the crowds. There are some faces I half-recognise: politicians, business people, a bloke who pops up on the teatime news to talk about whether interest rates will go up or down. There is even a TV presenter who does *Newsnight* sometimes, discussing something with a serious-looking young guy, but also looking around to see who else he should be talking to.

Near the stairs I pass an immaculately dressed man who is talking through pursed lips to a rather harassed-looking woman.

'Now darling, remember what we're going to say?' he hisses. 'That's right. "Thanks but I think I've had enough." Yes? "Thanks, but I think I've had enough." Got it?'

'Thanks but I think I've had enough. *Thanks* but I think I've had enough,' says the woman, concentrating hard. 'Thanks but I *think* I've had enough.' She takes a deep breath. 'Yes, don't worry darling.'

At that moment a waiter bearing a tray passes them and she grabs two glasses of champagne from him as though her life depends on it and knocks them back, one after another. The man rolls his eyes.

Other people are double-kissing each other and making unfunny jokes or talking money in loud, braying voices. Most of the women look like they've been very carefully put together from kits, every piece painstakingly assembled and polished up before being sent out. I try to work out who is my mum's age. I'm just thinking this when I bump into my dad. Unlike everyone else he is not in black tie. Instead he's wearing a black Nehru jacket, and Mari, or whatever the hell her name was, is on his arm.

'Charlie,' he says, looking very surprised, almost shocked. 'What are you doing here? You don't know James, do you?'

'No, I'm with a friend. How do you know him?'

'Well, why shouldn't I? I mean, some of his companies are clients of ours.' He smiles suddenly and pats my shoulder. 'Hey, looking good. You remember Mari, don't you?'

'Yes, nice to meet you again,' I say, trying to eradicate thoughts of my mum who is probably at home watching *The Bill*.

'So, where is Lauren?' He waves at someone and double-kisses a gorgeous blonde woman, asking her 'How you doing?' as she moves past us.

'Catch you later,' she purrs, squeezing his arm, so obviously an ex-fuck. Mari looks on benignly – or ignorantly.

'So, yeah, where's Lauren?' says my dad, coming back to me.

'She's at home.' At least I hope she is, not out with PBC again. Suddenly I feel a bit lonely without her by my side. You never have to worry about not having someone to talk to at a party with Lauren. People sort of gravitate towards her and she's always got something to say.

'Everything all right between you two?'

'Not too good. I'm just here with a work friend though.'

'From 2cool?' he says, sounding slightly concerned.

'Not exactly. Just someone who's helping me.'

'That journalist?' How did he know?

'Well, yeah.'

He looks anxious again, nervous even.

'Charlie, just be careful. She's a journalist. She's got loyalty to no one but herself. This thing is pretty big by all accounts – there's been a lot of money invested in it. People really wanted it to work, for it to make investing in the consumer side of the net sexy and fun again. Have you had a chance to look at the accounts yet?'

'What accounts? It's just chaos. Bills, final demands – I can't even find where they've filed all the bank statements.' I decide not to worry him about the police visit now. Anyway, I'm not sure that there is anything about that visit to worry about: they seemed quite happy with it all.

'Fucking hell.' He thinks for a moment. 'Well, I think you should just resign. Hand in your notice tomorrow. Get the fuck out of there.'

'Mmm,' I tell him thoughtfully.

'Charlie, did you hear what I said?'

Suddenly I'm transported back to being a teenager with the old man having a go at me again.

'Yeah, I did, Dad, but the thing is . . . the thing is, it's like when I was a kid, well fifteen, sixteen or something. What were you doing then?'

He looks, mystified, irritated. 'How do mean?'

'You were working all hours with the other two in a tiny attic in Brewer Street across the landing from a girl who charged twenty quid a go. Remember? We had no money. You had to go to Grandpa for a loan. No, I know you did, I heard you on the phone to him. And remember what Mum said, remember what your ex-boss told you? Everyone said you'd fail but you stuck at it, even when it seemed hopeless.'

'This is different,' says Dad, frowning sadly. 'Charlie, you've got to get out of this. Look, get yourself a solicitor and charge it to the company; you're quite entitled to under the law.'

'I don't think we can afford it.'

'I'll pay for it. I know a great guy. I'll give you his number.'

'Thanks, Dad.'

He is about to say something else when a big bloke with a Number One haircut and another young, blonde girl on his arm appears and says, 'Jared, mate, how are you?'

'Grey. Good, thanks. How are you? How's the movie business? This is my son Charlie.'

We shake hands and then, relieved, I say 'Excuse me,' and slip away to find Nora.

I end up talking to someone called Annabelle who works in management consultancy, specialising in the personal finance sector, read politics at Durham although she doesn't use her degree now, lives in Fulham where her flat has doubled in value over the past five years, likes to go skiing but was in Bali earlier this year where she spent the whole day lying on the beach and relaxing.

Yep, it's one of *those* conversations, so when another girl joins us I excuse myself and continue my quest for Nora.

I pass a woman with huge blue/grey hair and a ball dress with massive puffed sleeves, talking on her mobile.

'He wants Gonk. No, *Gonk*. The thing with the bug eyes and the blue hair above the bed . . . What's the matter? He said what to you? Well, I don't know where he picked up that kind of language. Look, I'm sorry but just give him his Gonk. Okay, let me have a word. Hello darling, it's Mummy. Maria will get it for you if you say sorry . . . no, I know, but you mustn't call her that . . . have you got it? Jolly good. Listen I can't say hallo to Gonk now because I'm a bit busy but . . . Oh hallo Gonk . . . how are you?'

Some people are dancing by now. A middle-aged couple are going for it with great seriousness. She looks like she is trying to stamp on armies of ants and he seems to be having a series of minor heart attacks in slow motion.

Finally I find Nora talking to a middle-aged woman and a young guy.

'Hi Charlie,' she says. 'Lady Philips, Alex, this is my friend Charlie.'

Alex is a hearty-looking rugger-bugger City type in his early twenties and Lady Philips looks like she sits on a lot of committees. I say hallo to them both and realise that the woman thinks 'friend' means 'boyfriend'. So does Alex. Perhaps he thought he was in with a chance, but then again he looks like he'd be more at home with someone in an Alice band.

I'm just thinking I might slip away and ring Lauren, not to check she's in, really, but just to say hallo, having a crap time, when Lady Philips and Alex bugger off and Nora asks me, 'Well?'

'Well, what?'

'Have you found out anything?'

'No, not really, have you?'

'No, nothing much. Except that apparently Piers and Lady H might have, you know, at one point.'

'What? Piers?'

'And Lady H.'

'She's old enough to be his mother. Actually, I did learn something: apparently Sir James might have invested in 2cool.'

'That's interesting. But I can't even begin to imagine how we're going to find out where Piers is.'

'No, unless Lady H knows something.'

'Oh, come on, even if they were having it off – and I find that very hard to believe – she's hardly likely to know where he is now, is she?'

'How do you know? Look, she's just over there. Let's go and talk to her.'

Before I can object, Nora has steered me over to our hostess.

'Lady Huntsman, we were just saying what a lovely party this is,' beams Nora.

I nod dumbly, fear having removed my ability to speak. The woman Lady Huntsman is talking to smiles at us both, again, no doubt assuming we're an item.

'Thank you,' says Lady Huntsman graciously. 'I was a little nervous because they're new caterers but everything seems perfectly satisfactory.'

'New caterers? Oh, such an anxiety,' says the woman she has been talking to, shaking her head knowingly.

'I was just telling Charlie that you do so much for badgers, don't you?' says Nora to our hostess. 'I mean protecting them.'

'Well, I play a small part; fundraising, flagging up the issue.'

'Charlie's been wanting to get into badger conservation for a long time, haven't you Charlie?'

What?

'Oh, we're always looking for fresh blood for our badger meetings,' says Lady Huntsman.

'There you go,' says Nora. 'I told you they'd be interested.'

'Yes,' I say robotically.

'What do you do for work?' asks Lady Huntsman. I tell her I work for a website called 2cool2btrue.com. 'Oh, the one that all the young people are going on about. I'm sure that's the one my daughter Anastasia is logged on to all the time. And I think James has got something to do with it too. Oh, well, if you had any time outside work to devote to our little group that would be absolutely super.'

'I'd love to,' I say. Oh, what the hell!

There is an embarrassing silence and then Nora says, 'We don't have them in America.'

'No, you have muskrats instead,' says Lady H authoritatively.

'Oh, look, let's have another drink,' says Nora. She reaches across me to the waiter who has approached us and this time it happens: she manages to bring with her half a dozen glasses along with the one she's picked up. Every single one of them falls onto me, it seems.

'Oh, Charlie, what happened?' she says.

I'm about to tell her exactly what the bloody hell happened, Lady H or no Lady H, when our hostess says, 'Oh, dear. So easily done. Come upstairs and we'll get you changed. Don't worry. Why don't you have one of James's shirts? He must be about the same size as you.'

I don't want one of James's bloody shirts, I really just want to go home and see Lauren. By this time the party is actually beginning to thin out.

'Listen, Lady Huntsman, it's very kind of you but I think perhaps I'd better be going, anyway.'

'Nonsense, it's only, what is it?' She tries to focus on her watch. 'Well, it's early, anyway.'

Fortunately we're quite near the stairs so my embarrassment at being led, dripping wet, by the arm like a seven-year-old who has disgraced himself on a school trip, is intense but short lived.

She opens the door of a large bedroom and I follow her in.

'Now, quick, take that wet shirt off and I'll have someone put it in to soak.'

'Really, Lady Huntsman, it's drying already.'

'Nonsense, it's soaked through. You'll catch your death.'

'Well, have you got a hairdryer or something?' I suggest. 'That would probably do it.'

'A hairdryer? Don't be ridiculous. Take it off. Quick, quick. I'll go and find one of James's shirts. Be right back.' She disappears through another door.

It is getting quite uncomfortable – cold and sticky – so I undo my tie and take off my cufflinks. I put them on a nearby table, slip off my shirt and make a gesture towards folding it. I lay it on the bed but then decide that it might soak through and so I put it on a chair. Bloody Nora! Bloody, buggering Nora.

Lady Huntsman shouts something from the other room.

'Er, sorry?' I call after her.

'I said I'd do *anything* for badgers, absolutely anything, wouldn't you?'

'Erm, well, it depends on what circumstances . . .'

She pops her head round the door. 'Mind you, I am a woman of extreme views,' she declares.

'Mmm, I'm sure,' I say. 'I can appreciate that.'

She looks at me for a moment and then disappears again.

Feeling slightly exposed, I fold my arms. Then unfold them. Then I swing them by my sides and then fold them again. Aren't arms a nuisance sometimes? I wait around a bit more and then call out, 'Lady Huntsman?'

No answer.

What the hell is she doing? I potter around the room a bit. Absent-mindedly I look into the half-open door of a wardrobe as if Piers might be lurking in there. I suddenly sense Lady Huntsman standing behind me so I turn round quickly.

'Oh, hallo,' I say unnecessarily.

She's there all right but where's the shirt?

'You obviously play a lot of sport,' she says, eyeing me up.

'Um, well, sometimes, er, you know, used to.'

'You certainly keep fit.'

Quite what happens next, I'm not sure, but it seems like she has fifteen pairs of hands. Her lips are on mine and I can smell her perfume and feel her soft, well-powdered skin against me.

'Lady . . . argh! . . . Huntsman . . . please.'

'Shut up. Make love to me.'

'I—'

But she's kissing me again, hard and deep, her hands pulling at my hair. 'You said you were going to make the party swing.'

'It wasn't actually *me* who said that, ow, if you remember, it was Nora. I don't know what—' A bit of a fine distinction given our current situation, even I must admit.

'And all that crap about badgers? People always use badgers to get to me.'

'What?'

Then her lips leave mine and she is on her knees unbuttoning my fly.

'Lady Huntsman, please. Oh, my God. Look, please don't erm, take this the wrong way.' Suddenly my trousers are round my ankles and she is pulling at my undies. 'Look, just—' Now I'm on the ground on my back, trying to drag myself away from her with my elbows. I don't want to be any more forceful in case I hurt her but she's quite strong for a woman of her age, especially one with such a slim build, and she's bloody persistent, I'll give her that.

With a sharp tug she has yanked my underpants down and her lips are travelling up my thigh, her hand finding my cock and beginning to work it manically. Just then the door opens and Sir James looks in. I'm partly horrified, partly relieved.

'Oh, my God,' wails a weak, high-pitched voice, which I suppose, by a process of elimination (he's not saying anything, she has her mouth full) must be mine.

This is it. What could a rich, powerful man do to you, if he found you assaulting his wife? He must have some of the best lawyers in the land at his disposal. He'd make sure I never worked at anything again. I'd have to leave the country. But instead of looking horrified or angry he looks vaguely disappointed.

'Oh,' he says. 'We'll use the spare room, then.'

'We' turns out to be Annabelle the management consultant who specialises in the personal finance sector. She peeps round the door after him and looks stunned for a moment before being dragged off to the spare room.

'There are clean sheets on the bed,' calls Lady Huntsman after him.

I make the most of this interruption, turn over and do a sort of sprinter's start away from her. I throw myself against the far wall and get my breath back. We eye each other for a moment. Then I reach over to the table and pick it up, legs pointing at Lady Huntsman, lion-tamer style.

'Honestly,' she says, pulling herself up. 'What's wrong with you boys these days? Is it all this new man rubbish or something?'

'No, I'm sorry, it's just that I'm going out with someone,' I tell her, gasping for breath and wondering if I can safely get to the door without her trying another rugby tackle on me. She looks remarkably unruffled considering the struggle we've just engaged in.

'Oh, so what? I'm *married* to someone. Live a little, why don't you?'

'Sorry, it's nothing personal.'

'Is it AIDS? I've got condoms.'

'No, it's . . .' I can hardly tell her she's old enough to be my mother and I don't fancy her. 'I'm, er, just not in the mood. I wasn't expecting . . . sorry,' I mutter girlishly, pulling up my trousers as well as I can with one hand and edging out of the door. I put the table down and scurry out. 'Sorry,' I mutter again. Outside I manage to do up my fly and get my shirt on.

'Crikey.' It's Alex. 'What the hell happened to you?'

'Just changing my shirt,' I gasp. 'Someone spilled something down it.'

'And your trousers, too?'

'Yes. Bit of an accident.'

'I was just looking for the loo,' he says, suspiciously.

'It's in here,' I tell him, jerking my head back towards the door I've just come out of. I move aside to let him past.

Warily, he nods a curt thank you. As soon as he's in and I hear him say, 'Oh! Lady Huntsman, I'm so sorry, I thought—' I pull the door shut and scamper off to find a quiet corner to finish getting dressed in.

I open a door further down the corridor and step into a silent, darkened room and switch on the light. I see a pair of female legs sticking upwards. In between them is my dad's friend Grey. He glances round at me and then looks at the owner of the legs.

'For Christ's sake, don't any of the bloody doors lock in this house?' he asks her.

'No, obviously not, now shut up and get on with it,' she says.

I withdraw, slip back into the corridor and bump into Nora.

'Oh,' she says. 'What happened to you?'

I laugh bitterly.

'I met you.'

She ignores this comment. 'You look worse than before. Did you get a clean shirt?'

'I got everything but.'

'She try it on?' asks Nora, looking slightly pained.

'Yeah, she bloody did. Fuck! How embarrassing, she just leapt on me. Hang on, let me do my shirt up.'

'It was the badgers thing, I think.'

'What have they got to do with anything?'

'Her badger meetings. It's well known: they just get together at country houses, all these so-called badger enthusiasts, and just, you know, get off with each other. It's like a code for upper-class swingers: "Are you interested in badger conservation?" It means, are you up for it? I was going to write a piece about it but—'

'All right, I get the picture.' I finish tucking in my shirt. 'I can't believe you knew she was going to do that.'

'I certainly had an inkling. Didn't you see her eyes light up when I mentioned you and badgers? Anyway, more importantly, did she mention Piers?'

'No, funnily enough she didn't, she had her mouth full, and I'm afraid I didn't manage to broach the subject as I was trying to force her lips off my di— off my, er, lips.'

'Shame.'

'Oh, shit, my mobile, where is it?'

'Who are you going to ring?'

'Never mind.' Why shouldn't she know? 'I'm just going to call my girlfriend, Lauren.'

'Is it not in your jacket?' asks Nora, blandly.

'No, it must have fallen out in the struggle.'

'It'll be in there then.'

'Well done. Good detective work.'

'Just nip in and get it.'

'I can't, not with her in there.'

'Oh, for goodness' sake,' sighs Nora, and she sets off along the corridor to Lady Huntsman's bedroom. I'm just about to call her back when I realise that in fact it will bloody well serve her right. I see her open the door warily and put her head round it.

'Oh, Alex, hi,' she says, and then I hear her gasp, 'Oh, is that you Lady Huntsman? I didn't recognise you.' She turns her head to one side. 'Sorry, don't mind me, I'm just looking for a mobile phone, ah, here it is, sorry, see you later. Oh, lovely party, by the way.' She emerges again, frowning as she comes towards me. 'That's a sight that'll stay with me for a while. God, she's supple for a woman of her age, though. I don't think I could manage that. She must do a lot of yoga. Anyway, here's your phone. It's a bit wet I'm afraid.'

'Thanks.'

She takes off her glasses and begins to polish them on her lacy black dress. Once again she looks like no one else at the party but she does have a certain style. Then she puts her glasses back on again and pushes her diamante hair-slide around a bit. She looks up at me with her big, dark, inscrutable eyes.

'Well, I'll leave you to make your phone call,' she says.

'Okay.'

'I'll keep mingling and maybe see you later.'

'Yes, sure,' I say. 'I'll go outside and ring from there.'

chapter nineteen

I leave Nora to carry on mingling and step on to the terrace which overlooks a bigger garden than anyone in London has the right to own. I look up at the house ablaze with light and then call Lauren. The phone rings a couple of times and then the answer machine clicks in. I knew it! I fucking knew it! She's out with Peter.

Then the phone is picked up clumsily. 'Hello?' says a sleepy voice.

'Lauren? Hi, it's me.'

'Oh, hi babe. Where are you? What time is it?'

'It's . . .' I check my watch in the light from the house. It's 11.45 p.m. 'Oh, sorry, it's nearly midnight.'

'Oh, Charlieeee. What's the matter? Are you all right? Why are you ringing so late? I've got to get up early tomorrow for a casting in Docklands.'

'Sorry, I just wanted to hear your voice.'

'Oh, right. When will you be home?'

'Very soon. Night, hon.'

'Night.' She puts the phone down.

'You in trouble with the missus?'

I spin round but can't see anyone in the gloom. 'Hello?'

'You shouldn't have fucked my mother then, should you?'

'Hello? Who's that?'

The smell of pot floats through the summer air. Finally a face emerges from the darkness of the shrubbery. A girl in her twenties, long dark hair. A face that is still girlish. Pale skin, pretty but for a sad, sulky mouth. She takes another drag on her joint.

'Feel better now you've rung your wife?' she asks knowingly.

'I haven't fucked your mother,' I tell her, more intrigued than cross.

'Really? Apparently she was last seen dragging you upstairs.'

'You're Lady Huntsman's daughter.'

'Well done.' She waits for a moment and extends a hand. 'Anastasia.' We shake.

'Charlie, Charlie Barrett.'

She looks at me for a moment. 'I know you, don't I?'

'No.'

'I do.'

'Perhaps from the website, 2cool—'

'2btrue, of course.' She takes a drag and looks at me again. 'So you didn't do it with my mother, then?'

'No, I . . . we didn't in the end.'

'Oh, I see. Was that your *boyfriend* you were ringing just now?'

'No, it was my girlfriend. I just—'

'Managed to fight my mother off. Gosh, you're now a member of a very exclusive club: the ones who've managed to get away from her.'

She offers me her joint. I'm about to decline but instead I reach and take it from her. I have a drag and hold it before handing the joint back.

'How do you know my parents?' she asks.

'I, er, I'm here with a girl called Nora. Know her? American girl, she's a journalist. Writes for the *Post*.'

Anastasia shakes her head without thinking. 'I haven't been inside much. Can't stomach it.'

'Sure. I can understand that.'

She takes another drag. 'It's quite fun, your website – I look at it quite a bit. Quite funky. Shame, though, apparently it's all going tits up, isn't it? Still, that's Piers for you.'

'You know him?' I feel a surge of adrenalin through my tired, aching body.

'Piers? Yes.'

'How?'

I curse myself for appearing too blunt, too interested. This is what I came to this stupid, awful party for, but I get the feeling I'm going to have to reel this one in carefully. I can tell, though, from way she's looking me up and down that there is something going on here. I give her the same frowny, 'come to bed' look as in the picture that ended up in the first *Post* article. I probably look like a tit but I might as well try to charm this sultry, cynical girl.

'I've known him for yonks,' she says. She flicks ash off the remainder of her joint and takes another drag at it. 'He's my dealer for one thing.'

'Really? Piers?'

'Oh, Piers can get you anything. Real Arthur Daley. You should know – he was selling this shit through your site.'

'What, drugs? On 2cool?'

'Derr! Didn't you notice? Go to "Extra Curricula", click on "What's in the cupboard?". You must know what that means? No?' She tuts. 'So innocent. Then you just choose "Charlie Says", "Pot Noodle", "Good Enough to 'E'at?", "Grass Cutters".' She laughs. 'I can't believe you've never looked.'

'I can't keep track of all the things that go on the site.'

'So what's happening to it? They say it's falling apart.'

'A few financial difficulties. That's why I'm looking for Piers.'

She glances around for a moment. 'Well, he doesn't seem to be here,' she says in an ultra-patronising tone.

'Thanks for looking.' I flash her a big smile to keep her onside.

'Don't mention it.'

'It would be really helpful if you could let me know if you hear anything. Seriously.'

She thinks about it, finishes her joint and throws it into the bushes. ''Kay,' she says in a strangled, post-drag voice. 'I think my dad would quite like to speak to him too. Piers is the one who persuaded him to invest in 2cool.'

'Well, if we find him, we'll call your dad, I promise. It's the least I can do.'

'For fucking his wife.'

'I told you—'

'Oh, I'm kidding.'

I put my hands in my pockets and walk around thoughtfully. 'So what else has Piers has invested in?'

'Oh, let me see.' She looks up at the few stars we can see above the London light pollution. 'A girl band. Oh, haven't we all? These were two Croatian models. Piers chatted them up in a bar. They couldn't speak English let alone sing, but Piers paid a couple of backing vocalists to take care of that little technicality, had them photographed and even got them a recording "contract".' She draws lazy, stoned, air-quotes. 'Then they went home to some remote village. He thought it would be funny if he got them into the charts. He loved the idea that they would be stars in this country and not even know it. It nearly worked, I think.'

'Very virtual.'

'Then there were Yukisakis or whatever they're called.'

'What?'

'These little creatures. According to Piers they were a cross between Tamagotchi and Hello Kitty. You know, cute little things with computers in them. He thought they'd be huge, bought thousands and thousands of them from a factory in China – you know, the kind where they employ five-year-olds for eighteen hours a day making sports gear, the kind my father invests in – and he planned to sell them on street corners, cutting out the middle man, a kind of guerrilla marketing thing. Make it an underground operation. Really hip accessory. Kind of thing that all your mates have, but too cool to be sold in any high street shop.'

'Don't remember them. What happened?'

'Apparently the head came off really easily and there was this sharp spike which also gave off an electric shock.'

'Nice.'

'Not really. So obviously he couldn't flog many in this country. Last thing we heard the Triads were using them to poke their enemies' eyes out with, oh, and I think some African dictator had bought a job lot.'

'So, not all bad news then.'

She laughs. 'Depends how you look at it. Piers always looks on the bright side.'

'Yeah, he does, doesn't he?' There is a pause as we both look up at the stars. Then I say, 'I would like to find him you know.'

'I'm sure you would.'

'I won't land you in it.'

'I don't care if you do. He won't hold it against me – I'm one of his best customers.' She mimes a rolling action with the tips of her fingers.

'Can I ring you about it?'

'I'll ring you.'

I go to find Nora. She is talking to a couple of people and seems ready to leave when I suggest it. We find a taxi in Kensington High

Street and although Notting Hill isn't strictly on the way we decide to drop her off first. Once inside I tell her what Anastasia Huntsman has told me.

'Great,' she says.

'It's not great, it's terrible. Piers is a total spiv.'

'At least we know something more about his business background. This girl, Huntsman's daughter, is bound to hear from him at some point. Give her a call tomorrow and have another chat.'

'She wouldn't give me her number, but she's got mine and said she'd call me when she heard from him,' I say, wondering what it must be like to be as angry and bored all the time as Anastasia.

'Okay, if you haven't heard by the end of the day tell me and I'll get her number for you.'

We sit in silence for a moment and then I say, 'I bumped into my dad and he basically just said get out of it.'

'The advertising man, was he there?'

'How did you know my dad was in advertising?'

'You mentioned it the other night,' she says quickly. 'Anyway, he says get out, does he? He's probably right, but you might as well follow up this Piers thing and then leave it. One more day can't do any harm can it?'

I think about it. The harm it could do is to get me sent to prison or beaten to a pulp, but something, some stupid, headstrong, irresponsible part of me agrees with her. Most of all, I just want to prove to my dad that I can do what he did. Even if it doesn't work, I want to show I didn't walk away without trying.

We set off up Kensington Church Street past the antique shops full of the kind of furniture we've just been walking past and sitting on and getting sexually assaulted amongst. After a few minutes I ask, 'Did you see your friend Anna in the end?'

'Anna? Er, no, I don't think she made it.'

'Probably because she doesn't exist.'

'Yes, she does,' says Nora, half-heartedly.

'No, she doesn't. You just made her up. We basically just crashed that party, didn't we?'

'And very successfully,' she says, turning to me and raising one eyebrow elegantly.

We reach Nora's and I get out to see her to the door. We do the key thing again. She rabbits on about what she's got to write tomorrow while she searches around what tonight is only a tiny dress handbag but seems to have a Tardis quality about it. Then she produces the key and holds it up.

'Knew it was in here somewhere,' she laughs breathily. She's like a little girl with her big, dark eyes and her cheeky grin. I suddenly wonder whether she has anyone to protect her, to put his arms round her, to listen to her when she's got herself into trouble at work – again.

I don't think she has.

This girl is trouble, I remind myself. She's lied to me, she's already got me into various horribly embarrassing situations, she's made the 2cool problem a thousand times worse, she seems to have only a light grip on reality and she is either unaware of or unconcerned about what problems she causes other people. But somehow I find myself wanting to get closer to her.

Looking up at me, she licks her lips, almost subconsciously. We're standing inches away from each other.

'Night then,' I tell her.

'Goodnight, Charlie,' she says.

I slip into bed with Lauren. She groans slightly in her sleep, turns and backs into me. I put my arms around her sleeping body and gently drift off.

Although there seems very little point in going to the office the next day, I'm there by 10 a.m. Scarlett comes in an hour later and Zac drifts in at lunchtime.

'I got you a carrot, apple and ginger to help you detox,' she says. 'After last night.'

'Thanks, doll,' I say, and tell her about the party, minus the Lady H episode. I came so close to kissing Nora last night and I still don't really know why. As I finish talking about the party, the phone rings with someone about payment again. I'm polite but firm. They'll have to wait.

'Fuck,' says Scarlett over her alfalfa sprout roll.

'Let me just finish this email and I'll be right over,' says Zac.

'In your dreams, net nerd.'

'What's the matter?' I ask.

'Have you seen the *Standard* today?'

'Oh, God, now what?'

'It's about your friend Nora.'

I'm at Scarlett's desk in a moment. She points to a piece in the 'Londoner's Diary'. It's a picture of Nora next to one of Piers.

> Post *columnist Nora Benthall has become something of an expert on style-over-substance website 2cool2btrue.com. At a party thrown by financier Sir James Huntsman at his Kensington mansion last night, she was seen on the arm of her latest squeeze, former male model and internet guru Charlie Barrett.*
>
> *But her connection with 2cool goes beyond Barrett, the public face of the fast-disintegrating luxury goods outfit. Her cousin, Piers Gough-Pugh, founded and financed the site but has since disappeared. In addition to a full-blown police investigation which now includes the Fraud Squad, American born Benthall, 27, has been carrying out her own enquiries into her cousin's whereabouts.*
>
> *'Nora is very tenacious and if anyone can find Piers it will be her. She's bound to be there before the police,' says a friend.*

'Latest squeeze?' asks Scarlett.

'No, no. Me and Nora? Not at all.' I look at the paper again. 'And they've got this wrong too. Nora isn't Piers's cousin – how can she be?'

But even as I'm saying it I realise how very possible it is. That's how Piers knew her in the first place. She's done it again. How could she? She's lied to me again. Tricked me again. Fucking betrayed my trust. The bitch, how could she? I think about that moment on her doorstep last night. We nearly kissed. Let's be honest, I wanted to kiss her. I actually felt very close to her, and all the time she was taking me for a ride. Lying to me. Again. I begin to feel more hurt than angry.

'You all right?' It's Scarlett.

I look round at her. She squeezes my hand.

'Yeah, just . . . why didn't she say?' Somehow, even though I didn't mention her much when I was talking about the party, I think Scarlett can tell that I feel something for Nora.

'She's bad news, that girl.'

'Tell me about it.'

'Why did Piers lie as well? I *knew* there was something funny about it when he first mentioned her – he couldn't seem to decide whether they were old friends or whether they'd just met.'

'Perhaps *she* told him to say that.'

'That's no excuse, it's just pathetic.'

Scarlett looks sort of pained and shrugs her shoulders.

I go back to my desk, take a moment to collect my thoughts and then ring her.

'Hello, did you get back all right then?' she asks brightly.

'Yeah, thanks. Look Nora. Have you seen the *Standard* today?'

'The *Standard*? Oh, that piece. Horrid isn't it? Talk about shitting on your own. And the thing about you being my squeeze. How embarrassing. I hope your girlfriend doesn't see it. Just blame the journalist if she does.' I let her gabble on for a moment.

'What about this stuff about you being Piers's cousin?'

'Oh that.'

'Yeah, that.' I give her a moment to say something but there is no response. 'It's not true, is it?'

'Oh, honestly, who really bothers about these things?'

I grip the receiver tight and my teeth are gritted. I know the others are listening in intently but I don't care.

'Nora. Tell me. Is it true? Are you and Piers cousins?' There is a pause. 'Listen. I don't want any more surprises, okay? I can't stand it. Either you're honest with me, completely honest and tell me everything, or we never speak to each other again, do you understand me?'

The silence at the other end goes on for so long that I'm just about to ask whether she's still there when she says in a small voice, 'All right, we're cousins. I just forgot to tell you. I'm sorry. I know it's silly, I know I should have but I just forgot and then it didn't seem relevant. We're not exactly close.'

'It doesn't matter if you're not close. You're still cousins, you're still related. Why didn't you fucking tell me?'

'Charlie, what difference does it make?'

'But you could have told me. What else are you lying about?'

'Excuse me, don't speak to me like that. I don't have to listen to this. We *are* cousins, yes, but as I said, we're not close. It didn't have any bearing on what I wrote about 2cool or our attempts to find him.' The best form of defence is obviously attack, she's decided. I can sort of see her point.

I take a deep breath. 'From now on we're completely honest with each other, you understand me? We tell each other everything.'

'Of course, Charlie.'

'No "of course" about it. Do you promise?'

'Yes, I promise. Now I've said I'm sorry so let's just leave it. I've got some more calls to make about Piers. Just because I'm his cousin and we share grandparents way back, doesn't mean I have any more of an idea where he is than you do. Less in fact. We've hardly seen each other since we were kids. Now, listen, I'm getting a number for that Huntsman girl so you can call her.'

'Okay, ring me when you've got it,' I tell her and put the phone down.

'I wouldn't trust that woman as far as I could spit her,' says Scarlett.

She's so right.

chapter twenty

The people I least want to speak to after Nora are the police, so naturally DI Slapton calls – on the entry phone. He's downstairs. It doesn't help that Scarlett, who picks up the receiver, announces him as the 'pig-lice' with the receiver inches away from her mouth. I hope he just thinks she's got a stutter.

'We need to take some documents away with us, as well as your computers,' he says, arriving at the top of the stairs and panting slightly. He is accompanied by three junior officers carrying large plastic boxes.

'You've got a warrant and everything then?' I ask, trying to make it sound like I'm not a total soft touch.

Slapton looks surprised at my question and then contemptuous. His sarcasm is all the more intimidating for its subtlety. 'Oh, yes, we've got all the right paperwork,' he says, standing very close to me. 'You see, we've done this before, son.'

The four of them move in.

'Stand away from the computers, please,' one of the other officers tells Scarlett and Zac. Uncertainly, they get up and move away from their desks. The officer takes out a polaroid camera and photographs the computer screens, then begins to pull plugs out of the wall.

'Hey,' says Zac, suddenly animated. 'Let me close these things down properly, will you?'

'Sorry, sir, can't do that. We have to take them as they are,' says the officer, grimacing slightly as he pulls at a particularly reluctant plug under a desk. The Macs and the other pieces of hardware die slowly in front of us, fans slowing, lights flickering off.

'It's standard practice,' Slapton informs me. 'We've got the photos to show what's on the screens when we unplugged them. You see we don't want it to look like we've changed any documents, or allowed you to amend or delete anything that could be incriminating,' he adds, snapping on some rubber gloves.

From their boxes the officers produce piles of clear polythene bags which they begin filling with our carefully sorted invoices, ripping off strips and sealing them, one officer laboriously filling in the form printed on each one of them, near the words 'Police Evidence' in big letters.

Slapton consults some printed notes, obviously telling him and the others what to take. I notice him fill in a series of forms to show where in the office the various papers and computers were seized from. After a couple of hours they've filled almost all the evidence bags and they seem satisfied. Loading the computers and the processing units into evidence boxes and bigger polythene bags takes some time. I offer to help one officer who is obviously struggling, but he grunts, 'Can't allow you, sir, I'm afraid,' and carries on.

Having packed up computers belonging to Guy, Piers and Zac, they're obviously debating whether to take the remaining machines when I jump in, because we'll need something to keep the site going and also, it has to be said, to continue making our own enquiries.

'There's nothing interesting on these. All the financial stuff is on the ones you've already got – Zac can give you the passwords if you want. If you could leave these it would mean we can still keep the site going.'

The other policemen look to Slapton for guidance.

'Look, erm, the thing is,' says Scarlett, getting up from her desk. 'It's not just about the money, we've never been much good at that.' She blinks and sniffs. 'The site means a hell of a lot to us; we've put our whole lives into it for the last month or so. We've been working on it twenty-four seven, hardly slept or eaten.' A single tear rolls down her left cheek. 'I know you've got your job to do but we'd really appreciate it if you could just leave us enough to keep 2cool going, keep our dream alive for a bit longer. That would be very kind, thanks . . .'

I'm more stunned than our visitors. I had no idea that it was so important to her. Slapton approaches her, smiles kindly at her and says very quietly, 'No.'

I see a couple of the other officers exchange glances and smother grins. Then Slapton asks me a few questions, most of which I can't answer, and gets me to sign his notes as well as a receipt for the goods taken.

'When do you think we might get them back?' I ask.

His bloodshot eyes narrow. 'You'll get them back when we've finished with them, son.'

As the door closes I hear a slow hand-clap behind me. I turn to see the ever horizontal Zac grinning and looking at Scarlett.

'Zac, just . . .' I tell him. But by this time Scarlett is grinning too and wiping away her tears.

'Thank you,' she says, bowing deep. 'Thank you, all.'

'And the Oscar for Best Actress Talking Bullshit goes to . . .' announces Zac.

'I'd like to thank my agent, my mother, Krishna, and all the producers I've ever slept with,' gushes Scarlett, clasping an imaginary Oscar to her breast.

We're all helpless with laughter for a few moments then I manage to say, 'You're unbelievable.'

'*Au contraire*,' says Zac. 'You're very plausible. Just not quite plausible enough, unfortunately.'

'Oh, well. Thank you, anyway. It helped slightly that I've got my clit ring caught in my knickers,' says Scarlett, wriggling around and pulling at her crotch.

We take it in turns to stay in the office and fend off the calls demanding payment while the others go out shopping or in Zac's case to play pinball. I try to ring Lauren but I just get her voicemail, and leave a message asking her to ring me. A magazine journalist rings up wanting to do a piece following up on our survey about the number of men spending more on clothes than their female partners, so I give her a quote, explaining that it is all part of broader, socio-economic developments in society and the changing self-image of men or some such bollocks.

When Scarlett comes back to do her shift and I'm unplugging my mobile from the charger, ready to go out, I tell her, 'Look, you don't have to keep coming in if you've got better things to do.'

She looks slightly embarrassed. 'Oh, well, I'll give you a hand for a while . . .'

'I know we're all getting paid but there's nothing else we can do.'

'No, but . . .' She pauses, looking down, and then says quickly, 'You're a good bloke, Charlie, I don't want to leave you in this shit on your own.' She looks up and smiles. 'Besides, you might need someone to protect you from those attackers.'

'Thanks, Scarlett. I appreciate it.' I give her a peck on the cheek and then go out.

Because we haven't got any computers I have to go to a café down the road to use the internet. I look in the online newspaper archives for something more about Sir James Huntsman. There is nothing particularly interesting other than various stories about his companies and a story in the *Daily Mail* about Anastasia getting chucked out of Roedean for possession of drugs.

Then I check for 'Nora Benthall'. Lots of her freelance writing comes up. But there is a piece in the *Observer* about her. Really it's about her father, a doctor who has worked with other doctors in Third World countries. 'Some of his friends have suggested that this extensive work abroad might be to escape personal and professional problems in the US,' it adds mysteriously. There is also a letter in *The Times* from him, berating the large drugs companies for not offering sufficient discounts to patients in the poorest countries.

I step back out onto the street, wondering what to do for the next few hours. The thought of shopping reminds me that even if my 2cool salary goes through this month, and that's looking increasingly unlikely, I'll need to earn something for the following month. I ring Karyn. Unfortunately, Brad from the women's division answers the phone instead of her.

'Jet Models. Can I help you?'

'Is Karyn there, please?' I ask.

'Sure, who may I say is calling?' he says, smoothly.

'It's, er, it's a personal call.'

'A personal call? One moment please.' I know he's recognised my voice but he can't prove it's me, can he? And anyway, I can't be bothered to talk to anyone else.

There are a few seconds of dance music and then, 'Karyn speaking.'

I realise how much I love her soft, clear voice.

'Hi, darling, it's me, Charlie.'

'Oh, hi.'

'You all right?'

'Yeah,' she says awkwardly.

'Can't talk?'

'No, that's right.'

'Sorry, shall I call back?'

'Er.'

'Or you could call me back a bit later? I'm on my mobile.'

'Yeah,' she says. 'Yeah, will do, babe.'

I end the call. I decide to sit at a café and ring Lauren again about the *Standard* piece.

'Charlie Barrett?'

I look up and am immediately blinded by a flash light. 'What?'

It happens again.

'Oh, fuck. Stop that! Who are you?'

'Just look over here, matey.'

A photographer is dancing around me, shooting from different angles before darting across the street and taking some pictures with a telephoto lens. I walk away confidently until I've turned the corner into the next street. Surely Nora hasn't put them up to this. It can't be her, can it? Not after our conversation this morning.

'Someone took pictures of you just now?' she says when I ring her.

'Yes, just as I was walking out of the building,' I say, adding sarcastically, 'You wouldn't happen to know anything about it, would you?'

'No, Charlie, I promise. I'm certainly not writing anything about 2cool at the moment. I'd tell you if I was. Let me ring the picture desk and see if they've sent someone.'

'Nora, if this *is* anything to do with you—'

'Oh, for God's sake, Charlie, believe me. Please! Let me find out and I'll come straight back to you.'

'Okay . . . thanks.'

A few moments later the phone rings again. 'Hi, Nora?' I say.

There is a pause.

'No, Charlie, it's not Nora.'

It's Lauren's voice.

'Hi, babe.'

'I saw the piece in the *Standard* today.'

'Oh, God, I know. Did you get my message? I'd have called you sooner but I didn't see it. Scarlett pointed it out and we've had a hell of a day. The police have been round again.'

'So what? What the hell's this piece about? When were you going to tell me that you and Nora are going out together?'

I laugh in disbelief and frustration. 'Don't be ridiculous, babe. It's completely wrong. Of course we're not going out. How could you think that?'

'Because I read it in the paper, like hundreds of other people we know probably have.'

'It's just bollocks; that was a troublemaking article that got it all wrong.'

'So your new girlfriend Nora isn't related to Piers then?'

'She *isn't* my new girlfriend! But, yeah, that other bit about Piers is right.'

'It's also right when it says that 2cool is going down the tubes, isn't it?'

'Yes, probably.'

'For God's sake, Charlie, just leave it will you? Walk away.'

'I know, you're right. Look, I'm waiting for a call from Karyn at Jet. I'm going to go back to modelling.'

'That's very sensible. I'm glad to hear it,' she says, like a mother talking to her son who's decided he will go back to college after all, this term. I always used to love Lauren's self-assurance, her absolute conviction, but at the moment it's just a bit annoying.

'First, though, I want to find Piers and Guy and find out what's going on,' I say.

'I don't believe it. Just forget it, will you?'

'I told you I *will* forget it – when I've found Piers and Guy and asked them some questions.'

'Well, I can't stop you,' she says quietly. 'But just stay away from that Nora woman, she's trouble.'

'Seeing Peter tonight are you?'

'No, as a matter of fact, I'm going out with Sarah, but my work with Peter is totally different to your, your *relationship* with Nora. He's helping my career, she's destroying yours.'

I think about it for a moment and then I hear the 'call waiting' bleep.

'I've got to go, I think that's Karyn from Jet.'

'I'll see you later.'

As I press the button to get through to the other call I wonder why Lauren and I cannot talk these days without rowing.

'Hi, it's me,' says Nora.

'Hi.'

'No one at the *Post* has sent a photographer, and I checked with the news desk *and* my editor, and no one is doing a piece about 2cool.'

'So it must be another paper.'

'Yep. I'll ask a mate of mine on *The Times* if they're doing anything.'

'Okay, thanks.'

'You all right, Charlie?'

I laugh bitterly. 'Oh, fine. My career's collapsing around me, my girlfriend has read in the paper that I'm seeing someone else, the police are visiting me almost every day and I've got no money.'

'See what you mean. Oh, well.'

'Oh well?'

'Sorry, I didn't mean it to come out like that. It's been a tough couple of weeks for you, hasn't it? Do you want to have a drink tonight and talk about it?'

This woman is trouble, like Lauren says – especially after the piece in the *Standard*. But on the other hand Lauren's out, and if she were in we'd only end up rowing. Nora, at least, knows what I'm going through at the moment.

We arrange to go to a place near hers at seven.

I sit at a café and order a cup of tea and a ham sandwich because I haven't had any lunch yet. In fact I haven't eaten much at all over the last few days. I've had no appetite recently, and Lauren normally decides what we eat even if it's not her turn to cook. Like I say, I've always loved Lauren's self-assurance and her no-nonsense approach, wherever you are, whatever you're doing, you just have to look at her and she'll know what to do next.

But now I'm doing something different, something she doesn't approve of, doesn't understand – and she obviously just can't stand it. Like one of those big, smart hotels that will offer you anything, as long as it's on the menu. If you ask for something a bit odd, there is no procedure in the customer care manual to handle it. I once wanted to go swimming in a hotel pool in France after we'd been shooting a catalogue all day and they just wouldn't let me. The pool and the surrounding area were empty. I'd be very quiet, I assured them, and I just wanted to do twenty lengths or so, but neither the smiley receptionist nor her smiley manager would let me. Guest. Swimming pool. After 8 p.m. Access Denied. Won't compute.

Perhaps that's the thing about Lauren. You can have anything you want as long as it's on her menu, within her sphere of competence. I think about Becky and her baby. I must have broached the subject three or four times but on every occasion I get this dismissive look as if I'm suggesting we get a pet snake or buy a holiday home in Bulgaria. It's not that mad, is it? I'm thirty, for fuck's sake. My dad already had two children at this age.

Perhaps there are some things that Lauren thinks are mad or inappropriate which, in fact, aren't. Perhaps, amazingly enough, she might not be right all the time.

Oh, God, I love her so much but I just need a bit of freedom to do my own thing after all these years. To do something that's not on the Lauren Tate list of officially approved activities. I realise how angry I am with her about 2cool. Okay, so she doesn't think much of it but she must see how important it is to me, how much I want to prove that I can at least do my best, clear my name and not just look like another model who tried to do something else and failed.

I think I deserve a little support here.

Karyn rings me back while she's out on a very late lunch break.

'Hi, Charlie, sorry about that. How's it going?'

'From bad to worse to disastrous. I was wondering, actually, if I could go back to modelling. Do you think Penny would take me back?'

Her reply takes me by surprise. 'I'm afraid not, Charlie. We were talking about you this morning. Penny saw the piece in the *Standard* and she called me in and said she doesn't want us to represent you again because of all the bad publicity.' I'm stunned. 'Charlie? Are you there?'

'Yeah, er, yes. You're kidding, though. I was one of her highest-earning models. I've made her a shedload of money over the years.'

'Oh, Charlie, of course you have, but you know what she's like.'

'The ungrateful bitch.'

'I'm sorry to have to tell you that but she's absolutely insistent.'

'Don't worry, it's not your fault.'

'To be honest she's forbidden me to talk to you. It's a good thing you didn't give your name to Brad. Sneaky little queen, he knew it was you when you called just now and I'm sure he's the one who's told her.'

'I don't want to get you into trouble, Karyn.'

'Don't worry about me, I'll be okay. Look, Charlie, Nevs or MOT or SoDamnTuff would take you in a second with your book, you know that.'

'But not with my business track-record and the bloody awful publicity I've had recently.'

'I'm sure they won't be bothered.'

'That's very sweet of you to say, I wish it was true. Look, I'll give you a call on your mobile in a few days or something.'

I set off back to the office. At one point a man with a TV camera walks alongside me. I decide to say nothing and carry on walking, trying to look relaxed and confident, although I feel like I'm going to throw up at any moment.

'Cheers mate,' says the cameraman nonchalantly, slipping the machine off his shoulder. In the office I suggest to the others that they go home. I tell them they should think about other jobs. Zac informs me that he's already talking to a web design agency and Scarlett says she's been asked to manage a new band that could end up being as big as someone I've never heard of.

I leave early with the phones ringing. We haven't got any money to give to these people so why bother even speaking to them? After half an hour mooching around at home, cursing Penny, I decide to go swimming at the health club where I'll soon have to give up my membership. The woman at reception gives me a lingering look and checks the name on my membership card. That's right, love, I'm the guy from the poncey internet fiasco. Ha, bloody, ha.

I spend quite a lot of time underwater, hearing my own breathing. Then I sit in the hot tub, which feels good on my stiff back and shoulders.

'Great thing about this is that you can fart all you want and no one else can tell,' says the other bloke in there with me. I smile politely and then get out quite quickly.

What inspires people to say these things?

*

Back at home I have a shave since I couldn't be bothered to this morning, and put on a black Thomas Pink shirt and faded blue jeans. Then I take that off and put on combats and my favourite B52s T-shirt. Then I change that for a long-sleeved, ribbed T-shirt and my faded blue jeans again.

I leave early, so that I don't see Lauren and have to tell her that I'm seeing Nora tonight. I arrive ten minutes early at where we've agreed to meet, cursing myself because I know Nora will be late. I pick up a paper; it's the *Standard.* A sense of horrid fascination forces me to look at the article about Nora and Piers. There it is. Who could fail to miss it? Half our friends must think that me and Lauren have split up – which we haven't, of course. Not technically, anyway.

Nora arrives almost on time. We've agreed to meet in a pub she knows. It's just an ordinary pub, nothing smart, glamorous or achingly hip. Nor is there any special treatment or free drinks courtesy of 2cool, and that's something of a relief. I'm glad to be able to go out for a drink without being an ambassador of cool. She's wearing a peasant blouse and she looks good in it; quite normal, I suppose, is what I'm thinking.

'Hi,' she says, reaching up and giving me a peck on the cheek.

'Hi, what would you like to drink? G and T is it?'

'Double please,' she says to the barman. 'Charlie, this is Cole. He's an art student.'

'I am *not,*' says Cole. 'I'm studying business finance.'

'That's very useful,' I tell him, with grim irony.

'But Cole's such a brilliant artist, he *should* be studying art,' says Nora.

'Nora, just because you'd like something to be true, doesn't mean that you can go round saying it is,' Cole explains, dropping ice into a glass and giving me a what-can-you-do? look. I know the feeling, mate. I order a bottle of beer and we go to a quiet corner table.

'Did you tell your girlfriend about the *Standard* piece?' she asks.

'Didn't have to – she saw it herself.'

'Ouch! Was she upset?'

'Just a bit.'

'Oh, dear. What does she do for a living?' asks Nora, taking a sip, quite a large one.

'She's a model,' I say. 'Too.'

'Beautiful couple.'

I laugh. Doesn't feel like that any more. 'She wants to get out of it and become a TV presenter. But you know that, don't you?'

'Do I?'

'You said so in that first piece.'

'Did I?' I'm trying to work out if she's really this forgetful or if she's just putting it on. Under the unruly dark red hair and through the black-framed specs, her eyes give nothing away. Instead she thinks for a moment and then groans, 'Oh, TV presenter. Doesn't *everyone* want to be one these days? I was thinking that today when I was having lunch. Everywhere you go now, people – waiters and waitresses, shop staff, bar staff, people on the street – everyone acts like they're, well, acting, waiting to be discovered. I was having lunch with an old college friend who's a TV producer and our waitress must have known what he did for a living – she was practically doing audition pieces between the courses. Anecdotes, funny observations, chatty little asides as she took our order. If someone had had a cigarette lighter she'd have been performing in the light from it.'

I smile. 'I know what you mean. I think Lauren will probably do it if she wants to. She's very determined.'

'Oh, I'm sure she'd be very good. I hope she makes it,' says Nora, quickly.

'She probably will.'

'I never watch TV myself. It just bugs the hell out of me.'

'Quite relaxing sometimes, though.'

'No, see, I don't think so. I hate it when you go to someone's house or apartment and the whole room is focused on the TV. Even when it's switched off, you sense this brooding presence, almost like you should be trying to pay it homage or at least bring it into the conversation. You know what I mean?'

'Blimey, you do hate them.' I suddenly feel I'm squaring up for a debate here. I wonder whether to take the opposing view just for the hell of it. 'Television can educate and inform. I've learnt lots of things from it.' Please don't ask me what, though.

'You couldn't have got it from a book?'

'Probably, but you can see moving images.'

'From your position lying on the settee.'

'And I should be reading some improving work, sitting on a hard chair, is that it?'

She ignores this comment. 'In fact, I think the size of a telly has a direct bearing on the owner's intellect.'

'Mine's fourteen inches,' I say. 'My telly, that is.' I'm not sure which is more embarrassing: the *Carry On*-style double entendre or the claim to some sort of superior intellect.

Nora is just staring at me with interest. I wish she'd laugh or something. Instead she says, 'Like this guy I dated in New York when I was at journalism school. He was a Wall Street trader, went to Stanford on a football scholarship or something.'

'A bit thick?' I ask. I'm keen to move on from my fourteen-incher comment.

'Could have rented his head out for storage space.'

I laugh.

'He caught me reading a book once, when we were staying with his folks in the Hamptons. You'd have thought I was doing drugs or picking my nose and flicking it at his family portraits. Finally told me, "I'm going to read when I'm too old to play sport." Can you believe it? I said, "Don't you mean you're going to stop playing sport when you're old enough to read?"'

'Very good.'

'That was that.' She drifts off for a moment.

'You're quite angry, aren't you?' I tell her.

'Sorry, am I moaning?'

'No, I didn't say that, I just said "you're quite angry".'

'I suppose so.'

'Anger's a good thing, isn't it?' It dawns on me. 'I mean anger, if it's directed properly, can be quite invigorating, energising, empowering?' Why am I thinking of Lauren and 2cool when I say this? 'Can't it?'

'Yeah, yeah it can. A lot of people do what they do, create things, change things, improve things, because of anger.'

She looks away and I watch her, wondering what she's thinking now. She tries to catch the eye of Cole at the bar.

'I'll get them,' I say, taking her empty glass.

'You've got to be quite angry to write,' she says when I come back. 'Even fluff like I knock out.'

'What do you mean? Just to stir it up?'

'Yes, I suppose so.' She takes a drink and looks around the pub. 'So you've had the police in.'

'How did you know that?' I ask defensively.

'You told me,' she says.

'Did I?' Shit, I've forgotten what I've told to whom. 'Yes, they've been in twice. They've taken away all the financial stuff we've got.'

'The Missing Persons Unit took all that?'

'It wasn't the Missing Persons Unit, it was the Fraud Squad.'

'Shit! That's serious.'

'I wish I hadn't told you that.'

'Why?'

'Why do you think? Because I don't want it in the paper.'

'Charlie. You still don't trust me?'

I can't believe she's just asked me that. My silence is more damning than any words could be.

She looks surprised, hurt. 'I promise I won't mention it. From now on I won't write about 2cool without talking to you.'

'I'd be very grateful,' I say, underwhelmed by her offer. I look at my watch: it's gone nine. 'Do you want to get something to eat?'

'Yes, I'd love to. I mean, that would be nice.'

'Where do you fancy?'

She thinks about it. 'Somewhere with pictures of the food on the wall outside.'

'Mmm, yummy, slightly faded ones.'

'Exactly, or better still a plastic model of them.'

'Deeelicious – and probably slightly dusty.'

'The waiters have name badges.'

'Printed with those dymo tape machines.'

'And where they say "Enjoy your meal".'

'And do their audition pieces between each course, just in case you're someone who can get them on telly.'

She laughs, but I'm wondering how far Lauren *is* prepared to go.

chapter twenty-one

After dinner in a little Italian place round the corner (one bowl of salad knocked onto the floor during an animated description of the behaviour of Mariah Carey's entourage during an interview, followed by a glass of wine while attracting the waiter's attention about the salad) I decide to walk her back to hers before I get a taxi home.

'Well, night then,' she says, looking up at me. We haven't done the key thing yet. We're standing so close that I can smell the alcohol on her breath, and then somehow I find myself kissing her. Her mouth is soft and she lets my tongue find hers.

I pull away – but not to leave – and she takes her key straight out of her bag without any difficulty and opens the door. Silently, I find myself following her in. We go into her living room where she switches on a lamp, before turning to me and kissing me again. I know I should leave now. Every second that this goes on will make it harder to say 'goodnight', turn my back on her, and walk out.

Her flat is crammed with ornaments and books. Three huge bookshelves dominate it. Well-used paperbacks, their edges scuffed and worn, are packed in any old how. I turn my head to read some of the titles: *The Beauty Myth* by Naomi Wolf, *Fast Food Nation* by Eric Schlosser, and *No Logo* by Naomi Klein are rammed in alongside *Pride and Prejudice, The Catcher in the Rye, Little Dorrit* and *Animal Farm* and even the Koran. I suppose quite a few people I know could claim to have the same titles on their shelves, but these books are so obviously well used. Read, re-read and consulted.

Having turned on one table lamp and switched the main light off, she walks up to me and stands expectantly in front of me. I look at her and smile. What would Lauren say if she could see this? Stupid question. But I'm wondering. Would she dump me immediately? Or would she be hurt and angry and want to know why I was doing this? Why am I doing it? I've never been unfaithful to her in our entire relationship, so why am I doing it now?

Because everything's different now. 2cool is unsafe, unpredictable and just a bit frightening. Modelling is safe, familiar, attractive. It's also sensible and well thought of – even my parents were won round to it in the end.

Lauren is modelling. Nora is 2cool. That's why I want Nora now. Like that moment at a teenage party when someone first hands you a cigarette and you know you shouldn't because it's dangerous and naughty and stupid and your mum and dad could so easily find out, but something makes you do it. Is it the environment, the mood you're in or just an angry, rebellious desire to hurt and disappoint the people who love you and think they know what's best for you?

I could argue that Lauren is pushing me into this but I don't believe that. Perhaps I'll feel better when I've done it. I'll realise how much I love Lauren, how I don't need or even want anyone else, and then I'll go back to her and all will be well.

When Nora reaches up to me I kiss her, but I'm much taller than her and it feels awkward so she giggles, embarrassed and then leads me to the settee where we sit down and continue to kiss, our hands exploring each other's bodies. I almost pull away a couple of times but something – that self-destructive, first-cigarette moment, perhaps – makes me want to carry on just a little bit longer.

I also want to get close to this girl, so close that I can see inside her, find out what makes her tick, see what else she hasn't told me. I run my forefinger over her smooth, clear, pale skin. Her eyes are wide, expectant, intrigued, drinking me in.

As she takes off her top, I realise I've been wondering for some time what her body would be like. She looks at me, nervously, very un-Nora. She has full, milky white breasts and dark pink nipples. Her stomach is rounded, so unlike Lauren's taught, tanned belly. For years now I've been sleeping with one of the most beautiful bodies any man could ever wish to see: that swan neck, those long legs with their lean thighs and gently rounded calves that have earned their owner a fortune. Those perfect, pert breasts that every woman who sees them under crisp, white shirts or soft, relaxed T-shirts in an advert would kill for – and most men too. Here I am with Nora, remembering what it is like to touch a real body, not a masterpiece of nature which has been carefully honed to perfection for commercial purposes.

I take her breasts in my hands and kiss one, then the other, running my tongue over her nipples, closing my eyes to give myself up to the experience but also to try to close off my mind from thinking about Lauren and how she would feel if she could see this scene taking place. Nora gasps and begins to run her hands through my hair, leaning down to nestle her face in it. I raise my head and kiss her again. She undoes my fly, massaging my erection. After a while I lift her away from me and stand up. She looks surprised, anxious. But when she sees me slipping off my T-shirt and jeans, socks and trainers, she takes her remaining clothes off too. We stand opposite each other. I'm so much taller than her that my dick is poking into her stomach. I lean down to kiss her again but she kneels and begins to suck my dick, working it gently with her hand.

Then she gets up and leaves the room, muttering, 'I'll be right back.'

If, *if* I was going to do the sensible thing, this would be the time to do it. Embarrassing, yes, ungentlemanly too, but she'd understand and I'd go home with only a mildly guilty conscience and we'd talk the next day. But instead I stand there, gently playing with my dick. I catch sight of my flushed face in the mirror and turn away quickly. Nora is back with a condom.

'I suppose we should . . . er . . .'

Silently I take it from her, tear it open and slide it on. I'd almost forgotten how to use one of these things. I realise that with the height difference she'll have to sit on me, so I lie on the settee, chucking some superfluous cushions on the floor, and she carefully straddles me, groaning and biting her lip as she slides down on me. I reach up and take her breasts in my hands. She gasps some more and then, after a while, reaches down to kiss me.

She comes pretty quickly and so do I. Then she kisses me again, bumping into my nose and smiling with embarrassment before she gets off me and goes into the bathroom. I pull the condom off and hold it carefully to make sure it doesn't leak. I'd forgotten how disgusting these things are. Not sure of what to do next, I wait there, holding the slithery manifestation of my wrongdoing in my hand until she comes back. Wearing a T-shirt and knickers, she smiles uncertainly at me and then sees the condom.

'Oh, right. Bathroom's just through there to the left.'

It smells damp and slightly mildewy. There is a scummy ring around the bath and sink, and some of the wallpaper is peeling off at the top of the walls. Next to the loo is a huge pile of glossy magazines, crinkly with condensation. I pull off some loo roll, wrap the condom in it and flush it away. The bastard floats to the surface again so I wait for the cistern to refill, chucking more paper down so that at least I don't have to see it. I shiver slightly, standing there naked in someone else's flat.

Looking around me I realise that this is perhaps my only chance to see the real Nora. The toiletries themselves come from Boots and Sainsbury's – none of Lauren's fantastically expensive French pseudo-scientific stuff in white bottles, but everything else in the room has a girlish prettiness about it. It is packed with things like frames with shells stuck on them; on the walls and around the mirror are starfish and scallop shells. The shelves are filled with little ivory carvings, blue Islamic bowls, a mother-of-pearl box and other little toys and knick-knacks.

Behind me is a huge collage with photos of people taken at parties, in a jungle, outside a gothic school building (from her time at Vasser?) and what looks like a Middle Eastern city somewhere. Nora with girls and boys – one square-jawed guy with his arm round her photographed on a skiing trip, which might be her empty-headed, football scholar ex, I guess. There are older people who must be parents and relatives, even teachers and college professors.

I flush the loo again and, finally, my waterlogged tormentor disappears from view.

In the other room, I kiss her on the lips once, less out of lust or even affection than because I can't think what else to do. I start to get dressed in silence as she watches.

'You can stay if . . .'

'Um, well, I'd love to but, well you know, I'd better . . . I'm sorry about this.'

'Oh, of course, yes. Do you want me to call you a cab?'

'No,' I say, too quickly. 'I'll pick one up in the street.'

'Right, sure. It shouldn't be too difficult. There's usually quite a few around this time of night in Ladbroke Grove.'

'I'll speak to you tomorrow,' I say, tiredness, confusion and an all-embracing feeling of guilt and seediness preventing me from saying anything more romantic or meaningful. The sex should have brought us closer but somehow, afterwards, we seem to have nothing but small talk – a trivial conversation about transport. We share a final, awkward kiss and then I smile at her and leave.

Like I said, I've never had an affair in the seven years I've been going out with Lauren. Not once. But then again, in my case, the old joke about not bothering to go out for hamburgers when you've got steak at home really does apply. Which makes what I've done all the more inexplicable – and weird.

When I get home Lauren is just turning off the lights to go to bed. She's opened all the windows and put the fan on to get rid of the smell of Sarah's smoke.

'Hello,' I say in a quiet voice, putting my head round the living room door.

'Hiya,' she says without looking up. 'Where have you been tonight?'

Luckily she doesn't make a move to kiss me hello.

'Just out for a drink with . . . with the people from the office,' I tell her in a daze. If she'd asked any more questions I'd have been stumped, unable to invent any more innocent but fictional details of my night out.

Instead she just nods her head slightly in acknowledgement. One thing about Lauren, she hardly ever sulks, she just comes out and says it, but this time she can't be bothered: she's just so obviously deeply pissed off with me – and us.

'I'm just going to have a—' I'm about to say 'shower' but it sounds too suspicious somehow as I usually shower in the morning, so I say 'bath' instead.

'What? Now?' says Lauren, looking at her watch.

'Yeah, I'm just so knackered, I need to unwind a bit.'

She nods again and walks through into the kitchen with the glasses.

I have a quick bath, washing my dick well. If only my conscience was as easy to clean. When I was a kid we'd eat peppermints after we'd smoked at parties. Years later my dad said he knew exactly what we'd been doing and he'd actually have preferred the smell of Silk Cut to the pong of all those Extra Strong mints.

I get dry, brush my teeth, sloosh round two shots of mouthwash and slip into bed, lying very still at the edge. Listening to Lauren breathe and trying not to breathe loudly myself, I try to get to sleep.

So, this is what adultery is like.

I pour semi-skimmed milk on my Rice Krispies, but instead of putting the empty carton back in the fridge as I normally do (oh, the bin's right over at the other end of the kitchen) I find myself carrying it across the room and carefully putting it in with the rest of the rubbish like a good boy.

Lauren calls me from the bedroom. I freeze for a moment but she shouts again. 'Come and look at this. Quickly!'

I go into the bedroom where she is watching telly in bed. My eyes sweep over the floor and the bed in case she's somehow found some proof of my unfaithfulness, but she gestures towards the telly. Sir Josh Langdon, the ancient and debauched rock star normally known for doing royal command performances and marrying teenagers, is being interviewed.

'Yeah, of course, I'm really BLEEP, BLEEP, off with the whole thing. I've lost a lot of money, yeah?' he says, stopping for a moment between the front door of his Chelsea home and a large black Merc, two men in sunglasses shuffling around uneasily behind him. 'I suppose there's no fool like an old fool and it sounded kind of young and funky and cool so I put in a few hundred thou. But now of course, I'll never see a BLEEP penny of that, will I?'

He gets into the car but before one of the heavies can close the door, the interviewer asks. 'Will you sue?'

Langdon looks up from his seat. 'Well, let's just say I'm thinking about suing 'em. I've got better things to do with my time,' he snarls and pulls the door shut.

Then there are shots of Sir James Huntsman, as the reporter explains that many big names from the City have also invested and have had their fingers burned. The next shot is of me, leaving our office and walking down the road. Once I've got over the shock of seeing myself I begin to take in what is being said.

'Although the police are still looking for the two men who arranged financing for the site, attention has been focused over the past few days on Charlie Barrett, seen here. A former male model, Barrett has been very much the public face of 2cool and is also being investigated by the police. We asked for an interview with him or any other spokesman from the company but there was no response from the 2cool offices.'

There is a shot of a computer terminal with our home page on it. The camera pulls back to reveal a female reporter in a bright green suit and shoulder-length blonde hair sitting on the desk next to the terminal.

'Whether Sir Josh Langdon sees any of his money again depends very much on the eventual outcome of the police investigations,' she says, giving us a frowning, head-tilting look of genuine concern, 'but one thing seems certain: what promised to be the coolest site on the web has suddenly become too hot to handle. Juliet Hargreaves, BBC News, Central London.'

I sit down heavily on the bed. 'Oh, fuck.'

As soon as I come up out of the tube station at Piccadilly Circus my mobile rings.

'Hi, it's me,' says Nora.

'Hiya,' I say gently, wishing I was somewhere that I could talk more easily.

'How are you?'

'All right, you?'

'Yeah, okay. I'm sorry you couldn't stay last night.'

'Yeah, so am I.'

'I'm so glad you came back, though, and we made love.' She sounds like she has rehearsed the comment.

'So am I,' I say. But I'm not, absolutely not. If you start to deceive your partner, you soon have to start deceiving the other woman too, I suppose. And yourself for that matter.

'Perhaps I'll see you tonight or tomorrow then.'

'Sure, I'll give you a ring later.'

'Bye.' I'm just thinking that at least I didn't mention love, when the phone rings again. 'Hello?'

'Charlie, it's me.' For a moment I hardly recognise the voice.

'Lauren?'

'The police are here.' Her voice is cracking; she is almost in tears.

'What?'

She swallows hard. 'The police are here. They've got a warrant and they're searching the flat, our flat.'

'Oh, fuck.'

'Could you please come home and deal with this?'

'I'm coming, I'm coming. Let me find a cab. I'll be right there.'

I find one coming down Regent Street and leap in, ringing Scarlett to tell her what has happened. She's had more calls from journalists already but promises to handle things till I get back. Almost as an afterthought she gives me some other news that is either terminally bad or quite a relief – I can't decide which.

The traffic is mercifully light at the end of the rush hour and I'm home in twenty-five agonising minutes.

Lauren is waiting in the hallway, arms folded, eyes red, motionless. She is wearing a cream V-necked pullover and jeans. Her hair is up. She looks gorgeous even in distress and I feel worse than ever – for putting her through this, for Nora, for everything. I put my arms round her and say, 'Are you all right?'

'Yeah, okay. They're in the bedroom.' She doesn't move, unresponsive to my embrace. I go into the bedroom and a young policeman who has been searching under the bed looks up at me, enquiringly. I'm enraged. This *my* bedroom.

'Oh, hello, *sir*,' says Slapton, who is wandering about, ostensibly supervising but also just poking around our personal things, I can tell. 'We won't be long.'

'Why the fuck couldn't you do it while I was here?'

He looks at me impassively. 'You'd left for work.'

'You could have called me.'

'Not our practice to call every time, sir. For obvious reasons. But we've got the necessary paperwork and we showed it to your girlfriend.'

'What are you taking?'

'A few papers and things. We're going to have to take your computer away with us, I'm afraid,' he says, nodding towards it.

'What else?'

'We'll know when we see it,' he says, his rubber-gloved hand poking at some of Lauren's neatly folded clothes which are sitting on the bed. 'You'll get a receipt.'

'You bastard,' I tell him. 'You're enjoying this.'

He half-laughs then steps up to me and his smile tells me that I've guessed right.

'Oh, don't try and get tough with me, pretty boy. It's pathetic to watch. You just stick to flogging your Prada handbags and your trendy champagne glasses. Leave the tough-guy stuff alone, it doesn't suit you.'

I sense some of the policemen sniggering.

After about half an hour, during which time they've even been in the bathroom, they leave and I go into the kitchen to find Lauren.

'Have they gone?' she asks without looking at me.

'Yes.'

She bites her lip.

'Can I make you a cup of coffee?'

'No.'

I wait for her to say something.

'I'm sorry about that.'

'I've never felt so dirty in my life. The *police* searching *my* flat.'

'I know.'

'How is this happening to us? I don't understand.' Her lip trembles. 'I was in the shower when they knocked on the door. I was terrified.'

'I'm so sorry, babe.' I put my arms around her but she is still unresponsive.

'When are you finally going to let it go?'

'The truth is, I have let it go. There's nothing left to hang on to. We had to give up our computers so we can't put in any more content. Worse still . . . when I rang Scarlett from the cab on the way over here she told me that the company that runs the site on the net has cut us off. There is no such site any more. That's it. Finito.'

'Really?'

'Yup. RIP 2cool.' I repeat the phrase over to myself to see what effect it has on me. I suppose it hasn't quite sunk in. Or else I just don't care any more.

'Good,' says Lauren. She takes a deep breath. Her face and shoulders seem to relax. 'Good. That's that then.' I can see her pulling herself together. There's not much that fazes Lauren, so she finds not being in control of any situation even more frightening than most people would. 'You've got a receipt for what they've taken, haven't you? If I've lost any work or anything because I can't get on to the computer I shall expect them to pay.'

I laugh. 'So they bloody well should.'

'It's not funny. Anyway, I think you're right going back to modelling. At least it's safe and you know how it works,' she says, picking up a cloth and wiping down the already immaculate work surface.

'Yes. The only problem is that when I spoke to Karyn at Jet yesterday she said Penny won't take me on again because of the adverse publicity.'

'That's her loss then. You'd have no problem with any other agency, not with your reputation and your book.'

'I was sort of hoping to move on from modelling though, and do something else.' I walk across the room towards her to try and catch her eye as she finishes wiping and puts some glasses in the dishwasher.

'Oh, I wouldn't rule it out. I suppose the point is that this has been a pretty horrible experience for us both, but at least you've learned something which could be useful for any other projects. Now, I think I *will* have some coffee. Do you want some?'

'Er, no thanks, I'd better get back to the office.'

She turns to look at me. 'Which office?'

'Well, 2cool – as was.'

'You're not going back there?'

'I've got to. I told Scarlett I would.'

She puts the jug of the coffee maker down again. 'What have we just been saying?'

'That I'll go back to modelling. But I can't just leave Scarlett and Zac on their own there, can I?'

'Why the hell not? You don't owe them anything.'

'I can't just desert them. I'm going to go in, we'll get our stuff, hand the key back to the landlord and wait till the police contact us about Guy and Piers and that's that. Look, the point is I'm a director, babe, I've signed cheques, I've sat on board meetings, well, I should have.' I don't feel protected any more by lack of control, lack of connection. I just feel like an idiot.

'Well, get yourself a good lawyer and let him take care of it all.' She picks up the phone.

'Who are you calling?'

'Mark. He'll know someone who can help you.'

I can imagine the conversation with Mark, who does complicated, important things in the City and has his own secretary: 'Charlie's got himself into a mess by trying to do something other than modelling, can you help dig him out of it, please?' So gently but firmly I take the portable phone out of her hand.

'No, *I'll* get a solicitor if I need one. Don't ask Mark.'

Lauren takes a deep breath and turns her back on me. 'I don't believe this. Charlie, don't go back there. Hasn't it occurred to you that all of them – Scarlett and Zac as well as Guy and Piers – have been stringing you along? They've *all* been conning you. Why should you help them? Get out now and save yourself.'

'I will save myself and I'll do it on my own.' I remember Scarlett's kind words about being there in case I needed protection, and the kiss on the cheek she gave me. 'I won't be late,' I say, turning to leave.

There is another piece about us in the *Mirror*, I notice at the news stand by the tube station. More puns about 2cool getting too hot to handle and people having their fingers burnt. There's a picture of me walking down the street – it must have been that photographer yesterday – and some older photos of Piers looking a prat in a dinner suit alongside some other men who have bottles of champagne in their hands.

A girl opposite me in the carriage who is reading the story looks up as she turns the page, sees me and does such an unsubtle double-take that I can't help laughing.

We spend the day finishing up our list of creditors with contact details, amounts owed and invoice dates. Although none of us says it, we all know it is probably pretty pointless. We tidy up the office and file whatever bits of paper the police didn't take away with them. We're doing something just to keep busy and also so that, in my case anyway, we can at least tell people like the small print shop round the corner which is owed £420 for photocopying and brochures, that we, the ones who are left that is, did our best to get them their money.

Zac unplugs some of his remaining equipment, including a laptop he has brought in so that he can at least play computer games and email his mates, and begins to pack it up. How much is his and how much he's just helping himself to I don't know, but he's welcome to it. He's worked hard. At one point when I'm looking for some stamps in her desk I notice that Scarlett is writing out a list of names.

'What's that?'

'Oh, it's just some record pluggers for this new band I'm managing.'

'Good,' I tell her. 'Good idea.'

I don't even mind Zac watching telly in the corner later in the day. It's some quiz show. I can tell this because every few seconds we hear: 'Elizabeth the first, you dickhead', or 'Newfoundland, you shit-for-brains', or 'Sodium chloride, fuckwit', or '164, ass wipe'.

chapter twenty-two

I get home just after five. The first thing I hear as I open the front door is Peter Beaumont-Crowther's voice. When I look into the living room he and Lauren are sitting very close to each other on the settee.

He gets up quickly and says, 'Oh, hi Charlie.'

I don't say anything. Lauren still has her back to me. I go into the bedroom and kick off my shoes. I wait for her to come in but she doesn't, so I go out and make a cup of tea and take it back to the bedroom. I switch on the TV and watch some woman saying, 'But when they got to the hotel, Jane and Michelle were in for a nasty shock . . .'

When I look up, Lauren is standing in the doorway.

'What's *he* doing here?' I ask.

'Shh!' she says, looking across to the living room. 'He'll hear you.'

'I don't care,' I laugh angrily. 'It's my flat.'

She pulls the door closed slowly. 'Peter came over because I asked him to.'

'How kind of him.'

'Charlie, I'm so worried about you. Peter saw that piece on the news today and lots of other people have called about it, including your mother. She's worried sick.' There is a pause. 'I can't bear to see you hurt like this.'

Oh, God, my mum, I must ring her. I turn back to the telly and switch over to watch a plump teenage girl in a boob tube singing 'Angels' by Robbie Williams in a strained, flat voice. Then I say, 'Perhaps I'll be okay.'

'What?'

'Perhaps I'll be okay, perhaps I'll get through this, handle it myself.

I might get bruised in the process.' I feel my chest where my biker assailant hit me but it doesn't seem to hurt at all any more. 'But I'll get through it.'

'What do you mean?'

I switch off the telly, throw the remote control down on the bed and walk over to the window. A man is taking a young boy for a ride on a bike. The kid wears a helmet and protective gloves as well as ankle, knee and elbow pads. When I was young we just got on and fell off.

'I've had the kind of career, the kind of lifestyle that most people can only dream of.'

'Yes, and think yourself lucky,' she says as if talking to a spoilt child – which she is probably is.

'I fell into modelling after college, unlike my mate Paul who wanted it so much, poor bugger. I get paid for doing what most people would consider a pleasure, things most people would probably *pay* to do. I've always had work. I'm not short of money. I've got a lovely flat, a beautiful girlfriend,' I say, looking at her. 'The only slight hiccup has been my parents' divorce, and really my sister dealt with most of that.'

'Exactly, so why throw it all up in the air?'

'Because it's all been *too* easy. Don't you see? I want to do something that will challenge me a bit, something different, a bit dangerous—'

'I don't believe I'm hearing this,' says Lauren, staring at the ceiling and shaking her head. 'You want to do something dangerous.'

'I want a challenge,' I bark back at her. 'I've *got* a challenge and I'm enjoying . . . what's the word? Meeting it. I can't remember when I last felt an adrenalin rush.' Lauren looks on, horrified. 'I, I want to be tested. I want people to say "God, Charlie really went through the ringer. Had all that shit thrown at him and he came through it. I never knew he had it in him".'

'Your career in modelling is nothing to be embarrassed about.' She's standing right next to me at the window. 'You certainly shouldn't feel ashamed of yourself.'

I have to look away from her. Ashamed? But I have got something to be ashamed of. I've cheated on her, had sex with someone else. I go back to what I'm more comfortable with.

'Don't you understand? I'm just fed up with being considered a lucky bugger, someone who's lived a charmed existence.'

'Oh, Charlie,' says Lauren, shaking her head and getting up. I can tell it's not a question of her not understanding me, it's just that she doesn't want to hear it. 'Look, we both think you should get out of this. Peter says he might be able to get you something in marketing or PR with a friend of his who runs a TV company. They make that cookery programme with Tania Bryer—'

I'm lost for words so I put my shoes on again and leave.

Walking back along the street I wonder where I'm going. My mum's? I will ring her, yeah, of course, but I can't bear to land on her doorstep and bring all this trouble with me. I'll go and see her properly when it's all sorted and she won't be nagging and worrying. I can't face trying to explain the situation to a friend, and now Sarah seems more Lauren's friend than mine so I decide to ring Nora. She's working on a big piece for tomorrow so she won't be around until about eight but we arrange to meet at hers then.

I buzz on her door at quarter past eight and she lets me in. The flat smells of scented candles or joss sticks and it's noticeably tidier than it was last night. She looks like she's just got back and tidied up. She gives me the kind of wicked, quizzical grin that annoyed me so much when we first met.

I'm doing this to hurt Lauren. Punishment for her unquestioning assumption that she – she and Peter, even worse – knows what's best for me. Proof as well that I can do dangerous things like have sex with wicked, untrustworthy women and get away with it.

We go straight through to the living room and onto the settee. She giggles. Then she stares at me with her wide eyes, any trace of that mocking, knowing smile disappeared. We tear at each other's clothes and make love. Then we lie back and cool off.

'Would you like a drink?'

'Yes, thanks.'

We both laugh at her polite hospitality following on so soon from our animal lust. She goes into the kitchen, her hand passing aimlessly over her buttock, slightly self-conscious about her naked body. A moment later she comes back with a bottle of champagne and two glasses.

'Wow,' I say, taking it from her and unwrapping the foil. 'What's this in aid of?'

'Nothing, just felt like it.'

The cork pops and she puts the glasses underneath it to catch the froth but there is nothing, just a plume of condensation.

'Twist the bottle, not the cork and do it very slowly,' I inform her, one eyebrow raised knowingly.

'Gosh, how clever,' she says sarcastically.

'Learnt that from a wine waiter on a modelling job for a hotel,' I explain, pouring the champagne. 'I suppose I have learnt something in eight years.'

She raises her glass. 'Here's to 2cool.'

'May it rest in peace.'

'What do you mean?'

'It's no longer on the net. If you go to that address you get a notice explaining that the site has closed, but thanks for visiting.'

'You're kidding?'

'Nope. 2cool is defunct, deceased and . . . I don't know . . . something else beginning with "de".'

'Shit,' says Nora. She looks really upset.

'Oh, never mind, it was fun while it lasted and at least it's helping to bring the whole thing to an end. A conclusion.'

'Why don't we have a bath?' she says suddenly. 'I've got some lovely new bath oil. Hot bath, cold champagne. Very Jackie Collins.'

'Okay. Sounds good.' I'm not sure it does, though: Lauren and I used to have baths together a lot during the early years. Those condescending 'Peter and I' comments have been ringing in my ears all evening. Who the hell do they think they are? My fucking parents? Perhaps that's why the sex with Nora is so much better, so much wilder this time around. Revenge sex – there's nothing like it.

'You run it. I'm just going to make a phone call,' she says, checking her watch and dashing out into the kitchen.

We order in some takeaway Chinese to go with our champagne and eat it in front of a video of *Some Like It Hot* because, as Nora reminds me, she can't stand watching TV.

When it gets to the moment where Marilyn Monroe, as Sugar, knocks on the door to borrow the bourbon from Jack Lemmon and

Tony Curtis because she's been dumped by her 'millionaire' and she says, 'Hi, it's me, Sugar,' Nora grabs the remote and pauses it.

'That took eighty-three takes.'

'What? That one line?'

'Yep, she was so off her head, so worked up, in such a state that she needed eighty-three takes before she got it right. Kept saying "Sugar, it's me" and things. Can you imagine being like that?'

I try and think about it. 'Almost,' I tell her.

'Oh, poor baby,' she says, resting her head on my shoulder and then turning to kiss me.

Towards eleven I'm beginning to have this feeling of dread. Nora will ask again if I'll stay the night and I'll have to decide. It's late and I'm so tired but it would really escalate tensions between me and Lauren. Not coming home is more than just provocative, it's insulting. I can't do that to her.

Just as I'm thinking this, the film ends. An exasperated Jack Lemmon is trying to explain to his millionaire why it might be difficult for them to get married. Finally, despondently pulling off his wig, he admits, 'I'm a man.'

'Well, nobody's perfect,' says his rich suitor.

'That was one of Billy Wilder's favourite lines. It's not actually a gag as such, is it? But he knew that it would work, because it's so bland,' says Nora looking at the credits. 'When they first showed the film to a test audience somewhere in the midwest it just bombed. They sat and stared at it in total silence, apparently, and there was panic at the studio, but Wilder was still confident – he knew he'd made a great movie. So then they brought in a bunch of college students to see it and apparently you couldn't hear half the lines for the sound of their laughter.'

I watch the light of the telly flickering over her face with its wide forehead and large, expressive eyes. How many times has she seen this film before? How did she get this doctorate in it? I wonder if she's rather lonely in London. Not that being American singles you out but being very bright and rather eccentric does. I know she's had boyfriends but she seems almost new to this kind of simple, domestic intimacy, almost excited by the novelty of it. There is something about her that makes me wonder how difficult it might be to get really close to her.

I can't stay, though, Nora. I'd love to curl up with you and watch you fall asleep next to me but I can't. What I've done to Lauren this evening is bad enough but to stay the night would be too much, too cruel. To both of you. I'll have to go home and either try and make up or continue the sulk, neither of which I'm looking forward to.

'Listen, it's late, I've got to go.'

'Stay.'

I bend down and kiss her shoulder sadly. 'I'm sorry, I've really got to . . .'

'Of course,' she says, getting up. 'I'll ring you a cab.'

'No, don't worry. I'll get one outside.' But instead of sounding considerate it sounds like I'm keen to get away as soon as possible – and that's probably it.

Lauren is out when I get back at eleven-thirty. Where the hell is she? Out committing adultery like me? I suppose she and Peter couldn't risk doing it here. They can't be doing it. How could she? What could she see in him? A TV presenter's contract, probably.

I brush my teeth and get into bed. Right at the edge again. As I wait I suddenly realise that I smell of Nora's bath oil. Girlie bath oil. Oh, shit. I swing myself out of bed and get into the shower and soap myself all over, standing under the running water for a while. Then I get out and dry myself. I sniff around my arms and bend down to sniff my stomach. I even sniff my knees and feet just in case, nearly falling over in the process. This is ridiculous. I can't decide if I can actually still smell it or whether I just remember the smell. I have another shower and use some of Lauren's expensive exfoliating lotion.

I go back to the bedroom and sniff the sheets. They definitely smell of it. Oh, fuck. Where does Lauren keep the clean linen? I find some in the drawer under the bed and change the bottom sheet which is the worst offender, but baulk at replacing the duvet cover which would be too obvious. And too difficult at this time of night. I want to get these little details of deceit over with as quickly as possible.

I don't hear Lauren come into the flat. When she gets into bed I instinctively make to put my arm round her but stop myself at the last minute. In the pale light of the street lamps outside I can see her face looking straight up at the ceiling, eyes wide open.

*

There is no other reason for going to the office than to get away from her. That is why I'm there before nine. Scarlett and Zac won't be in for hours, if at all. I think they're only coming in to use the phones and free internet connection and to help themselves to any stray 2cool goodies. I don't blame them. Every day there is less and less that needs to be done but more and more I can find to do just to kill time. The most vital, pressing thing that needs to be done – finding Piers and Guy – looks less likely than ever. I've rung the solicitor my dad put me in touch with and he has contacted the police, who just explained that they're continuing their investigations. When they've got something to say (does that mean charging me with something?) they'll contact him and he'll advise me on what to do next.

This morning's pointless activity involves collecting together the press cuttings ready to make copies of them so, as Lauren suggests, if I ever get the offer of another job I can show the positive publicity I've achieved for the site, before it all collapsed. I quite enjoy reading through some of the stories we've generated. Looking back, it is obvious that it really was, well, pretty cool. But perhaps *2*cool. Did Piers and Guy appreciate the irony? Are they laughing about it together somewhere now?

I suddenly feel a wave of anger. How could they dump me in it? If only I'd smiled and said 'No thanks', when we started discussing it at that modelling job.

I make a list of the model agencies I could approach. There are three that I think I'd be prepared to go with. It seems like a very short list on the laptop screen, the cursor blinking underneath it expectantly. Even adding the phone numbers doesn't seem to bulk it up. My options appear pretty limited to say the least.

I pick up the cuttings and go out to the copy shop down the road. The woman there smiles and asks me how I am.

'Fine, thanks,' I say.

'I saw the piece about you today,' she says as the copier zips back and forth, flashing light over her face.

'Yesterday? In the *Mirror*? That was pretty embarrassing. I don't think we'll be including that one in the file.'

'No,' she says, taking a press cutting off the glass and replacing it with another one. 'Today. I'll have to put this one on A3, is that okay?'

'Today?'

'Yes, in the *Post*, I think it was.'

My first reaction is that she doesn't know what she's talking about, but I've so had so many surprises – most of them horrible – over the last few weeks that I realise she's probably right.

'Can I pick these up later? I'll pay you cash.'

'Of course, if you want to, but I've nearly finished.'

I race out of the door and rush across the road to the newsagent's, missing a taxi by inches.

It's the main story in the features pages.

The dream finally ended yesterday as the smartest website on the internet closed. Post *reporter Nora Benthall who has followed the 2cool2btrue story from the start, talks exclusively to Charlie Barrett, the man at the centre of the controversy.*

There is a photo of me from the site, looking cool and pleased with myself.

Charlie Barrett seems relaxed for a man at the epicentre of what has been described as the South Sea Bubble of the noughties. Wealthy celebrities ranging from financier Sir James Huntsman to pop star Sir Josh Langdon and theatrical impresario Martin Preston have lost millions after investing in the website 2cool2btrue.com and many other investors are promising legal action.

With the real financial whiz-kids behind the site in hiding, hotly pursued by Fraud Squad officers, former male model Charlie Barrett is now the focus of attention and has found himself holding the fort against creditors and reporters. The last few days have certainly been tough on Barrett – his office has been bombarded by photographers and his every move watched by police and angry investors – but he has managed to stay cool, 2cool, perhaps?

He is sanguine about the eventual collapse of the site which kept its millions of fans around the world in touch with the cutting edge of cool.

'It was fun while it lasted,' says Barrett, thirty, over a glass of champagne. 'But I'm glad it's closed, it's finally reached a conclusion. May it rest in peace.'

His good looks are more than matched by his easy charm, and it's not difficult to see why in a career spanning almost ten years he has worked in London, New York and Milan, promoting everything from smart suits to whisky and Italian designer labels to fast cars.

'It was time for a career change,' he tells me. 'I'd had enough of modelling.'

Later on I say (apparently):

'We really thought that 2cool could be different, something that would appeal to young people wherever they are and show them what is on offer in the way of clothes, music, food, architecture. It was like we were reinventing youth culture, relaunching it for the twenty-first century, the biggest statement since it had been invented in the sixties.'

Did I really say that? It sounds more like Guy or Piers. I certainly sound eloquent. Daft and pretentious, but eloquent.

His naivety is remarkable at times, but has the effect of making him all the more endearing, even charismatic. You can suddenly understand why normally shrewd business people would want to be involved in 2cool, a project that he so clearly believes in and sells with such effortless cogency. Barrett freely admits that he had almost no marketing experience other than a degree in the subject from Leeds University, and his knowledge of internet entrepreneurship is also almost non-existent.

However, he reveals the thinking behind this. 'It meant that I came to it fresh, with no preconceptions, no baggage,' he says. He argues that being a successful model also requires a certain skill in marketing. It's a tenuous connection but, again, Barrett's obvious sincerity and enthusiasm carry you over the treacherous, rocky terrain of his illogicality.

It goes on to talk about Lauren and my flat before concluding:

Given the cool, casual elegance of his own lifestyle, almost every aspect of which – from his blonde model girlfriend Lauren to his elegantly understated Chiswick flat – looks like a shoot from the pages of a glossy magazine, it's quite understandable that he should want many more of us to share in the wonderful world of luxury and style that he inhabits. It's just a shame that boring things like basic economics and balance sheets got in the way.

I walk to the office building and up to the second floor feeling almost dizzy with confusion and disbelief as much as anger. I've been so close to this woman, emotionally and physically, and now she's done this to me. How? Why? Did I think our making love might make a difference? I skim through the piece again just to make sure that there are no references to my body or performance in bed.

At that moment my mobile rings. I don't recognise the number shown on it but, in something of a daze, I answer it anyway.

'It's me. I'm outside,' she says.

'Erm, come up.'

I buzz her in and sit down at my desk. I don't want to shout at her, I'm too stunned and perplexed for that, I just want an explanation. I just want to know how I got it so wrong. Perhaps this is normal behaviour, perhaps people often do this kind of thing in life and I'm just not aware of it.

'Hi?' she says, putting her head round the door.

'Why?' is all I can say.

'Oh, Charlie,' she sighs matter-of-factly, putting her bag down on the desk and sitting down. 'Look, I was debating whether or not to tell you last night.'

'Why didn't you? Hang on, why the hell did you write the thing in the first place?'

'Because they told me to write a piece about it after that *Mirror* story and the TV report and . . . ow, do you mind if I take my shoes off? They're killing me.'

'Why didn't you tell me? Why didn't you ask me?'

'I don't have to ask you. I can write whatever I like, it's a free country,' she reminds me, as if I'm being the unreasonable one.

I slam my hand down on the desk. 'Nora, you and I made love last night. You can't do this to me.'

'Why, do you feel violated?' she says, enunciating the last word with exaggerated passion.

'Don't push it,' I say, raising my finger at her.

She takes a deep breath and looks down at the floor. 'Look, I didn't ask you because if I'd asked you, you'd have said no. Or, if you'd let me do it, you'd have been too self-conscious. It wouldn't have worked right. Anyway, the point is it'll do a lot of good, it's just telling your side of the story.'

'I don't need you to tell my side of the story.'

'Just read it,' she says, reaching over the desk and flipping the paper round to face her. 'Read it and tell me if there's anything you don't like, anything that I've got wrong.'

'Of course! That call last night.' It comes back to me, making me feel even sicker, even angrier. I was just feet away from her, naked, running a bath. 'You rang the paper to get them to put that line in about it being taken off the net. You checked your watch to make sure that you could still catch them before it went to print. Christ, you bitch. How could you?'

'There's no point in going on about it now, it's too late to change it. I think it'll do you a power of good.' She puts her left foot on to the desk. 'I also think I've crippled myself with these bloody shoes. One of the fashion assistants leant them to me. Some new guy just out of college who's going to be very hot, already been recruited by Tom Ford or something but God, ow, he must hate feet.'

'Just stop talking.'

She looks round and stares at me, affronted.

'Don't you know, don't you care what you've done? I can't tell if you're serious or not. Do you think this is funny?'

'No, I don't think it's funny. I just think your reaction's over the top, that's all.'

'Oh, for fuck's sake Nora. I wish to God I'd never met you. I regret this whole 2cool shit but what I really regret is ever getting involved with you.' I'm inches away from her face now, leaning over the desk. 'I wish I'd never met you, do you understand, Nora?' I sense a jolt of adrenalin. This feels good. 'I just can't believe anything you say to me. You're a compulsive liar, aren't you? How could you have sex, make love – is that was it was? – to me one minute, *literally* one minute, and then trick me, shit on me the next?'

I can feel tears pushing their way up into my eyes. My hands are trembling.

'What else are you lying about, Nora? If that's your real name. Or is that just another lie? What kind of name is Nora anyway? I'm sure a bright girl like you could have invented something more convincing than Nora,' I tell her. 'Can I believe that you went to Vasser and you had a boyfriend who said that stupid thing about reading when he was too old to play sport? Those are pretty convincing lies, I could fall for those, yep, quite easily.'

If I still don't know the real Nora, still can't get close to her after we've slept together, then perhaps upsetting her, making her cry will do it. She looks away, but not at her foot this time, and when she turns back at me, she is blinking away tears like a little girl trying to be brave.

'I *did* go to Vasser, I *did* have that boyfriend. All that I've told you is true, Charlie. I've been, well, less than honest about the articles, but then I had to be. I've never lied to you about who I am . . . or how I feel about you. And I *am* called Nora.' Her voice is suddenly cracking. Are those tears real?

'Oh, yeah,' I say, less angry now, suddenly a bit concerned at what I've started.

'If you must know, my dad gave me my name. Quite simple. Why are you called Charlie?'

I look at her for a moment. Okay, not a good comparison. 'Never mind,' I tell her.

She takes a deep breath, made ragged by tears. 'If you must know, if you think it'll help, Nora is an anglicisation of my name. Really I'm Noor.'

'Noor?'

'Do you know that name? It's Arabic.'

She stops and swallows hard. She looks in her handbag for something and I realise she wants a hanky. I go across to Scarlett's desk and pick up a box of tissues. Nora takes one, saying 'Thanks,' almost inaudibly. What have I done here?

'My father is a doctor and my parents were living in Cairo when I was born, because he was working there as part of an aid programme. My mother went into labour unexpectedly when Dad was out with some colleagues and medical students at a party. She was rushed to hospital and the servants went out to tell him but it was hopeless, they couldn't find him anywhere, so they had to wait until he got home after midnight. Then they gave him the news. In fact, all they could tell him, all they knew, was that she had gone to hospital.'

She pauses and bites her lip. I stand back and watch her.

'Unfortunately, though, there had been . . . there had been a complication. It wasn't the doctors' fault . . . a one in a million chance . . . and my mother . . .'

'Nora, you don't need to—'

'When he finally got there ready to see his wife and his first child he was told that they had both died. Can you imagine? Instead of having a wife *and* a child, a family, all he ever wanted, he had nothing, no one. So he was taken upstairs to see the bodies – his wife's that he knew so well, and the tiny corpse of this complete stranger, someone he'd created, who was part of him, someone he'd listened to and felt kick, but he'd never met before and would never know now.

'But I wasn't dead. Somehow I'd made it. I'd started breathing. The nurse had just noticed this and was so busy trying to revive me that she hadn't had time to tell anyone else yet. When my dad came in and she saw him she started crying, apparently, even though she was used to seeing life and death everyday. My dad says as soon as she handed me to him and he held me in his arms he knew what to call me – Noor. It means "light" in Arabic. Standing with the body of his wife in that terrible darkness, I was his only light.'

She sniffs again and wipes her nose. 'You see the irony was that my dad was an obstetrician, the best in the city, probably the best in North Africa. If he'd been on duty at the hospital that night he would probably have been able to save her, save his wife.'

We sit in silence for a moment. Then I walk round the desk to where she is and kneel in front of her, taking her hands in mine. I kiss them gently. She leans down and I feel her rest her face on my head, still sniffing back tears. I don't know how long we stay like that. It's my mobile that brings us out of our trance.

'Answer it,' whispers Nora, huskily.

'No, don't worry.'

'Get it. I'm okay,' she says, sniffing and unfurling the soggy tissue.

Still watching her, I get up slowly and pick up the phone from the desk. It's showing another mobile number that I don't recognise. I press 'OK' to answer it.

'Hello?' I say, and cough to get my voice back.

'Charlie Barrett?' barks a throaty voice that is vaguely familiar.

'Speaking.'

'Anastasia Huntsman.'
'Oh, hi Anastasia. How are you?'
'Good, thanks. Listen, I know where Piers is.'

chapter twenty-three

I'm not quite with it so this information takes a moment to sink in. I look round at Nora.

'You what? You know where Piers is?'

'Yes, I made a few phone calls after we spoke and a friend has just come back to say he knows where he's living at the moment.'

'You're kidding.'

'No,' she laughs, clearly revelling in the power this knowledge is giving her, a bored rich girl looking for a thrill, something to tell her other bored, rich friends about. 'I'm deadly serious.'

'Well, where is he?'

'It's a squat in south London. Piers in a squat, can you imagine it?' She laughs again.

'No, I can't.' I laugh too, but really just to humour her. I look across at Nora, who is staring intently at me. She mouths something but I ignore her, anxious in case Anastasia rings off.

'Can you give me the address?' I ask.

'That I'm waiting for,' she says in her luxurious drawl.

'You haven't got it?'

'No, patience, my boy.' She is definitely playing with me now. I roll my eyes heavenward and say "Oh, fuck" silently. Nora is now standing up and trying to attract my attention.

'But you could get the address for me?' I ask, mainly for Nora's benefit. 'I'd really appreciate it, Anastasia.'

'Oh, sure. He's staying in a house owned, well not quite owned, but occupied from time to time by some guys who get my gear for me if you know what I mean. I'm not sure where they're hanging out at the moment, that's all. I can call them after seven this evening and they'll give me the address then, I'm sure, no problem.'

'And you'll ring me then?'

'Sure, don't worry,' she says smoothly.

'Thanks, Anastasia.'

'You're welcome, love. Speak soon. Bye.'

'Oh my God, she knows where he is,' says Nora, hanging on to my arm, eyes still red but now wide with excitement. 'I don't believe it. She knows where he is.'

'Yeah.' I'm wondering whether, when I do get this address, to tell the police.

'Amazing news! That's *so* great. But why couldn't she give you the address now?'

I'd feel bad handing Piers over to the police, but then again, why not? He's landed me in it. If he has defrauded people then he deserves to face the consequences. On the other hand, if he hasn't done anything wrong he's got nothing to fear. It would also avoid getting further embroiled with Nora.

'Why didn't she give you the address now? When is she going to call you?' she asks.

But the idea of handing him to that mean, ugly bastard Slapton on a plate is too much. I have a vision of him standing in my bedroom. He'd have such a coup. Nora is pulling at my arm like a kid. I look at her, wondering how she could turn me over again with this new development.

My thoughts still elsewhere, I tell her, 'She doesn't have the address at the moment. She needs to get it from her dealer and she can't ring him until after seven tonight.'

'Seven tonight?' Nora looks distraught. 'We can't wait that long.'

'Well, Nora, we're going to have to, aren't we?'

She thinks about it for a moment. Then she says, 'You're going to the police.' She looks horrified at this sensible option.

'Well, let's face it. I should do, shouldn't I?'

'What?' She stomps across the room and throws her hands up in the air. 'Are you crazy? This is huge. This is what we've been waiting for. How can you give it all away?'

'Because the police will know what to do.'

'Don't be insane. This is such a massive story.' She stops when she realises what she's said.

'That,' I tell her, 'is exactly what I'm afraid of.'

She looks guiltily at me. 'I'm sorry, I shouldn't have said that.'

'Oh, Nora. I just want to get out of this. I want to call the police, give them the address when I know it, let them arrest Piers or whatever and get my life back.'

'Charlieee. Look . . . look,' she runs her hands through her hair, thinking. 'You can tell the police *after* you've spoken to him. After all, you don't even know if he really is where Anastasia says he is until you've seen for yourself.' She does have a point. She realises that she's making progress here. 'If it is him, if he is there, we'll go outside and call the police immediately, okay? And, I promise, I won't speak to anyone else about it.'

'All right.' It does make sense, I suppose. 'You'd better not write anything, though.'

She looks at me for a moment. 'I won't write anything until I've spoken to you about it.'

'Until I've approved it.'

'Approved it? Oh, honestly—'

'Or I don't tell you the address.'

She looks at me hard. 'Okay,' she says. 'Okay. We'll work on the piece together.'

Nora goes back to her office after another severe warning from me. We've arranged to meet back here at seven to await Anastasia's call. Even then, I decide, peering out of the window at the traffic and people below, I don't have to tell Nora where Piers is. I could just ring Slapton straight away and hand the whole thing over to him.

I sit down at my desk and spread my hands out before me. What would Lauren do in this situation? If you think you know the answer, ring this number, calls cost fifty pence per minute, and don't forget to get permission from whoever pays the bill. Hey, I think I do know the answer.

But I'm not Lauren, though, am I? So am I Nora? Or is it Noor? The light of his life. Oh, God, that poor man.

I shuffle some more bits of paper around. No sign of Scarlett or Zac. I realise I'm missing them so I go out and do some window shopping. A couple of people in the street take a second look at me and the people in the sandwich shop exchange very unsubtle glances as I order a turkey salad sandwich to take away.

It's funny, so many people at my agency, I mean my old agency, want to be celebs. I remember a guy called Dave, a complete tosser, had five pages of editorial in *The Times* magazine, beautiful stuff –

winter coats shot in Scotland, I think – but he spent almost the whole day it appeared standing by the bar in a café in the King's Road, looking around, waiting for people to recognise him.

He was there at 10 a.m. when Lauren and I were having a quick coffee before we tackled the shops, and he was still there at gone four o'clock in the afternoon when we went past on a bus on our way home. Like anyone was going to recognise his face from the magazine.

'People just look at the clothes, go "Blimey! I wouldn't pay that", and turn the page,' said Lauren in a rare moment of cynicism.

I watch telly in the office a bit. The same quiz show that Zac was watching the other day. I can do the abuse – 'you pea-brain', 'you dingbat' – but I can't always get the answers right like he can, so I turn over and watch a woman telling another woman how much she hated her former, fat self. I flick over again and another woman is telling yet another chat show hostess about how dieting took over her life and how she is now, finally, happy with who she is – a size twenty. The hostess, a stick-thin blonde, smiles sweetly and invites the audience to give the fat woman a round of applause.

The door buzzer goes. The police? Reporters? Creditors? Not again. I look at my watch; it's a quarter to seven already. I let Nora in. She rushes upstairs, throws her arms around me and gives me a passionate, slurping kiss, pulling me towards her. Then she pushes me away.

'Has she rung yet?'

'No, it's only quarter to seven.'

'Good, good,' says Nora, taking off her coat. She sits down on Scarlett's desk, still breathing heavily from the running up stairs and the kissing and leans back. 'Isn't this exciting? Got anything to drink?'

'No and no,' I tell her.

'Oh, Charlie, don't be boring.' She comes over to where I'm sitting behind my desk with a sultry sashay.

'I'm not, I'm just . . . a bit anxious, that's all.'

'So am I. I've been thinking about it all day.'

'I just hope we're doing the right thing.'

'I'm sure we are,' she says, too quickly to sound convincing.

I sigh deeply and start an aimless tour of the office.

'What have you been doing today?'

'Erm, just pissing about here really. You?'

'Oh, I've had one of those days. A lot of firefighting, you know, crisis management, trying to sort things out for people,' she says, shaking her head.

'What? Where they've cocked things up?'

'No, where *I've* cocked things up,' she says blandly.

'That figures.'

Just then my mobile rings.

'Oh, my God. That'll be her,' says Nora, leaping up off the desk and rooting around in her bag. 'Quick, take this. You stick it on to the back of the phone and it records what she says. Oh, fuck, where's the tape? I'm crap at technical things. Hang on, here it is.'

I wave Nora and her recording gear away as I answer the phone.

'Hello?'

'Charlie? It's Anastasia.'

'Hi, thanks for ringing back.'

'No, probs, I said I would. Right, I've got this address . . .' I scatter papers around my desk as I find a pen and something to write on, then I swap hands to stop Nora trying to listen in, but she goes round to the other side of me.

'Sorry, Anastasia, go on.'

'Right, I've never heard of it, I never go there myself, always get a mate to do it, or a bike from one of Dad's companies; it's the absolute back of bloody beyond. You'll need passports and injections to go there.'

I laugh encouragingly.

'Oh, get on with it,' whispers Nora from beside me.

'It's number seventy-nine Fairisle Road, SE twenty-seven. Where the hell's SE twenty-seven? Never been very good on my SEs.'

I repeat the address to make sure I've got it. 'That's great, I really appreciate it.'

'So, you're going to go down there?'

'Well, we'll go and have a look.'

Nora is already feverishly consulting an A-to-Z.

'Be careful, Charlie.'

'Of course, don't worry. I'll let you know how I get on. Thanks again, Anastasia. Bye.'

'Bye. Oh, and Charlie, try and get me some stuff while you're there will you, I'm running dangerously low.'

I laugh. 'Will do.'

I finish the call and look round at Nora.

'Found it,' she says triumphantly. 'It's near . . . near . . . absolutely fucking nowhere. Don't worry, though, I've got a car.'

'A car? That'll be useful.'

'Right. You can map-read, I'll drive.' She is already half out of the door.

I'm wondering again whether I should just ring the police and give them the address. It would make life easier. But I can't bear to speak to Slapton again, let alone help the bastard in his stupid enquiries, so I pick up my stuff and follow Nora out. We'll talk to Piers and then perhaps ring the police and tell them his whereabouts. It's already getting dark and and a large spot of rain lands on my face as I step outside.

She is illegally parked – horribly, outrageously, illegally parked so that a couple of passers-by stop in disbelief to look at the little blue Renault sitting next to, almost on, the zebra crossing but of course she has managed to avoid getting a ticket.

She lets me in just as the rain really gets going. We set off down Charing Cross Road ready to cross the river. She is silent and intent. We haven't been going long before I realise that she isn't going to pay much attention to traffic regulations and other drivers.

'Fucking hell, Nora,' I say, leaning back in my seat as we seem to be driving straight towards a bus. Traffic lights are a minor hindrance and she seems to pass most as if they were at green. She also seems to think that she has right of way, whatever the road markings and the position of other vehicles might suggest. But her erratic performance is clearly not just a result of her excitement and determination to get to Fairisle Road as soon as possible. As we hurtle over a mini-roundabout, causing a couple of other cars to screech to a halt on my side, I find myself saying what has been dawning on me since our last near miss but two.

'Nora, you can't drive, can you?'

She laughs uncomfortably. 'Derr! Huh! What do you think I'm doing now?'

'No, I mean you don't have a licence. You haven't passed a test, have you?'

'Oh, honestly.'

By sheer fluke we seem to be heading down the road without any obvious crises for a moment but I don't let it go. 'Nora, whose car is this?'

'A friend from work. She *does* know.'

'That you've got it, yes, but she doesn't know that you haven't got a licence.'

'Oh, Charlie, for goodness' sake. Who knows whether I've got a goddamn licence or not?'

'Well, everybody else near us on the road, I'd say. Look, just stop the car and we'll get a taxi or something.'

Face set in grim determination, she carries on.

'Nora, I said stop the car. You can park in one of these side streets and we'll get a taxi.'

'We're nearly there now, aren't we?'

'No.' We *are* actually but I can't stand this. We must have used up our luck by now.

'It's at the end of this street, isn't it?'

Outside it is dark and wet. I look in vain for cabs but there are none.

'Okay, but let's take it slowly from now on.'

'Of course,' she says, putting her foot down.

We find Fairisle Road soon afterwards and decide to leave the car at the beginning of it, just off the main road. I do the parking since even Nora admits she's not too hot on that.

Fairisle Road is a Victorian terrace in which most houses are shabby but still inhabited. There are five that are seriously dilapidated and number seventy-nine is in the middle of them. There is no sign of life from it whatsoever. My first thought is that Anastasia must have made a mistake. Surely even a squat must have something to show that it's inhabited. I walk up to the gate and open it. The downstairs windows have been boarded up with corrugated iron and there is a pile of litter, Big Mac containers and rubbish around the front door.

'This place looks deserted,' I say to Nora, willing this to be the case.

'What a perfect place to hide, then,' she says brightly, a drop of rain hanging off her nose. 'Go and try the door.'

I look at her for a moment, wondering whether there is still time to call the police and get out of here.

'Go on.'

I walk up to the door and knock gently, hoping that if there is anyone inside they won't hear me.

'Oh, for fuck's sake,' she says, pulling me out of the way. She boots the door as hard as she can, staggering backwards with the impact.

'Nora!'

'Well, what are you? The Avon Lady?'

Unfortunately the door, obviously rotten and with a knackered old lock, *has* given a bit. There really is no excuse for not trying again.

'Psst,' hisses Nora.

I look round and see a couple walk by, giving us a surreptitious glance as they pass. After a few moments I give it another assault. I have to admit to a touch of macho self-satisfaction as it opens properly with a shove from my shoulder.

'I hope whoever's in here is deaf,' I whisper to her.

We both peer in. I shudder involuntarily at the thought of rats. The place smells of rotting wood, damp and urine. I nearly gag. 'We can't possibly go in without a . . . torch,' I say, as Nora produces one from her bag. Oh, shit.

'Luckily someone's come prepared,' she says.

In the light of the torch the place itself doesn't look too bad. It's very grimy, with wallpaper and even bits of plaster hanging off the walls in the hallway, but the floorboards look sound. Nora steps inside and I follow her.

'Close the door,' she whispers.

Reluctantly I push it closed behind us. We move further in, and on the right is a doorway to the living room. I'm so close to Nora that I'm almost pressing up against her. She flashes the torch around. The room is empty except for a deckchair and some old lager cans dotted around a filthy rug. The hearth shows signs of a small, incompetently constructed fire.

We move on along the corridor. In front of us are the stairs and behind them the way to the kitchen. We choose the kitchen route, a tense, shambling, two-person conga. I'm beginning to think about a big drink after we get out of this. *If* we get out of this. There are more old lager cans and wine and whisky bottles in the kitchen plus some cardboard boxes. Oh, shit, obviously full of giant rats. They say you're never more than ten feet away from a rat in London; we're probably inches away from them. Don't they go for your jugular? Or your genitals? Or is that wild dogs?

'Go back,' hisses Nora.

'Why?' I gasp.

'Because there's nothing here.'

'Oh.' I turn to head backwards and it's then that we hear a creak from above us.

I turn to look at Nora and she holds the torch up to her scared face. Suddenly all the comparisons with the Blair Witch Project which I've been suppressing come flooding into my mind, and I'm ready to just sprint out of there – what the hell.

'Did you hear that?' says the mask of terror in front of me.

'Yes, it came from upstairs,' I say, taking the torch from her and holding it in such a way as to give her a more gentle, flattering light. Which is, of course, for my benefit, not hers. 'Let's get out of here.'

Even she seems to be contemplating a fast exit for a moment.

'There must be someone up there.'

'Exactly! So let's get out of here.'

She takes the torch off me and moves back towards the hallway. I'm breathing more steadily already at the thought of escape but she stops at the foot of the stairs.

'Come on,' I tell her.

'Just a quick look upstairs.'

'No, for fuck's sake. I told you, this isn't *Scooby Doo*. Let's just go . . . Nora?' The step creaks and by the light of the torch I can see her beginning to walk up. 'Come back.'

But she ignores me and carries on up. Helplessly, I follow her. There is another creak from the first floor. We get halfway and she turns round for a moment, but it's obviously just to check that I'm still here behind her. Finally we are on the landing. The street lights throw a gentle yellowy light into the front bedroom. It is empty apart from the obligatory cardboard boxes. The torch is shaking in Nora's hand, I notice.

Although there is no actual noise, somehow we both sense it at the same time: there *is* someone in the room next to us. The door is closed, and there is total blackness at this end of the hallway. Again Nora turns to look at me, her face a mixture of fear and curiosity in the harsh torchlight.

This is the moment. I'm a big bloke, I've got the element of surprise. Don't think about it, just do it. I turn the handle and throw the door open as fast and as hard as I can.

Initially it moves smoothly and easily but a split second later it comes into contact with someone or something. From behind me I hear Nora scream and she drops the torch, a flash of light revealing a shadowy figure in the room. Already reeling from the impact of the door, it has no chance of seeing off a badly aimed but forceful blow from my right fist. It feels like I've hit someone's head or cheekbone.

'Awwwfff!' There is a crack as a head hits the crumbling plaster of the wall. I stagger back for a moment but realise that it isn't *my* head so I take a deep breath and look round for Nora. She is nowhere to be seen in the inky blackness of the hallway.

'Nora?' I'm still whispering.

'Yes?' she gasps.

My heart and lungs are both hammering away so hard that I can hardly get the words out. 'I think I hit someone.'

'Sounded like it.'

We both stand in silence. I'm almost bracing myself for my assailant to come back at me but there is nothing except the sound of the traffic outside and the distant thump of a reggae beat from across the road. The pain from my hand begins to kick in, a dull, throbbing ache. I hope I haven't broken something.

'Where's the torch?' I whisper.

'I don't know, I think it's broken.'

'Oh fuck, it'd better not be,' I say, stepping back very slowly and bumping into her. We both crouch down and begin to feel around on the damp, rough floorboards for it.

'Got it,' she says. A second later the light begins to flash around crazily as she shakes it back into life.

'Give it here,' I hiss. I take it and shine it into the bedroom.

There is a figure on the floor, lying motionless. I think I'm going to be sick for a moment, then I'm conscious of Nora looking round from behind me.

'Who is it? Is he all right?' I can hear her words and I want to go and find out but somehow my body won't move.

After what seems like hours but can only be a few moments, she pushes past me and walks gingerly into the room, looking behind the door. I've at least managed to shine the torch in there. She looks around for a moment and then crouches down by the body.

'Oh, my God! It *is* Piers,' she says in a strange, husky voice. I see her touch his face and then reach down towards his wrist. She holds it for a moment and looks back at me.

'Well?' I hear myself whisper.

'He's dead.'

chapter twenty-four

'What made you think I was dead?' asks Piers brightly.

'You had no pulse,' snaps Nora as if he's not playing fair by still being alive.

'Well, obviously he had a bloody pulse,' I tell her.

'Oh, very clever, Dr Doug Ross. Next time you knock someone out cold *you* can check they're still alive.'

'I will, don't worry.'

'Actually,' says Piers. 'You might be right. I play a lot of squash and I'm pretty fit so I've probably got a very slow pulse, that's all.'

'Oh, shut up,' Nora and I chorus. We look at each other in surprise and then look away crossly. Why the hell didn't I call the police right away? I decide I'll do it as soon as we leave, whatever Nora says. How did I get talked into this, anyway? I'm still feeling a bit sick and faint after the shock of thinking I'd killed someone.

'Gosh, my head hurts, though,' says Piers, rubbing the side of his forehead which is already beginning to swell.

'Good,' I say. My hand is killing me. I can hardly straighten out my index finger. Bang goes any more hand-modelling work.

'Charlie,' says Nora. 'I think you should apologise to Piers.'

'What? *Me* apologise? After what he's put me through?'

'Yeah, sorry about that.' says Piers.

So far we've ascertained that after deciding to go AWOL Piers stayed in a cheap hotel in Earls Court for a few days before realising that with his picture over so many newspapers he wasn't safe. 'I wore a false beard but it kept falling off,' he told us, sadly.

'How annoying,' I say.

'It was pretty embarrassing, especially when you're having a curry. Obviously I couldn't even take it back to the shop after that, either.'

The fact that all the stress, humiliation and misery I've suffered over the last few weeks has been caused by this idiot makes me feel a whole lot worse. I can't even boast that I've been exploited and tricked by a proper villain.

According to Piers he bumped into Anastasia in a late-night supermarket in Earls Court Road and being a very shrewd sort she recognised him through his fiendish disguise. They started talking drugs, of course, and so she came up with the idea of staying at one of the squats used by his drug contacts. A bloke called Twange or something found him this place.

'It was pretty grim at first but I've made it quite cosy, haven't I?' he says, pointing to the tent he's erected in one corner of the room. Inside is a sleeping bag and there is a tiny gas stove set up in the middle of the floor. I might have known he'd been a Boy Scout. 'Loo facilities are bit basic. It's round to the right if you want to go.'

Nora and I, sipping whisky out of brightly coloured plastic camping cups, decline. With the whisky warming me, I feel ready to ask Piers some more questions. I just can't think where to begin but, of course, Nora starts first.

'So, Piers, can I just check, have you actually done anything that's against the law?'

'Erm, not really,' he says thoughtfully, feeling the side of his head again. 'It's not our fault that 2cool didn't actually make any money, well not enough money, anyway. We told all the investors exactly what it was and how it worked, they saw the prospectus, it was all legal and above board.'

'But they're not stupid. There are some very shrewd, experienced business people who've put money into it,' I point out.

'They knew what they were laying themselves open to. The point is that it was young and hip and fun and glamorous, and so everybody wanted a piece of it. Pop stars, movie stars, designers – they all thought it was going to be like the best sex they'd ever had, which it was, of course. And as for those older ones, it was their children or mistresses or whatever who persuaded them. It all made sense. We were just a bit vague about revenue streams, that's all.'

'You mean how it would actually make any money?'

'Yeah, I mean it did make *some* money, you know, through selling those luxury products and things, just not enough. The punters were always using the site, reading the articles, doing the competitions, looking at the porn, but the buggers just weren't buying anything or giving us any of their cash. We did sell some advertising space on it but even then it wasn't enough.'

'But didn't the accountants say something about all this money we were spending, you know, with the launch party and everything?' I ask.

'Oh, all the time, you know what they're like. Penny pinchers!'

'So you've done nothing wrong?' repeats Nora.

'Oh, no,' says Piers. 'More whisky?' We both accept another splash.

'So, if you did nothing wrong, why are the Fraud Squad all over us?' I ask him, taking another sip.

'I don't know. One of the investors must have said something to them I suppose. Or perhaps the accountants became suspicious because they'd never seen anyone spend money so quickly and go into the red so fast. Also, let's face it, for the police, it was a high profile case – can you imagine if they *had* managed to make an arrest?' He whistles and pours himself some more whisky. 'It would have given them huge a PR coup.'

That arrest could have been me, I realise. 'So they won't find anything dodgy in the accounts?' I ask.

'Well,' says Piers, frowning thoughtfully. 'The accounts *are* a bit of a mess, as you know.'

'I did notice.'

'But there is nothing actually illegal.'

'So when Josh Langdon says he's thinking of taking us, I mean, 2cool,' I say choosing my words carefully, 'to court to get his money back, because it was obtained under false pretences, he's talking rubbish?'

Piers smiles enigmatically. 'Oh, I don't think Josh'll be taking us to court somehow. I don't think any of our main investors will be rushing to cause trouble. Don't worry about that, mate. Anyway, *caveat emptor*, I say.'

'What?'

'Let the buyer beware,' says Nora. 'It's Latin.'

'So why did you disappear and leave me to handle it all?'

'Sorry about that, mate. It was all getting a bit too hot to handle and then Guy disappeared—'

'Where is he?' asks Nora before I can get the question out.

'I don't know,' says Piers, looking, for once, as if he has realised how serious the situation is. 'That's the thing. He just vanished that night. I haven't heard from him since.'

'We thought you'd both gone together,' I say.

'Oh, no.'

'That morning, you came into the office looking like shit and said you'd had a bit of a night of it. That was when—'

'I *had* had a bit of a night of it, a hell of a night of it in fact. I'd been looking for him everywhere: at his flat, ringing his phone, asking his friends. All night and nothing. I didn't hear a word from him.'

'Why didn't you tell us?' I ask.

Piers shrugs his shoulders. 'I didn't want to worry you.'

'So you have no idea where he is now?' asks Nora before I can question Piers's logic.

'No. Mind you, bit of a funny character, our Guy. Never could quite suss him out,' he says, conspiratorially. This just gets worse and worse.

'So, are you going to come back then, to the office I mean?' I ask.

'We-e-e-ll, bit difficult. I'll think about it if you don't mind.'

'For God's sake Piers, you can't just leave me to handle it on my own. The police are on my back every day. Not to mention the press.' Nora seems to ignore the dig.

'Old Bill being a bit of a nuisance are they?'

'More than that, they've taken away the computers, half the paperwork – all those bills,' I say, suddenly remembering the drawers and boxes full of paper that had given me such a heart attack. 'I've never seen so many bits of paper.'

'Did you manage to sort that lot out? I always was a bit crap at filing. Kept meaning to ask Scarlett to do it.'

'They've been to my flat, and yours and Guy's,' I tell him.

'Oh, dear. What *will* the neighbours say?' He laughs. 'Anyway, like I told you, we haven't actually done anything wrong, it's just that we spent rather a lot of money rather quickly, that's all. 2cool could still come back with a vengeance, like a phoenix rising from the—'

'Don't be stupid,' I tell him.

'Oh, okay.' He takes another sip of whisky.

'I could just ring the police now, of course,' I say slowly.

'No,' says Nora. 'That's not fair.'

'Fair? What's fair? I've been hounded, humiliated, beaten up—'

'Beaten up?' says Nora, looking at me, concerned.

'Some bloke tried to.'

'Ooh, nasty,' says Piers. 'But you gave as good as you got, yeah?' He mimes a left hook.

'I didn't have to,' I say, too overwhelmed and confused to be macho about it. 'He walked into the door and then fell downstairs.'

Piers looks quizzical and then suddenly roars with laughter. 'Hang on, was he about my height, bit thinner?'

'Yes, I suppose so.'

'Orangey brown hair?'

'I couldn't tell really, he had a biker's helmet on.'

'Oh, that's definitely Shagger,' he laughs. 'Old Shagger Potts. We used to call him Shagger because he never got any. God, he's a clumsy bastard. Worse than you,' he tells Nora. 'Specially with that stupid helmet on. So he wants his money, does he? Huh, back of the queue for you, Shagger!'

'Anyway, Piers, the point is, are you going to the police or are you going to stay here?' I ask.

'If you don't mind, I think I'll stay here. Lie low for a bit.'

'I *do* mind, actually.'

'Charlie, come on,' says Nora. 'Like Piers says, they haven't actually done anything wrong, just been a bit spendthrift.'

'And I *am* trying to find Guy for you,' says Piers. Of course.'

'How?'

'I've got people looking for him as we speak, and if he contacts anyone it'll be me.' He sees my sceptical look. 'I've got my mobile, it's just that I don't leave it on, I collect my messages a couple of times a day.'

'I take a long look at Piers. Wearing a blue and white striped City shirt, a pair of chinos which are remarkably clean given his squalid surroundings, and a pair of scuffed docksiders, he stands next to his schoolboy tent, in this derelict, rat-infested shit hole. I decide to leave him to wallow in it. Besides, at least he can't wreak any more havoc here. I get the feeling that if he were interrogated by Slapton – even with a good lawyer present – he would end up digging himself into a hole that he couldn't get out of, and somehow I'd end up falling into it as well.

'Come on, Nora, we'd better be going.'

'Cheers then,' says Piers, putting down his cup. 'Good to see you again.'

I laugh bitterly. 'Yeah, and you.'

'Keep in touch,' he says. 'Just leave a message on my mobile if you hear anything and I'll call you right back. Oh, Nora. You haven't got any chocolate, have you?'

'No, Piers, sorry,' she says.

Even she seems a bit exasperated by him by now.

With me holding our torch and Piers illuminating us from overhead with another one, we carefully make our way out. I really do hope there are giant rats in that place. Lost in thought, I wander back down the road. At least it's stopped raining. We get to the car and I stand by it, waiting for Nora to open the door.

'Want a lift home?' she says.

At this point I come back to earth. 'No, 'course not. Sorry, Nora, but we can't risk you driving this thing again without a licence or insurance or anything. Look, let's get a taxi and your friend will have to pick it up tomorrow.'

'Oh, okay,' says Nora, clearly relieved that she doesn't have to repeat her hair-raising performance behind the wheel.

We find a minicab office and an enormously fat man, overflowing a typing chair, assigns a driver who, even before we've got north of the river, has offered us a selection of good quality leather coats which his brother imports, together with a mobile phone, cheaper than we can find in a shop, and some CDs. In a break during the sales pitch I say to Nora, 'You're not going to write about that, are you?'

'About Piers? No.' I'm trying to work out what she's thinking, but she's looking out of the window and won't look round at me.

'I mean, in some ways it doesn't matter to me whether you do or not,' I say.

'But I wouldn't. We agreed, remember?'

We drive on in a silence broken only by a special deal on some carpets which are going for just £20 each.

'What did Piers mean about Josh Langdon and people not taking us to court? I was glad to hear him say it but I don't quite understand why he's so confident.'

'I've no idea,' she says, looking out of the window.

By the time we've reached Vauxhall Bridge it's decision time. Do we go to hers or do we say goodbye in a minute and go our separate ways? The fact that she's fiddling furiously with a stray piece of thread from her jacket suggests that she's also aware of the dilemma. As we zip up to Victoria at frightening speed, a shit-hot deal on portable CD players falling on deaf ears, I make my choice.

'I think I'll get out here,' I tell her. 'And get the tube.'

She looks at me and for a moment I think she's going to ask me to stay like she did the other night, but instead she says, 'Oh, sure, of course.'

'We'll speak tomorrow, decide what to do next.'

'Yes.'

I ask the driver to stop and let me out and then I move to kiss her but she's not expecting it.

'Oh,' she says. I pull away but then she turns to me and moves to kiss me. It's all a bit awkward and when the driver swerves into the kerb I end up with a mouthful of her hair while she ends up kissing my neck. I get out and walk towards the tube, turning to wave goodbye, but the car has already darted in front of a bus and is off. I haven't even given her some money towards the fare, I realise.

I get home at nearly ten. It's the second cold, dark, apparently empty house I've walked into this evening. Somehow it feels even more uninviting. I put the lights on, put the heating on, even though it's not exactly chilly outside yet, and pour myself a glass of wine. There is no note from Lauren. I check my mobile – no message. I do the same with the answer phone and there is nothing except something from my mum hoping that I'm all right. Why hasn't she left a message? I'm hungry but nothing in the fridge or the cupboard appeals. Anyway, there's a funny smell in the fridge. It's the milk. It's off. Sour milk in our fridge. In our cold, dark flat. Oh, God, what's happening to us?

I ring Lauren's mobile assuming I'll get the voicemail. It's worse than that – it rings once and then goes onto voicemail. Can she have seen it was me and decided not to take the call? What is she doing that means she can't even say 'Hi, I'll ring you back'? I don't know whether to be angry or hurt. I'm probably both.

I switch on the telly where a woman is giving some advice on how to choose bathroom furniture. 'Make sure there is enough room for you to sit on the loo,' she says, posing on the bog herself and moving her legs around her to demonstrate exactly what she means as she looks up at the camera seriously. TV makes me think of Lauren, the new Lauren, these days.

I switch it off and ring Nora. Half an hour later I'm getting out of a cab and buzzing on her door.

We've been drinking warm white wine and talking about Piers and Guy and the usual stuff, turning it over as we try to work out where Guy could have gone and whether 2cool could ever have made any money. Suddenly it's gone midnight and we both know that I'm not going home. As I brush my teeth with her toothbrush I'm trying to work out to what extent I'm doing this because I want to be with Nora and how much it is simply to spite Lauren. At the moment, standing there naked in Nora's bathroom, a bathroom that's not even as nice as mine and Lauren's at home with its wicker basket bought from a catalogue, warm white towels and classic chunky basin and shiny taps, I wonder whether spite is the main motivation – after all, she's out doing it with that fat, ugly twat Peter – but when I slip into bed with Nora and she lifts her head for me to put my arm around her, I realise that it's also a desire to be with this woman who doesn't bother with details like driving licences, was so much braver than me this evening and was the only light in her father's terrible darkness.

When I wake up, disorientated by the feel of different pillows and sheets and a strange bed underneath me, she leans over me and smiles.

'Morning,' she says.

'Oh, hi, morning,' I mutter, swallowing and closing my eyes again.

She reaches down and kisses me. Her mouth is cool and fresh and tastes of toothpaste.

I pull her down on top of me and she giggles. We kiss again and I feel her breasts pushing against me. I'm naked and in a moment I've lifted her T-shirt above her head. I've still got my morning erection and I push it against her. She groans and closes her eyes, reaching down and biting my ear. I'm thinking about condoms and wondering whether there are any in the drawer, but in the next moment I'm inside her and she is beginning to move up and down.

After I've come she falls down beside me, sweating slightly.

'Did you . . . come?' I feel embarrassed asking it, but I want to know.

'Eh? Oh, yes, of course,' she laughs and looks away. Then she reaches over and kisses me some more.

It's nearly nine o'clock, so she makes me toast while I have a quick shower and then she has a shower herself. I kiss her goodbye outside the tube station as she sets off for work and watch her walk up the steps, then I begin to trudge up Ladbroke Grove. The unfamiliarity of the streets makes me feel unsettled. I shouldn't be here, now. Despite a feeling of sickening uneasiness about what I've done, I realise that I'm actually still quite hungry, having eaten nothing last night, so I find a greasy spoon and order scrambled eggs, bacon, sausage, tomato, beans, toast and a large tea for £3.50.

I spread the newspapers across the next table and try to decide what to do next. I really, really don't want to go home. I don't want to face Lauren if she's there but neither do I want to find that she's not there, that she's done what I've done.

Even though Nora and I made love this morning, even though we kissed as she went into the tube station like a proper couple, the simple truth is that when I woke up in that strange bed and saw Nora's face, not Lauren's, looking down on me, I felt a sudden stab of depression.

I get home at nearly ten-thirty and open the front door. She's in. She's on the phone, talking to her booker at the agency it sounds like, checking the venue and fee for a job the next day. I know she's thorough but it seems to take ages. I wait in the living room, staring at the wall.

Finally she says 'Bye, Lou, take care,' and puts the phone down. Then there seems to be a lot of paper shuffling. Oh, come on. Finally she walks in and jumps slightly when she sees me.

'You gave me a shock.'

I say nothing.

She puts some papers in her bag, which is on the chair next to me. 'Where were you last night?' she asks, not looking up.

It doesn't really matter how we start this thing, we both know roughly where it's going to go.

'I was out.'

She stops what she's doing for a moment.

'Yes, I know that. Where?'

'Never mind, where were you?'

She looks at the far wall. 'I was here, Charlie, in our flat. In our bed.'

'Not when I came home.'

'Obviously not, but I came back just before midnight and went to bed. Now where were you?'

'I was out with someone from work.' We don't have to say who. 'You were with Peter, weren't you?'

'Yes, I was as a matter of fact. We had a drink with a friend of his who's a commissioning editor at Channel Four and then I got a taxi home and went to bed.'

It all sounds so reasonable. Oh, my God, how could I have doubted her?

'Lauren, I know you're sleeping with him.' It comes out more considered, more assertive than I expected.

She finishes putting her stuff in the bag and turns towards me. 'That's complete crap. How can you say that when you've been out all night, fucking that weird, horrible woman who's knifed you in the back time after time?'

I stand up and walk over to the window.

'Charlie,' she says more quietly. 'I want you to move out. For a while at least.'

'So that Peter can move in?' As soon as I say it, I regret it. It sounds cheap and silly – and I don't mean it. Perhaps I just want to hurt her. Why can't Peter just take his silly, floppy fringe and his TV talk and his commissioning editor friends and leave us alone?

'No. I just need some space, that's all. I think we both do. Last night was just . . . just the final straw.'

chapter twenty-five

Having stuffed some carelessly chosen clothes and a handful of toiletries into a bag I walk out of the flat and slam the door behind me without saying anything to her. I stomp purposefully along the street into the main road and then stop and look around.

What the hell am I going to do now?

I walk back down the road parallel to ours ('ours?' – can I still say that?) and sit down on a wall. A woman with a briefcase marches along and gives me a suspicious glance as she passes me. That's right, dear, I'm just casing the joint.

Where can I go? I don't want to move in with Nora; that would be too much. I could never go back to Lauren if I'd been staying there. Anyway, it's not like I want to set up a new life with her, it's just that . . . Just that what? I'm enjoying playing away from home? Getting at Lauren. Perhaps. Etiher way, it's no reason to try and set up a new life with someone. Lauren's words, sensible words, come back to me: 'That weird, horrible woman who's knifed you in the back time after time.'

I decide to focus on practical considerations again. I can't land on Sarah and Mark or any of mine and Lauren's common friends – it's just not fair on them. I can hardly arrive at Becky's with her new baby and a boyfriend I haven't met yet.

I find myself thinking about me, Lauren and children. It seems further away than ever. A pointless daydream. Being unfaithful and staying out all night is hardly the best way to prepare for kids.

I realise that I have few other friends that are close enough just to crash out for a few nights with anyway. I can imagine my mates' girlfriends who I hardly know, whispering in the kitchen about how long I'm going to be sleeping on the settee. I fidget at the thought of a settee and a sleeping bag. Why are living rooms always so cold at night, colder than bedrooms, somehow? I even contemplate the office – there's a loo, a kitchenette and a long sofa there. What an awful thought. Somehow it's only one step up from a doorway.

I need a bed and preferably my own room. I can't land on my mum and anyway, that house is too depressing, so I consider the other parent. His spare room is en suite. With a jacuzzi. And a forty-inch plasma screen. What am I waiting for?

I dig out my mobile from my bag and ring him at work. He comes on the phone via the squawk box. He says, 'Yeah? Oh, shame,' when I tell him about Lauren. I would have quite liked some paternal words of comfort or advice but, then again, this is a man whose TV commercials last longer than his relationships.

'Nothing lasts for ever,' he adds profoundly, his voice distant and distorted through the loudspeaker.

'No, I suppose not. Hang on, isn't that a line from that beer commercial you made a few months ago?'

'Yeah, well spotted, kiddo,' he says, delighted. 'It just won an award at the TV ads international festival in Toronto. Our third!'

'Well done.'

My dad's secretary arranges for a key to be waiting for me at the block's marketing suite. I set off up the road and decide to pop into the shopping centre in Hammersmith to buy some magazines to read on my never-ending tube journey to the other side of the world. My soft leather holdall by Loewe looks slightly out of place in Hammersmith mall amongst the Safeway carriers and Burger King bags. It'll probably get snatched and then I'll be completely unencumbered, with literally nothing but the clothes I'm standing up in.

There is a strong stink of piss by the entrance to the mall and as I walk in, an enormous teenage girl in black leggings and a bomber jacket is coming out shouting, 'Leave my fucking dad alone, you slag. Go on, fuck off, I know you're sleeping with him.'

At first I think she's just bonkers, shouting at the world in general, and I really wouldn't blame her for that. Then I see the object of her tirade: another girl, also a teenager, who is now shouting something back.

I buy *GQ*, *Vogue Hommes* and *FHM* plus the *Post* and *The Times* and set off to the tube station. As I wander along the street, replaying my last (last ever?) conversation with Lauren in my mind, I pass a dirty nappy lying on the pavement, a tiny smear of shit nestling in the stay-dry fabric. Nearby, a mother is changing her baby in a pushchair, humming to herself and blithely throwing dirty wipes down on the ground. The smell makes me feel sick.

At the station I flick through a magazine and manage to read the whole of it without a train coming. I wait a bit longer and then walk up the platform and find a London Underground man.

'What's the delay?'

'There's no delay.'

'There must be, I've been waiting for over twenty minutes.' Small exaggeration.

'There's no delay.'

'So, when's the next train?'

'Don't know, probably not for another couple of hours.'

'A couple of *hours*?'

'Yep, eastbound Piccadilly line services are suspended until further notice, from here as far as Green Park due to a person under a train at Knightsbridge. Harrods sale again. Like this every time – they go down like ninepins.'

'Oh, right.' I sigh and consider my options. 'Wait a minute, I thought you said there was no delay.'

'Aha,' says the man triumphantly. 'There isn't a delay, there's a suspension of service, which strictly speaking, is not a delay.'

I decide to take the bus into town and go to the office to start calling round model agencies. Eventually a bus comes. Needless to say it's absolutely packed. I'm just about to get on when a little old lady pulls me off. I step back on to the pavement.

'You will let me get on first, I think,' she says in a heavy Eastern European accent.

'Yeah, sure,' I say, allowing her to go ahead with a melancholy flourish of my hand.

I wait nearly an hour outside the bus station for the next. This is ridiculous, but what else have I got to do?

I get to the office and speak to a very nice French journalist who is waiting at the bottom of the stairs. She wants to know more about the site but I explain that it's over, *kaputt, fini*. She asks for an interview and I say no and smile sadly. She looks disappointed and wanders off. You're not the only one who's disappointed by the demise of 2cool, love, really.

I make myself a cappuccino from the machine in the corner – the first time it's ever been used. Now it will have to go back. We told our readers it was the chicest thing to put in your open-plan kitchen, which the manufacturers must have been pleased about, but then we suggested another, more expensive, brand a couple of days later. Immediately a freebie arrived from that company. I wonder where the new one went.

Then I take a deep breath, pick up the phone and ring round the three model agencies I've been considering working with. I leave messages for the head booker in each case. Then I try a couple more that I hadn't originally considered contacting.

'We see new faces between ten and twelve on Wednesdays,' says a girl when I explain why I'm ringing.

'I'm *not* a new face,' I tell her sniffily, and put the phone down.

What am I, then? An old face?

By three I've had enough. I'm beginning to get sick of this place, anyway. I don't even like it, I don't think I ever did. Coming here is like an addiction. I hate it but I can't stop doing it.

I get to Docklands at nearly half past four. As usual the cab driver has never heard of the development and we drive past it a couple of times on the wrong side of the dual carriageway with me pointing frantically, trying to make him understand where I want to go. Finally he deposits me by the barrier, next to the skip and the burnt-out car. I walk over the unfinished road along to the marketing suite. It smells damply of filter coffee and dodgy gas heaters.

'I've come to pick up a key from Mr Barrett in the penthouse,' I tell a girl with shoulder-length blonde hair, a dark suit and lots of make-up.

'Oh, yes of course,' she says, smiling ecstatically. 'Now, I'm afraid the penthouse has actually been sold but—'

'Sorry, I don't want to buy anything; I'm staying here with Mr Barrett, he's my dad. I've come to pick up the key. He said you'd have it.'

Her face falls. 'Oh.' She opens a drawer in her desk and takes out an envelope with my name on it. Then she pauses for a moment. 'We do have some properties with a river view on the fourth floor, though.'

I look at her, bewildered. 'No, I'm just staying here. I don't want to buy anything.'

'Of course.' She hands over the envelope.

'Thanks.' I open to check that the key is in there but she is saying something else. 'Sorry?'

'Would you like to go on our mailing list?'

'No, thank—'

'Please,' she says. She looks desperate. 'I need three more names by the end of today.'

So I give her my address in Chiswick and trudge off over the loose rubble and broken bricks to the special penthouse entrance. Once inside I dump my bag in the room and go over to the stereo. It's so minimalist that it looks like a rectangle of brushed stainless steel with one dark circle in it, but fortunately I was there when my dad first got it and we spent a Saturday afternoon together working out how to operate it.

I choose some music – a dance compilation that I'm kind of guessing Nikki, Mari, Toni, Traci or one of the 'i's probably bought – and turn up the volume with the remote as far as it will go, which is pretty loud. My ears are almost ringing. I potter around the apartment and wait till the music ends. Then I ring Nora. She hasn't heard anything from Piers. I don't tell her about Lauren even though she must be wondering after our night together.

'You're not writing about him are you?'

'What? Piers? For a piece? No, honestly Charlie.'

'Sorry, just wondered.'

'And you haven't called the police?'

'No, no, don't worry. I think he'd cause trouble if he did speak to them.'

'Just wondered.'

I'm about to say 'bye' when she says, 'You all right, Charlie? You sound really down.'

'No, fine, don't worry, just tired.'

'Will, erm, I see you tonight?'

I think about it. I need some time on my own.

'Oh, er, no, sorry I'm going out with a friend—'

'Sure, no problem. I'll speak to you tomorrow, then, perhaps.'

'Yep. Bye babe.'

*

I look out across towards the City and central London just as the sun is setting in a glorious pink and blue mess like a strawberry ice-cream melting on a pale blue plate. The lights are coming on in the office blocks and along the roads. I can see the appeal of living up here in this ethereal sanctuary, watching the rest of the world as if it was all happening on giant TV screens.

I decide to have a jacuzzi. While it's filling I get myself a drink. One fridge is full of nothing but champagne, I discover, but another has a few bottles of white wine so I open one and take a glass into the jacuzzi. Cold wine and a hot jacuzzi – it should be wonderfully, luxuriously self-indulgent but in fact, sitting alone in this vast, white, echoey sensory-deprivation tank I feel like crying.

My dad gets home around eight, still on his mobile to what, I guess, must be his New York office. I mime a drinking action to him and he mouths 'white wine, please' back at me. I suddenly notice the vintage of the bottle I've already opened – 1982. Oops, I hope he wasn't saving it for a special occasion. Then I remember that my dad's whole life is a special occasion.

He takes the glass from me, gives me a wink of thanks and goes into his bedroom, telling New York, 'We'll need to see the last five years' billings at least, together with future projections for this year and next plus . . . oh, bullshit, Marty, 'course they can. Get them over to me and I'll have a look at them later tonight.'

When he comes back he is wearing a sort of kaftan and smelling of cologne.

'So what kind of day have you had?' he asks, collapsing on the settee.

I give him an exasperated look. 'Well, pretty shit actually.'

'Mmm? Oh, yeah. Lauren. Women just suddenly get these things into their heads. So, what's the matter with her? Time of the month?' He flicks on Bloomberg Business News on the telly. I feel quite indignant on Lauren's behalf.

'No, she's not like that, she's very level-headed, as you know,' I say, hoping he'll remember that he has met her frequently over the last six years. 'She's just got this thing about getting into television. Met this awful bloke called Peter Beaumont-Crowther.'

'Oh, right, Freak Productions.'

'That's him. Do you know him?'

'Met him a couple of times. I think he's produced some infomercials for us.'

'What do you think of him?'

Still watching the telly, Dad shrugs his shoulders dismissively. Either he doesn't know much about PBC or he doesn't think much of him.

'Where's, erm . . .' What's her bloody name?

'English lesson,' intercepts Dad. 'I told her I could get someone over here to do it but she insists on going to this school in Soho or something.'

A cynical thought about her desire to get away and mix with her own age groups in the bars of Soho crosses my mind. But Dad is asking me about 2cool. I don't tell him about Piers. I just tell him that the site is no longer up on the net and that we're waiting to hear back from the Fraud Squad.

'But you've done nothing wrong, you're sure of that?' he asks, looking at me severely.

'No, I told you – I signed a few cheques.'

'But that was before the other two disappeared, before there was any suggestion that finances might not be healthy.'

'Yes, I said.'

'I did tell you about those revenue streams,' says my dad, flicking over to CNN Financial.

'Yeah, I know,' I say sadly, wondering suddenly what Nora's doing tonight.

'What do you want to eat?' he asks.

I'm about to ask what he's got in the flat but then the absurdity of this notion strikes me.

'Whatever.'

'There's this new online sushi place,' he says. He presses a button on the TV console. A keyboard appears from the table next to him and the TV screen turns to an internet homepage. He types in an address and suddenly a picture of a sushi bar appears before us.

The chef, looking mildly surprised, bows and says, 'Harrow, may I take your ordah?'

'You can see it all being made in front of you on webcam before it's sent off to your home,' Dad explains to me. Then he says into the mike, 'What do you recommend today?'

'The brue marrin is very good.'

'What? Oh, blue marlin? Yep, give us a couple of those. Any fugu fish?'

The chef looks alarmed. 'No fugu fish today,' he says decisively.

'Fugu fish is the poisonous one. If it isn't filleted in exactly the right way, the venom remains in the flesh and you'll be dead in seconds,' explains Dad.

'Shame they haven't got any, then,' I say.

'What else do you fancy, kiddo?'

'I don't know. Salmon? Tuna?'

'Good idea.'

My dad orders lots of things I've never heard of and then we watch them being prepared on screen, the paper-thin, surgically sharp knives stroking the fish into tiny strips and cubes and the rice being patted and cut into shape. The only slightly disconcerting thing is the one non-Japanese member of the team who stands at the back, watching the other chefs at work and picking his nose disconsolately from time to time. Unfortunately the camera pans away from him just as he has finished the extraction process so we don't see where his quarry ends up.

Anyway, twenty minutes later our sushi, beautifully laid out with intricately carved vegetables and mysterious fronds of greenery, arrives with a slightly overwhelmed guy on a bike and we set it out on the coffee table before us.

Dad puts the screen back to television mode. He's got over 600 channels I've already discovered. On one we find a rerun of *Fawlty Towers*. We smile and sit back, mid-sushi. We used to watch it when me and my sister were kids and he and Mum were still together. But he just wants to check what's on the other 599 channels and by the time we've scanned through all of them and got back to *Fawlty Towers* on 178, the seventies sitcom channel, it's over and instead there's *Are You Being Served*? which we don't like.

At about eleven I announce that I'm going to bed and he says he's going to do some work until what's-her-name comes back. (He doesn't call her that, of course, but I just *cannot* remember this girl's name. Read into that what you will.)

I brush my teeth in my own bathroom and get into bed. Was ever any bed too big for one person? I feel as if I'm in a hospital ward. Lauren will be in our bed. I hope she's on her own. The idea of Peter, with his head on my pillow, looking lovingly across at her, inches away from her face under our sheets, makes me shudder.

I stare at the ceiling for a while, gently torturing myself, and then I reach across to the lighting control panel. I press a button and the ceiling lights dim slightly, but some others by the dressing table come on. I touch another nob and the ceiling lights come back on and so do the ones by the jacuzzi. I try a third and the jacuzzi lights go off along with the main lights, but some others by the bedside tables come on. The fourth puts the main light on dimly and the jacuzzi lights on brightly. The fifth and sixth still leave lights on in various places in the room. By this time I've run out of buttons – and patience – so I whack the whole panel a couple of times and finally I'm in complete darkness.

chapter twenty-six

I sleep surprisingly well, probably because of the intense silence and darkness of my new room which, because of the design of the building, has no windows. When I wake up next morning at just after nine, I lie in bed for a while trying to decide whether my dad has gone to work yet. He must have. I get up, put on a T-shirt and boxers in case what's-her-name is still here and open the door to the main reception room. The sunshine streaming in through the wall of glass opposite me hits me like a bucket of cold water after the intense darkness. I stagger back and close my eyes for a moment.

Slightly more accustomed to the light, I open them again. It really is the most beautiful day. Oh, God, why hasn't someone told the weather about what's happening in my life. I've got no job, no money, no career prospects, my girlfriend has chucked me out, I'm known by millions as that tit from the up-its-own-arse website which has bitten the dust, and yet standing here, I'm bathed in glorious, golden, late summer sunshine.

I find some orange juice in the fridge and flick on the telly to interrupt the gentle, monotonous roar of the air-conditioning. I open the window but even though it's a relatively calm day, this far up, this near the river, it's just too windy to stand outside in your underwear. When I step back inside again, Dad's current girlfriend is just emerging from their bedroom. She looks at me for a moment, her long blonde hair all over her face, wearing nothing but a man's shirt which is undone. Her breasts are clearly visible underneath but she makes no attempt to button up the shirt. They are pert and tanned and remind me of Lauren's.

'Oh, hi,' she says.

'Hi,' I say. 'Erm, I'm just staying for a while, did my dad mention it?'

It's definitely the one I met at breakfast in Knightsbridge. She looks blankly at me. Perhaps she doesn't understand. Or even remember me.

'Oh,' she says, finally, without smiling. Then she walks over to the kitchen unit and gets herself a bowl of cereal and takes it across to the settee. She switches on MTV. I get some cereal myself and then go into my bathroom, visualise those breasts and have a wank.

My plan, such as it exists, is to spend the next few days at my dad's just chilling. I'll call the model agencies again, keep in touch with Nora, check in with Piers a few times, wait to hear from the police and see if Lauren rings me again. I don't think I've got a cat in hell's chance of finding Guy, frankly. The more I think about it, the more I realise that he is very sensibly just getting out of it. As soon as I can, I think I'll do the same.

I watch more telly with the girlfriend who has established herself Guardian of the Telly Controller, and turns over quite arbitrarily without any consultation or consideration.

I go for a swim in the vast, empty pool in the basement of the building. Then I have some lunch of smoked salmon and scrambled eggs. I offer some to her. She smiles acceptance and scoffs it hungrily as soon as I put the plate down in front of her. In fact eating things – and watching MTV, VH1, The Box and some bizarre Brazilian soap opera – is what she seems to do all day.

Nora rings in the early afternoon to ask 'how it's going'.

'How's what going?' I ask, laughing.

'Things,' she says, sounding hurt.

'You mean, how's it going sitting here in the middle of nowhere with a girl who just watches telly all day and stuffs her face and can't speak a word of English,' I say, looking across at her, wondering if she might understand this bit and react. Instead she slowly puts another Pringle in her mouth and stares at the screen as two women set about each other screaming and pulling each other's hair.

'What do you mean "in the middle of nowhere"? Which girl?' asks Nora.

I mutter 'Oh, fuck', remembering that she knows nothing about this. I suppose I can't pretend I'm still in Chiswick but I don't want to get involved in a long explanation so I say, 'My dad's girlfriend. I'm staying with him for a while.'

There is a pause as she takes it in and considers what to say. She obviously can't think of anything appropriate so instead she just says, 'Right, I see. So you're not in your flat.'

'No, I've . . . I'm not.'

'Oh. Well, I haven't found out much more about Guy. I rang and left a message for Piers just to see if—'

'Do you *know* where Guy is?' I ask her suddenly.

'What are you talking about?'

'You really don't know where he is?'

''Course not, don't you think I'd have told you if I did?'

'I'm not sure.'

'I would. Charlie, what are you saying?' I don't answer. 'Look, I've been ringing round his friends and acquaintances from Cambridge. We've got a stringer, you know, a local reporter, working in the area too. I've even spoken to his brother in the Galapagos Islands.'

'And?'

'He didn't seem that bothered. Obviously not a very close family. So the trail's gone a bit cold. You haven't heard anything more then?'

'No, nothing at all,' I sigh, getting up and walking around the room.

'Your dad hasn't said anything?'

'My dad, no. Why should he?'

'Just wondered. They're getting a bit tired of the story here at the moment. They're asking me to do other things. Don't know anyone who had an affair with their cleaner do you?' Suddenly she starts talking to someone away from the phone. I hear a shout in the background. 'Well, you shouldn't have left it there, should you? It was right by my elbow,' I hear her say. Then she comes back to me. 'Sorry, where was I?'

'Little accident?'

'Honestly, what a stupid place to leave a cup of coffee.' Someone is talking to her again. 'Just turn your keyboard upside down and pour it out. I'm always doing it, it doesn't do them any harm. Except for the "b" that sticks a bit. Oh, and my "v" has been playing up recently but you don't even take sugar so you shouldn't have any problems.' I'm laughing now. She whispers to me, 'She can't even bloody write anyway, it's probably a blessing. So, where was I? Oh, yes, you don't know anyone who's had a thing with their cleaner, do you?'

'With their cleaner? No, 'fraid not.'

'Anyone who'd be willing to say they had. What about some of your model friends? We need some good-looking young men, twenty- to thirty-year-olds. We'd pay them.'

'*I'll* do it.'

'Erm, I think you're a little bit too famous now,' she says.

'Oh, don't say that,' I groan.

'Besides, I thought you didn't like being in the paper.'

'Nora, I still haven't forgiven you for that,' I say, seriously.

'I know, I said I'm sorry. So what's on TV?' she asks, obviously hearing the screams and dramatic music in the background.

'It's a Brazilian soap opera.'

'Hey, what's happening in it? We used to get them on cable in New York. I love 'em. It was the only TV I ever watched.'

I squint over at the telly.

'This woman is running through a house screaming for some reason. Every time she opens and closes a door all the scenery moves . . . Oops, she's just slammed the door straight into the camera . . . oh, no, a little hand's come up and opened it, that's lucky . . . for some reason you can't see her face, we're just getting a shot of her bum. I don't think the cameraman can keep up with her.'

She laughs. 'God, I miss them. They're so mad. They have to do everything in one take and they never even have time to rehearse I don't think.' There is a pause. I know she's going to say it: 'Will you stay at mine again tonight?'

'Let's have a drink, shall we?' I know I'm not answering the question.

'Sure, okay.'

I suggest somewhere in town, midway between hers and my dad's.

I get to the bar at seven, glad to leave the flat, I mean penthouse, and relieved to be going out before my dad comes back, in a way. I haven't really spent much time with him since I was a kid, and the new him, although it's quite a few years old now, still takes some getting used to. Nora doesn't get there till nearly half past. I roll my eyes and look at my watch. Pushing her way through the crowd, she makes a face and mouths the word 'sorry' at me.

As she nears me, she transfers her bag from one hand to the other and, in the process, manages to swing it like a croquet mallet, sending a bowl of pistachio nuts flying off a low table. I can just hear her tell the girl who was about to take a handful of them before they shot off, 'They're actually *really* fattening, full of calories.'

When she gets to me she says, 'She'll thank me next time she gets on the scales.'

We kiss lightly on the lips.

'You took your time,' I tell her. 'If I'd waited here any longer they'd have turned me into a Starbucks.'

'Ha, ha,' she says sarcastically. 'I'd love a drink, thank you. Large G and T.'

'Good day?' I ask.

'Oh, fuck,' she says, making a face.

I laugh. 'Do you ever have a good day?'

'Sometimes but, oh, today, I'm in so much trouble. Did you see my piece in the paper?'

'Erm, sorry, I didn't buy it.'

'Don't worry. Anyway, I had an interview in it with this little old lady who'd hitched, can you believe, *hitched* all the way over to Tangier to see the grave of her war hero husband because she couldn't afford to get there any other way.'

'Amazing.'

'Oh, she is, I was so impressed. Does charity work and everything, really lovely woman. But unfortunately in the piece there's a spelling mistake in the third par. Oh, God, *third* par—'

'Par?'

'Paragraph. Right at the top of the piece. The subs should have picked it up but they didn't. Damn them! Anyway, I describe her living room and then it's supposed to say that she offers me tea and gets up to water her plants but I left the "l" out of plants. Think about it.'

'Water her pants?'

'Yes. She was wandering around her tiny, immaculate living room watering her pants. What was she? Incontinent?'

Just then the barman puts down her drink in front of her.

'Oh, God, do I ever need this.'

We don't spend long in the bar as it's too noisy. We go to a pizza restaurant round the corner where she orders a bottle of Chianti before we've even sat down.

'You like your booze, don't you?' I say.

'No, I don't,' she says defensively. 'I mean I do, but not excessively.'

'Sorry, just saying.'

'Besides, all journalists drink quite a bit – or nothing at all if you know what I mean. I suppose models have to watch it; you know, keep your skin clear and your weight down.' She purses her lips and sucks in her cheeks absurdly.

'Ha, ha. I don't think I'll ever be a model again, though.'

'Really? Why not?'

'I've left messages at all the main agencies, well, the ones I'd work for anyway, and none of them has rung me back.'

'Why not? With your reputation, your portfolio, they'd have you like a shot.'

'My reputation's the problem, I think. They don't like all the stuff that's been in the papers about me.'

'And that's my fault?'

'Well, some of it, yeah,' I laugh bitterly.

She begins to consult the menu. Around us groups of girls are meeting over white wine and garlic bread for gossipy, giggly evenings. I catch a couple of them looking at me. I give them a convincingly cool smile. 2cool? They giggle to each other and look away.

'Do you want me to say sorry *again*?' she says from behind the menu.

I sigh. 'No. What difference would it make anyway? I just fancy having a moan. Thing is, I don't know what the hell I'm going to do.' She looks sympathetically at me. 'Oh, don't worry, there's nothing *you* can do. I'll find something. I thought I might go back to college and refresh my marketing skills.'

The waiter comes over and we order.

'I spoke to Piers this afternoon,' she says.

'Really? What did he say?'

'He's had to move.'

'Why? Did someone discover where he is?'

'Not exactly.' She stifles a giggle. 'It's not funny actually.'

'What happened?'

'He burnt the house down.'

'What?'

'You know that little Calor Gas stove he had? It must have caught on something and the whole house went up in smoke.'

'You're kidding. Is he all right?'

'Funnily enough, he got out unscathed.'

'Typical Piers.'

'I saw a report about the fire on the local news this evening. Now he's found a deserted warehouse that a club promoter he knows was using for illegal raves.'

'Well, that news has cheered me up a bit,' I tell her, refilling her glass.

After our food arrives I ask her about their common grandparents.

'Piers's mum is my dad's sister, that's all,' she says dismissively. 'There were six brothers and sisters altogether. One died in a car crash ten years ago. Piers's mum, my aunt Lucille, lives in South Carolina now with her second husband, Piers's stepfather.'

'So, Piers is half American?'

'Yeah, fifty per cent Yank, though he always plays the Hugh Grant role whenever he goes there.'

'Very shrewd.'

'Oh, yes, he knows how to charm the right people, what to say to take them in. But then you know that, don't you?'

By the end of dinner the issue of whether I'm going to go back to hers is hanging in the air between us. Our conversation is getting vague and disjointed with short, half-finished sentences as a result. Of course, I could easily go and stay with her now that I'm not living with Lauren, but somehow that fact makes it worse. It would be like a double betrayal. Even if she is cuddling up with Peter tonight I can't go back with Nora. I do actually enjoy talking to Nora; she makes me laugh, she's so different from anyone I've ever met before, we never seem to run out of things to say, she's so sharp it's scary, she's got that dangerous unknown quality about her – I feel like I'm playing with fire just having dinner with her, let alone having sex with her. But I can't go and sleep with her again, even though Lauren wouldn't know about it this time, of course. I just can't do it.

'Shall we get the bill?' I say, bringing things to a head.

'Yes, of course.' She looks round very energetically for a waiter while I watch her. Sometimes she's so in control, so cool, like when we first met and had lunch and then, sometimes, she's like an insecure teenager. I wonder how many boyfriends she has had. I wonder if the Wall Street broker with the parental home in the Hamptons was the only one. I wonder if he really exists at all.

She insists on putting it on expenses. It's only twenty-five quid a head, so I let her. Besides, I'll have to start saving my money now. We step outside and I realise that getting back to my dad's is going to be a hell of a schlepp. Notting Hill is just fifteen minutes away. But still I can't do it.

'I'd better be getting back,' I say, touching her cheek.

'You don't want to come back to mine?' she says, looking down at the ground, kicking an old crisp packet gently.

'I, er, I can't. Sorry.'

'Not even for a quick fuck?' she says. I see a muscle in her jaw jump angrily.

'Nora, don't say that.'

'Why the hell not? That's all it is.'

'It is *not*. Look, I really like you, Nora, but—'

'But not that much.'

'Just let me finish, will you?' Suddenly the street seems very crowded, very public. 'I've been going out with Lauren for seven years, it's a big chunk of my life.'

'But you're not with her now.'

'Well, I'm not living with her but—'

'But when you feel like doing it with someone else again, you'll let me know.'

'Don't say that.'

'Well, why did you do it with me then?'

I can't think of how to put it, so we stand in silence as people push past us.

'Nora, I was angry and confused, you were kind, you were there. I really appreciate that.'

'And I was a useful way of getting back at your girlfriend when she was pissing you off, is that it?'

'No, no.' I touch her cheek again but she looks away angrily. 'Nora, I really like you. I don't want to hurt you and I promise I wasn't just using you, but I'm in a relationship, or perhaps I'm not any more, perhaps I'm just getting over one, I don't know. Either way, I just need some space at the moment. I don't want to mess you around.'

She takes a deep breath and looks around her. 'Sure,' she says in a whisper.

'The point is, if I did come back now and we had sex, it *would* just be a quick fuck. And I really don't want that either.'

'Okay.' She looks up at me and says the worst thing she can say: 'I love you.'

I smile as kindly as I can. Oh, Nora, I'm so sorry. I kiss her on the lips. 'Let's find you a taxi then.'

What I didn't say, because it seemed too cruel to say it at that moment, is that I still don't trust her and I'm not sure that I ever will.

Finding a cab for Nora is no problem but it takes three attempts to find one who's willing to go anywhere near my dad's. The first two obviously think they're going to fall off the edge of the earth.

'What the 'ell do you wanna live there for?' asks the driver as we shoot out along Commercial Road, the meter clicking up the fare rhythmically.

'I don't,' I yell at him from the back seat. 'My dad does.'

'Oh, right.' As we drive on, I notice him look at me again in his mirror. 'I thought I knew your face. You're that guy from that website, arncha?'

I think about it for a moment. 'No, that's not me. That's my brother.'

'Really, you don't half look alike. Bet he's keeping a low profile somewhere, is he? He must feel a real prick.'

'Yeah, I think he does.'

'Unless, you know, no offence intended, he's in on the whole thing. Waiting to get his share and then scarper, know what I mean?'

'I don't think he is. I think he's just a helpless pawn in a bigger game.'

'Well, you'd know.' He drives on a bit more with me willing him to shut up. 'But what about all these big names? They must be livid. They'll be suing the arse off him, won't they?'

I think of Josh Langdon's little bit of backtracking on the news report and Piers's odd laughter when I mentioned legal action to him.

'I don't know,' I say, and then I introduce the subject of traffic congestion around the Blackwall Tunnel, and that keeps him busy until well beyond Limehouse.

When I get back just after eleven my dad and Thingy are curled up together watching the climax of a Tom Cruise action movie at deafening volume.

'Hi, kiddo,' says Dad sleepily. Thingy remains glued to the set eating Jaffa cakes.

The next morning my dad is tearing around the flat because he has overslept. His driver is waiting awkwardly by the door to the apartment, shuffling from foot to foot. I nod hello to him and then sit quietly out of the way until the Armani-clad whirlwind has left in a cloud of expensive aftershave, still cursing and swearing. I have a swim and use the gym. I get back up to the apartment at eleven and Thingy is putting away the groceries that have been delivered from Harvey Nicks. She smiles and offers me a biscuit. I smile back, shake my head and point to the cereal which is in the box she's currently unpacking. She laughs, pushes away the box with the cereal packet in it and opens the biscuits anyway, shaking the packet around in front of me temptingly.

I snatch them from her and run away to the other side of the room with them. She shouts something and comes running up to me, giggling, trying to grab them off me. I hold them above her head and she jumps up. Then she pokes me in the stomach and I crumple up, startled, winded, laughing. She makes for the biscuits but I'm too quick for her, yanking them away again.

Then I dash off back down the living room towards the kitchen, but on the way I open the window and throw them out. The wind catches them and we both look down to see a confetti of tiny bickies blowing across the urban landscape. Harvey Nicks bics – chucked away just like that. Lauren would be furious at such silliness, my mum would be shocked at the waste. How much? Just for biscuits? But over the last few weeks I've been drinking vintage champagne at five o'clock in the office for no reason, wearing Comme des Garçons shirts once and stuffing them in the drawer, never to look at them again, and chucking expensive freebie toiletries in the bin because there's no more room in the bathroom cabinet. So what the heck?

I look down again. The biscuits are still falling, blowing around, some disappearing from view.

I've set them free. The poor little Harvey Nicks bics.

What's-her-name looks horrified and begins to punch me playfully. It's our longest exchange since I got here.

A bit later on I ring directory enquiries and get the number of the PR company that Sarah works for and, after some debate, during which I watch more MTV and The Box than any sane person should in their entire lifetime, I ring her and ask whether she's spoken to Lauren.

'Yes, I saw her last night.'

'How is she?'

'Hang on, let me close the door to my office.' She comes back a moment later. 'Charlie, she's really upset.'

I feel my throat tighten slightly. 'Yeah, well.'

'She can't believe how you've changed.'

'She's the one that's changed, Sarah, all that TV crap.'

'I know, but it's what she wants to do, you know how determined she is. She'll get it in the end. But the thing is she doesn't want to lose you.'

'It's driving me mad, though. That ghastly bloke.' I can't even bear to say his name.

'Look at it from her point of view – all this 2cool stuff, she says you just won't leave it alone.'

'Sarah, I'm implicated in it. I'm a director. I might go to jail.' I don't really believe that but I want to make the point.

'Mark can get you a good lawyer—'

'Don't worry, I've got one thanks. Look, I've left really anyway, it's all finished now.'

'But also, you know . . .'

'What?'

'You slept with that journalist.'

'I . . . well . . . so? She's sleeping with *him*.'

'She's not, believe me. Look, actually I think Peter's— What? What? Now? Sorry, Charlie. Got to go, crisis. Erm, call me later will you?'

'Sure,' I tell her, sitting in my empty, white room with my few clothes strewn around me.

*

I stand out on the balcony and let the wind buffet me for a while. I look out at the Canary Wharf tower and the 'Gherkin' with their backdrop of fast-moving clouds. Sometimes if you position your eyes right, it looks as if the sky is still and the towers are falling over. Trains snake their way between buildings and I can even see people in the streets like little dots. Real human beings, dwarfed by what they've created around them.

When I step back in again, slightly punch-drunk from the wind, my hair all over the place, a phone is ringing. It's a mobile lying on the industrial stainless steel kitchen work surface. It's not mine. I don't think it's Thingy's. It must be my dad's. He must have left it this morning in his mad rush to get out the door.

There is no number showing on the screen, just the word 'Unavailable'. I pick it up and answer it.

'Hello?' says a voice. 'Jared? Sorry, have you got a sec? I need to ask you something. Hello? Is that Jared?'

'No, it's not, it's his son. Can I take a message for him?'

There is no response from the other end, just a pause, and then the caller clicks off.

It's not much to go on, and there was a lot of background noise, street sounds, people talking, cars, buses, but it was just enough for me to recognise the voice.

What the fuck is Guy ringing my dad for?

chapter twenty-seven

I put the phone down. It *was* Guy's voice. I know it. I recognise those clipped vowels, that strangled urgency. Thingy comes in and smiles sweetly, then goes to the cupboard and gets out a bag of Kettle Chips before sitting down in front of the telly, flicking between the twenty or so music channels that my dad's got. A girl in a bikini top and mini-skirt dances manically around a computer-generated backdrop and sings to a thumping Europop beat:

> *'I'm your pretty little dolly, dolly*
> *Pick me up and put me in your trolley, trolley.*
> *Bend my arm, bend my leg*
> *Do it till I scream and beg.'*

I watch her for a moment then I look over at Thingy. I wish I had someone to talk to.

'What?' says Nora. 'You're kidding, that can't be right.'

It's so much easier to discuss this with her than to talk about us, our relationship, if that's what it is and, worst of all, why I can't sleep with her again.

'I'm sure it was him,' I tell her. 'I know that voice too well.'

'And it was your dad's mobile?'

'Yeah, he left it behind this morning.'

'What does he say?'

'My dad? I haven't asked him about it.'

'Why the hell not?'

'Because . . .' I don't want it to be true? Because I don't want him to lie to me? Because I don't want him to be involved? I'm not sure whether I'm shocked or angry. 'Because he's been in a meeting all day,' I lie.

'Have you left a message for him?'

'Yes.'

'Good. As soon as he gets out of the meeting and you speak to him, call me. I'm going to ring Piers to see what he thinks. You couldn't hear anything in the background that would indicate where Guy was?'

'No, just traffic and people.'

How many times have I heard this kind of exchange in stupid cop shows? This time it's real.

'I wonder if the mobile phone company could tell us what incoming calls your dad has had recently.'

'It's possible, I suppose.' More cop show stuff.

'Find out from your dad, can you? Look, I'm on deadline for another piece. Speak soon.'

Nora the hard-nosed journalist is a lot easier to handle than Nora the lover, I decide, slumping down and staring at MTV Dance.

I don't ring Dad, but just after seven he comes home. Thingy looks up from the settee and aims her face at him. He bends down to kiss her and there is rather a lot of tongue action so I head into the kitchen area.

'Hi, son,' he shouts through to me.

'Hi, Dad,' I shout back. 'Want a drink?'

'Um, yeah, get me a glass of champagne, will you?'

'Champagne?'

'Yeah, why not, we've just closed a deal and acquired another US agency. Cronkite, Lipchitz, Winckel, Schwimmer. Heard of them?'

'They're the talk of Chiswick,' I mutter, popping open a bottle.

After Dad has settled down and bored us with the details of his brilliant acquisition strategy (I say 'us' – Thingy doesn't move her eyes from an episode of eighties vintage *EastEnders*), I say to him, 'You left your mobile at home this morning.'

'Did I? Oh, thank God for that, I thought I'd have to get another one. I just can't seem to hang onto them. Did anyone ring me on it?'

'A couple of people. Your reflexologist to confirm Thursday at six.'

'Oh, fuck! Can't make it, I must ring and tell her.'

'Cathy?'

'Oh, I'll ring her. Anyone else?'

'Yeah, Guy.'

'Guy?' He takes a sip of champagne and changes the channel to the annoyance of Thingy, who looks round at him from her position in his lap and frowns. 'Guy who?'

'Guy from 2cool.'

He switches channel again. 'Your former business colleague ringing *me*? What are you talking about?'

'It sounded like him,' I say, staring at my dad.

'But I don't know him. Why would he be ringing *me*?'

This time when he tries to change channel Thingy snatches the remote away from him.

'Right. Must have made a mistake.'

'Well, what shall we eat tonight? French? Italian? Chinese? Fusion?' He kisses Thingy, during which time she manages not to move her eyes away from the telly.

'Actually I'm not very hungry,' I say, getting up and going to my room. 'I think I'll just have a bath and go to bed.'

I haven't felt so homeless since I first walked out of our flat in Chiswick.

As soon as I lie down on my bed I leap up again. I feel physically sick. How could he tell me crap like that? Why is he lying to me? Why *would* a father lie to his son, and so unconvincingly? To protect him? From what? I've been exposed to so much shit over the last few weeks I can't believe there could be anything else. Could there be? Something worse? Something that he knows about, that he's involved with?

I decide to have a jacuzzi; at least it will kill some time. Above the noise of the bubbles and the pump I hear a knock on the door.

'I'm in the jacuzzi,' I yell.

'Oh, right,' says Dad. 'I, er, wanted to check that you don't want anything. To eat, I mean. We're going to order some food.'

I'm suddenly reminded of the time when he was leaving Mum. His clumsy attempts to win me over, to make me understand why he was doing this terrible thing. He kept arranging these trips and outings for me and my sister. Big, planned things. His anxiety as he took us to the Planetarium or a special kids' screening of that year's Bond movie or a pop concert (we always had a box, or special seats –

shame it was never an act we liked) was contagious. By the end of the day I felt sick with nerves as well.

Eventually he gave up on my sister who, being a bit more forthright than I am, made her feelings very plain. Then it was just me and him. If he'd simply sat down and said to me, 'Please forgive me, please can we go on being father and son,' it would have been so much easier but, instead, he kept manifesting it, clumsily acting it out, with his expensive, meticulously planned treats. Even more desperate, more intense now with just the two of us. His jolly commentary and self-conscious enthusiasm. Perhaps I should have said something. Like 'stop it', for instance. But I couldn't bear to, in case it hurt him.

'No, I'm fine thanks, been eating all day,' I shout back.

Even above the noise of the jacuzzi I can sense him hesitate outside the door before he goes back to Thingy. I watch *Raiders of the Lost Ark* on my own massive stereo surround-sound plasma screen before launching my now nightly assault on the hi-tech lighting control panel and slipping under the sheets.

The next day I'm awake by seven but I lie in bed until I hear my dad leave at eight. Then I get up and have some orange juice. It's raining softly outside. The huge wall of windows makes me feel slightly exposed and I want to pull a curtain or get away from them but, of course, it's impossible. I shiver slightly as I finish the juice. I haven't got a pullover, just a couple of T-shirts, a couple of short-sleeved shirts, some jeans, some undies and five socks, none of which match. I wish I'd been better organised but then again I'm not used to walking out like this.

The mist and fine rain means that you can hardly see beyond Canary Wharf. The Thames is slate grey, flecked with white. A barge moves almost imperceptibly in the choppy water. I think of Lauren and wonder what she's doing now.

My mobile rings.

'Charlie Barrett?'

'Speaking.'

'It's Detective Inspector Slapton here. We just wanted to return your papers and computer terminals.'

'Oh, yeah.' I'd almost forgotten about them.

'Also I need to ask you some more questions.'

'What kind of questions?'

'Just a few simple ones to help us with our enquiries. I'm sure they won't prove too demanding.'

'No, sure.'

'Right, when can we deliver these things?'

'Where do you want to deliver them?' I ask, thinking out loud.

Not surprisingly Slapton is a bit confused by this question. 'Well, that's up to you, isn't it?'

'Yeah, I suppose it is.' I watch the rain on the windows for a while and then make a decision. 'Can you deliver them to my flat in Chiswick?'

'If that's what you want.'

'You know the address,' I remind him pointedly.

'I've got it. What time?'

I look around the apartment, shiver again. I see the big plasma TV which will go on again very soon when Thingy wakes up and I say, 'Soon as poss?'

This takes Slapton by surprise. 'Hang on a sec, let's think. How about eleven-thirty?'

'Sounds good to me.'

'See you then.' He rings off.

I go back into my room, think about having a shave but decide I can't be bothered. I text my dad to tell him what's happening and ten minutes later I'm downstairs waiting for a minicab from the one company that will pick up from this godforsaken place.

The taxi takes me to Tower Hill and I let the end-of-rush-hour crowds pass either side of me like shoals of fish past a snorkler. I buy a coffee and a bacon roll for the tube journey, feeling nervous but sort of elated. I'm going home even if I do have to face Lauren. I pick up the *Post* at the tube station. There's a story about some footballer getting thrown out of a nightclub and then something about a little girl who died because she was turned away from a hospital by a doctor who thought she just had a cold when she had something much more serious. The parents are threatening to sue. Someone has called for an enquiry.

Nora has a piece about a woman who left her husband and went off with her stepfather. I hardly recognise Nora from the postage-stamp-sized photo of her by name. She looks quizzically over the top of her glasses. I feel I should ring her. If this thing gets sorted out, or even just fizzles away to nothing, what will happen to us? I wonder.

On the next page there is an advert for anoraks featuring Steve, one of my old mates from Jet Models. He'll be taking some stick for that. He looks like a right berk, standing there in a horrible fawn anorak, all zips and toggles and pockets, smiling inanely into the middle distance. 'A special offer from the *Post* – just £29.99 including postage and packing.' Not exactly one for your book. Still, at least he's earning.

By the time I reach our tube station, I'm really feeling nervous. I take out my phone to ring ahead. Hang on, why the fuck should I? It's my flat. I check for my keys in my pocket. They suddenly feel very sharp, like an offensive weapon. I'll be stabbing them into the lock in a few minutes.

As I walk down our road, I find myself looking out for changes, like a soldier returning after the war, or someone coming back to a childhood haunt. Needless to say, it hasn't changed at all over the last few days. But something stops me in my tracks.

Peter's car. A dark blue Lexus, parked just down from the flat. I peer in the window as I walk past, just to make sure. Yep, there above the dashboard are some sunglasses that I've seen him wearing. I check my watch – just gone ten. He could have arrived this morning, certainly, but somehow I don't think so; the car looks like it's been there all night. There are rain-sodden leaves on the windscreen. My heart thumping with shock, anger and an explosive, paralysing unhappiness, I carrying on walking until I reach what used to be mine and Lauren's home.

It looks innocent enough. But the curtains are still closed.

Just as I'm putting my key in the lock, some devious, masochistic part of me tells me to do it quietly. I slip it in surreptitiously, open the door in silence and step inside. I close the door very softly behind me and put my bag down. I can smell his aftershave already. I feel my breathing becoming irregular as my heart starts beating faster.

In our bed! The two of them.

Putting my head round into the living room I see a bottle of champagne and two glasses on the coffee table. While I was drinking champagne at my dad's last night they were doing it here. Then I hear Peter's voice. Very quiet, slightly muffled. Then a giggle. I have to stop for a moment. I feel dizzy and physically sick. This is *our* flat.

How could she do it here? In our bed? How could she swap him for me so easily?

It's too much. I burst into the bedroom.

Peter looks round in alarm. 'What the—?' is all he can say before I grab him by the hair and drag him out of my bed. Out of the corner of my eye I see Lauren's slim, tanned leg slip back under the duvet.

Peter is lying at my feet, contorted as he tries to look up at me and move away from me at the same time.

'Charlie!' he says, trying to cover his genitals while holding his head where I yanked his hair. There are still stray hairs in my hand. 'What are you doing here?'

'You fucking bastard,' I yell at him. 'You fucking, *fucking* cunt. How dare you?' My voice is cracking as anger and unhappiness surge through me. A good kick sends him sprawling across the floor.

'Ow, shit. Please. Stop it.' He crawls away from my foot. 'It's not what you think, it's not—'

'What the fuck is it, then?' I sniff back tears and look across at Lauren.

Except that it's not Lauren.

chapter twenty-eight

It's a lithe, tanned body and there's blond hair but it's not Lauren's. The legs are a bit more sinuous and quite a lot hairier than Lauren's. My mind is reeling and I'm not sure I'd recognise my own mother at the moment. But I do realise pretty quickly that this is a bloke. I look a bit harder and see his dick, nestling in its light brown pubic hair by the edge of the duvet. I look further up and there's the face of a young guy with a nose stud, regarding me with a mixture of terror and shock.

'Who the fuck are you?' he asks, sliding out of the far side of the bed and protecting his groin with the duvet.

Dumbstruck, I look down at Peter, who has by now edged over to the dressing table and is curled up half-underneath it.

'I told you,' he says, still terror-stricken.

'What's going on?' I say, a little unnecessarily. 'Where's Lauren?'

'She's gone away with Sarah. To France. They're staying with Sarah's parents. She said the flat would be empty and I could borrow it. I've got friends from the States staying at mine. Scott has a roommate so we . . .'

'Scott?' I mutter, moronically.

Peter nods in the young, blond guy's direction again. We stand there like a tableau for what seems like ages. I feel faint. Perhaps I'm just dreaming this, hallucinating, even. I slump down on the bed and sense both men shrink back further. I take a deep breath, put my head in my hands and find my arguments with Lauren during the past few weeks repeating themselves. My stupid, sneering comments. You pillock. You stupid, stupid bastard. Oh, God, Lauren, I'm so sorry, I just thought . . . what a fucking idiot. Peter's sexuality was probably obvious if only I hadn't been so paranoid and suspicious.

Finally I look across at Peter and say to him, 'You're gay?'

Peter appears baffled, as if to say: look, I know you're blond and a model but . . .

'Oh, thank God.'

I let it sink in for a moment. I suddenly feel wide-awake, relaxed, full of energy, euphoric, as if nothing bad could ever happen again. I stand up and move towards Peter. He flinches and edges further under the dressing table but I pull him out and lift him to a standing position. 'Oh, thank God,' I say again, and I nearly hug him, but then don't quite, given that he's naked. Instead I just look at him for a moment and walk around the room trying to take in the full significance of my discovery.

'You've never slept with Lauren?'

'With Lauren? Well, no. Not at all, I don't really . . .'

'No, sure,' I say, running my hands through my hair, trying to come to terms with this new situation. 'And Lauren doesn't fancy you? No, of course not.' It's only afterwards that I remember Peter looking a little bit hurt at my instant supposition.

We all three stand in silence for a bit longer. Two naked, terrified gay guys, one clothed, embarrassed, relieved, oh, hugely relieved, straight guy.

'Oh, God, I'm so sorry Peter. Are you all right?' I look up at his hair and then down further at his plump, mottled flesh to where I kicked him. He smoothes his hair slightly, fingering his scalp. He checks for blood as I discreetly rub away any remaining hairs from my fingers. Then he puts a hand on his back and stretches gently, assessing the pain.

'Yes, I think so,' he says. 'Shall we, er?'

'Oh, sorry, carry on,' I say, overwhelmed with bonhomie. 'I mean, if you feel like it.'

Neither of them look like they're exactly panting with lust at the moment.

'I meant get dressed,' says Peter.

'I'd better get going,' says Scott in an American accent. He locates his underpants on the floor and begins to put them on without taking his eyes off me, probably concerned that I might flip again and turn on him. 'I have school,' he explains, smiling nervously.

'Would you like some coffee?' I ask them. 'I'm going to make some.'

'Um, well I'd better get going too,' says Peter.

'Oh, stay, have a cup of coffee,' I tell them. I want to celebrate.

'Um,' says Peter, looking across at Scott. They obviously decide to humour me – no sudden movements, now.

'Have a shower and coffee will be up in a minute,' I say, making my way towards the kitchen.

Peter. Gay. It was so obvious. I just thought that any man who came within feet of my beautiful girlfriend would want to jump into bed with her. How can I ever apologise to her? Poor Lauren, I'm so sorry. I stop in my tracks as I think of her. She's done nothing wrong, other than spend a bit too much time with Peter. When I think of all my pathetic, jealous comments. And I was wrong all the time. Fucking idiot. She's innocent of all charges.

And then there's Nora. Oh, God. I've used Nora to get at Lauren for something Lauren hasn't done. Poor Nora. I think of her that first night after we made love, wandering around naked – demure, self-conscious.

What? What am I talking about? She's deceived me time after time. Articles she's written. Her connection with Piers. There are probably other things that I'll have the pleasure of finding out about, too. Casual deception seems to be a way of life for her. I strayed, I admit, but I so, so regret it. I've got to win Lauren back whatever it takes, I decide, filling the coffee machine with water.

I make some coffee and a few rounds of toast into the bargain. I'm just putting it out on the breakfast unit when the others come in, looking slightly anxious, slightly sheepish.

'So, did you have a good . . .' I ask, realising that I'm not quite sure what the end of this jolly bit of small talk will be. Luckily I manage to think of 'shower?' just in time.

'Yes, thanks,' they mutter in unison. I get the feeling they're doing this just to keep me sweet – and stable – as if they're taking part in a siege and if they decline my hospitality or offend me in any way, I'll go for them again. But I'm in such a good mood I don't really care what they think.

Scott, who is dressed in a sleeveless, red Abercrombie & Fitch sweatshirt and very baggy, ripped jeans, is a film student it turns out.

He takes his coffee black and looks at Peter a lot for guidance – and protection, presumably.

'Why didn't she tell me? That you were gay, I mean?' I ask, spreading a piece of toast liberally with Lauren's mother's home-made marmalade.

'Well, I didn't tell her until recently and by that time you and her weren't talking to each other. I only mentioned it at all because we bumped into an old lover of mine in a bar,' he says, cutting a piece of toast corner to corner. 'I did suggest she should tell you because I sort of got the impression you thought that there was something going on between us, but she said why should she? It was your problem and . . . well, she was really angry with you by that stage. You know what Lauren's like.'

I smile at the thought of Lauren standing on principle, not wanting to be pushed into saying or doing something she didn't feel she had to.

'So she's gone to France, then?'

'Yes, with Sarah. It was a last-minute thing. Sarah organised it. They'll be back on Saturday.'

We both stop for a moment as we realise what this means. For all my confidence and determination, I'm not sure where I'm even going to begin to apologise adequately and to see how we can rebuild our life together. On the other hand, even if she hasn't been sleeping with Peter, she's been doing everything else with him almost every waking minute of the day, and I can't stand that any longer.

'Saturday,' I repeat dumbly. That's what? Three days away. I take a bite of toast and say, almost to myself, 'I'll be here when she gets back.'

The guys loosen up towards the end of our little impromptu breakfast. Peter's got quite a nice line in self-deprecating humour, I discover, and the way Scott gazes at him, laughing anxiously at all his jokes, is quite sweet. They're just getting up to leave when the doorbell rings.

I look at my watch. Eleven-fifteen. They're early.

'Oh, it's just the police,' I explain. The others look horrified again. 'They're just bringing back some computers and papers they took, you know, for this whole, stupid investigation thing.'

'I'll tell you about it in the car,' says Peter to Scott. 'Charlie's had a nightmare time of it for the last few weeks.'

'Harsh,' says Scott, sympathetically. 'Way harsh.'

They pick up their stuff: car keys and blazer for Peter, rucksack and walkman for Scott, and make towards the door.

'Listen, Charlie, mate, I hope you and Lauren do get it back together, you're a lovely couple,' says Peter.

I'm about to say 'Thanks' or something but suddenly my throat feels tight. Instead I just smile and nod.

The bell rings again, and I open the door to Slapton.

'Thanks, Peter,' I cough at him. 'I appreciate it. Sorry I started kicking the shit out of you like that, just didn't understand the situation. Saw red, you know?'

Peter deftly touches his hair again and, finding it's all still attached to his head, smiles.

'Good to meet you, dude. Sorry about the bed thing,' says Scott. He holds up a hand and I give it a high five.

'No worries, mate.'

They squeeze past Slapton. He looks confused and suspicious as he tries to make sense of the exchange he's just witnessed.

'Come in,' I tell him. Two junior officers, both struggling with large boxes are obviously very pleased to hear that. Slapton comes in and they follow. 'Just dump it all on the floor, here,' I say, pointing to a place by the coat rack.

One of the policemen goes out to get another box while the other produces a piece of paper and asks me to sign to say I've received them.

'What's the next stage in the investigation?' I ask Slapton.

He sucks his teeth for a moment and then says, 'Our investigators can't actually find any evidence of wrongdoing. We've informed your solicitor of that so he'll be giving you a ring about it soon. Also, none of the investors is willing to assist us with any future action.'

'Really?'

'Yes,' says Slapton through gritted teeth. 'Really. They all seem quite happy to have thrown their money away. Apparently they're very glad to think that you and the others have spent it all on designer clothes and champagne and . . . and . . . flower displays,' he snarls.

'Oh, thank God for that.' My second huge relief of the day and it's only eleven-thirty. I feel like I'm on drugs, punch-drunk with good news. All I need now is a lottery win.

'We're really just back to a missing persons investigation, which doesn't affect me,' he says bitterly. 'I go after criminals.'

'Well, thanks very much,' I say. I go to open the door.

'There is just one thing,' says Slapton, who hasn't moved from his position in the hallway. 'I'd just like you to have a look at something for me. If you don't mind.'

'Sure.' I don't like the sound of this.

'Can we . . .?' He looks towards the living room.

'Of course,' I say, leading him in. There is an awkward moment as Slapton sits down before me. I just want him out of here, so badly. I want this to be a happy, trouble-free place for when Lauren gets back so that we can talk about everything.

He hands me a list of names. 'Do you know any of these people?'

I glance down the list. 'I've heard of most of them,' I say, noticing Sir Josh Langdon, Sir James Huntsman and various other wealthy, glamorous, important names who were at our launch party together with some others who were also at the Huntsman party.

But then, towards the end, strangely out of alphabetical order, is one name that makes me gasp, almost audibly. I read it again to make sure, before handing the list back to Slapton.

He's smiling, the bastard.

'Any that jump out at you?' he says, casually.

'No,' I say gruffly. 'No, like I say, I know *of* them, well, most of them, and I've met Sir James and Lady Huntsman once but nothing more than that.'

'I think there's at least one there that you know.'

I look down again just to check. 'Yes.'

'Recognise some of them as investors in 2cool?'

'Some of them, yes.' They were on the list of names that I printed off from Piers's computer just after they disappeared.

'Oh, well. Just wondered,' says Slapton. He pulls himself up, groaning slightly with the effort. 'Thanks again for your help.'

'You're welcome.' I lead him out into the hall. The other policemen have already left.

'Sorry to interrupt when you had visitors,' he says, raising one eyebrow very slightly. 'Your girlfriend away is she?'

'She's back Saturday,' I tell him.

'I might well be in touch again about that list,' he says. 'Goodbye, Mr Barrett.'

I know why he's smiling. It's not my 'visitors'. He saw me look down that list and notice that name, the one he wanted me to see, the one name that neither of us mentioned.

John Barrett.

Why is my dad's name on that list?

I knew it was too good to be true. Two lots of good news in one day. Then one bit of awful, confusing, disturbing news. I go into the kitchen. My dad's appearance on this list doesn't necessarily mean he's done anything wrong, does it?

I pick up my cup absent-mindedly and take a swig of stone-cold coffee. But that's certainly the implication. It also means that he probably invested in 2cool – without telling me – and it means that Slapton and his mates are probably keeping an eye on him. What if he has done something dodgy? My poor mum. Bad enough having me all over the papers, but my dad too . . . And at least I've been proved, well, am *being* proved not guilty, whereas I don't know that that will be the case with my dad.

Then there's the Guy thing. This morning I was beginning to think that perhaps I was wrong, that perhaps that wasn't Guy on the phone, that I was just getting obsessed with the whole thing, but now I'm sure it was him.

I take another mouthful of cold coffee, the milk separating on the surface. Urrch! What am I doing? I pick up my phone and ring Nora in the office.

'Hiya, babe,' she says. 'How are you?'

'All right? You?'

'Okay.' I'm glad we can talk about 2cool and not us. 'Listen, I've just had the police round again. They cancelled the fraud investigation. They're just concentrating on a missing persons thing now.'

'That's great news,' she says. 'I mean, especially for you.'

'Oh, yeah I know, but there was something else.' I tell her about the list.

'So what is your dad's name doing there?' she asks. 'Did he invest in 2cool?'

'Perhaps, but if he did, why hasn't he told me? And anyway, I don't even know that the people on that list are all 2cool investors. It might be something else.'

'What else could it be?'

'I don't know, I just don't like the idea of my dad being on a list of names put together by the police.'

'Sure, I can understand that. By the way, did you ask him about Guy?'

'Yeah, he denied it.'

'Mmm. Interesting. Why would he be lying?'

'I don't know if he is,' I tell her. 'Perhaps it wasn't Guy.'

'Charlie, you were absolutely certain yesterday.'

'I know, but . . . Oh, I don't know.'

'Look, I think you should talk to your dad about that list and ask him about Guy again. Go and see him at his office today.'

'No, I can't—'

'You've got to speak to him. You've got to warn him about this thing.'

'*If* he needs to be warned. It might not be anything.'

'He should still know. Tell me who else was on the list.'

I give her the names I can remember: business people, captains of industry, society ladies, a couple of earls, some ageing rock stars and a few media barons. She scribbles away.

'Another thing: why do you think none of the investors is suing?' I say. 'Why would they suddenly decide just to kiss goodbye to their money like that? Did you see the TV interview with Josh Langdon? He was asked if he was going to take legal action to get his money back, but he just dodged the question, even though he was obviously really pissed off about the whole thing.'

'Mmm,' says Nora. 'Perhaps it doesn't matter to them. Perhaps if you're that rich you just think what the heck?'

I think about it for a moment. 'No, that doesn't make sense. It's the principle for these people, isn't it? Even if it's just the equivalent of a couple of hundred quid for them, they won't want to look stupid in front of their mates, like they've been conned, will they?'

'That's true. Not with their egos.'

'And you remember when we went to see Piers I asked him about that, and he just smiled, laughed in fact. Odd, isn't it?'

There is a moment of silence and then she says, 'You talk to your dad while I go and see Piers. I know where he's staying now. I'll go down there right away.'

'All right. Can you just leave the office like that?'

'Of course. It's a story, isn't it?'

'I'm not sure that it is.'

'What? With these names? If they're connected in any way this is huge!'

That phrase again. Like when we went to find Piers. A massive story, she said.

'Yeah, but look, Nora, my dad's on that list and I don't want—'

'Oh, don't worry about that, I'll make sure he doesn't come into it. Now go and talk to him and let me know what he says.'

'But Nora—'

She's hung up.

I ring my dad's mobile but it goes straight to voicemail, so I leave a message asking him to ring me and then I call his secretary, Amanda, a girl too smart to let him fuck her. Apparently he's in a board meeting now, but she'll ask him to ring me as soon as he gets out. I tell her it's important.

The call comes from my solicitor as Slapton predicted, giving me the all-clear from the police. The guy sounds a bit disappointed that there's nothing more to say on the subject. I'm not.

I set up my computer again and check my emails. One from my mum's sister, my auntie Emily, bless her. Hoping I'm okay. Email Emily, we call her. She's got friends all over the world now. I suddenly wonder if she ever looked at 2cool. She must have. Did she see that porn? Did she appreciate the irony? Oh, Emily, irony or not, I really hope you didn't see it.

I write her a breezy reply hoping she's well and explaining that the site has closed and that I'm out of trouble now, but my mind's not really on it.

There is only one thing I can think about at the moment: what I'm going to say to Lauren. So I start to type out some thoughts: 2cool is over now and I'm going to stop behaving so selfishly and help with her new TV career, but I think she should spend a little less time with Peter, because much as I like him (and I really did warm to him over breakfast) she's going out with me, not him.

Well, that's her career plan sorted out, but what the fuck am *I* going to do? I hope Lauren will have some ideas – she always does. I also start writing about why I slept with Nora, and how it was partly to get at her for sleeping with Peter and partly because I was . . . was what? Going bonkers? Going on a bender? Trying to hurt the one I love because that's what you do when you're angry and confused.

It all looks a bit daft set out on the screen, complete with typos. I find myself checking the Thesaurus for another word for sorry because I've written it so many times, sprinkled uselessly across the text. I read through it again and then delete it all.

I bung some washing on, change my clothes and put new sheets on the bed. Then I open Lauren's wardrobe and go to the little bit at the end which is full of her casual clothes rather than her work outfits. I stick my head in amongst the neatly hanging jeans, shirts, trousers and jackets and breath deeply, inhaling her.

My dad rings at 12.45. He's in the car. 'You all right?'

'Yeah, fine.'

'Sorry I didn't see you this morning.'

'I'm back in Chiswick at the flat.'

'Made up with Lauren?'

'She's not here, she's back on Saturday. She's been in France with friends. Dad, can I come and see you this afternoon?'

'See me? I'm pretty booked up this afternoon.'

'Tonight?'

'Erm, can't make it tonight. I've got a . . . a . . . business thing. What about tomorrow?'

'Oh, never mind.'

'Okay, okay, I've got something at fourish that I can move. Ring Amanda and book yourself in.'

'Thanks.'

Dad keeps me waiting until twenty-five past four. I sit on one of the giant, black leather, Bauhaus-style settees in the lobby, listening to the two receptionists answer the phone.

'Matthewman Kendall Barrett, good afternoon.'

'Matthewman Kendall Barrett, can I help you?'

It's funny to hear my name repeated over and over again. Sometimes there's a pause as they both stare out of the giant picture-windows in front of them or exchange a comment with each other ('*EastEnders* on tonight?' 'No, tomorrow. Matthewman Kendall

Barrett, good afternoon. I'm taping it because we're going out. Should be a good one.' 'See it last week? Matthewman Kendall Barrett, good afternoon. What a bastard what's-his-name is. Engaged, will you hold?'). Sometimes they overlap with their greeting, sometimes one follows the other immediately. On a couple of occasions they say it in perfect unison. What are the chances of that?

Unable to take any more MTV I ignore the monitors on the wall and read *Campaign* and *Media Week*. I see the name of dad's agency in a headline and read the story underneath. Another acquisition. I'm just about to turn the page when I realise that the guy in the photo next to it, moody, unsmiling, his face slashed with light filtering in from the Venetian blinds behind him, is my dad. He's like a stranger.

Finally I go up to the top floor. Amanda asks me to wait again; he won't be long. We make small talk but my throat feels almost too dry to speak. Then suddenly my dad is waving for me to go in.

'Hiya,' I say, as casually as I can.

He finishes scribbling something, shouts to Amanda for some coffee and then gets up and gives me a hug. 'So. Everything all right?'

His office is huge. White walls, black and white prints, Wenge wood furniture. TV screens along one side: Bloomberg, MTV, a shot of the House of Commons. Framed awards along the other. His desk is huge and filled with papers. An Apple Mac computer screen faces him. In the corner of the room is a Charles Eames recliner.

'I think so, Dad. I had a visit from the police again today.'

'Yeah?'

'They've called off the investigation, well, the fraud bit, anyway.'

'Oh, thank God for that.' He looks genuinely relieved. 'That is excellent news,' he says, accepting a coffee from Amanda. I smile and shake my head in answer to her offer.

'Water?' she asks.

'Oh, yes, that'd be great, thanks.' I turn back to Dad. 'But they showed me this list of names.' I'm trying to read my dad's expression but, leaning back in his huge, black leather chair, he looks slightly quizzical, that's all.

'And?'

'Yours was on it. Along with a lot of other people, big names, rich and famous people.'

'And what was this list about?'

'I don't know.'

'Didn't they say?'

'No.' Amanda brings in a tray with a glass, a bottle and a dish of ice. It's that water again: Glacial Purity. 'But almost all of them, I remember, have invested in 2cool.'

'Sure.'

'Well, have you invested in 2cool?'

When Dad stands up and walks over to the window I know the answer.

'I put some money in, yeah. So did a lot of people, as you know.'

'Why didn't you tell me?'

There is no answer.

'That *was* Guy on your phone, wasn't it?'

My dad sighs. 'Yes, it was.'

'You know him, don't you?'

'I've met him a few times.'

I take a sip of water, hoping he'll say more, but he doesn't. He just stands by the window, his back to me, looking down at the traffic halting and pushing its way around in Berkeley Square.

'Was it your personal investment or was it Matthewman Kendall Barr—?'

'It was my own money.'

'How much?'

'Fifty grand.'

'Dad, that's quite a lot of money.'

'I can afford it,' he says defiantly, turning round and watching the TV monitors. I give up on the hope that he's going to answer the big questions unprompted.

'Why didn't you tell me?'

He says nothing.

I can feel anger and tears welling up inside me but I keep control. 'Why didn't you say when I first got involved with 2cool? You must have been in from the start. You knew all along. Why did you pretend not to know Guy and Piers? No wonder you popped up at the Huntsman's thing. You got that first article about it faxed to you in New York. Why have you lied to me?'

When Dad turns to look at me there are tears in his eyes and his jaw is shaking. 'I wanted to protect you. I, I've just been caught up in this thing.'

'Caught up in what thing? 2cool? How? Why?'

'Something bigger.'

'What?'

'Charlie, I can't tell you. Please don't ask.'

'For God's sake, Dad, what is it?'

'Never mind. Why don't you and Lauren go on a holiday. Get away from it all, now you've been cleared and this whole thing is all over. You could go somewhere nice – relax, talk about your relationship—'

'Dad, what're you talking about?'

'I'll pay for it.' He opens a drawer and takes out a chequebook. 'Remember last year, I went to the Gazelle D'Or with, er . . .' He starts writing. 'With . . . er . . . what's her name? We had a great time. Why don't you take Lauren there?'

However weird and alien this conversation might seem, I can recognise my father now – practical solutions. Do something. Identify the problem and develop an effective response to it. After all, that's why those hip, funky, off-the-wall guys in the offices further down the corridor employed him. That's why he thought little trips to Thorpe Park would sort out his relationship with his children when his marriage was breaking up.

I watch him write the cheque, tear it out and hold it out to me. It's for £5,000. Bloody hell, what kind of holiday would that pay for? I look up at him. He has blinked back the tears and his face is set with a positive, upbeat look. It must be killing him. I take the cheque and put it down on the desk between us.

'I don't want to talk to you again until you tell me the truth,' I say, and walk out of the office.

chapter twenty-nine

Out in the street again I ring Nora at the office. Someone else answers, sounding rather hassled, and snaps that she's not there, could I call back later? I end the call without saying anything and then try her mobile. Voicemail. I leave a message for her to ring me immediately.

I walk around the streets of Mayfair for a while, thinking. There are smart offices in old houses with brass nameplates below the entry phones. Some of them are just surnames or initials – solicitors? PR companies? Accountants? Others have more obvious names such as West African Oil Exploration Inc. or Anglo-American Data Solutions Ltd.

I make my way down to Green Park tube and go home to Chiswick. I potter around trying to decide what to do. Then I pour myself a whisky and lie in the bath where I can think. A couple of times I think I hear Lauren's key in the lock and I sit up.

As well as being angry with my dad, I also feel very sorry for him. Watching your father cry is a weird experience. He's seen me cry thousands of times when I was a kid. A kid? I bawled my eyes out when I discovered that that cow Karen Sutton was seeing my mate Tony behind my back, and I was sixteen then.

Having the roles reversed is strange, though. Like when you realise for the first time that your parents are not the all-knowing omnicompetent beings you thought they were. Like when you explain to *them* how some bit of technology works, or what something means that they've read in the paper, or when you say goodnight to them but they're the ones who are going to bed.

When the father helps the son, both smile. When the son helps the father, both cry. It's a Chinese saying, I think. Watching your father cry while you're dry-eyed is even worse.

You sort of assume that a wealthy man behind a big desk is safe, but perhaps not. Oh, Dad, what is it? Why can't you tell me? What have you done? Something illegal? Criminal? No, surely not. Did you just get a bit greedy? Has someone got something on you? If so, what? And what – or who – are you protecting me from? I slip underwater and stay there as long as I can manage. When I come up, my mobile is ringing.

I reach across to the towel rail and dry my hands, then pick up the phone. It's a breathless Nora, obviously out on the street.

'I've just been talking to Piers. We've had a long, long talk. He's been talking, really talking. Spilled his guts, man. I had to bully it out of him – told him I'd tell everyone where he was – but, my God, what a story! I know why all those people, including your . . . I know why they haven't sued.'

'Why not?'

'Because he and Guy have got something on them.'

'Blackmail?'

'That's what I said, and Piers said, "What an ugly word" or something. He called it "encouragement".'

'So what has he got on them?'

Nora laughs hysterically. 'You won't believe it. Let's just say it's about badgers again.'

'Badgers?'

She is still laughing. 'Yeah, look, we're going to another party tonight.'

'Nora, what are you talking about?' I'm hanging over the edge of the bath now. 'What did he say about my dad?'

'He and Guy *do* know your dad. It almost certainly *was* Guy who rang for your dad that day.'

'Yeah, I know, I spoke to Dad this afternoon.'

'What did he say?'

'He told me he was involved in something. Something more than just 2cool.'

'That would be it!' says Nora. 'Charlie, this is huge.'

That phrase again. I shiver in the steaming bath water. 'Stop saying that. What have you found out?'

There is a rustle of fabric and a muffled cry. 'Oh, shit, sorry,' I hear Nora say. 'Are you all right?'

'What's going on?'

She comes back to me. 'Sorry about that, bumped into someone. What else did your dad say?'

'Nothing.'

'Nothing at all?'

'He suggested I . . . Lauren and I go on holiday.'

'Well, you'd better wait till tomorrow. After then it will all have blown over and it won't really matter.'

'Nora, what the fuck are you talking about?'

'A big, big story. We're going to a party in Mayfair. Tonight. Meet me, where, where? Umm. Meet me in the bar of the Metropolitan Hotel in Park Lane at eight-thirty and I'll tell you everything. Better still, you'll *see* everything for yourself.'

'Nora, what do you—? Hello? Hello?'

I drop the phone on the floor and slump back in the bath.

To my surprise she's already there when I arrive at eight twenty-five. She smiles broadly, throws her arms around me and kisses me on the lips, pushing her tongue into my mouth, playing with my hair. I respond mechanically, not quite with it, not quite sure why I'm here, but sure I don't want to kiss her.

'What will you have to drink?' she says, eyes dancing with delight.

'I'll have a glass of white wine.'

'Excuse me,' she bellows across at the barman, who makes a great show of looking shocked at such over-excitable behaviour in this temple of cool.

Her elbow catches her own glass, but I manage to rescue it just in time.

'Hallo? Yes, white wine, over here. Make it a big one.'

She is wearing a simple, black, close-fitting dress with a fur collar. And a lot of diamonds.

'Do you like it? Got it from the fashion department. Mustn't get it dirty or ripped or anything.' She giggles maniacally. She's scaring me now. 'These rocks are paste of course, but they're so glam, aren't they? They're mine. I bought 'em in New York.'

'Nora, what is going on?'

'You look very nice.' I'm wearing a black dress-shirt and a black

Armani jacket courtesy of 2cool, and some faded, stitched-up blue jeans – 'model's own', as they say.

'Thanks, now what on earth is going on?'

'This party . . . ooh, here's your drink.' She more or less throws it at me and then clinks her own against it so hard that I end up licking wine off my fingers. 'This party should answer a lot of questions.'

'I wish *you'd* answer some questions.'

'For goodness' sake, I don't know anything. All I know is what happens at this party will tell us a lot about 2cool, and why all these people who have coughed up aren't that bothered about trying to find out what happened to their money.'

'So what *is* going to happen at this thing?'

'I don't *know*,' she says, opening her eyes wide. 'But we'll see. Just have patience. Here, look at this.' She holds up her handbag.

'What about it?'

She looks around and then points to what looks like a large sequin on one side of it.

'Hidden camera.'

'What?'

'The picture desk sorted it out for me. You just squeeze the catch here. Hang on, I'm doing it the wrong way round. Yep, that's it, you just squeeze the catch here and it takes a picture.'

'Why? A picture of what?'

'What goes on at this party.'

'And you still won't tell me—?'

'I told you, we'll have to wait and see.'

'Nora, you're really beginning to—'

'Here he is,' she says, looking over my shoulder and waving.

I look round. A guy in a baseball cap and sunglasses is walking straight towards us. Not surprisingly, most other people in the bar have spotted him too and are looking discreetly but intensely to see who it is. Robbie Williams? Will Young? Oh, no, they almost certainly won't know him, but I do.

'Piers!'

'Shhh,' he and Nora say in stereo from either side of me.

'What are you doing here?'

'Hello, matey,' he says, looking around, coming up close to me and shaking my hand while clutching my elbow as if he's trying to stuff my arm into the black bomber jacket he's wearing.

'What do you want to drink?' whispers Nora.

'Oh, a real drink. Thank God,' he whispers back.

Fortunately the barman is being a bit more attentive this time, obviously wanting to check out the 'celeb'.

'G and T' he hisses at Nora. 'A large one. Lots of ice.'

She relays this to the barman who has in fact already heard and is looking at Piers closely.

'Good disguise,' I tell Piers, as more people turn to look at him.

'Cheers,' he says, winking behind his sunglasses, oblivious as usual to my sarcasm.

'Tell Piers what's happened today,' says Nora. 'To you, I mean.'

I leave out the Peter and Scott episode but explain about Slapton's visit and the computers. He's pleased and tells me that he knew it would all work out okay. Then I give him an edited version of my conversation with my dad.

'Your dad,' laughs Piers as he takes his drink from the barman.

'What about him?' I say, staring intently.

He looks surprised. 'Well, it's just unfortunate that . . . you know . . . he's mixed up in this.'

'Unfortunate?' I say, moving closer to Piers. He takes a step back.

'Just saying. I'm sure he won't, you know, get into any trouble.'

'He'd better fucking not.'

'Stop it, boys,' says Nora. 'Aren't you glad to see each other again?'

She really is bonkers, this woman.

'I'm so glad to be out of that bloody warehouse. Full of rats, I'm sure,' says Piers.

'It must be,' says Nora.

'I'm looking forward to this party, as well,' sniggers Piers.

I'm not.

We leave about ten and walk up Park Lane a bit before turning down a side street.

'It's Wareham Street which is just . . . about . . . here. Here we are,' she says, leading us into a little thoroughfare of flat-fronted Mayfair houses, near Frederica's where we had our launch, a lifetime ago. I look round for Piers and see him flattened against a wall looking furtively around him before making his next move.

'Oh, try and keep up, you tit,' I tell him.

'Number twenty-five, this is it,' says Nora. She stands still for a moment and then looks round at me. She takes a deep breath. 'You ready?' Now I'm feeling really nervous. She checks her hair and then her handbag camera. 'What time is it?'

'Ten past ten.'

'I've got to be out by midnight to file. I'll read it over to the copy takers from my mobile. That's the very latest time I can do it. Don't let me forget, for God's sake. Things should have got going already with a bit of luck.'

I grab her arm. 'You're really going to write about this?'

'Derr! Why do you think we're here?'

'I don't want you writing about it.'

She laughs irritably. 'What's it got to do with you? How can you stop me? I can write about anything I want.'

'What's the problem?' says Piers from behind us.

'My dad. Even if he's not here tonight, he's involved, isn't he?' But he did say he was doing something tonight, didn't he? This was obviously it.

'Oh, for God's sake,' says Nora. 'I won't mention him, if you don't want me to. There are plenty of other important people, after all.'

'But it'll get back to him. Other journalists will be looking for every name connected with it. People will talk, won't they?'

'Piers, get the door. You'd better stand by that security camera. You're the one they'll be expecting.'

'Nora.'

'Just fucking go home then. Go on.'

'No.' I think about it for a moment. 'I'm coming with you to see if my dad's here. And if he is, I'm going to get him out and I'm going to make sure you make absolutely no mention of him.'

'I said I wouldn't.'

'But you're a liar, Nora, I don't trust you.'

She looks at me for a moment. Hurt? I bloody hope she is. I begin to wonder if I'm here with her as moral support. Perhaps she needs me to come with her, to look after her, since she can't trust Piers, who is now looking around furtively in a way that would attract the attention of anyone who happened to be in this darkened little side street.

'I told you, I won't mention him. Now look, I invited you because we've been a team so far.' A team? Is that how she sees it? Sensing that I need convincing on this one she adds, 'We've worked very well together on this but if you don't want to see it through then fair enough, just go home and I'll speak to you later.'

'I'm coming in,' I tell her. It's meant more as a threat than an offer.

She thinks about it and then says, 'Piers, get the buzzer.'

Piers squeezes between us and hits the intercom. A harsh white light comes on from above us.

'Hello?' squawks a woman's voice from the entry phone.

'It's Piers. I'm here for the badger meeting.'

'*Piers? Piers Gough-Pugh?* You naughty boy, come in.'

The door opens.

'Oh,' says the woman, looking at the three of us.

'I brought a couple of friends,' says Piers, kissing her on both cheeks.

'Well, I'm not sure . . .' She takes a look at me. 'Oooh, I dunno.'

She moves aside and lets us in. She's wearing a tight black dress. It's only as we walk past her and go inside that I see it's made of rubber. And backless. Very, very backless.

'Get yourselves a drink and come on in,' she says, peering around outside carefully before shutting the door. 'Well, Piers, this is a turn-up for the books, we didn't expect to see you here again. I think there are rather a lot of people who are just a teensy weensy bit cross with you,' she says, pulling down his shades with a long, slim, bejewelled finger. 'I think they might want to spank you.'

Nora laughs. 'I think they'll want to do something worse than that.'

'Even better,' says the woman, looking me over again. 'Get changed upstairs if you want to.'

We move down the hallway. The living room, and the rest of the house, as far as I can see, is decorated very much like the Huntsmans' – antiques, classic upright sofas, huge lamps, marble-topped tables, silver photograph frames, landscape paintings alongside some abstract pieces on dark, heavily patterned wallpaper. There are big bookcases full of leather-bound volumes which look as though they've been bought wholesale by an interior decorator and never read.

But despite the classic furnishings there is something odd about this place. I can smell it before I even see it. Bodies, sweat. I can sense a certain electricity. As I peer further into the living room, wondering whether I'll see anyone I know, I notice a coffee table like the one Dad used to have, except that underneath it is a man in a leather basque. A real man.

We walk through, looking into a couple of other rooms further towards the back of the house. In one I notice a naked bottom. In fact it's a large woman on her knees giving a man, half-hidden by the shadowy light, a blow job. Wide-eyed and trying not to laugh, Nora turns to look at me. It would be funny, except that I know my dad is connected with this in some way. The idea that I might confront him in a moment doing something like this couple (no, wait a minute, there's three of them, now that I look carefully) is too horrible.

Piers has started to talk to some people in a quiet corner by the stairs, his cap pulled down over his ears, but when he sees us move off he follows.

'Wait while I get rid of my coat and put on my disguise.'

'Disguise?' I ask. 'Aren't you disguised enough?'

'No, that woman at the front door wasn't kidding. There are quite a few people who'd like my balls for marbles.'

'Why are you staying here, then?'

He shrugs his shoulders and looks at me as if it should be obvious.

'Because it's fun. Best free peepshow in London.'

The risk appeals, I guess. Part of me hopes that one of these irate investors recognises him and decides to vent his spleen.

'Piers, go and put your disguise on and then come back quickly. Coats are in there, I think,' says Nora nervously, pointing to a door beside us. He is back within a few seconds.

'That's better,' he says.

'Piers?' I say. 'What are you doing? What's that for?'

'What's what for?'

'You're wearing a gas mask.'

'I know – disguise.'

'Don't you think it looks a bit odd?'

Piers gives a muffled laugh. 'You're so innocent.'

I sort of see what he means.

'Come on, let's look upstairs. If anyone asks you to, you know, get involved, just tell them you're getting a drink and you'll be right back,' Nora instructs us.

'Roger, Wilco,' says Piers.

I look at him but it's impossible to tell now if he's taking the piss or not. We move towards the stairs, keeping as close together as it's possible to be without tripping over each other.

But before we go up we look into another room where some people are having sex over tables, hands grasping desperately at each other, looking to grab some new piece of flesh, some appendage or erogenous zone that they haven't experienced yet. Just then there is a farting noise, as an old guy is pulled along a polished dining table by two young girls, his skin alternately sliding and sticking on the polished, dark wood.

I pull Nora and Piers out of the doorway and we go up. A woman is giving a man a blow job on the stairs as another man takes her from behind, his thighs slapping rhythmically against her quivering buttocks, generating waves of flesh. Without acknowledging our presence they shuffle over to one side to let us pass. I find myself saying 'thanks', which makes Nora laugh.

On the landing there are two giant Chinese vases and a huge, imposing portrait of a young girl. Obviously recently painted, her face is frozen in a look of self-conscious seriousness. The owners' daughter? She must love coming home and seeing that. Better than coming home and seeing this lot I suppose. I'm aware of someone staring at me. An older guy with bouffant, blue-rinsed hair and a black polo-neck is inches away from my face, looking at me provocatively. I step back into Nora and Piers.

'Care to join us?' asks the man, squeezing my bicep. I pull away. 'Us' seems to refer to a sad-looking young guy wearing only a pair of navy blue Y-fronts. With his solid build, pale skin and round face, he looks Russian or Middle European. He stares impassively at me. 'Mmm?' enquires the older guy, who is holding him by the hand.

'Er, no thanks,' I mutter.

The older guy shrugs petulantly and leads his friend off into another room.

'Spoilsport,' says Nora.

'It *was* tempting,' I tell her.

'You should,' she says, smiling wickedly. 'That guy's minted, what's his name? He owns half a dozen theatres and he's got shows all over the world.'

It occurs to me that everyone we've seen so far is either over fifty or under twenty-five. Nora, Piers and myself are a sort of demographic hiccup: neither young and desperate enough to be paid or old and desperate enough to be paying.

We look into the master bedroom, continuing our ritual: a quick glance, a moment to analyse exactly what is going on, a wave of relief on my part that it's not my dad, followed by another sensation of revulsion at which I drag a smirking Nora and Piers out. Scented candles blend with the smell of sweat and pot. A searing stink of amyl nitrate meets us suddenly.

On the floor of this huge room, with its chandelier and elegant mahogany fitted wardrobes, a middle-aged, Rubenesque woman is riding a very thin young guy who looks more scared than turned on, her huge legs almost crushing his narrow thighs. Still bouncing energetically she shouts across to a grey-haired bloke who is jerking off furiously as he watches two young girls kissing listlessly on a settee.

'Jeremy, uh, uh, you'll have to feed, uh, uh, the meter in a minute, you know,' she says.

Thinking that this might be slang for another sexual position, I look away and drag the others out again. We turn and bump into a bloke I've seen on the telly a few times but I can't think when.

'What a fantastic dress,' he tells Nora. 'I love it. Where *did* you get it?'

'Thanks, it's Hussein Chalayan,' says Nora. 'What about yours?'

'It's just a little Vivienne Westwood number,' he says, touching her arm. Then it comes to me. Of course – he's that rugby commentator.

'Don't leave me alone,' she says to me after he's moved off.

'Let's go up another floor,' I tell her. 'And then we'll get the fuck out of here.'

We bump into a rather drunken Lady Huntsman, her arms round two young men. One, a skinhead, has a tattoo of a spiderweb across his neck, while the other is in camouflaged combat pants and is drinking champagne out of a bottle, letting it pour down over his neck and naked torso.

'Huh,' she says, looking me up and down. 'Changed your mind, have you?' She moves on haughtily. We pass a girl, totally naked, doing coke off a marble-topped consul table.

'Oh, my God, can you believe this?' hisses Nora at me as we move into another room. 'I just hope I remember all the names. Wait.' She rather clumsily holds her handbag up in front of her and fiddles with the catch. 'Look, there's Josh Langdon.' Langdon, drunk or stoned or both, is with three young girls. 'Oh, fucking hell, there's Sir Peter Townsley, he owns the *Informer*; now that would be funny.' She holds up her bag again.

'Nora, someone's going to notice you doing that in a minute,' I tell her.

'No,' she says, 'they're all too trashed. Talking of which, I could do with a drink. Can you get me one?'

'I'm not sure . . . oh, wait a minute, there are some bottles over there.'

'Charlie.'

'Yes?'

'Get me a large one, will you?'

'Sure.'

'Er, yep, whatever's going,' says Piers when I ask him.

'Will you be able to drink it through that?'

'When it comes to alcohol, mate, where there's a will there's a way.'

I notice a table over the other side of the room, complete with snowy white tablecloth. There are cut crystal glasses, a huge ice-bucket and a silver dish with elegant slices of lemon. Bottles of Tabasco, Angostura Bitters and Worcestershire sauce are gathered in a little triangle. Everything else is neatly arranged, but the ultimate absurdity are the canapés: exquisite squares of brown bread with smoked salmon and gravadlax, little cocktail sausages, and what looks like foie gras on crackers. Who, tell me, *who*, is here for the food?

I shake my head in disbelief. In a way, this very ordinary sight seems more bizarre than anything else I've seen tonight. I pour a nicely chilled Chablis into three heavy-cut crystal glasses. As I replace the bottle in the silver ice-bucket I notice a face peering up at me from beside the table. It's a middle-aged man with a moustache and neatly cropped grey hair. He winks at me, then closes his eyes and opens his mouth. Feeling slightly embarrassed and not wanting to be a party pooper, I take the bottle out and pour some of the wine into his open mouth. He gently squirts a bit out and lets it trickle over his face and down his neck, before drinking the remainder.

'Don't you want to piss?' he asks sweetly.

'Erm, not at the moment, thanks.'

'Oh, well, you know where I am if you do,' he says, smiling.

'I'll bear it in mind, thanks.'

I get back to the others and give them their drinks. Piers tries unsuccessfully a couple of times to get at his through his gas mask before giving up and pushing it over his head. Nora knocks hers back almost in one go and then looks around again.

'You're right,' she says. 'I shouldn't waste my time writing this one silly article. I should blackmail these people. I'd get a hell of a lot more for it that way.'

We watch a bit more, backed up against a wall, hoping there is safety in numbers. I realise that not many people seem to be actually enjoying themselves. Those that aren't obviously too pissed or stoned to know what's happening are looking around to see what else is going on and what other activities they should be involved with. It's like one of those parties where everyone is looking past everyone else to see who they should be talking to.

'I'm going to the loo,' says Nora after a while. 'Do you know where it is?'

'No,' I tell her, 'but there's a bloke by the drinks table who'll be happy to oblige.'

'Oh, he knows, does he – oh, I see what you mean.' I don't look round but I assume from her expression that someone is indulging the guy. 'Actually I just want to make some notes.'

I catch her arm. 'Nora—'

'For goodness' sake, your dad's obviously not here, and don't worry I won't mention anyone associated with him, I told you.'

'Please don't do this. It could still get back to him.'

She rolls her eyes and breathes deeply. 'Charlie, face it: it fucking serves your dad right – stupid cunt shouldn't have got mixed up in all this shit, should he?'

Her vehemence takes me back for a moment but then I say, 'It's not my dad I'm worried about. Don't you understand? It's my mum.' I can hardly bear to think of her, here, now. 'It would just kill her.'

She gives me a look of contempt.

'Nora!' But she has disappeared. I turn to Piers, who is chatting to a well-preserved woman with long blonde hair. She's wearing a leather waistcoat, riding chaps and cripplingly high stilettos.

'Hello,' she says, extending a hand. 'Sabrina. I'm mistress of pleasure.'

'Hi,' I say, shaking it, wishing she'd bugger off, mistress of pleasure or not, and let me talk to Piers.

'We're having our own little thing up on the next floor, front bedroom. Hope you'll be able to join us.'

'Very kind. I'll certainly try and make it,' I tell her.

She moves off.

'You'll enjoy that, all right. She gives the best blow jobs ever. Makes you feel you're sort of melting. Her husband's very senior in—'

'Piers, I'm not going to join her bloody party. I'm pretty sure my dad's not here so I'm going in a minute and I'm taking Nora with me. But look, just to get this straight: you went to one of these things with Guy and then blackmailed half the people you saw there to get them to invest in 2cool, is that right?'

Piers looks surprised. 'Oh, no,' he says. 'We didn't have to blackmail anyone to start with. Everyone wanted to put their money into 2cool. They were falling over themselves to invest once we'd described it to them and given them the presentation. But, I have to say, when a mate brought me along to one of these and I saw half our investors here it was quite useful for later. See what I mean? Reminding them of this when they started nagging us about dividends and returns on investments and things and crapping *on* and *on* about where their money was going.' He tuts and shakes his head as he remembers. 'God, it was *so* boring, but one little mention of the badger meetings and we never heard another peep out of them.'

I nod, taking it in. 'I see.' How sensible. Is it? I'm not sure any more.

'I don't know, perhaps it would have been better if we had listened to them nagging at us. Who can say? 2cool2btrue dot com might still be up and running.'

'But why does the Badger Preservation Society, or whatever it's called, meet? I mean, why do these people, all these rich, famous, influential people do it all together like this?'

'Well,' says Piers, rocking on the balls of his feet and finishing his drink. 'In a way you've answered your own question: they like to do it with people of equal social standing, movers and shakers, I suppose. People they can do business with, quite literally – so many deals are struck at these things, you wouldn't believe it – plus there's safety in numbers, you see. No one's going to blow the gaff, if everyone's got the same amount to lose.'

'Unless someone *does* give the game away.'

'Ah, but they wouldn't, would they? Besides some of the best lawyers in the land are here, along with a couple of judges too, I see,' he says, smiling a 'hallo' at someone taking part in a manic groping session in a corner. 'Yep, the legal establishment would be down on any squealers like an avalanche on a school skiing trip. They wouldn't stand a chance.'

'What about the other people? The young girls and boys?'

'Oh, half of them have just arrived from Eastern Europe or Brazil or somewhere yesterday; they don't even speak English, let alone know who these people are that they're having sex with.'

I'm just about to ask who organises these events when Nora comes back, carefully carrying three glasses of wine.

My wine looks a bit cloudy. I taste it carefully.

'You sure this wine is okay?' I ask her.

'Yes, of course it is. Just drink it.' She turns away and looks around the room. 'Let's go and see what else is going on. I'm bored with this.'

'Let's go up one more floor. I think there should be a pretty cool little gathering in the attic space,' says Piers. Out of Nora's line of vision, he nudges my elbow and mimes a blow job. I'm beginning to get a headache and feel dizzy.

We push past people sitting and lying on the stairs. A man is banging a young girl from behind. Her eyes are closed and her face is a mask until she opens her mouth and is violently sick. The guy behind her doesn't miss a beat as his thrusts synchronise with her spasms of vomiting. A woman nearby tuts and says, 'Oh, really.' A naked man with huge metal vices on his nipples stops me at one point and barks, 'Do you know where the coats are?'

'Er, no, sorry,' I mutter, feeling even queasier at the sight of his pinched, bruised flesh. We get upstairs and Nora, who has just obliviously knocked wine over a couple of women snogging passionately in a chair, disappears to find some more names and dubious activities for her story.

'She's a funny one,' says Piers, shaking his head.

'Why do you say that?' I ask. *I* know she's a funny one, as he puts it, but I'm wondering why he thinks so.

'It's the way she doesn't relate to other people. Doesn't understand what effect she has on them. Can't read them. Turned over lots of people for stories and can never understand why they feel so hurt and angry afterwards.'

'A typical journalist, I suppose.'

'Not even that, I don't think she's particularly ambitious. I mean, this is a great story but she's not what you'd call a newshound. She's very bright. Guy says she's got a very low boredom threshold. She'll do anything to amuse herself, never mind what effect it has on other people.'

I listen in silence. I think of our sex together and our cosy evening in with a takeaway and *Some Like It Hot*. Close, cosy. Affection if not love – and then she stabbed me in the back so callously, so coolly. I find myself feeling even sicker at the thought of it.

'Got no real friends, you know,' Piers is saying. He shakes his head dismissively. 'Not really a woman's woman, is our Nora. I knew she'd go for you. You slept with her? Thought so. That's what she does. She has sex with men and then has rows with them. Great one for these dramatic, stormy affairs, then she gets tired of the whole thing and moves on to the next one, God help him.'

I'm beginning to feel really sick to my stomach now at the thought of our relationship.

'Guy says even that clumsiness thing is put on. You know, she loves going to posh parties and restaurants, smart store openings and galleries and things, then physically demolishing them in case she doesn't get the opportunity to do it in writing.'

'Why did you lie to me about how you know her?' Piers looks confused for a moment but then, completely unembarrassed, uncontrite, he explains:

'It was her idea really, said she thought it would look a bit too cosy to you if we all knew each other. Anyway, why be boring and just tell the truth when you can make something up? Much more fun.'

I take another mouthful of wine and then a deep breath and say, 'She told me about her father.'

'Ha,' says Piers. 'Her mother's a better story.'

'Her mother? She died when—'

'Dead? No, she's still going. Amazingly. Drinking New York dry. Have you noticed Nora's going the same way?' He tuts. 'That woman drank all through her pregnancy, my ma says. They thought Nora would be stillborn because her mother was doing a bottle of vodka a day, almost. Then again perhaps that's why Nora's the way she is. It *has* had an effect, I suppose.' He taps the side of his head and rolls his eyes.

'I used to hate having to play with her when we were kids. All the cousins did. She'd be playing something perfectly normally then, without any warning, she'd throw everything up into the air – Lego or whatever – and just wander off. People who didn't know her thought she was tired or upset, or that we'd been bullying her, but no, that's Nora for you.

'Then there were her stories. She rang the police when she was seven and told them she'd been kidnapped by some frightening men. Gave exact descriptions of each of them. Major alert. APB or whatever, police kept her on the line until they traced the call to her pre-school. She'd sneaked into the office when she should have been doing PE.

'She told my little sister that she, I mean my sister, was adopted and that her real mother was married to a giant who was coming back to eat her up. Poor Sophie had nightmares for months afterwards. Chaos. Chaos and trouble, that's what Nora likes, and she doesn't care who she hurts.'

'What . . . what about her father? They were very close, weren't they? She told me how she got her name.' I can hardly get the words out.

'How she got her name? What? Nora? Nah, her mother called her that. Her dad wasn't around much when she was born.'

'It's from Noor, meaning "light" in Arabic, isn't it?' I say, forcing out every syllable now.

Piers laughs. 'Where d'you get that from? No, it's Leonora, meaning, I don't know, "the stupidest name I can give my daughter because no one can stop me". Guy's theory – want another drink? No? – Guy's theory, you know, he's really into this psychology guff, is that she's trying to get at her mother all the time, she's constantly hurting people and knackering things because she's trying to get revenge on her mother.'

'What about her father?'

'She hardly knew him. Left her mother when she was quite young. Nora always idolised him. I suppose she wanted at least *one* parent to look up to. She's only met him a few times. I think he's not very interested. He's got a new life and a new wife, now.'

'Oh, come on boys, you going to join in or what?' says a ruddy-faced man with white hair. 'It's not a spectator sport, you know.'

'Be with you in a minute, Sir Michael,' says Piers, winking cheerily. 'Where was I? Oh, yes, her dad.'

'An obsti . . . obstet . . .'

'Yeah, a doctor. Until he was struck off. Touching up the patients apparently. Especially as an obstetrician, plenty of opportunity if you think about it. Went to Cairo or somewhere like that and practised there for a while. Nora visited him a couple of times I think, but like I said, it wasn't a very happy meeting apparently. Not according to my mother, anyway.'

The room really is moving now, rising and dipping. Or am I? I can't seem to stand still.

'You know, I think I feel angrier with you for introducing me to Nora than I do for getting me mixed up in the 2cool thing,' I say, trying to focus on him.

Piers looks surprised. 'Really? Well, you shouldn't have slept with her then, should you, matey? Look, do you want to do something here? Quite welcome if you want to. I'd better stay out of it – I think that guy has recognised me. Might have to get out of here pronto. But there's some quite decent totty and I'm sure you'd be in great demand. Yeah, I'm going to push off; he's looking a bit shirty. Never mind, booked myself into a nice hotel for tonight under an assumed name. You all right?'

But I'm not. It's as if his last few words have been coming to me through a long pipe. His face and the gas mask perched above it appear blurred and distorted. He begins to look like *The Scream*.

My legs seem to be giving way under me. I can't control them. I'm sliding, falling and there's no one to catch me where's my dad he can help me but I can't see him can't see anyone I know just bodies and laughing teeth and glasses of champagne and diamonds and people lying around me but now I'm floating gently downwards I can just feel the wall behind me it's the only firm thing what's Piers saying now I can't hear him someone has taken hold of my legs and they're stretching them out I feel like my body weighs a hundred tons someone's undoing my shirt no I don't want to join in leave me alone to lie here and die they're taking my jacket off that's my Armani jacket my 2cool Armani jacket be careful with it you don't want to damage it there's Nora hallo Nora what are you doing what you saying oh God I wish I'd never met you Nora some woman in a low-cut dress more tits fucking hell I've seen a lot of tits tonight Piers haven't I what is Nora saying to you why is she walking out of the room some other people are looking at me and then walking out as well I want to go out I want to go home Lauren will be home soon I want to see her tell her I love her where's my dad hello dad is that you where is he I want to go home I'm tired so tired I just want to close my eyes and sleep for ever

chapter thirty

A huge, flat, glassy eye stares at me, unblinking. The woman says something in Spanish that I don't understand. I laugh and shrug my shoulders.

'No, gracias.'

Is that right? Must be. Wish I'd brought the phrasebook. She holds up the fish enticingly, its tongueless, sharp-toothed mouth lolling open between her cracked, reddened fingers. I laugh again and shake my head, frowning apologetically.

What am I going to do with such a huge fish? Take it back to the hotel? Put it in my suitcase? It does look very good, though. I've watched enough cookery shows over the years to know what to look for – the bright eyes, the shiny scales, the pink gills.

Piled onto the crushed ice are mounds of fish. I think I recognise red snapper, one particularly gruesome bugger – must be an eel, I suppose, just from the shape of it – and that's monkfish, I reckon. I certainly know the squid when I see them, grey and shiny and semi-transparent, eyes drooping with apparent boredom. Something about the way they're piled on top of each other adds to the sense of casual abundance. Luxurious, somehow. Not a word I can use lightly. I find myself wondering how this woman is going to sell all this fish today. Still, it's only just gone one and the market stays open late, like everything else in Spain.

The next stall sells fruit and vegetables. Technicolor piles of them. Red peppers, tomatoes, onions, oranges, glossy purple aubergines, courgettes – everything bigger, fatter and juicier than I've ever seen before. A surfeit of taste and colour. Shamelessly exposing themselves. Looking gorgeous. Subtlety, reticence and discretion have no place here. More, bigger, every inch of every stall covered in them. Like cheap prostitutes garishly dressed, pushing their breasts out at the punters. Vulgarly seductive.

I almost want to stop and tell someone that I've never, ever seen so much gorgeous food in all my life, share my feelings with them.

There is a stall with nothing but olives, a little sign above every plastic container describing its contents. Why didn't I bring that bloody phrasebook? How many olives do you need, for goodness' sake? This is ridiculous. In a second the man behind the counter swoops one out of a tub in a tiny sieve and offers it to me – salty, garlicky. Is that rosemary, too? Lauren would know. It makes me realise how hungry I am. I have to buy some. With a combination of sign language, plus 'si' and 'no' at the appropriate moments I manage to buy a small pot of the ones I've just tasted.

I throw the stone down under the stall like everyone else does. This is not the place for politeness or niceties. This place is about big gestures. Even the floor is alive, full of colours, shapes and smells: rejected fruit and vegetables, bits of paper, newspapers and magazines, cigarette ends, brightly coloured wrappers, half a croissant, a lurid-coloured ice-cream.

And the noise. People shouting, laughing, talking, haggling, someone singing, tinny pop songs playing out of a battered old radio hanging from an awning. Knives banging down onto counters as chickens are quartered, fish decapitated and vegetables chopped up for display. A cacophony of human life at its most energetic, all echoing up into the cast-iron and glass ceiling. Someone shouts just behind my right ear and I scoot aside to let a guy rush past with a trolley full of boxes bursting with fruit and vegetables. Coming towards me are a middle-aged couple, obviously English – the sallow complexions, the sensible, dowdy clothes, the diffident manner, in dramatic contrast to the raucous colour and racket around us. We smile a conspiratorial acknowledgement of pure joy at each other.

I buy some bread from another stall and choose a couple of small cheeses from the one next door. We could eat these at the hotel before we go out at midnight for dinner. That would be a nice surprise for her when she gets back. Or I could just chuck them away. It's the buying, the being part of this amazing event, that counts.

'I love markets, don't you?' says a voice behind me. I spin round.

'That's because you're an economist,' I say.

Guy laughs. 'No, it absolutely is not. I love the noise and life of markets. I thought if you came to Barcelona this was the one thing you should see. The Gaudí cathedral is interesting in a slightly bizarre, surreal way and the view from the top at dusk is breathtaking, but this is the best thing about this city. No one should ever leave without experiencing the legendary Mercat Sant Josep.'

We walk on a bit as Guy points out some of his favourite stalls, smiling and speaking in authentic-sounding Catalan to the owners.

'Are you hungry?' he says after a while.

'Starving.'

'There's a great tapas bar just round here.'

'Brilliant.'

'Where's Lauren? Is she coming?'

'She's shopping across the other side of the Ramblas. We're meeting later back at the hotel,' I say.

'Oh, okay. I was hoping I might see her again.'

'Well, she's a bit cross with you.'

'Really?'

I laugh. 'You know, what with the whole 2cool thing?'

'Ah, that.'

'Don't worry, I've forgiven you.'

'Have you?'

'Yeah. I think so. I mean, it would be different if it had got serious, if I had been arrested or prosecuted. Oh, fuck, when I think of all the things that could have happened to me.'

'Actually they wouldn't really. If I'd thought you were at real risk of conviction or anything, I'd have come back.'

'Thank you.' We stroll on a bit. 'So you just let me sweat a bit.'

'I can only apologise, Charlie. It was a cowardly act.'

Guy's formal phrase could be just Guy or it could be a way of avoiding the fact that he really does feel guilty. I let him think about it for a moment as we walk, passing a cheese stall where a spectacularly toothless woman in a headscarf is gossiping indignantly with the owner.

'Oh, don't worry about it,' I say at last. 'It was pretty horrible at the time but in fact all that happened to me in the end was that I grew up a bit. The end of my charmed life.'

'How ironic, given that that's what we hired you for,' smiles Guy. 'Here we are. Look, it's only half past one so the Spanish haven't even started lunch yet.'

We take a seat each at the tapas bar in the middle of the market. The counter in front of us is packed with dishes and plates: there are golden-crusted tortillas on a display and various stews with fish, beans and great bony chunks of meat. Guy orders us both a glass of Cava.

'Try the tomato and courgette tortilla,' he says, so I nod at the woman looking expectantly over the counter at us.

'I have to say I think I was most pissed off when you rang my dad's mobile and then hung up when I answered.'

'Oh, that. That was a bit of a shock, I must say. Sorry, I panicked but I just couldn't think of anything else to do but hang up.'

'Why were you ringing him?'

'I wanted some advice, wanted to know how to get out of this. Of all the people we'd roped in to 2cool he seemed the most sensible. You look surprised? Well, perhaps not in his private life, but in business he's a very savvy operator, actually. I thought he might be able to help.'

'He lied to me.'

'He thought it was for the best, Charlie. It was agony for him but he thought that if he could just hang on the police would find nothing to charge you with, 2cool would be wound up and you'd be safely free from it all.'

I think about this. The tortilla arrives and I'm distracted for a moment by the rich sweetness of the tomatoes, courgettes and peppers. All my senses seem to be heightened today.

'Are you still speaking to each other?' says Guy, sticking his fork into his own potato and onion tortilla.

'Yes, oh, yes. He is my dad afer all.'

'Bet you're glad he wasn't there that night, then.'

'Yeah, mind you, everyone got out safely in the end.'

'Yes, I heard,' says Guy, intrigued. 'Something went wrong with the camera, is that right?'

I smile and roll my eyes. 'Nora's camera. She, um . . .' I laugh.

'What?' says Guy. 'What was it?'

'She forgot to put any film in.'

He bursts out laughing and within seconds we can hardly sit on our stools, tears running down our cheeks. Even some of the Spanish stop their shouting and smoking to look over at us.

'You're joking,' says Guy, wiping his eyes with a very old, dirty hanky.

'Yeah, the bloke at the picture desk on the paper showed her how it all worked and gave her the film cartridge but she was so over-excited that night that she forgot to put it in the camera.'

'But they still had the story.'

'I know, but according to Piers, they didn't dare run it without the proof of the photographs. Can you imagine the risk? Nora's word against the great and good from politics, the City, the arts and everywhere else. The law. They'd have shredded her.'

'I'd love to have seen her face.'

'Glad I didn't. I hope I never see her again.'

'*That* I did feel very guilty about. I mean when Piers told me what she was doing to you – writing about you without telling you and things.'

'And then the final insult at the party. God I was ill for days after.'

'What was it in the end?'

'It was a drug called GHB. Heard of it?'

Guy shakes his head. He looks both intrigued and alarmed.

'Gama Hydroxy Buterate,' I explain. I know all the details – I've been thinking about it quite a lot. It's like my war wound. 'It's a recreational drug which she'd begged or nicked from some dealer there. It's got no smell but just a slight taste, which you know, I do remember, now I come to think about it. Anyway, I got a double dose and that, plus the alcohol I'd already drunk, knocked me out completely. I'm lucky to be alive.' Again the nearness of my escape hits me. I'm here, now in this noisy, lively market – a day I should never have seen. 'A double dose the doctors said. She wanted me to come and help but once she was in and had got some stuff, she suddenly got so terrified that I'd try to stop her filing her precious story or screw it up for her in some way that she . . . she poisoned me. Risked my life. Can you believe it?'

Guy thinks about it and then nods slowly. 'Yeah, yeah, in a way I can.'

'She didn't even have to really. I couldn't stop her sending her story to the paper, even if I'd really wanted to, but she was so desperate not to let anything get in the way.' I find myself reliving that evening for a moment before I pull myself out of it. 'I knew that wine tasted weird.'

We finish our tortilla.

'Have some fish,' says Guy, getting up from his bar stool. 'Look, come over here and choose what you want. It's so fresh! It was still swimming in the sea just a few hours ago.'

We choose a fillet of salmon for him and some swordfish for me. Guy orders them in his effortless Catalan and meanwhile we chew on fresh bread, ragged with tomato and garlic and drizzled with olive oil.

'But in fact it was lucky for everyone else,' I explain. 'Rumour went round the place in no time that someone had OD'd and died. They shot out of there like rats out of a trap. The photographer the *Post* had positioned outside, by the front door, was away for five minutes getting a cup of tea or having a pee. When he came back the place was empty. Only picture they got was the ambulance taking me away.'

'Shame.'

'Piers says,' I take a deep breath. Might as well tell him. 'Piers told me afterwards when he came to see me in hospital that Nora wanted to write the story around me – after all they had the pictures of me. The story was going to be that I was so upset about the whole 2cool thing that I had taken an overdose.'

'You're kidding.'

'She told Piers that it would be good for me really. Win me the sympathy vote.'

'I was going to say how evil of her, but I'm not sure that it is.'

'No, Piers told me his – and your – theory about her. I was already drugged and he was wearing a gas mask – don't ask – but it made sense to me. I honestly think she never really understood why I'd be upset.'

'You're probably right,' he says. 'She didn't actually want to hurt you, it just didn't register with her that you'd be upset and angry. The more I got to know about her the more I realised she just uses people to amuse her. Even if you never spoke to her again, which I'm sure you wouldn't, she wouldn't care that much, I'm afraid.'

'Yeah, I'm sure you're right and yet . . .' Why has this suddenly come to me now? 'When I was out of it in the hospital the next day, semi-conscious, delirious, before Lauren had got back and heard from my dad what had happened, I'm sure Nora came to see me. I'm sure I saw her face looking at me, saying something and then kissing my forehead.' I try to remember more, taking myself back to that hospital bed, but it doesn't come to me. The doctors warned that I might have memory loss and even hallucinations. 'I don't know, perhaps I'm just imagining it.'

'Perhaps you did, you know, touch her. Connect with her.'

'I wonder.' We watch the staff at work for a while, dishing out food, reaching over each other, shouting orders, banging out coffee dregs, joking and gossiping with the regulars who stand at one end of the bar smoking and drinking glasses of beer. 'I suppose having parents like that must screw you up. Was it true about her father and mother, do you think?'

'Was what true?'

I tell him what Piers told me. He thinks for a moment.

'I heard about her father because a friend of mine is a doctor in New York. Piers is half-right, I think. Her dad did have a habit of touching up his patients which was a trifle unfortunate, but he was, well, could have been, a great doctor. He was very bright, had huge potential, but I suppose it was a kind of undirected, undisciplined intelligence. He couldn't put it to any positive use. Bit like Nora. You sometimes need a sheepdog for intellect. You know, round it up and point it in the right direction.'

I smile, but it's just so fucking sad. For both of them.

'So you've made it up with Lauren, then?' he asks.

For a second I panic that Lauren's not with me. Perhaps I dreamed that too. Perhaps we're still not speaking.

'Yes,' I tell him. 'My dad got her mobile number from my phone and rang her in France where she was staying with a friend. Told her what had happened. In fact, by the time she'd got back I was out of hospital and I'd been given the all-clear by the doctors – they'd pumped my stomach and checked me over.'

'So you managed to sort things out between you?'

'Yes. She and Sarah, the friend she was staying with, had done a lot of talking about us and our relationship, and all the things that have happened over the last few months, so I think that helped.'

I don't tell him all the details about the meeting that Lauren and I had at the flat when she got back. I can hardly bear to think about it now, in case I've dreamt it or in case by going over it yet again in my mind I'll somehow undo it.

*

It was early evening, the last rays of the sun were filtering in through the windows and it was still quite warm. My mum, who had been fussing around, had just left, finally ejected by me. Oh, I was really grateful to her. She had brought round a shepherd's pie. If chicken soup is Jewish penicillin, shepherd's pie must be Barnet's Nurofen, I suppose. But I didn't want her there when Lauren got back and I think she understood that.

So I sat with the telly on, not taking anything in, rehearsing what I wanted to say to Lauren, trying out phrases, thinking of an apology that would really convey how sorry I felt, explaining why I'd done the stupid things I'd done but also setting out what I wanted from our relationship if it continued, and trying to test these terms to see if they sounded reasonable.

For some reason I didn't hear her key in the front door and so one minute I was watching telly, thinking about her, praying that she would come back, would be willing to see me, and the next minute she was there, standing in the doorway of the living room. I got up slowly and faced her. She was tanned, beautifully dressed as always, but her eyes looked like she'd been crying quite a bit and not sleeping much.

She looked at me for a moment in silence and then muttered something about putting her bag in the bedroom. I nodded and stayed put. She was back moments later, saying something.

'Sorry?' I whispered.

'I was going to have a glass of wine, would you—?'

'Yes, oh, yes please. There's some in the fridge. Are you hungry? My mum brought a shepherd's pie, you could microwave it—' I was gabbling.

'Erm, no, thanks. I'm not hungry.'

'Sit down, I'll get the wine.'

She came into the room to let me pass and I went out into the kitchen, trying to work out from what I had seen so far whether she simply wanted to discuss arrangements for splitting up and moving out, or whether something more positive was possible.

I came back with the wine and she asked, 'So, how are you?'

'I'm okay, thanks. The doctors checked me out and they think I'm fine. No brain damage,' I added, goofily.

She smiled gently and nodded. 'Good, I'm glad.'

'How was France?'

'It was, it was . . . good. Yeah, lovely.'

I sensed we were skating around this huge hole in the ice: desperately sticking to the periphery in case we went too near the middle and fell into that icy water that could have drowned us both.

'Lauren,' I paused for a moment, trying to think when I'd last used her name rather than 'babe' or 'honey'. The formality and unfamiliarity of it threw me for a moment. 'I'm sorry.' All my arguments, defences, explanations and carefully honed phrases went completely out of my mind. 'I'm just so sorry that I thought you and Peter were sleeping together. I'm sorry I slept with Nora—'

Her face hardened at the name.

'What's happened to her?' she asked briskly.

'I don't know.'

'She put something in your drink?'

'Yeah . . . something she was given at the party, except she used a double dose.'

Lauren shook her head in disbelief. 'She should be prosecuted, the police—'

'I know, but I couldn't necessarily prove it *was* her in a court and frankly, I just want to forget all about her, about the whole thing.'

She seemed to be thinking over my implied question: would she forget about it as well? She sighed heavily and put her glass down as I watched her closely, trying to read her thoughts.

'I still can't believe you did that – slept with her.' She could hardly bear to say it. I was silent. What could I say? 'How many . . .?'

This, I really couldn't bear to go over. 'Twice. Look, there's no excuse, Lauren, I was angry with you. I was feeling lonely, you weren't around. Everything seemed different, I didn't know what I was doing.' She nodded again. 'Oh, God, Lauren, I'm so sorry. Really, it was also because I was going . . . I don't know . . . a bit bonkers, I think, with the whole 2cool thing and, like I said, I was just feeling so angry with you for spending so much time with Peter.'

She laughed gently. Sensing my surprise at her reaction she said, 'He told me about you finding him . . .'

It took a moment to realise what she was referring to.

'Oh, fuck, that was embarrassing. I can't believe I didn't realise he was gay. I think Sarah was about to tell me when I spoke to her on the phone at her office but she got called away. Oh, God, poor bugger – I really kicked the shit out of him.'

She laughed again. 'Don't worry, he doesn't hold it against you. Poor Peter, Scott's left him for some girl on the same course at college. He's heartbroken.'

'Oh, no,' I said. 'They seemed like a nice couple.' The phrase stopped us both for a moment. 'Are we still . . .?' I asked.

She looked me directly in the eyes. 'I'd like us to be, Charlie, if you do.'

I couldn't believe she thought I might not. I stared back at her. That familiar face, that way of sitting, one long leg elegantly crossed over the other, her glass cradled in her lap. So composed, self-assured. Suddenly I was brought back to the thrill I got on our first dates together.

'I've changed since this whole 2cool thing, you know that, don't you?' I told her.

She smiled sadly. 'Yes. Don't forget, I've seen most of it at first hand.'

'Of course. But can you live with it? I mean, could you love this new Charlie?' I wondered if I was talking her out of it. 'But I haven't changed completely, though, you know.'

I could see her blinking back tears and smiling.

'I'll still leave my underpants lying on the bedroom floor, I promise. I'll never remember when you've invited people round for dinner and you'll always have to do the dusting again after I'm supposed to have done it. There's still a lot of the old Charlie around, believe me.'

She opened her mouth to say something but nothing came out, then the tears began to flow. In a moment I was kneeling in front of her. Unsteadily, she put her wine down, slopping it slightly on the carpet, and rested her forehead against mine, sobbing gently. I held her head in my hands and smelt her hair. I kissed her cheeks, her eyes, tasting the saltiness of her tears and then my mouth found hers. To think I'd nearly lost her, this wonderful, gorgeous person who'd been my life for nearly seven years.

After we'd held each other for what seemed like hours, we began to talk. It was like we'd just started going out together. She told me things about her I didn't know and I told her about the whole 2cool thing and Nora and my dad and everything. At some points I'd stop and say 'But you know this, don't you? Do you really want to hear it again?' and she'd say 'Yes, yes, tell me.' She said it was like 'going behind the scenes', finding out what was really happening.

Although most of it came out effortlessly, like a stream of consciousness, telling her about Nora was harder. I had to explain that I wanted to do something dangerous, mad, unpredictable, as well as getting revenge for the Peter thing and her 'adultery'. The look in Lauren's eyes showed how painful it was for her to have to hear about our relationship and I kept wondering if I should censor bits of it, but I knew I had to be completely honest, and in fact from her own point of view she found Nora intriguing too. 'Why did she do that?' she asked again and again. Finally she said, 'I feel sorry for her.' Whether her judgement was damning or understanding I don't know.

When I listened in the quiet, calm place we'd both finally reached, to her talking about Peter and what they had been doing together, I found myself understanding more about their friendship. Peter had offered her something I couldn't, both professionally and personally, but I began to realise that that was nothing to feel jealous or resentful of. Peter had, *has*, I should say, a part in her life and so do I. Thank God.

Then we talked about the future, what we both wanted from now on. Sarah had done the groundwork, explained to her why I wanted to do something so tough and challenging. I think coming from Sarah rather than from me, over a glass of wine on a sunlit terrace in France rather than the familiar surroundings of our flat during one of our many rows, it had been easier to take in. Sarah also explained to Lauren, she told me later – and this must have tested all her PR skills and experience – that Lauren could be just a bit overpowering, a bit controlling at times, and perhaps that's why after nearly seven years I had felt the need to rebel a bit, break out on my own and do something that she didn't understand and didn't approve of. My own seven-year itch.

Suddenly the quiet intensity of that living room conversation is shattered by the noise of the market. Guy smiles at me, realising perhaps why I have drifted off suddenly like this.

Our next course arrives. Two plates are casually banged down in front of us. The fish is grilled to a crisp brown and is glistening with olive oil and lemon juice. There's a little pile of finely chopped garlic and parsley on top of each piece.

'Has Lauren got a job in television, then?' asks Guy, having ordered two more glasses of Cava.

'Oh, yeah. Funnily enough, Peter managed to sell a one-off to the BBC about 2cool. The rise and fall of it. They were so keen to get an exclusive that they accepted Lauren as the presenter, despite her lack of experience. She's good, though, everyone who knows about these things says. I've seen her practice tapes, her show reel. She really comes across well. Peter's producing it. Anyway, she's going to interview me and Piers and we persuaded lots of other big name investors to take part.'

'Persuaded?' says Guy, smiling wickedly.

'Oh, some were a bit unwilling, but just we just mentioned badgers and funnily enough they became much more approachable. It'd be great if you'd do an interview for them. She asked me to ask you about that. You could really explain the thinking behind it.'

Guy smiles again and looks away. 'No, thanks. 'Fraid not.'

'Fair enough.' I take a mouthful of fish and let the powerful, fresh flavours wash through my mouth. Oh, God, who needs drugs? But then I come back to 2cool again. Was I really the only one who thought it would ever work? I think of Zac's comment that day when we first began to get worried about Guy and Piers's disappearance.

'Did everyone but me know it was going to collapse?'

Guy looks thoughtful for a moment.

'No, sometimes, some of us . . . in our wilder moments . . . I suppose, thought that it might succeed.' So I *was* the only one – just like Zac said. I chew for a minute and think of another question I've had for Guy. 'What *was* the thinking behind it?' I ask. 'I mean, if it had worked, did you want to get rich or was it all just a joke, an economist's prank? Ha, ha.'

'We economists are known for our sense of humour,' Guy informs me gravely.

'Of course. Seriously though . . .'

'I don't know. Perhaps I've also got the kind of intelligence that needs a sheepdog to keep it on the straight and narrow. If we had made some money it would have been great, really nice – certainly that was Piers's idea. But I think really I was just carrying out an experiment. Everyone wants to be involved in something cool, glamorous, stylish, something that everyone else is involved in.'

'But you had some very intelligent, financially acute people throwing money at you.'

Guy smiles wickedly and suddenly his eyes are wide with excitement. 'Have you heard of Charles Mackay? He was a nineteenth-century economist who developed the theory of the "madness of crowds". Basically a person wouldn't necessarily invest in something if they're the only one asked to do it, but if they see others investing in it, especially people that they admire or equate themselves with, they'll put their money into it as well. Even if – small detail, this – it doesn't actually exist.'

'And I was just a useful tool in your experiment.'

He puts down his knife and fork and raises his hands defensively. '*Mea culpa*. It was just that you were used to selling something virtual, something that wasn't real – a lifestyle, an image in a magazine – so it was perfect.'

'And what about the badgers, the blackmail thing?' He carries on eating. 'That was Piers, wasn't it?'

'Of course. I had to admire him. We were getting stick from various people about their money, about returns, and the way they could see us spending it. He'd recently suddenly stumbled on those, erm, parties, and realised that most of the people who were hounding us were at these little do's, so he had something on them. He even managed to persuade a few of our more troublesome investors who hadn't been to them to go along to one. Then, of course, they were caught.'

'How did that fit into your little experiment?'

'It didn't, that's one reason why I had to get out of there.'

I'm wondering whether to ask how desperate this desire to get out was. Was it a breakdown? But then he asks me, 'So what are you going to do now?'

'I'm going to start a model agency. Karyn, my booker at my old agency, is going to be my business partner. My dad's investing in it. Scarlett is doing some scouting for us, you know, going to clubs and bars and finding people who might have the right look – as well as managing this band of hers. Zac's doing all the IT stuff because we're going to be more web-enabled than any other agency.'

'And Piers is?' Guy asks, smiling enquiringly.

'And Piers is not coming within a million miles of it.'

He laughs. 'Oh, dear old Piers,' he says. 'Thing is, he had the contacts, he's got the charm, the chat.' Guy shakes his head thoughtfully, chasing some stray fish around his mouth with his tongue. 'All he needs now is a jail sentence.'

'He certainly has the chat. I spoke to him briefly on the phone just before we came here.'

'How is he?' asks Guy, with what looks like genuine interest.

'Apparently he's setting up a company to sell these talking lavatorials.'

Guy looks mystified.

'You know, lavatorials? Those adverts above urinals that you end up reading for a couple of minutes? He's met some kid who invented a little electronic device that fits into the bowl and when it's peed on, it broadcasts a message. There's another one for the cubicles so that when people sit on the seat, the device senses the pressure and begins the spiel there too.'

Guy looks at me, still more mystified. 'Well, I'm sure there's a demand for it,' he says.

'Piers seems to think so.'

We eat. Then I ask, 'And what are you going to do?'

Guy finishes his last piece of fish and then shrugs his shoulders. 'I don't know.'

'You don't know?'

'No, I don't know. Is that a crime?'

'Not at all, it's just that I always thought of you as being quite, you know, driven, organised.'

He looks down at his plate. 'So did I. Once. But you don't always have to know what you want to do, where you're going. Sometimes you can just *be*. I've got some money put aside and it doesn't cost much to live here. I might teach English, or even economics.' He grins to himself at the thought of it.

'So you're going to stay here, in Barcelona, then?'

'Oh, yes,' says Guy, looking around him and taking a deep, contemplative breath. 'I love this place. It's just so real, isn't it?'